Antioch's Daughter

PRAISE FOR ANTIOCH'S DAUGHTER

"Jenna Van Mourik has done it again—created a family that draws you in and touches your heart. Van Mourik shines with a powerful story of grace and forgiveness that's timeless ... Libi and Cassius both have hearts to serve the downtrodden, but will their similarities be able to withstand the truth in their differences? Don't miss this family adventure and sweet romance. Saul and Barnabas make appearances as well as Asa from *Jerusalem's Daughter*. Another story that shows the grace and love of the One True God."

— Barbara M. Britton, author of The Daughters of Zelophehad series and *Defending David: Ittai's Journey*

"Jenna's sophomore novel delivers a moving message of God's redemption that is strong enough to reach even the hardest lost souls. The love story between Cassius, an imperfect man who believes himself beyond redemption, and Libi, a selfless young woman with her own set of imperfections to work through, will both inspire you and cause you to examine your own heart. Wholesome, uplifting, and thought-provoking, *Antioch's Daughter* is perfect for readers young and old alike!"

— Ashton E. Dorow, author of The Royals of Acuniel series

PRAISE FOR JERUSALEM'S DAUGHTER

"I truly believe this author brings a sweetness to Biblical fiction that is hard to describe. These characters have become vivid to me and I have loved seeing the passion week through their eyes. This story has an even moderate pace that slowly allows you to get to know the characters and then brings you to a climax that has forever changed the world."

— Nicole, host of *The Unending TBR Podcast*

"Rich in historical fact, memorably lovable characters, and inspiring reminders of faith. It's an encouraging story of overcoming fear and learning to trust God. This is easily one of my favorite books and I can't wait to see what Jenna has in store for the rest of the series."

— Audrey Bodine, author

"I loved being in Jerusalem during passion week, the crucifixion, and the resurrection!! Jenna did a wonderful job telling that story while still telling us the story of Shamira and her family ... I know so much research, prayer, and heart went into this book and it definitely paid off! It was beautifully done!"

— Alysha, blogger from *For The Love of Christian Fiction*

Antioch's Daughter

JENNA VAN MOURIK

GLOSSARY

Abba—Father
Agora—Marketplace or large, open meeting place.
Ahav sheli/Ahava sheli—A term of endearment, "my love" or "loved one"
Atrium—Central courtyard of a Roman house
Auxiliaries—Soldiers in the Roman Army who were not citizens of Rome
Bat—Daughter of…
Ben—Son of…
Centurion—A rank in the Roman Army; leads 80 men
Century—A group of 80 men in the Roman Army, led by a centurion
Circus Maximus—Chariot racing course in Ancient Rome
Cohort—A group of men in the Roman Army made up of six centuries
Culina—Kitchen in a Roman house
Dodah—Aunt
Dodh—Uncle
Domus—A kind of grand Roman house, typically within a city
Hamud/Hamuda—A term of endearment, "cute one"
Hippodrome—A course for chariot races or sporting events
Imma—Mother
Insula/Insulae—Roman apartment/apartment style building
Ketubah—Marriage contract
Legionnaire—Soldier, member of a legion in the Roman Army
Mater—Mother
Mezuzah—A small box traditionally affixed to the doorways of Jewish homes, containing a parchment inscribed with Hebrew words from the Torah
Mohar—Bride price
Pater—Father
Pax Romana—Roman peace
Pilus Prior—Senior centurion of a cohort
Principia—Headquarters within a Roman Army camp
Sabba—Grandfather
Savta—Grandmother
Shalom—A greeting, meaning "peace be with you"

Vestibulum—Entrance hall in a Roman house

Via principalis—Main street in a standard Roman Army camp, along which the headquarters were situated

Via praetoria—Cross street in a standard Roman Army camp, leading from the headquarters toward the main gate

Villa—Large residence, typically removed from a city

FAMILY TREE

ELIYAHU
HODIYAH
ELISHEVA
AHARON
DEVORAH
BINYAMIN
CHAVA
TAMIR
ELIANA
MATTHAN
RUT
BENAYAHU
YUVAL
GILAD
LIBI
ASA
SHAMIRA
ELIEL
YEMIMA

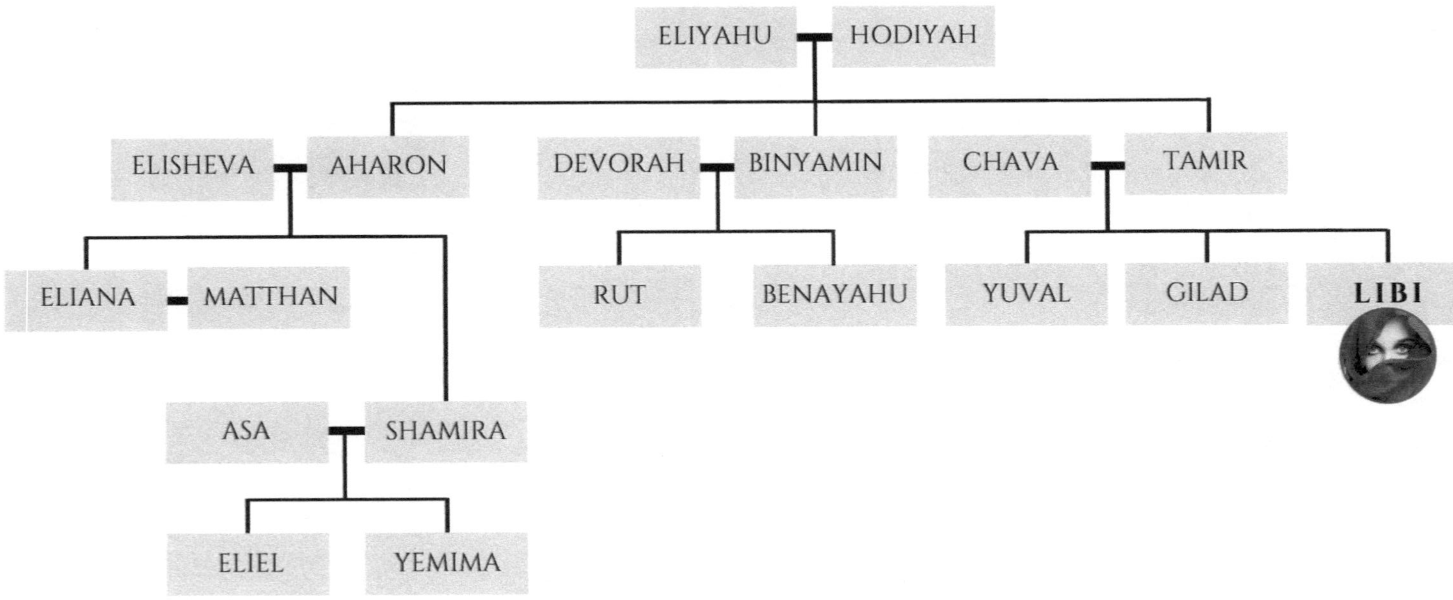

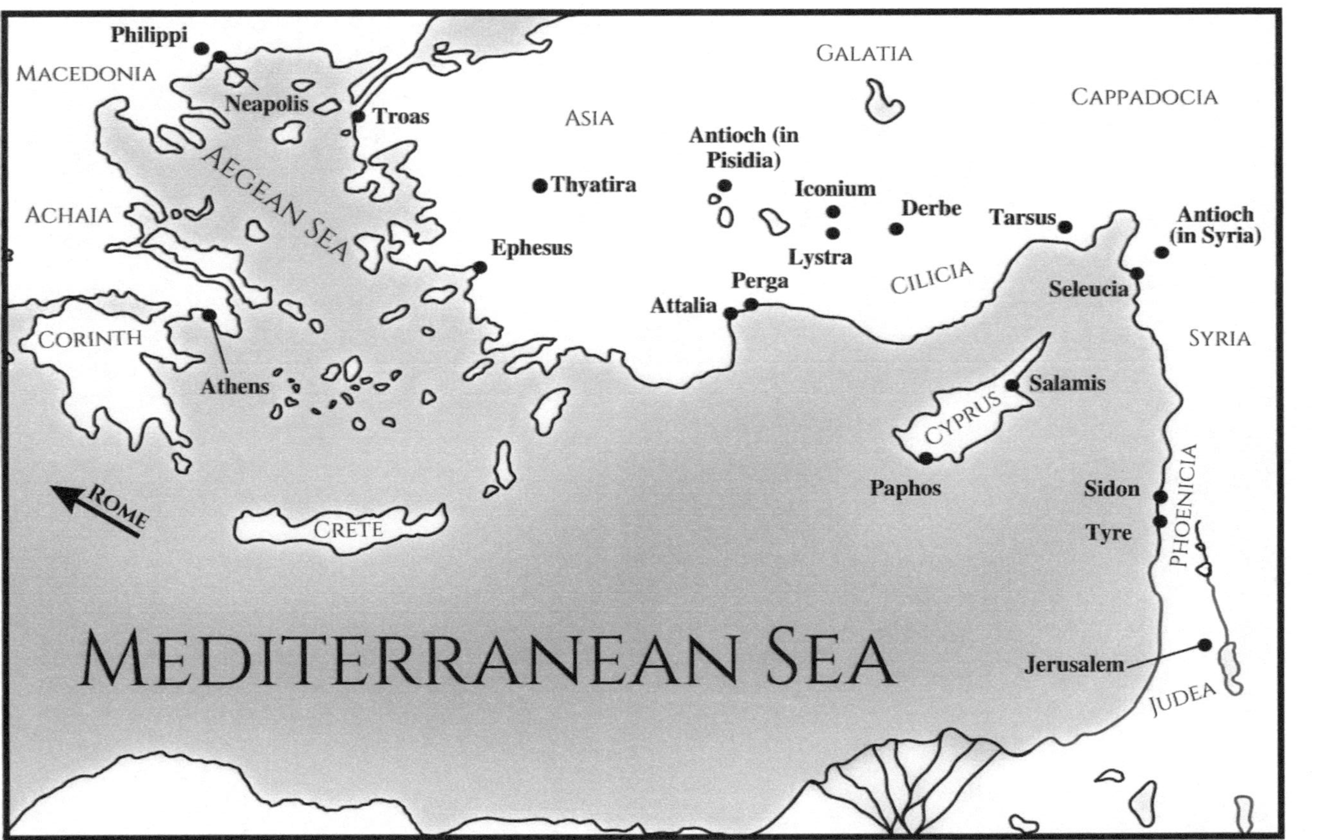

Philippi
MACEDONIA
GALATIA
CAPPADOCIA
Neapolis
Troas
ASIA
Antioch (in Pisidia)
Thyatira
Iconium
Derbe
Tarsus
Antioch (in Syria)
ACHAIA
AEGEAN SEA
Lystra
Perga
CILICIA
Seleucia
Ephesus
Attalia
SYRIA
CORINTH
Salamis
CYPRUS
Athens
Paphos
Sidon
ROME
Tyre
PHOENICIA
CRETE
MEDITERRANEAN SEA
Jerusalem
JUDEA

THE ANCIENT ROMAN DOMUS

The "domus" was a popular style of home architecture for the Ancient Roman family, usually reserved for the wealthy or upper class. The domus was typically built along city roads, and was either one level, or had a staircase leading to another level or rooftop space near the back. Entering through the *vestibulum* at the front of the house, you would immediately find yourself in the center of an *atrium*. The roof would be open so that water could fill the square-shaped pool, otherwise known as an *impluvium*, in the middle. Surrounding the atrium on all sides were various *cubiculum*, or bedrooms, that could be modified to suit the occupants' needs and turned into offices, dining rooms, entertaining spaces, and more. Near the back of the house, you would usually find the *culina* or kitchen. The larger houses may have also had enclosed gardens or an additional atrium farther removed from the street.

Figure 1 (left) and Figure 2 (next page) represent possible layouts for the lower level of a domus.

Figure 1

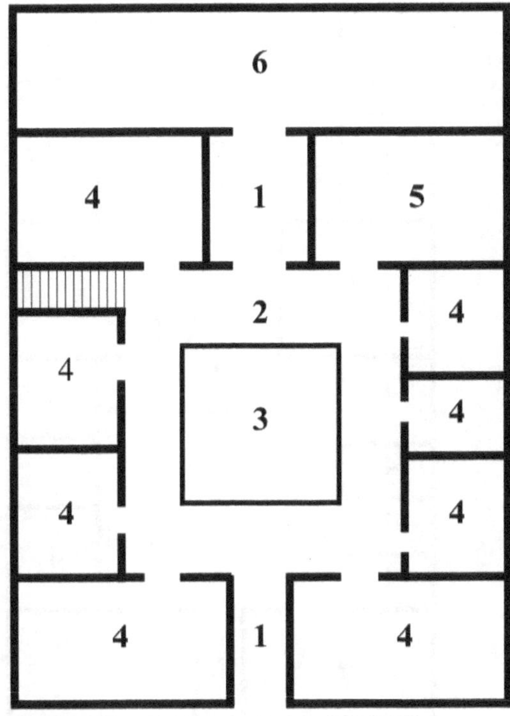

Some members of the upper class may have lived primarily in a domus, but more often than not, the domus was used as a secondary residence. Although they were typically grand in design, they were still much smaller in scale and afforded the occupants less peace and quiet than the elaborate villas located outside of town. Sometimes, the street-facing rooms of the domus had separate entrances from the outside, and were rented out to merchants or craftsmen as places of business. Those who lived the majority of the year in villas may have used the domus as a place for entertaining visiting guests, hosting parties or events, or operating their own businesses.

Key:
1. Vestibulum
2. Atrium
3. Impluvium
4. Cubiculum
5. Culina
6. Enclosed Gardens

Figure 2

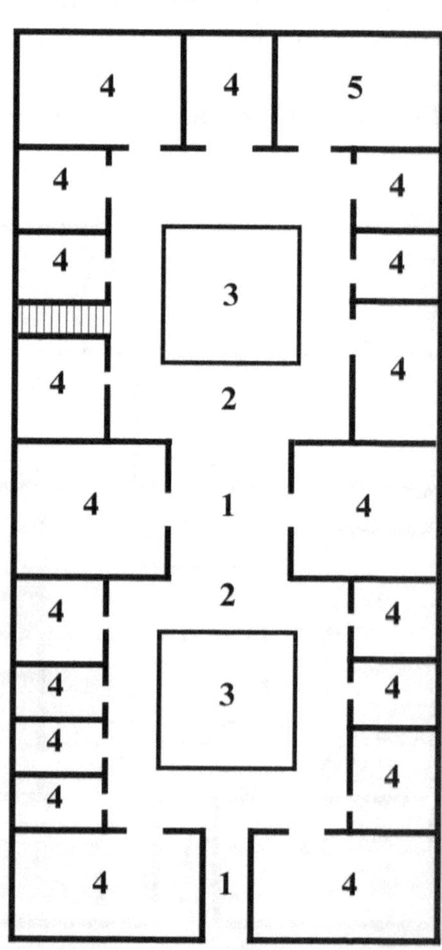

DEDICATION

To the men who have been role models and leaders in my life: Grandpa Graves, Dad, Brandon, my uncles, and more. Each of you are strong and courageous and embody what it means to put on the full armor of God. I have watched you "fight the good fight" throughout my life and overcome obstacle after obstacle with God on your side.

In addition to embodying leadership, you have also each taught me something about what grace and forgiveness looks like, and that sometimes being strong means getting down on one's knees and asking for help from the One who is stronger than us all.

Most of all, you have shown me what redemption looks like.

"Grace Greater Than Our Sin"

Marvelous grace of our loving Lord,
Grace that exceeds our sin and our guilt!
Yonder on Calvary's mount out-poured,
There where the blood of the Lamb was spilt.

Grace, grace, God's grace,
Grace that will pardon and cleanse within;
Grace, grace, God's grace,
Grace that is greater than all our sin!

— Julia H. Johnston, 1910
(Public Domain)

PART ONE

"After the priests had assembled with the elders and agreed on a plan, they gave the soldiers a large sum of money and told them, 'Say this, 'His disciples came during the night and stole him while we were sleeping.' If this reaches the governor's ears, we will deal with him and keep you out of trouble.' They took the money and did as they were instructed, and this story has been spread among Jewish people to this day." — Matthew 28:12-15 CSB

"When I was a child, I spoke like a child, I thought like a child, I reasoned like a child. When I became a man, I put aside childish things." — 1 Corinthians 13:11 CSB

27 A.D., The Imperial City of Rome

"I told you never to come here again…" the man who Cassius had been told was his father growled from the ornate doorway of his *villa* just outside the city of Rome. Cassius allowed his eyes to roam over the lush landscape and grand architecture while the tension ensued.

"But I thought that if you could see him and see how much he looks like you, then things would be different," his *mater* pleaded.

"Laelia, women who find themselves in such a position as you did get rid of their children. If they are smart, they don't fall into such a way at all. You are the one who kept him."

"Please… I bear the shame for what we did, but he is *our* son."

"Don't you dare say such a thing again—especially not in front of my own home! Do you know what could happen to both of us for even suggesting that boy is my son? I was already promised to another and about to be married when you and I were together. I had ambitions to think of, and I still do, along with plenty of my own legitimate children from a marriage that secured my place in society. The position you are in is entirely your fault."

"How can this be my fault alone? You made me promises! You said you would always love me, and that you would always take care of me. You said we were destined to be together, no matter what."

"Did you honestly think I would break off my betrothal to marry you, when both of our families would have been opposed to the match? I have kept my end of the bargain. You remain fed, clothed, and sheltered because of me."

"Please, I am begging you—"

"Begging for what? Is it more money you want? Do you wish to blackmail me, or simply ruin me as a part of some bitter thirst for revenge?"

"No!"

"Then what?" he probed. Cassius pulled back behind his mother, his little lips quivering with fear for the man his mater told him that he was meant to like. Cassius didn't like him at all, nor did he understand why he was so angry. Had Cassius done something wrong?

"J-j-just give him your n-n-name. Your name is all I ask. Give him your name, be a *pater* to him, and he might have a chance at a future!" Cassius had never heard his mother stutter before. He sensed she must have been frightened as well.

"My name? You want me to publicly acknowledge him?" As the man said it, he seemed to almost laugh at the suggestion. Cassius' brow furrowed. "You are mad, Laelia. If it was found that I had been unfaithful, even before I was formally married, I would be ruined. I have my own reputation to consider!"

"Your reputation? What about my reputation? My family treats me as though I am dead! No other man will look at me."

"I'm sure plenty of men will look at you, Laelia. I never said our relationship needed to be so… exclusive. You are free to do as you please."

His mater's spine straightened. "Please don't say such a thing in front of our son. He is still a child."

"He is not our son. He is a mistake. As I have already said, he is a problem that should have been dealt with before he was ever born. I'm warning you, Laelia, do not come here again. I want no part in this."

The man closed the door in their faces, and Cassius, still a boy, closed off a part of his heart that day.

29 A.D., The Imperial City of Rome

Two years passed, and Cassius still didn't know his father's name, but he didn't want to know it either. He dreamed of having a pater, but after the way things ended between them all, Cassius' new dream was to never see that man again. He got his wish, but he suspected his mater still went to him. Every time she returned without saying where she had gone, she cried for hours, and Cassius knew it must have been because of that man. He learned to associate her tears with him. Eventually, they were forced to move from the only house Cassius had ever known as his home, to an even smaller space—a cramped *insula* at the top of several flights of stairs. Food became scarce, and what money they did have, Cassius' mother spent on stone idols to improve their fortunes.

They both grew thinner, until one day Laelia began sending Cassius out on long errands. Sometimes he was given a list of things to purchase, while other times she would send him out to find news on the latest races at the great *Circus Maximus*, or explore the surrounding hills and riversides to look for specific plants or flowers. Whenever he returned, he would often cross paths with strange men coming down the stairs as he went up. Men who didn't resemble any of the other residents of the *insulae*. Once, he tried to speak to one of them and ask them who they were, but they slapped him across the face. He learned after that not to make eye contact or attempt conversations with any of these visitors. If possible, he would try to stay out long enough that he could avoid them.

Even though he did not like the visitors, circumstances were not so dire after they began to visit regularly. There were proper meals again, and dinners in the evenings. Although his mother had visitors during the afternoon, the mornings belonged to him, and it was the time he looked forward to most. Cassius would sit beside his mater and listen to her explain the names of the little statuettes she filled their insula with, what offerings they liked, and what things to ask of them. The stories fascinated him.

"First, we pray to Jupiter. He is the supreme ruler over all of the gods, and all of mankind," his mater explained, gesturing to the small statue in the windowsill as the sun rose behind them. As she talked, Cassius' eyes focused beyond the little figures to the view from the small upper room they inhabited. He felt like he could see the entire Imperial City from the top of the insulae. He could see the part of town where they used to live, and he could just make out the villas in the rolling hillsides where he'd seen his father for the first and last time. Still his eyes drifted farther and farther out. He wondered what kinds of lands were beyond Rome, and wished with all of his might that he could take his mother and go. He could find work and be her protector, making sure no one ever hurt her again.

"Then to Neptune, the god of the sea, and to Ceres, that Rome may be bountiful and that we may never want for food in our bellies." She tickled the young Cassius as she said it, and he couldn't help but laugh. "Then to Juno, who protects women…"

One by one, she went down the list of gods, the ones that had statues, the ones that didn't, the ones of Rome, the ones of other countries, and then she taught Cassius about the nameless gods.

"Nameless? How can they be gods if they do not have any names, Mater?" asked Cassius. "They can't be very powerful or important without names."

"Of course, they can!" his mother objected. "We must send up special prayers of forgiveness to the gods whose names we do not know. Just because we do not know their names does not mean that they do not exist. We do not want to incur their wrath by ignoring them, so we pray to them also."

That didn't make very much sense to Cassius. "How can you pray to someone without knowing if they exist?"

"Hush now, Cassius. It is getting late in the day—run along and see about those errands I mentioned earlier. If you have time, perhaps you could head toward the river and see how many perfectly smooth stones you can find. I will see you at supper."

Cassius was approaching the insulae to join his mater after his afternoon of exploring the city when he saw two men hurriedly climbing the stairs ahead of him. Cassius was used to seeing people coming *down* the stairs at that time, but never going *up*. Something in their hurried manner made him pause. Rather than follow them, he crouched down in the shadows at the bottom of the stairs, peering up at the many doors. He watched as they threw open the door to the room he shared with his mother, the glow of the lamplight casting even more shadows for Cassius to hide in. He climbed up the stairs and jumped into a discarded crate outside the door, propping the top open just wide enough for his fingers to squeeze through, enabling him to see into the dimly lit room that smelled overwhelmingly of fragrant perfumes and spices.

"Where is he? Where is the boy?" the cloaked men shouted over and over again.

His mother screamed and screamed, but no one came to her aid.

Cassius remained in the crate, barely breathing.

"You tell me where he is, woman, or so help me I'll—"

"Or you'll what? 'Take care of him,' as you always said I should have?" she choked out the words between sobs. Cassius wanted to jump from his hiding spot and save her, but he couldn't move his limbs. Was this some cruel trick of one of the gods his mother taught him to worship?

"You should not have kept calling after me, Laelia."

"You're right," she cried. "From the very beginning I have been a fool… I took your words as trustworthy, and I let you take everything I had… I loved you."

"I never asked you to love me! Tell me where the boy is so that I can end this and do what you never could."

"If that's what you want," his mater continued, "I'll never tell you where he is. Never! We made mistakes, but he is not one of them. I will never give him up!"

The man grabbed his mater by the hair and pulled her head back. Cassius squeezed his eyes shut at the sound of a metal blade being unsheathed, and after that, he heard his mater's sobs no more.

When Cassius heard the men coming toward him again, he dropped even deeper into the crate, hoping they would not spot him. Their heavy footsteps as they passed him were like thunder that shook Cassius to his very core.

"Aren't you worried about the boy?" asked the companion.

"Laelia was the only one who could have identified me to him. I don't care what happens to the boy now. We need to get out of here before we are seen; and remember, no one must ever know of this night."

That was the last thing Cassius ever heard his father say. When he opened his eyes again, all he saw was a trail of blood from his mother's room, and he didn't dare look inside. He knew he had no pater or mater now. The streets would become his home, and with no one left to take care of him, he would find a way to take care of himself.

"'Take guards,' Pilate told them. 'Go and make it as secure as you know how.'" — Matthew 26:65 CSB

32 A.D., The Imperial City of Rome

Cassius knew the streets of Rome well enough to find a new home for himself every night. Sometimes he found cover, but most nights he slept under the stars. That is, when the city was dark enough to see the stars. Some parts of the city never went dark.

Years had passed since his mother's murder. In numbers, Cassius was just becoming a man, but the horrors he had seen and the days spent on the streets forced him to mature faster than most boys his age. As was his morning routine, teenaged Cassius began the day by walking through the densely populated Roman Forum. It was the perfect opportunity for a street urchin like Cassius to make off with some goods. He could swipe enough food to keep his belly satisfied, stuffing bread and fruits into his sleeves, and if he was lucky, he could pilfer some gold or silver jewelry to sell later. The coin from such a transaction would keep him fed for a long time, and that would be good. The less he had to steal, the better.

It wasn't so much that he minded the stealing or carried any kind of guilty conscience about the behavior. It was the risk; if he ever got caught, he could lose a hand or even his life. Neither of those options sounded appealing to Cassius, whose heart was growing harder and harder by the day.

The voice of an older man caught his attention. "Men of Rome, who among you will serve the empire? Serve the empire and earn wages, land, titles, and more!"

Wages meant money, and land meant stability. Those were two things that Cassius didn't have, but they weren't nearly as appealing as the last option the man had listed.

Titles.

Cassius never had a title. He didn't even have his father's name. By joining the Roman Army, he could make a name for himself. He could become a leader, perhaps even a *centurion*. The idea of becoming a great warrior to spite his father's dismissal made a part of Cassius come alive—a part of himself that he had believed for a long time was as dead as his mother.

He could be a son of Rome, no longer a mistake.

With that spark of ambition, Cassius clumsily dropped his loot and approached the soldier. He was a taller man. His face was tanned and weathered, probably from years of battle, seafaring, and travel. Cassius could see some of his hair from behind his helmet and took note of how dark it was, except for some scattered gray and white hairs throughout. The man didn't appear to be particularly advanced in years, but even if that was the life awaiting Cassius, it was better than the life he lived now.

"Me. I'll serve the empire," he said, boldly approaching the soldier.

"You?" said the man, squinting at Cassius. "How old are you?"

"Old enough," Cassius said.

"Live to see another day, boy. Military life isn't for you."

The man turned away from him, but Cassius couldn't let this opportunity pass. Enlisting suddenly meant everything to him. He needed this.

"I am eighteen!" He shouted knowing it was an erroneous answer even as he said it, but the lie rolled off his tongue easily enough.

"And I'm the Roman emperor," said the man sardonically, rolling his eyes. "I told you, boy, you're not getting in."

"You're looking for recruits, aren't you? I don't see anyone else lining up." If Cassius couldn't convince this man that he was competent in a battle of swords and fists, he would show his abilities by engaging in a battle of words.

The man's demeanor changed. He folded his arms over his chest and almost smiled at Cassius. Cassius himself knew that he was right, and the older man couldn't argue with his point.

"Fair, but you're still not getting in. Not that simply."

The man left an opening in the conversation for Cassius to plead his case, and that was exactly what he would do next.

"I'm strong and I'm able. I don't have a family. No one is going to miss me. You need recruits, and I am a willing volunteer. Live or die, I don't care, but when I am dead, I want to be remembered, even if only as part of a greater army."

The man looked at Cassius, looked at the ground, and then back up at Cassius. He cracked a half-smile before replying, "You're certainly not eighteen."

"You already said that," said Cassius, confused.

"But you're going to be." The words were spoken with authority.

"But that won't be for—" Cassius started to object, thinking the man had every intention of telling him to go away and come back in a few years.

"You're *going* to be eighteen. Make your mark here, and stay by my side," commanded the man, unrolling a scroll and giving Cassius a writing instrument. Cassius did as he was told. The man leaned in closely, and added in a hushed voice, "You don't need to tell people how long it will be until that happens."

"Thank you!"

"Don't thank me. Not yet, anyway. Thank me when you survive." A smile flashed across the man's face for a brief moment, before he resumed his stoic stance. Cassius bowed his head respectfully. "What's your name, soldier?"

"Cassius."

"What is your *family* name?"

"Just Cassius," he shrugged awkwardly. His recruitment had been tenuous; would his lack of a family name be its undoing?

To Cassius' surprise, the man merely nodded in understanding. "I'm Servius Arrius, and you'll be under my command. I'll show you later where you will make up your bed and complete your training. You could go far, Cassius, but you must remember: failure to appear when you are called or deserting your *cohort* at any time could cost your life. It isn't just the enemy who threatens you. You could be just as large of a threat to yourself."

"I won't desert. I swear it on my life. I'm joining up because I want to make something out of myself. I want to be great," Cassius responded with determination.

Servius chuckled, "Let's start with teaching you how to wield a sword. Then we'll teach you how to be great."

33 A.D., Jerusalem

The last year of Cassius' life passed by in a blur. He completed his training quickly under Servius' instruction. A few weeks after that, Servius Arrius was designated as the *Pilus Prior*, the commander of their cohort, and given orders to lead their men to Judea. None of them, neither Cassius nor Servius Arrius nor any of the other members of their cohort were very happy about the posting, although Servius was rarely happy anyway. Not in front of others, at least. Servius had taken him under his wing and

Cassius looked to him like the father he never had. Sometimes he liked to imagine that Servius was his father, and that his name was really Cassius Arrius.

Jerusalem wasn't a very exciting post most of the time. Aside from religious quarrels or common thievery, nothing ever happened that was worth them being there. It was that type of quarrel that brought them to Golgotha that day, with the Jewish people requesting the execution of a teacher with a growing following. With one mallet and three nails, and the help of a few other men, Cassius had hung that man on the cross himself. With each swing, he looked up and searched for Servius' eyes. Was Servius watching him? Would he notice how in command he was of the situation, or the precision with which he carried out the gruesome task, and raise his rank as a result?

Together, they hoisted the cross upwards and let it fall into place. "Father, forgive them, because they do not know what they are doing," said the man who was called a king.

Cassius spat on the ground at the foot of the cross. "If you're the king of the Jews, then why don't you save yourself?" Cassius shouted up at the man.

The men with him laughed and jeered, and Cassius' whole body felt energized by the attention. They were laughing with him, because of him, and because he had entertained them. A rush of adrenaline seized him. His stomach growled, hungry for his day's portion but also yearning for more praise from his peers.

Quickly, he grabbed the clothes and robes they had taken from the man and brought them over to the group. "Here," he directed, tossing them into the middle of the group, "Let's not tear it, but cast lots for it. Who shall keep the 'king's fine clothes?'"

He continued to laugh and shout with the other men. He'd always felt like the outcast, but here, now, at the center of attention? He felt accepted. Wanted. Like he had a place of some importance in the world. He turned to face Servius Arrius, standing with another centurion whose expression was equally grim, and suddenly his feelings of elation came crashing down.

Servius' face stared on at him with dismay. What had he done wrong? Leaving the small circle, Cassius approached him, sensing that he had words he wished to exchange.

"What is it?" said Cassius.

Servius nodded at the crosses behind them. "Can't you have a shred of respect?"

"For who? Them? They're criminals. Why should I care about any of them?" Cassius replied, still holding onto the attitude he'd had when he was with the other soldiers.

"Cassius, you forget yourself," said Servius, hardening.

Cassius knew he wasn't meant to use that tone of voice, especially with someone as high in rank as Servius, but he couldn't understand why the man he'd become so familiar with was suddenly sympathetic to these men. Surely they all deserved to be on their crosses. Cassius bowed his head, but only out of respect for his commander—and out of shame.

"Go back to the camp," said Servius.

"But I am needed here!" Cassius objected.

"That was not a request from your friend, that was an order from your Pilus Prior! The other soldiers and centurions can handle this."

Cassius didn't move his feet. The other men had laughed and smiled with him. He'd earned their approval. Why hadn't he earned Servius Arrius' approval as well?

"Go!" Servius shouted again, and at last Cassius relented, stomping off. He passed the mourners as he walked down from Golgotha, noticing their tears and their wailing. All this for a few criminals who would probably be forgotten on the morrow seemed like such waste. Cassius refused his evening meal, preferring to go straight to his cot.

The next day, Servius summoned him to his quarters. Cassius entered the tent, holding his tongue for once. It would not last long.

Servius continued the conversation from earlier, "Jewish, Roman, innocent, guilty—it matters not to death. Death will come for all of us eventually. Have some reverence for that at least. These are their final moments. I should imagine this is not how you would like to leave this life, with cackling hoards and insults."

"Well, I would never do something so stupid to land myself on the opposite side of Roman justice," Cassius huffed.

Servius groaned, slamming his hand down on the nearby table, "This was a mistake. I should not have allowed you to enlist. I should not have encouraged you."

"What do you mean?" Cassius' blood boiled, and he felt his fingers curl and clench into a fist.

"You're too arrogant. You enjoy all of this too much. You're not mature enough for this job," said Servius.

Cassius raised his voice. "*I* drove the nails through their bodies and into their crosses myself. *I* can handle this."

"I allowed you to enlist and I took you under my wing, but maybe that was a selfish thing to do. I saw in you what I had been at your age; ambitious, quick-thinking, eager to prove oneself. Perhaps I saw myself as some sort of a father figure to you, but now... Now I'm not sure if I've done the right thing. I did something that a Roman soldier must never do. I allowed my emotions to get the better of me."

"A good soldier should be able to act on impulse," argued Cassius. "Split-second decisions in the thick of battle are often based on instincts and feelings."

"Remember what I told you," said Servius. "A good soldier can be just as much of a threat to himself as any enemy."

Cassius didn't say anything in response. He had a feeling that Servius wasn't finished with his lesson yet.

"So that is why I'm doing what I'm doing, Cassius."

"What?" said Cassius, narrowing his eyes.

"The man that was crucified—they've requested soldiers to guard his tomb."

"Tomb?" Cassius balked. "He should have been thrown into a pit with the others. What makes this man worthy of a tomb?"

"Why do you always have to question everything, Cassius?" snapped Servius, rubbing his temples. "It's been a long day, and I refuse to answer your questions."

"I'm sorry," said Cassius, although he didn't really mean the apology.

Servius must have been able to sense his insincerity. He sighed before replying dryly, "I'm sure."

After a few more silent moments passed, Servius went on, "Pilate has promised a guard of soldiers. I'm sending you as one of them for tonight's watch."

"Why me?"

"You will do this assignment, whether you like it or not."

"Assignment?" Cassius questioned. "This isn't an assignment. It's a farce! You want me to watch a dead man's tomb, and for what exactly? To make sure he rots?"

"This wasn't my idea, but as Pilus Prior of this cohort, it is up to me to select guards for this post. If you want to avoid my wrath or any punishment for dereliction of duty then I would advise you to do as you are commanded and not give me any more grief on the subject. While you are there, I suggest you give some serious thought to your actions, and return with a different mindset."

"Yes, *Pilus Prior*... I will do as you command," Cassius acquiesced, but remained frustrated.

The watch was long and Cassius' military uniform and cloak did little to shield him from the chill of the night air. By the time the moon reached its highest point in the sky, his anger at Servius had long-since worn off and been replaced by boredom and tiredness. He told himself that no one would dare come to this tomb, not with the display of Roman Justice still fresh in their minds. During the watch, Cassius kept shifting his weight from one foot to the other, but he soon felt his own alertness slipping away.

The faintest hints of daylight were barely beginning to spread across the deep blue sky when Cassius' eyes drifted toward the horizon, anxious to see any sign of the next group of soldiers coming to relieve them from their post. Although he did not see anything, a strange noise startled him. Footsteps? Voices? Movement of some kind? He wasn't sure, but he wasn't the only one who heard it.

"What was that?" said one of his fellow soldiers whose name Cassius did not know.

Each of them slowly moved to draw their weapons, and Cassius' heart began to race. All of a sudden, a violent earthquake shook the ground beneath his feet. Pebbles moved. Rocks moved. He and the other soldiers began to shout, although no intelligible words came out. He turned his attention toward the tomb, the thing he'd been instructed to protect at all costs, and immediately raised a hand to shield his eyes. A bright, blinding white light, brighter than any sunrise Cassius had ever seen, flashed like lightning. From within that lightning, he saw a figure of some kind.

The noise of his fellow soldiers shouting, the earth moving, and stones cracking grew more and more intense. Cassius dropped his weapons as he fell to the ground. The last thing Cassius remembered was being full of terror, and then in stark contrast to what he had just seen, all went as black as death.

When he awoke sometime later, that feeling of fear had not subsided. He jumped up, gathering his wits. He tried to make sense of his memories, but he could not reconcile them in his mind. The other soldiers still lay asleep behind him, and the sun had risen much higher in the sky. When Cassius turned around to face the tomb again, he realized his problems had only begun. The stone had somehow been rolled away! He ran toward the tomb, stubbing his toe on a boulder in his haste. The pain he felt then was nothing compared to the feeling of shock and devastation when he looked inside the dark tomb and saw... nothing.

The body was *gone*.

The followers of the so-called king must have taken it. He convinced himself that what he saw must have been hallucinations. Dreams. Perhaps he'd been hit on the head by the radicals he'd been warned about, or maybe they'd used some sort of trickery. What would Cassius do if he had no explanation for what happened? No one would believe him if he confessed to the events as they happened. He didn't even believe himself.

What he did know was that the punishment for falling asleep on duty was death. He could try to run, but the punishment for desertion—if he was caught—was also death. At least if he ran, he could try to prolong the inevitable, and he'd been used to running before. Cassius took his chances, and left the other soldiers to fend for themselves. He abandoned his armor and cloak then and there, while dawn was still breaking. He cast aside anything that would identify him as a soldier in the Roman Army, and never looked back. No longer a son of the empire, he was once again a coward, ashamed and aimless. He ran like he'd run from his mother's body, and he'd been running ever since.

Part Two

"Now those who had been scattered as a result of the persecution that started because of Stephen made their way as far as Phoenicia, Cyprus, and Antioch, speaking the word to no one except Jews. But there were some of them, men from Cyprus and Cyrene, who came to Antioch and began speaking to the Greeks also, proclaiming the good news about the Lord Jesus." — Acts 11:19-20 CSB

ANTIOCH'S DAUGHTER

"Blessed are the pure in heart, for they will see God." —
Matthew 5:8 CSB

43 A.D., Antioch in Syria

Libi settled down onto the cushion in the corner of the room, clapping her hands to draw the children's attention to her. "All right, let's quiet down so we can begin. Which story would you like to hear today?" she asked, although she already knew which one she wanted to tell them.

"Not another *love* story," Rufus groaned. "I'm tired of those."

"I *love* the love stories!" Phoibe cheered. "Those are my favorite, *Dodah* Libi. Can't we hear another one of those, please?"

"Why do you call her 'Dodah' Libi?" asked Felix, settling down next to Rufus. "She's not *really* our dodah, you know."

"I know, but if I did have a dodah, I'd want her to be like Libi! She's the best storyteller there is, and she knows the words to almost every song that's ever been written," explained Phoibe, whose eyes followed the sounds of the movement around her, but never quite focused on anyone or anything in particular.

Libi laughed. "Well, I'm not entirely sure I know the words to every song, but you may call me Dodah as much as you like, Phoibe. My brothers have no plans to marry anytime soon, so you're the best chance at a niece that I've got!" Libi gave the girl's hand a tight squeeze to show her affection in a way that Phoibe could understand, even without sight.

Truth be told, none of these children were related to Libi by blood, nor were they even related to each other, although they called themselves brothers and sisters. Rufus, Felix, and Phoibe were orphans who had been taken in by Taliah and Keinan, a young couple with one child of their own. They were also believers in Jesus and followers of The Way, and since coming to Antioch years ago, Taliah and Libi became fast friends. It was unfortunately common for unwanted children to be abandoned on the streets in Antioch as infants or very young children. For those like Phoibe who had been born with a disability, they may have even been seen as curses from the pantheon of gods the Greeks and Romans worshipped.

Libi knew all too well that it wasn't only the Greeks and Romans who believed such things. As a child, Libi herself was looked down upon by others for being deaf, and even though she couldn't hear the things that were being said about her, she could understand enough to know what hid behind someone's expression. That was all before the miracle that healed her—before *Jesus* healed her. Now in Antioch, Libi served with all of her heart and had a special fondness for these children, especially Phoibe. She would do anything in the world to make sure they knew that they were just as loved as any other child would be by the adults who took them in, by Libi herself, and most importantly, by God.

"I agree with Rufus. Why can't we listen to the stories of warriors or kings today? I want to hear something exciting," said Felix, and Rufus nodded his agreement as he shifted on his cushion.

"Now, boys, Phoibe brings up an excellent point. While you

may prefer some of the stories of thrilling battles or fighters who prevail against their enemies, all of the stories I tell are love stories in one way or another. They tell of God's love for each of us."

"As long as it's not the kissing kind of love, I think any story you tell us today will be fine," agreed Felix.

Libi laughed and reached across the space between them to muss his hair, and he turned red in the face, reaching up to smooth the mess.

"Very well. I shall tell a love story, for Phoibe, but *not* the kissing kind, for Rufus and Felix," Libi nodded, clasping her hands together.

At that moment, the hurried sound of two tiny bare feet smacking the hard packed floor interrupted the conversation. "Wait for me! Wait for me!"

"Omri!" Libi exclaimed at the sight of Taliah and Keinan's only natural-born child, who was himself only a few years old. "I thought you were right behind the others. What happened to you?"

"I was," he explained as he ran toward Libi and jumped to sit in her lap, "but then I stopped."

"And why did you stop?" Libi raised an eyebrow, encircling him with her arms.

"Well, I… Well…" he said, licking his lips.

"Would it have something to do with that trail of sticky honey dripping from your chin?" Libi raised an eyebrow as she wiped his face with the edge of her own sleeve as though she couldn't already surmise the answer to what had stolen little Omri's attention.

"Maybe…"

"Well did you at least have your *imma*'s permission?" Omri nodded in reply. "All right, then. We'll not dwell on it."

"Quiet down, Omri," said Rufus, the oldest of them all. "*Dodah* Libi was about to tell us a war story."

"Wait," said Libi, "I never said it was a war story; only that it was *not* a romantic love story."

"Aw…" all three boys sighed, but Phoibe glowed from within. Libi took the little girl's hand in her own, giving it another squeeze of reassurance.

"Omri, sit here next to your sister and I'll get started." She gave him a bit of a nudge and then adjusted herself on her own cushion, trying to get as much distance between her body and the floor as she could.

"Will you at least tell us what this story is called?" pleaded Felix.

"This story is called," she paused for dramatic effect, "The Good Samaritan!"

"Where is Samarita…. Samaritania?" asked Omri.

"Samaria," Libi corrected, "is a land north of Judea, but farther south than Antioch."

"Have you been there, Dodah Libi?" asked Phoibe.

"I travelled through it once with my family before we came here," said Libi, recalling those days from long ago. Libi looked around at the group of children surrounding her and couldn't help but feel nostalgic for the childhood she had in Jerusalem, surrounded by all of her siblings and cousins in their humble Judean home. Whatever it lacked in grandeur, it made up for tenfold in love. The children before her now were so innocent and content to listen to stories and play together in harmony without ever worrying for the future. Libi's last day in Jerusalem had been as such, but in the span of a few short moments it turned into a nightmare. Though rarely spoken of, Libi could recall the events of the persecution that separated them as if it was yesterday. Persecution led by a man called Saul.

The name still made Libi shudder, but after nearly ten years, the majority of Libi's fears had been replaced with peace. They were far away from Jerusalem now and God had protected them from Saul's wrath, though her family did not remain untouched from the consequences of that persecution. She stopped her mind from reliving those memories any longer. How could she ask for more than what she had right now—the opportunity to share hope and show love to these children?

Except that there were other things she still wanted. Things only God knew.

"Oh, please, Imma Taliah. Can't Dodah Libi stay for one more song? I so love to hear her sing," begged Phoibe. "And when *she* tells stories, I feel as though I can almost see them!"

"Phoibe, you know I would stay if I could, but it is getting late in the day and my brothers have come to fetch me after doing their business. I have some errands to run myself, but I'll be back as soon as I can. Next time, I'll try to tell another love story… *Maybe* of the romantic kind."

Phoibe's eyebrows shot up. "You mean the one about Ruth and Boaz? That's my favorite!"

"Well, you'll have to wait and find out, won't you?" said Libi, smiling.

"Go on now and head into the other room. Dinner will be ready soon," Taliah directed the children, then turned to Libi. "I'd like to speak to you too, before you go, but it seems I must always wait to have a turn until the very end. The children adore you."

"And I adore them," Libi replied, turning her eyes toward the faint sound of Phoibe's hand brushing the wall. Once she could no longer hear the sound of her careful footsteps, she turned her attention back to Taliah.

"Well, that much is plain from the look on your face every time you're around them."

"I don't see how anyone could not love them! Felix with his sense of humor is incorrigible, but also a delight. Rufus can seem difficult, but he's really as sweet as honey when you get to know him. Phoibe is just precious, always looking for love and light in every situation. She even sings some of the songs more confidently than me these days! She made remarks earlier about me knowing all the words, but truly, I'm starting to think my memory pales in comparison to her passion. And of course, little Omri… Well, Taliah, he takes after both you and Keinan so much. All of them are so blessed here in your home!"

Taliah smiled and asked, "How are things with you, Libi? And don't tell me what you'd say if the children were around. I know you; you only ever talk about the good in every situation, and there have been many times that I've been grateful for that. You always are able to help brighten my perspective with a bit of your contagious joy whenever I am feeling low, but do you ever need any encouragement of your own?"

"Really, Taliah, I am doing well. Every year I think to myself, 'This is it. This is the best year we've had as a family since coming to Antioch,' and this year is no exception. The Lord has been abundant with His blessings, and I am continuously grateful."

"Good." Taliah nodded in understanding. She knew of the circumstances under which Libi's family had come to Antioch, but she did not know every detail. Still, Libi was closer to Taliah than anyone else in the city, and even if they didn't share everything, Libi was grateful for her company.

Taliah straightened her back. "What about socially… Have any young men caught your eye?"

Libi blushed. Every so often, the believers gathered, usually in Taliah's home or in the foothills outside of Antioch when the weather was clear and they were expecting a larger group. That would have been Libi's only time to seek out anyone for the purposes of getting to know them for marriage, but no one had ever *"caught her eye"* in that way, not that she hadn't been looking.

"No, nothing like that." Libi laughed. Although every so often, feelings bubbled up within her, making her wonder what it would be like to have someone look at her the way Keinan looked at

Taliah, or the way her *abba* looked at her imma, she made sure to stay busy enough that she rarely had time to be discontented. "Jehovah Jireh—The Lord will provide for me when the time comes if it is His will, but there is no one as of yet."

"As of yet," Taliah repeated, "but maybe soon!" She winked.

"Taliah!" Libi gasped.

"Well, there was something else I wanted to tell you before you left. I know your brothers are outside talking with Keinan and waiting for you, but I had to speak to you about—"

"Immaaa!!!" A young boy called out and Libi recognized it at once as the voice of Felix.

"Imma! Dodah Libi! Come quick!" shouted Phoibe.

"What is happening?" said Libi, already moving toward the commotion.

Taliah jumped ahead of her and ran toward the children, who were in the other room leaning out the back door, except for Phoibe who sat on a cushion beside them. "What is it, children? Is someone hurt?"

"Not one of us, Imma. I heard a cry come from outside," Phoibe explained.

"So, I jumped up to see what it was," said Felix.

"And I followed him," added Rufus.

"And we found a baby!" little Omri announced.

"A baby!" The color drained from Taliah's face and she motioned for the boys to step aside.

"Go and sit down with Phoibe, boys. Your imma and I will see if the child is all right," said Libi, reassuring their wildly curious minds. After a few more stern looks, they did as they were told.

Libi and Taliah went through the door to the alleyway where the fire pit was located for cooking. A stew boiled above it and Libi moved it off of the heat so that it would not burn. Taliah went to gather up the little bundle beside the door.

"Praise the Lord that this child is all right and that Phoibe heard her cries."

"Her?" Libi moved toward Taliah, who rocked the babe gently. "Oh, she's beautiful!" Libi exclaimed.

"She most certainly is."

"Who would leave such a perfect babe here?" said Libi.

"Perhaps the mother couldn't keep her, or they hadn't planned on…" Taliah didn't finish the sentence, but Libi knew what she meant all the same. Perhaps this child was born outside of marriage.

"How did they know to bring her to you?" Libi asked, genuinely puzzled.

"It may be that they know the God we serve and the faith we follow, and assumed that we would try to find a home for the child or raise it as our own. Or perhaps they chose our house at random. Nevertheless, this child shall have a home here."

They carried the nameless infant inside and checked to see if she had anything else with her. Although if their supposition was true and the mother was unwed or from a house of ill repute, she probably didn't know how to read or write either.

The child came with nothing except what she was wrapped in, but Libi was struck by how incredibly small she was. "She's so tiny!" she whispered. Libi remembered when Omri was a newborn, but even in the weeks immediately following his birth, he had never been as small as this child. "Is she a newborn?"

"I don't think so. I think she's underfed. I'll do what I can to fix that," Taliah promised as she swaddled the child.

"Does she have a name?" asked Phoibe, leaning forward on her cushion.

"Not that we know," explained Libi.

"How can we keep her if she doesn't have a name? We all had names when we came to live with you," Phoibe continued.

"That's true," agreed Taliah. "Each of you were old enough to know your own names by the time we found you, but this child here has been given to us before she has even learned to speak a word."

"What will we call her, then?" asked Rufus, furrowing his brows.

Libi smiled. "I think she should be called Tirzah, because she is so lovely."

Taliah nodded her head and beamed. "I think that's a wonderful idea! She has bright, wide eyes like yours, Libi."

"Can we play with her now?" said little Omri, suddenly coming between Libi and Taliah.

"Not yet, my son," said Taliah. "I need to speak to your father and tell him about our newest arrival."

"Is this how you found me, Imma?" Omri asked with wide eyes.

Taliah laughed, "Not quite. Now, all of you stay here for a little bit longer and we'll have dinner soon."

The children began to talk among themselves in excited tones while Libi and Taliah went to the front room to go and seek out Keinan and Libi's brothers.

"Do you think Keinan will be pleased with the arrival of another child?"

Taliah's eyes widened. "Oh, I know he will. We could never refuse a child in need, but this is what I wanted to tell you earlier, Libi … I am with child again! Another child is one thing, but two is… Well, that's eight of us in this house, and with only Keinan's work and the small portion of funds we receive from tithes to help take care of the children, not to mention the very limited room we have, I'm just not sure how we'll manage it."

"Oh, Taliah," Libi sighed. "I am so happy for you!"

"I am too. It is as you said, the Lord has blessed us abundantly, but that does not stop me from being worried."

"The Lord will provide as He always does. I *know* it."

"Yes, but that doesn't make the waiting any easier."

Libi bit her lip, trying to think of something she could do to help, but nothing immediately came to mind. "I will pray for you and see if I can think of anything. In the meantime, you must try not to worry. I know it's hard, but it's the best thing for you and the baby."

"You're right of course. I don't know what I would do without your calm nature to remind me to always look to God whenever I am in doubt," Taliah replied. "I don't want to separate any of the children we've taken in. Even if they aren't our blood, they are our family, but it will take a miracle to sustain us."

Taliah may have been unsure of the idea of a miracle, but Libi was no stranger to miracles. It was a miracle that had given Libi the ability to hear. She knew that feeding eight mouths and finding a place where orphaned children could thrive was nothing for the God whose son conquered death. "We should all pray, Taliah. Barnabas may return soon from his travels. Perhaps by then, we will have the answers you need. Remember, nothing is impossible with God, and He will take care of you *and* Keinan *and* the children *and* the little one you carry with you that we have yet to meet."

Taking longer than she should have, Libi and her brothers bid farewell to Taliah and her family. They would need to make haste to get to the market before the merchants closed their stalls if they intended to bring Imma the herbs she needed for the evening meal. There would be a great deal to discuss with her mother and father as they sat around the table that night.

"For the Son of Man has come to seek and to save the lost." —
Luke 19:10 CSB

Antioch was a cosmopolitan metropolis known for its wild nature. The walls teemed with people of all backgrounds, cultures, and religions. No desire was strange here, which made it the perfect place for a man like Cassius to go unnoticed.

Cassius spit on the ground beneath his feet after taking a bitter swig of warm water from the animal skin he kept tied around his waist. He tightened the closure before putting it back on his belt. Then, stopping briefly to pull his covering down farther over his face, he continued through the gridded streets. Within a city like this, a man could find every form of entertainment that he could imagine. Food, religion, art, sport...

"That hood looks heavy, and you must be hot on a day like this. Come inside and I'll help you take it off," offered a woman suggestively.

Cassius didn't bother responding. He had no interest in her particular business.

She was right, of course. The heat was sweltering and Cassius was miserable, but he wasn't *that* miserable. It was with a woman of such a reputation that an important Roman aristocrat sired a disgrace of a son, Cassius himself. Even now, well over a decade later, he could hear the words his father spoke the last time they saw each other reverberating in the dark corners of his mind. He called Cassius a mistake, told his mother, Laelia, that she should've found a way to get rid of him, and forbid her from ever trying to find him again. Cassius never did learn his father's name, but he knew it was an important one. Why else would he have gone to such great lengths to see to it that his name was not tarnished?

Without a pater or a mater in his life, Cassius tried instead to make a name for himself through the Roman Army. Though brief, Cassius had been proud of the empire he served during that time, and enjoyed feeling as though he were a part of a powerful, elite group. Then the empire asked him to guard the tomb. Whatever power and pride he thought he had vanished on the morning of the third day when he woke up and tried to make sense of what happened… What he did remember of that night could not be reconciled to the rational mind. All he knew for certain was that on the morning of the third day following the man's death, Cassius had woken up to see two things: his fellow soldiers, still sleeping, and the tomb, empty.

Even if he could put into words the terror he'd experienced, who would believe him? There was no good excuse for disobeying orders. Falling asleep while on duty was a crime punishable by death, but so was desertion. Sometimes he wished he had simply taken the punishment, because then it would be over.

That was how he ended up in Antioch in Syria. It was not a visit for pleasure; it was another city on the list of places Cassius had chosen to hide in since the incident. He was no stranger to life in the shadows after his unusual upbringing. In a city of this size, he might be able to stay for several months pick-pocketing passersby and committing small thefts before people grew suspicious. He could never stay long enough to be comfortable, however. Comfort bred laziness, laziness bred foolishness, and foolishness would lead to being caught.

He left the more unsavory parts of the city and made his way toward the agora. He knew that would be the best place to start to get the lay of the land and make decisions about what kinds of businesses would be the easiest to loot and where the safest place would be for him to lay his head at night. The marketplace in Antioch was busy, but not busy enough. As a youth he'd been thankful for his height and stature because it allowed him to appear older than he really was and assume more authority over boys his own age, but as an adult and one wanted by the Roman Army, he cursed the way it inhibited him from blending in with his surroundings. He stayed in the shadowy areas between stalls, not daring to walk out into the street. He did, however, keep his eyes peeled for an easy target. An unsuspecting man that he could filch some money from, a merchant he could loot when he wasn't paying attention… Cassius would take whatever he could get.

A larger man shouted into the crowds about fresh fruits and bargain prices. Cassius sauntered over to the stall and began turning over small fruits as though he were inspecting them, despite the fact that he had no intention of making an actual purchase. Out of the corner of his eye, he saw the merchant move closer to him, possibly suspicious of his motives. Cassius didn't allow even the slightest shadow of fear to cross his face. He simply continued conducting his "business" until, after a short bit of time, the merchant grew bored of watching him look meticulously over each item and turned his attention toward something else.

It was exactly as Cassius had planned. While he'd been turning the pomegranates back and forth, he really had his eye on the smaller figs to his left. He could hide one or two of those somewhere on his person without the man noticing. As Cassius was about to snatch some sustenance with his opposite hand and turn to go, a vision caught his eye. A young woman wearing a red shawl around her shoulders walked in the distance. The color was bold and stunning enough, but that wasn't what drew his attention to her. It was her eyes, wide and gray and full of light, as well as her voice. She was singing a song as she walked down the street and through the middle of the agora, half-dancing with one hand casually resting on the satchel at her side.

"Senseless girl," Cassius whispered.

She was beautiful, tall, and possessed striking features, but she should have been paying better attention to her surroundings. In a city like Antioch, one needed to remain on their guard at all times. Who was she and why was she walking alone? He could tell from her garments that she was a modest woman, not so low in class as to be in poverty, but not so high as to require fancy adornments and jewelry. The style of her clothing reminded him of the Jews, simple and functional. She definitely wasn't affluent, otherwise she would have been clothed in much finer cloth. The dress she wore was of a thick weave and more durable than fashionable, but it still managed to show her figure. What Cassius couldn't stop staring at, however, were her eyes. Her sparkling gray eyes seemed to reflect the silvery clouds that floated overhead.

"Ehem," the merchant grunted. Cassius had almost forgotten he'd been standing there. "Is there something I can help you with?"

Now there was no way for Cassius to pull off a successful heist, and all because he had been briefly distracted by some girl and her silvery eyes. He turned away and kept walking, although the image of the statuesque young woman was still in his peripheral vision and the sound of her voice continued to haunt his ears with its melodies.

Two figures moved to his right, catching Cassius' attention. He looked at them and saw that they too had taken notice of the gray-eyed girl, though their intentions did not seem to be of an innocent nature.

Cassius followed their sightline to see if she had noticed them.

Predictably, she had not. "Look around you," he muttered through gritted teeth. She stopped instead to admire a bit of cloth on the outside of some weaver's stall. Her song continued, but she paid little heed to her surroundings.

The two thugs flanked the gray-eyed girl on either side. Now she was most definitely aware of them.

Cassius watched as they said something unintelligible to her, probably warning her to be quiet. Her eyes widened, which Cassius didn't even think was possible. He saw her songs turn to cries until they covered her mouth and dragged her into a hidden space between two closed merchant stalls.

She should have been paying more attention. Still, his conscience kept nagging at him. As hateful as he'd become and as dark as his heart had grown, something about her appearance captivated him. Her eyes, her wistful demeanor, and her voice like birdsong… He was compelled to take action on her behalf, and he had a hard time believing that it had anything to do with his own sense of morality which dwindled low after all these years.

"Agh," he grunted, knowing that his mind wouldn't let him have any rest if he didn't do something. Stealing a piece of fruit or a loaf of bread was one thing, but holding a woman against her will? That was another thing entirely.

Giving up all notions of eating that day, he adjusted his course so that he would come right around the corner where the thugs probably thought they'd be hidden. As he approached, their voices grew easier to hear.

"Please, I'll give you all of the money I have. Here," she pleaded, trying to reach her coin.

"That's a good girl. Give us your money without making a sound, and we'll be on our way."

Her whole body trembled. "I'm trying, but the ties are stuck."

The larger man clearly got tired of waiting, and pulled the whole satchel from her shoulder with such force that she nearly fell over. Her shawl fell to the ground and Cassius briefly took notice of the long, fine tresses that fell well past her shoulders. Although Cassius had been and was willing to commit a number of crimes, including theft, his never involved terrorizing women.

"That doesn't belong to you," said Cassius, alerting them of his presence.

He jumped the first dastardly man from behind, throwing him against a nearby wall. Meanwhile, the larger man had let the girl go and was coming after Cassius. Cassius assumed a combat stance; the man was tall and strong, but Cassius was stronger still. Three punches—two to the gut and one to the face—was all it took to knock him backwards and make him rethink his choices. In the struggle, he dropped the satchel, and Cassius quickly grabbed it in one hand, still keeping his other fist curled and ready.

"Come on, let's go before we're seen!" Hissed the first one, who seemed so confident moments before. He spat blood onto the ground and took off in another direction, his comrade following closely behind him.

Cassius heaved several deep breaths as he watched them leave. After he calmed down a bit, he turned around to see the girl standing completely still and staring back at him with those same wide, gray eyes. He looked down at the ground near her feet where her shawl had fallen next to his own cloak. Bending down, he picked up both.

"I believe this is yours," he said, handing her the crimson cloth as well as the satchel.

She timidly grabbed them, tying the satchel to her waist and wrapping the shawl around her once again. "I don't know how to thank you…"

"We should move back into the middle of the marketplace. It's not good to stay in these dark corners for long."

As they did so, two other men who were startlingly alike in appearance ran toward them, calling what Cassius could only assume was her name. Cassius cleared his throat and took two steps backwards, adjusting his own cloak.

"Libi! Are you all right?" As the men got closer, Cassius noticed a few distinguishing features. Although they were clearly brothers, maybe even twins, the first one was slightly taller and much more muscular than the other. His face was also longer, and his cheek bones were more defined.

"Yuval, Gilad, two men tried to rob me, but I am fine now thanks to this man. He fought the attackers off bravely," said the girl called Libi. Cassius liked the name. It was simple, sweet, and suited her well, but he expected her to be more shaken by the encounter.

"We must thank you," said the second man. "My name is Gilad, this is my brother Yuval, and our sister Libi."

Inside his mind, Cassius chided himself. Why was he pleased to learn that this was their sister and not a wife?

"Thank you for your kindness," Libi whispered. "I prayed and asked the Lord for help, and there you were."

Cassius observed the trio, not quite sure what to make of their relationship, although he had no siblings or close friends of his own for comparison.

"Cities like Antioch are dangerous places. She should not have been alone," replied Cassius sternly, trying to avoid her gaze. Her eyes were beautiful, but perhaps dangerously so.

"We're always telling her not to get ahead of us. Praise the Lord that you were here."

With that, Cassius knew he was right in his assumption that these people were Jewish.

"What is your name?" said Yuval.

"I... I am called Cassius." His name was valuable information, but he supposed people like this were no threat to his identity, and no doubt there were at least a dozen others in this city alone who shared his name.

"Cassius, please allow us to thank you somehow," replied Yuval.

"Yes, will you join us for our evening meal? Our father will want to thank you as well." Gilad was quick in his speech.

Cassius raised a hand. "I wouldn't want to put you out." Cassius could tell these were humble people, and he could hardly intrude on their hospitality. All he had done was fend off a few thieves.

Beyond that, they didn't even know him. If this was how they treated all strangers, Cassius could see why the girl had been so vulnerable.

"We're already at the marketplace. It will just mean purchasing a few more things," said Gilad. "You must."

Cassius looked at each of the brothers, and then at their sister, all three of whom were of above average height. Libi blinked at him, her wide eyes seemingly compelling him to accept.

"Yes, it really won't be any trouble at all." Did her voice ever not resemble a melody?

"You don't even know who I am. I am a stranger to you," Cassius said with concern, still skeptical of these people. If they weren't going to protect themselves, Cassius somehow felt like he had to try.

"Any man who would perform such an act of kindness is more than welcome in our home. Our father and mother would feel the same. Consider it an invitation from a new friend," explained Gilad.

"All right, if you insist."

"Wonderful news!" exclaimed Yuval. The three of them turned toward the main road.

"Yes, wonderful," Cassius repeated under his breath. At least he was getting a meal out of this, though he sensed it would be an awkward dinner, and all because he couldn't ignore the gray-eyed girl in the marketplace. Even so, a hot and free meal was far better than any stolen pieces of fruit.

Cassius hadn't expected much when he'd accepted the Jews' offer for dinner. The three siblings led him to a narrow building without too much grandeur that faced the street. The surrounding area wasn't bad; they were within walking distance to several inns and other specialty shops in Antioch. In fact, it was a fine part of the city, seemingly reserved for more skilled craftsman. They were in close proximity to the Circus of Antioch, which was the greatest hippodrome in this part of the empire. The innkeepers of the area likely profited greatly off of the tourism the games and chariot races attracted.

As he stepped inside Cassius took note of the space and quickly identified their business as carpentry. The workshop was well-maintained and quite spacious for being cramped between so many other buildings. The arrangement of the area made good use of it, with separate work spaces for larger carpentry projects, and walls of tools for woodcutting and carving. He saw finished and half-finished wheels leaning against tables and chairs, piles of scrap wood sorted according to size and source, and several smaller projects that sat suspended in time, waiting to be completed. The covering over the workshop looked new, although light still managed to find a way through some cracks. The beams and walls that surrounded the structure were weathered, but they still seemed strong.

They came to the end of the workshop where there was another door and some windows. Going through the doorway, Cassius found himself in a courtyard, which was also very well maintained. There were enclosures for animals on one side, and a fire pit and clay oven on the other from which several savory aromas permeated the air. Cassius was half-tempted to ask if they'd be dining right there in the courtyard with the goats, donkey, and chickens with which he'd made uncomfortable eye contact.

Across the courtyard, however, Cassius saw where they were really leading him. Farther removed from the street stood a second structure, probably where they lived. They likely slept more peacefully without being so privy to the nighttime activities of the city. The building was at the other end of the courtyard, with its entrance directly opposite the door from the workshop, and stood just two stories tall.

"Libi," an older woman's voice cried out. "Libi, did you get the herbs I asked for?" The woman came out from the main house. She was quite regal and refined looking herself, but her hands were worn and she had lines around her eyes and on her forehead. Cassius could see that this family had not always lived so comfortably. The women of Rome would have kept their skin soft with ointments and creams as his mother had done, but these women had nothing to spare for such luxuries, be it time, money, or a combination of both.

"Oh, I didn't realize that you had brought a guest!" the woman exclaimed when she noticed Cassius' presence. At that moment, he'd expected to be eyed suspiciously. Any individual having half their wits about them would have been wise to be wary of Cassius, but again, no one showed any signs of trepidation.

Would all of the prey in Antioch be this easy to ensnare?

"Imma," began Yuval, "this is Cassius. We met at the agora."

"Come inside and tell me about it," said the woman, their mother, with a slight upturn to her voice.

Cassius followed the others into the house, or rather, the room. There was only one on the lower level of the house, mostly empty with a few mats rolled up in the corner, a low-lying table in the center that was probably used for eating, and some threadbare cushions scattered about.

"Well, what really happened was that Libi kept wandering ahead of us. You know how she gets when she's distracted," continued Yuval once they were all inside.

"I'm sorry, Imma." Libi bowed her head as though she were a child. "Everything was my fault. It was such a beautiful day and I couldn't help but take it all in. I was lost in my thoughts and caught off guard by two thieves who tried to take our coin. By then, Yuval and Gilad were too far behind me. Thank God for sending Cassius. He stopped them, saving me and our money."

The mother pursed her lips and turned to Cassius. Did she have tears in her eyes or was he imagining things?

"You are clearly a good man, Cassius. Not many others in Antioch would have done the same for our Libi."

"Libi," a much deeper voice resonated from the ladder on the right, which led up to the lofted upper level of the home. Cassius turned to see an older man who towered over them all. Cassius assumed that he was the father and man of the house. "You know how your mother and I feel. We send you to the marketplace with your brothers to protect you."

At once the girl nodded her head, this time with respect. "Yes, Abba. I apologize that I put Yuval and Gilad in such a situation. I am truly sorry. I promise—*really* promise—that next time I will try to do better."

Cassius had a flash of understanding of why she did not seem too startled. Things could have been so much worse, but if this was the kind of life she had been used to then it was likely she was sheltered from a great deal. Her family was loving and protective of her. Cassius' own life experiences on the other hand left him necessarily calloused. Perhaps if he had grown up like this, with a loving mother *and* father, he would not have grown so cold.

The family continued to chat with each other, hardly noticing his presence. Mixed into their conversation were constant references of praise to their God. Cassius eyed the door and wondered if he should leave, suddenly feeling incredibly awkward.

The mother held her daughter tightly. "You are safe, Libi. That is all that matters. Now I must put the finishing touches on dinner."

So that was that.

"Imma, did I smell my favorite lentil stew on the way inside?"

Gilad tilted his head to one side, throwing an arm affectionately around his mother's shoulder as he walked with her toward the courtyard. Her eyes once again seemed to light up with delight.

"Don't try and trick me, clever boy," she said as Gilad moved past her. "You won't be tasting a bit of it until it is ready."

"Oh, I'm not going to taste it, Imma," he said in a teasing way. "Although my nose is telling me that it needs a bit more cumin…"

"One cook at the fire will do, Gilad," she said, laughing lightly.

"I had better go with Imma," said Libi. She smiled at her father, Gilad, and then at Cassius, her gray eyes once again full of light. Then she too went out to the courtyard, leaving Cassius alone with the older man, whose name Cassius still did not know, and Yuval.

"My name is Tamir." At last, a proper introduction. "You've already met my wife, Chava, when you came in, and you are Cassius?"

"I am," he said, extending his arm for a respectful greeting. The gesture was unpracticed. Cassius couldn't recall greeting anyone in such a formal manner since his days as a soldier, although even those had been brief. He barely spoke to others except when necessary to lie or cheat, and he was even out of practice at that.

"What is this I hear of you rescuing my daughter in the marketplace this afternoon?" Tamir inquired with a protective instinct that made his voice drop to a low growl at the end of his sentence.

"It is exactly as she said," Cassius replied.

"Yes, but what do you say?"

"Two thugs came after her," said Cassius. "I merely fended them off."

"Such a humble explanation for something so extraordinary! My sons invited you to our home to share our dinner then?"

"Yes, I accepted only on the basis that I would not be an intrusion." Cassius' stomach roared from within him, giving away his other ulterior motives for joining their family for their evening meal.

Tamir continued, "Never you mind it. Chava makes more than enough for the five of us. She'll hardly even notice the addition to our table."

Cassius tittered, "She barely even noticed me when I walked in."

That made Tamir smile, which was good. The less these people suspected of him, the better.

They already invited him into their home, and while it wasn't much, he'd also seen their entire business. They must have made good money from their carpentry, for it seemed as though they had many projects going at one time. Perhaps he might be able to get more than a free meal from these people. If he could find where they kept their money, he could take enough to get off of the streets, and if not settled in Antioch, then well on his way somewhere else.

"Father, I'd like to check on Judah. I noticed on the way in that he's still refusing to put weight on that leg," said Yuval.

"Mm." Tamir nodded. "It doesn't seem to be getting better."

"Stubborn beast…" Yuval muttered.

"Is he lame?" Cassius didn't mean to interject, but he did have some knowledge of livestock. The Roman Army travelled with its fair share of horses and donkeys.

Yuval turned, surprised by Cassius' question. "A manservant came and paid to borrow him for an afternoon on behalf of his master. I think they may have overworked him, or perhaps he suffered some kind of injury. Since he came back, he's had a lopsided gait."

"I see. Shall we all go and take a look?"

"You know about donkeys?" asked Yuval, raising an eyebrow.

"I know about animals." Cassius' offer of help was nothing more than a military tactic. He was determined to gain their trust and conquer, as he had been trained to do.

"Yuval, lead the way. We might as well let Cassius have a try."

"Of course, Abba," Yuval responded, exiting back through the doorway from which they had come. Yuval was tall and strong; the spitting image of what Cassius assumed his father must have looked like at a younger age.

Briefly, Cassius wondered if he resembled his own father at any point in his life, but he banished the thought from his mind.

He had no father.

"Provide justice for the needy and the fatherless; uphold the rights of the oppressed and the destitute." — Psalm 82:3 CSB

"I think it's almost ready," declared Gilad, as if their mother needed his approval. Reaching into a nearby bowl, Gilad pulled a roasted date from within and bit into it, honey dripping down his chin before it could be stopped.

"Gilad, those are for dessert," Chava reprimanded, swatting at the air, "*and* you're making a mess." She tossed him a cloth and Libi smiled as she watched the scene, which had played out almost the same way with small variations here and there nearly every day since they first settled in their Antioch home.

"Imma, you have plenty of dates. No one will notice if one goes missing." Gilad winked.

Their mother's lips slowly curved into a smile before she answered, "One, just one, and that is all!" Imma shooed him away from the basket.

"Thank you, Imma," said Gilad, tossing the other half of the date into his mouth.

Dates. Libi was reminded of her *Savta*'s dates. As much as they tried, they had never been able to exactly replicate their Savta's specific process of roasting dates with honey and spices to bring out their natural flavors, cooking the fruit long enough to be chewy and sweet, but not long enough to become tough and tasteless.

Briefly, Libi's mind was assaulted with visions from her last days in Jerusalem. She thought of the basket of Savta's dates that she had carried, then the way that basket had been dropped to the ground in the commotion of the attack. She saw in her mind's eye the dark red splatter from the dates as they were trampled, and then the dark pools of blood that formed nearby.

That pleasant morning had been the last she would spend singing songs for her grandmother.

34 A.D., Jerusalem

The household was bursting with commotion on that particularly cool morning. Outside the walls of their family home, Jerusalem also awoke from its rest, but Libi didn't mind the noise of the city. After living in a world of complete silence for her entire life before the miracle, she delighted in every sound she heard; her brothers playing in the courtyard, the sound of her mother humming as she readied her things, even the sounds of people yelling and bartering in the busy marketplace down the street as they set up their carts for another day of business. Every sound was a thrill to Libi after Jesus had given her the gifts of hearing, understanding, speech, and song—song especially! She loved to sing. Even as she completed her last morning chore of sweeping the area where the family had just gathered to break their fast, she sang songs of praise to the Lord.

As she was going to put the broom away, Libi heard her grandmother call to her from the corner. "Songbird," she said softly, but still loud enough for Libi to hear the endearment in her tone and turn toward her.

"Yes, Savta?" Libi spoke respectfully, smiling at her grandmother Hodiyah whom she loved with all of her heart. Even in her silent years, Libi had always found comfort in her arms, assurance within her smile, and a sense of calm in her presence.

"Come and tell me where you learned that pretty song that you were singing," said Savta, gesturing for Libi to sit at her side. Libi did so eagerly and placed her hands in her grandmother's. She leaned in and closed her eyes, wanting to keep the memory in her heart for always. Savta's hands were cold, not because it was cold outside, but because they were always like that. She smelled of honey, like the honey she roasted her dates in, and although her hands felt like cool river water rushing over Libi's, she still felt warm and safe in her embrace.

"Oh." Libi blushed. She hoped her answer would not displease Savta. "I just sing the words that come into my head. I guess I made it up."

"You made up the tune as well?" Savta asked, her eyes widening.

Libi nodded. "Is it all right, Savta?" She hoped it was not considered rude or misbehaving to do so. Perhaps only adults were allowed to write songs. "I could sing a different song if it's not. One of the ones that you sing to me at nighttime?"

"All right?" Savta gasped. Laughing lightly, she continued, "Yes, my little songbird. It is good to know that the Lord is writing songs on your heart. It is even sweeter that you can share them. I would sound like an old goat if I tried to sing some of your pretty melodies."

Libi put her hand to her mouth to suppress a giggle. "Oh, Savta! You could never be an old goat!"

Giggles turned into robust laughter. Since Libi's *Sabba* Eliyahu had died, it seemed that Savta Hodiyah's smile had been rarer. Even from within the depths of such great loss, however, the family continued to choose the joy that Jesus had given them when He rose from the grave. Along the way, the family also had other exciting moments and milestones that brought them happiness, like the day Libi's elder cousin Shamira had wed her betrothed, Asa. Even so, it was the everyday moments like these, sharing happiness with her Savta, that brought Libi the most fulfillment.

Chava, Libi's mother, entered the room and joined in the merriment. "Libi, *hamuda*," said her mother, placing a hand on her shoulder, "we're getting ready to depart for the upper room where the disciples have called us to gather this week. I wanted to say farewell to you before we left. From the looks of things, you and Savta are going to have a most enjoyable time together!"

"Oh, yes, Imma... Farewell, and *shalom*," she said, approaching her mother to hug her tightly before she left. She tried to attempt a soft smile, but she could tell by the look on her mother's face that it was lacking something. She buried her face in her mother's side, not wanting to disappoint her.

Chava bent down to Libi's eye-level. Libi winced; her mother had clearly noted her downtrodden expression. "What is it, hamuda? Why the sadness? We'll only be gone for a few hours."

"Oh, nothing." Her voice was soft and small-sounding, like Libi herself who was the youngest child in their family.

"You can tell me, Libi," Chava said, gently rubbing Libi's shoulder and smoothing out her hair.

Libi pivoted on one foot and then the other, bowing her head before finding the confidence to look her mother in the eye and the courage to speak what was on her heart. "I thought we were all going to see the disciples today. I didn't know that I would be the one left behind."

"Oh, my miracle child," said Chava, pulling Libi closer. "Your abba and I think it is safer for you here. Savta is staying as well, so you can keep her company."

Libi nodded. She was not one to challenge the authority of her parents, or anyone for that matter. When she had been deaf-mute she had relied on others to lead her, and her family had always taken care of her. It took great courage for her to speak her feelings, even to those who were closest to her.

"I so love being with everyone else, hearing the disciples speak, and singing when we worship. I like hearing the melodies and trying to match my own voice to the others, and when they talk about Jesus…" Libi let her voice trail off, not finishing her sentences. She knew her mother would understand.

Chava took a deep breath. "Let me go and speak with your father. Perhaps it will be possible for you to join us. Go and tie your sandals just in case, all right?"

This was enough hope to restore Libi's countenance. She skipped blissfully off to the room she shared with her older cousins until Shamira married Asa and the two newlyweds moved to the rooftop of the house. Now it was only Rut and Libi, and while she missed the extra time with Shamira, she loved Rut equally. Rut also had a beautiful voice, and often taught Libi the harmonies to some of the family's favorite songs. When Libi returned downstairs to where the rest of her family waited, Libi searched her mother's eyes for some signs of approval.

"Libi, your father and I," Chava began, pausing to gaze at Tamir. Libi liked seeing them happy together. In the times when she couldn't hear, she was still able to tell that her parents hadn't always been so close, but since Jesus' resurrection they shared more smiles than ever before. "Your father and I have agreed that you may join us today."

"However," her father intervened, "we don't want to leave your Savta alone in case we are gone longer than expected. Yuval, you will stay behind."

Libi looked at her eldest brother, who was only older than Gilad by mere moments. According to her mother, they had been picking fights with each other even from within her womb. To this day, Yuval was the tough, mischief maker who favored their father, while Gilad favored their mother and had often borne the brunt of his brother's teasing. Libi liked the idea of walking with Gilad to meet the disciples, as she had always been closest to him.

Yuval's shoulders dropped at the announcement and his eyes narrowed. He opened his mouth to object, but Gilad spoke first.

"Abba, I would be willing to stay. I know that Yuval also wanted to go today, even more than me. We could switch places if it would not displease you and Imma," suggested Gilad.

Their father looked back and forth between the two of them, nodding his head in agreement with Gilad's suggestion. Libi wasn't surprised that Gilad had made such a kind offer. It seemed that she would be walking with Yuval after all.

Libi heard her mother turn to Savta Hodiyah and whisper, "I know it must seem as though we indulge her too much, but she so seldom asks for anything."

"Chava," she heard Savta reply, "I am delighted that Libi will be joining you. I know that the melodies our little songbird carries will delight the hearts of many of the believers today, and truthfully, I don't think I've ever spent a day with just my youngest grandson. I am looking forward to it. Aren't you, Gilad?"

"Yes, Savta," he replied.

"Perhaps you can help me choose the vegetables for the stew and chop them up? My hands are not as strong as they used to be, and your help would be so appreciated." Savta winked at him.

"I would like that very much!" said Gilad, leaning forward on the tips of his toes. Libi knew he would probably end up eating more of the vegetables than adding them to any stew, as both of her brothers had unusually large appetites, but she wouldn't dare call her brother out.

"Well now that it is settled, we really must be going. I hope Gilad doesn't cause you any trouble, Imma," said Tamir.

"Gilad? Never! Oh, Chava—don't forget to take the dates I prepared for the others."

"Yes, thank you for reminding me. Libi, would you carry the

basket?"

Libi did as instructed. "Yes, Imma. Farewell, Savta!"

"Farewell, songbird!"

Libi ran out the front door to lead the way and stumbled upon Shamira and Asa sitting close together underneath the courtyard tree, hands intertwined and heads close together as they whispered secret conversations. They laughed and pulled apart when they saw the others, but still kept a tight grasp on each other's hands despite the distance between them.

"I feel like them," Libi heard her father say from behind her. She could tell from the hushed tone to his voice that the words were meant for only her mother's ears, but she couldn't help listening.

"I know what you mean," Chava whispered back at him, softer still.

Libi's aunts emerged last with baskets of food of their own. The baskets contained what would be their lunch and their gifts to the disciples and other believers. They all assembled in the street and began the journey with the women and children walking first, and the men at the rear.

Libi walked beside Yuval, guarding the dates she carried as though they were valuable gems and coins.

"Oh, I want one of those," said Yuval as more of a demand than a request.

Libi's brows moved closer together as she considered his words. The dates were her responsibility, meant to be saved and shared at the gathering of The Way. Would it be wrong to allow Yuval to take one treat? If she relented once, would he keep asking and taking? Libi knew as well as anyone that no one could refuse Savta's dates.

"Shouldn't you ask Imma if it is all right?" said Libi softly.

"Nah," Yuval muttered, "I'll wait until we get there." He paused and scowled a bit, but then his demeanor changed in a flash to something much more amicable. "Libi, if the basket is too heavy, I can carry it for you."

This kind of care was natural for Gilad, but coming from Yuval was a surprise and delight. Libi beamed, thinking she had the kindest brother in the world. "Oh, thank you, Yuval! We can take turns if you'd like."

Yuval nodded his head and didn't say a word. He simply took the basket and kept walking. Libi felt a tiny twinge of sadness at losing the responsibility she had only just been given, but she quickly pushed it aside, not wanting to be selfish in her thoughts. At least he was helping her, and she knew that between the two of them, actions spoke louder than words. After a while Yuval handed the basket back to her and she prepared her arms for its full weight. She must have made an error in her estimations, because upon impact she noticed that the basket was much lighter than she recalled it being.

"Thank you, Libi," said Yuval, wiping his face on his sleeve.

"You're thanking me?" asked Libi, perplexed. "Why? I should be thanking you for— "

Libi was interrupted by a terrible sound. A sharp, ear-splitting sound. A woman was screaming! The shrill noise startled Libi, and she dropped the basket. The contents spilled over and out into the street. "The dates!" she gasped, but no one else seemed to notice.

The sounds grew louder and what was once one scream morphed into a thousand and one screams, followed by shouting and the drumming of many rapid footsteps. She tried to convince herself that it might have been from a festival of some kind, but judging by the reaction of the others she was with, she concluded that it must not be.

"Children, come here!" her imma called out. "Quickly!" Libi and Yuval raced to their mother, reacting to the urgency in her voice. It was a tone Libi had never heard her use before. What's the matter, Imma?" She turned to see her family members clutching onto one another. Asa and Shamira stayed near her parents, *Dodh* Aharon and Dodah Elisheva. Cousin Rut and her mother, Dodah Devorah, linked arms. Meanwhile, cousin Benayahu, his father, Dodh Binyamin, and her own father stood erect, craning their heads to see what was happening.

"Abba, what's wrong?" called out Rut to her own father.

"Binyamin, tell us what you see," echoed Dodah Devorah to her husband.

Dodh Binyamin didn't have to tell them what was happening, nor did anyone else. The crowds did that for them. "Stephen was a blasphemer! He got what was coming to him!"

Stephen… Libi knew the name, but from where? The Way?

"These followers of Jesus are nothing but troublemakers! Seize them!"

"Follow Saul's lead!"

Libi's abba's eyes widened like she had never seen before. "We have to get out of here, now!" Abba's voice boomed as he started to usher them back up the streets from which they had come. Libi tried to convince herself that she was playing a game like one she played with her brothers which involved chasing each other around the tree in their courtyard, but she knew in her heart that this was not a time for play, and she was afraid.

Somehow their entire group made it back to their home safely, but Libi did not relax once she was inside their walls. Their gate appeared broken down, signaling trouble. Even here, where Libi always felt the most secure, darkness entered.

"Savta?" Libi whimpered.

"Imma," she tried again, "where is Gilad?"

Panic flooded her mother's eyes and the whole family remained silent, shaking in fear. No one was able to form answers to the questions Libi was asking. They were all too busy taking in the sights of the aftermath of the violence against Christ-followers.

The tree that grew in their front yard still stood strong, but it seemed to lean to its side as though it were mourning something. The fire remained lit in the pit, despite the fact that the food which had been warming over it had been cast down onto the dirt. Broken shards of pottery surrounded the main door into their home.

Her father and uncles were the first to approach the house, fearing the worst. After a few moments, Libi's abba called out, "Chava! Come at once!"

Libi's mother, Dodah Elisheva, and Dodah Devorah followed immediately.

"Wait here, Yuval, and watch over your sister," she told them.

Turning around, Libi approached her cousins. "Shamira? What is going on?"

No answer came.

"Rut? Has something happened to Savta? Like what happened to Sabba?" Libi asked, the memory of her grandfather's passing suddenly very fresh in her mind.

"Don't be afraid, Libi. Pray for peace. In fact, why don't we all sit down and pray together? God will hear us and protect us," explained Rut, pulling them into a circle and beginning her own prayers.

Libi knelt in the rubble and prayed silently, her lips opening and closing as she called on God for protection and asked for another miracle. Seconds passed like hours until the adults emerged from the house, Savta's weight supported by all three of her sons.

"Savta!" Libi gasped, "You are all right!"

She darted to her beloved grandmother, ready to jump into her arms, but as she got closer, she became startled by the way Savta's face drooped. Her Sabba's face had looked much the same after he had suffered the pains which brought about his final days on this earth. She was not as well off as Libi first surmised, but Libi wasn't ready to lose Savta too; not like this.

Letting go of Savta Hodiyah for a moment, Libi's Dodh Binyamin leaned to correct the bench that had fallen over. Dodh Aharon and Libi's father helped her sit down, where she rested her head on Tamir's shoulder.

"What happened here?" Dodh Aharon asked his mother with a

tremor in his voice.

Shamira ran to get some wet cloths, being faster than any of them. Shamira had always been one for action.

"People, *angry* people, came here shouting and broke down the gate. I told Gilad to hide and run at the first chance he got. I tried to run into the house myself, but my old legs are no match for a swarth of younger, impassioned men. They said they knew that this house was a house of Christ-followers, and they asked me whether I was one too. Then they asked where the rest of you were, and I couldn't tell them. I wouldn't give up Gilad, and I honestly didn't know where you were. You could've been anywhere in the city for all I knew. They muttered something— one of them struck me. That's all I remember. Where is Gilad? Is he all right?"

Her gray hairs were stained scarlet. Libi convinced herself it was the juice of dates, even though she knew the fruit was still back on the road somewhere.

"I'm right here," said Gilad from behind them. "I did like Savta said… I ran and hid, but came back when I thought it was safe."

Chava's eyes flooded with tears as she sprinted toward her other son.

"You… are… well," Savta said, panting for air between words. "Good…" Savta's eyes started darting back and forth, never stopping long enough to focus on anything.

"Savta?" Libi asked. "W-w-what's happening?"

"Imma," said Libi's abba. "You need to rest."

Savta straightened herself and turned toward Libi, but Libi could tell that each word was a great labor for her, and the date juice that trickled down Savta's forehead seemed to grow darker. "It is like your Sabba said, Libi. I think my strength has run out in this life, but I will soon have strength ten-fold in the next."

"Savta, no!" Libi began to cry and shake, her emotions taking over.

"You must never stop singing your songs, Libi. Never stop

singing the Lord's praise. He will protect you as He has always done, and He will give you peace. Take Him with you, wherever you go, and never stop sharing His light."

"Savta!" she cried again, reaching out to hold her grandmother. Rut held her back in her own arms. Savta's eyelids fell for one last time and Libi knew she was gone. Soon they were all gone, for they immediately made plans to depart Jerusalem forever.

43 A.D., Antioch in Syria

Libi recalled the painfully vivid memories of their travels to Antioch, and their life in hiding as they moved from city to city, afraid of letting anyone know who they were or establishing any roots. They witnessed too much horror in Jerusalem to call another city home so quickly after the day Saul of Tarsus laid waste to those who believed in the divine authority of Jesus of Nazareth. Unfortunately, her family had been scattered. While the rest of them settled in the Phoenician hills and started farms, Libi's father took her, her brothers, and their mother even farther. It was hard, but they found ways of keeping in touch as much as they could, and Libi always looked forward to when the next letter would come, bringing with it news of Shamira and the rest of her cousins.

Eventually, as Savta had said, Libi did find the peace of the Lord. She was comforted by the knowledge that Savta lived a long, good life, and in truth, she missed Sabba dearly. Now she was in Paradise where she would want for nothing, and her strength would never run out. The nightmares and the tears came to an end, and gradually God had taken what the devil had planned for evil and turned it into a blessing. The Lord provided as He always did. Since then, they had been serving in Antioch with a large number of believers, both Jewish and Gentile. She witnessed the beauty of God's design and the glory of seeing His plans come to fruition on an almost daily basis. Although at times she found the memories of her childhood to be bittersweet, she was happy alongside her brothers and parents. Songs of praise to the Lord, their redeemer and deliverer, never ceased.

She still didn't understand how or why people could be so cruel, but she thanked God for blessing her family and protecting them always from those who persecuted them, as Cassius had protected her from the thugs on the street. Her eyes drifted to the other side of the courtyard, where Cassius, Yuval, and her father stood talking surrounding their donkey, Judah. She lost herself in observing his demeanor.

"Libi, did you need something?"

Libi smiled congenially, blinking her eyes and refocusing her attention. "No, Imma, I was lost in my own thoughts. I only came to make sure Gilad didn't ruin your stew, and to give you the herbs you asked for. In all the commotion of our arrival, I nearly forgot. They are here in my satchel," said Libi, pulling them out from the bag at her side. Imma took what she needed and dropped it into the pot. Gilad continued to stir while Imma went to store the rest to be used in the days to come.

"Pull that pot off the heat and help me take everything inside," their mother instructed when she returned. "Be careful not to drop it."

"I would *never*!" said Gilad, clutching his heart and feigning a wound. Libi and her Imma took baskets of already prepared food in their arms. Together, all three of them went inside and began arranging the food on the table and tidying the main room of the house.

Turning to Libi, she continued, "Hamuda, how were Taliah, Keinan, and the children?"

"They are well, Imma! Taliah is expecting again."

"She is? That is exciting news." Imma beamed as she added some finishing touches to their meal. "And the children?"

"They're wonderful, as always. Today I told them the story of the good Samaritan, as I remember it being told by the disciples in Jerusalem. Oh, but Imma, I haven't told you the most shocking part of the day."

"More shocking than what happened at the agora?" Imma raised an eyebrow.

"Well, this was in a different way. We found a baby left outside of Taliah's house! At first we thought she was a newborn, but Taliah thinks she is hungry and small for her age," Libi explained.

"It's true, Imma. I saw the child myself, and she was the tiniest baby I'd ever seen," said Gilad, now lounging on a cushion directly in front of the stew.

"Oh, and you've seen so many babies," said Libi, tossing another date to her brother who caught it in his mouth.

"That's enough with my dates!" Chava said, a hint of warning mixing with laughter. "Are they going to keep the child with another on the way?"

Libi nodded. "They plan to for now, but Taliah is not sure how many more children they can take in."

Chava pursed her lips. "I don't know many other people who would be as generous as Taliah and Keinan, except maybe you, Libi."

"That's what she asked me to pray about. We are hopeful that by the time Barnabas returns, God might provide some kind of an answer to their situation. Perhaps more money, or more resources, or another family that might be able to help…"

"Well, I shall pray for all of these things too, Libi. If God can provide an honorable man like Cassius within a few moments— honor being a rare thing in this city—surely He can supply what is needed for all of those orphaned children."

"That's what I said!" Libi beamed. Taliah and Keinan were good people. How could God not bless them?

Her mind concentrated on Cassius as she watched her mother gather what was needed to serve the meal. Cassius was not unpleasant to look at by any means. Libi couldn't deny his good looks, strong, muscular physique, and the attention commanded by his forest-like eyes, brown with green and yellow flecks. His most distinguishing feature was the scar across the left side of his face that cut through his brow and made its way down below his eye, hitting his cheekbone. She let her mind wander, imagining what heroic act might have led to that scar. He had been noble to rescue her, but Libi could sense by the way he acted after the fact that not all of his scars were physical. Some came from emotions. Cassius seemed all too familiar with the kind of darkness that possessed her attackers. He bore a great weight upon his shoulders, and Libi strongly desired to find out what it was. Perhaps if he knew who Jesus was, he would know what warm light was waiting for him if he only chose to step into it. The light Libi chose to live in each and every day, just as Savta told her.

"Libi, please go and tell your father, Yuval, and Cassius to wash up. I don't want the food to get cold."

"Yes, Imma," she replied, and quickly turned back toward the courtyard as her mother requested.

62

"After the priests had assembled with the elders and agreed on a plan, they gave the soldiers a large sum of money and told them, 'Say this, 'His disciples came during the night and stole him while we were sleeping.' If this reaches the governor's ears, we will deal with him and keep you out of trouble.' They took the money and did as they were instructed, and this story has been spread among Jewish people to this day." — Matthew 28:12-15 CSB

Yuval coaxed the donkey to a better position that enabled Cassius to get behind him. From that vantage point, he got a clear view of the problem and moved in closer to the hoof where Yuval had gestured with his eyes. Although Cassius was grateful, he didn't need a hint to tell that the donkey's hindlimb was in severe pain. He reached down to touch it and could feel the heat coming off of it, along with pulsing directly above the hoof. "Do you have warm water?"

"Yes, in the trough," Tamir replied.

"Bring me a bucket of it," he urged, a part of his voice still mimicking the military commander he'd never become.

In no time at all Tamir returned with the bucket, only for Cassius to make another request. "Do you have a cup or a ladle? And a small knife or a pick?"

Again, Tamir left and returned with the requested items without saying a word.

"He may have stepped on something, or gotten something stuck in the hoof wall that is irritating it. If we can't find a way to relieve the pain, there could be serious consequences," Cassius explained. In the journey from Rome to Jerusalem, they'd had to treat more than one horse with similar abscesses. Taking the simple wooden cup, Cassius began to pour the water on the donkey's hoof, and started picking away at the dirt and debris. At first, the donkey let out a displeased sound, but Yuval settled him again. When the hoof was fully cleaned, Cassius slowly lowered the hoof into the bucket, soaking it with the warm water. The donkey resisted, but relaxed over time.

"The water will help him relax for now, but you should have… Chava?" Cassius looked up for confirmation and then continued, "You should have Chava boil some milk over the fire." He nodded to the other side of the courtyard. "Allow it to cool until it is merely warm and not scalding hot, then mix some pieces of bread in it until it becomes like a soft clay. Apply it as a poultice to the base of the foot, then wrap the leg securely in cloth. Hopefully that will draw out the puss and allow the hoof to heal."

"Thank you, young man," said Tamir, watching as Cassius slowly and methodically continued his bath of Judah's leg. "We might be able to save this old donkey yet!"

"Don't thank me now. The poultice should be changed daily, and his hoof should soak for a bit in warm water between applications. It could take at least a week to know if he'll make a full recovery." Something in his heart pulled at him, and he hoped he hadn't come across as dry or hopeless. A bedside manner had not been a part of his military training.

"Abba? Yuval?"

There was that gray-eyed girl again. *Libi.* Her gaze burned into his soul. He felt like she was seeing right into him. Did she know the inner-workings of his mind? The violence he'd seen—even enacted himself—and the crimes he still planned in his head? Impossible.

"Libi, Cassius was taking care of Judah. He thinks we will be able to save him," explained Tamir. Cassius wanted to roll his eyes. Had he not already explained that he wasn't certain about the animal's fate?

"That would be such a blessing! We must add that to the list of reasons to thank the Lord for sending Cassius to us, and pray for that stubborn animal," Libi added with a smile.

"I've a mind to go after that manservant for not watching what he was doing," said Tamir. "We need him for hauling materials and delivering finished pieces to our buyers."

"Abba, you know it won't do any good. Besides, Judah is too stubborn to let himself go lame," Yuval joked.

Cassius felt like he should have joined in with their laughter, but he seemed to not know how. The pleasant conversation came so naturally among their family, but it was as foreign to Cassius as every city he'd travelled through since leaving Rome.

Libi cleared her throat. "Imma told me to come and fetch you. It is time to wash up and sit down for dinner. The table is set."

"Ah, so my twin finally stopped arguing over seasonings, eh?" asked Yuval.

"Only after Imma threatened to deny him any food at all," Libi said, laughing alongside her brother.

"Easy now," interrupted her father. "Both of you should go inside, and I will follow shortly. Cassius, are you almost finished here?"

"Yes, I'll be right there."

"Very well then, the water for washing up is by the door. Thank you again for your work with Judah. I was a shepherd before I became a carpenter, and while I know a fair bit about animals, larger beasts are not my specialty."

"I've said before, it might not work…"

"But you also said that it might! That's hope, and hope leads to faith. Faith, even the size of a mustard seed, can go a long way…"

The size of a mustard seed? That wasn't very much. This was a strange family indeed; Cassius wondered if perhaps he might feel more at home with the livestock after all. At least they didn't utter strange proverbs and confusing, if not unbelievable, sentiments. Nevertheless, he finished his work and went inside to join them.

"Come, Cassius," said Chava, motioning toward an empty cushion around the other side of the table.

"I apologize for my tardiness. That *is* one stubborn donkey you have."

"It is of no matter. Judah will be grateful to you in the coming days, I am sure." Tamir smiled.

"I have already set some milk to heat over the embers outside, as you requested." Chava smiled as she began ladling the stew into smaller bowls and passing them around the table, accompanied by pieces of flatbread.

Cassius shuffled around the table, making his way over to the empty space the woman of the house had pointed out for him. "Are you sure…"

"He's old, but he'll pull through. Now sit. You are more than welcome at our table after all that you have done for us."

"I meant, are you sure it is all right for me to dine with you? I have heard that your people…"

"Jews?" Tamir corrected, raising an eyebrow.

"Forgive me if I am being rude, but I have heard that you have restrictions about dining with people who do not keep your same laws. Are you sure that my eating with you will not cause problems between you and your God?" asked Cassius.

"Ah, well, Cassius, you will find that we are not as strict about the old laws as other Jews." Something in his response made Cassius narrow his eyes. "Besides that," Tamir continued, "we would be hard-pressed to live in a city like Antioch and not associate with Gentiles. I meant it when I said you are welcome."

"Very well," Cassius said submissively. He reminded himself that how these Jews chose to keep their commandments was no concern of his. He was just there for the food.

"Let us pray," said Tamir.

Prayer. Cassius scoffed inwardly. With his mother's guidance, he had prayed all of the prayers to all of the known and unknown gods in the Roman world and none of them had ever done any good. What would be required of him now? Were there words he needed to know? Rituals or actions he would be expected to perform to earn his plate?

Tamir bowed his head and closed his eyes respectfully. Briefly, Cassius locked eyes with Libi. She clasped her hands and nodded to him, almost as though she were showing him what to do. He copied her movements and nodded back to her, raising an eyebrow in question to search for confirmation. She cracked a small smile before closing her eyes, and he assumed he had done everything correctly.

The prayer that followed was unlike any Cassius had ever heard. Tamir spoke to his God as though he knew Him personally. The informality, which should have put Cassius at ease, only made him feel more out of place. A feeling settled in his stomach like the kind he felt during the earliest days of his military training, when he seemed to be the only one who didn't know how to conduct himself.

"Our father in heaven, Your name be honored as holy. Your kingdom come. Your will be done, on earth as it is in heaven. Give us today our daily bread, and forgive us our debts, as we also forgive our debtors, and do not bring us into temptation, but deliver us from the evil one. We thank you for the stew set before us, and for Chava, whose hard work has given us this delicious meal. We also thank you for Yuval, Gilad, and Libi, and for their good health and successes. They bring honor to us through their faith in You, and we pray that they would continue to honor You for all the days of their lives. Finally, we thank You for Cassius, for bringing him into our lives at just the right time. We pray that we can be a blessing to him, as much as he has been to us. We ask all of these things in Jesus' name, amen."

Jesus.

These were no ordinary Jews. They were Christ-followers. They were the very same group of radicals who created the resurrection myth. It had to be a myth, because Cassius had seen the Nazarene's dead body with his own eyes, and what he remembered of the morning of the third day was too terrifying to have been real. It had to have been a trick. These people were exactly the kind of people that Cassius had spent the last ten years despising.

"Is the food not to your liking?" Chava asked, her voice sounding as though she were wounded or injured.

"My apologies, I forgot where I was for a moment. It has been a long day of travel for me, but this stew is delicious." Cassius hungrily took a spoonful of the broth, quenching a desire in his stomach that he nearly forgot existed after the startling revelation. Whatever seasonings Chava or Gilad added did not matter—it was the best meal he'd tasted in years.

And it tasted of revenge.

These Christ-followers had brought him into their home, offered him food, and sat with him at a meal. By technical definitions, they had aided a Roman soldier in evasion of justice. That made them criminals like him, whether they realized it or not. If he were to be captured while in Antioch, or even come close, they could be implicated.

Chava smiled politely, and the clanking of dishes resumed at a moderate volume. Again, the remains of his conscience tugged at his heart and mind. Did these people deserve his hatred? All that he knew of them aside from their religious affiliations was their inexplicable kindness and generosity.

Cassius mentally took a step back and reexamined the situation from a military perspective. Their kindness was likely just an offensive tactic, nothing more than a ploy to distract him and convince him to join their cult. Cassius willed himself to believe that the only attraction he felt was not to these people or to their God, but to their food.

"So, Cassius, you seem to have travelled far. Where do you come from?" asked Tamir.

Cassius should have said nowhere. "I am originally from Rome."

"Is that where you learned about animals? I hear they have large circuses there, even larger than the hippodrome of Antioch, with chariot races and such."

He learned about animals in the same place he learned about being a soldier, but he could hardly tell them that either. "Yes, the Circus Maximus is most impressive."

Tamir leaned backwards. "Was your father in the livestock business?"

Cassius forced himself to unclench his jaw. "I never knew my father." That was the truth. "My upbringing was much more… nomadic. I picked up a few things here and there as I travelled." That was a stretch, but it was close enough to the truth that he could say it with meaning and intonation in his voice, and enough of an interesting story to garner these people's sympathies.

"I see," said Tamir.

"What brought you to Antioch then?" asked Yuval.

Turning to the other side of him, Cassius continued, "A fresh start. Antioch is a large city. There is much opportunity for trade here."

"That is true. What trades are you skilled in?"

"A bit of handling livestock, horses especially." Which really meant raising and riding military horses. "A bit of smithing." Which really meant weaponry. "A bit of carpentry." Which translated to making makeshift barricades for the Roman Army and assisting with the setup and tear down of camps. "I know a decent amount about many trades, but not enough of any one particular skill to call myself a valuable asset. Still, I can make myself useful."

"Have you a place to stay this night?" asked Tamir.

"No, but I'm sure I will find something," Cassius said, leading them all to make their offer as an army would lure the enemy to the optimum position for victory.

"Why don't you stay here for tonight?"

"Are you sure?" replied Cassius.

"There is room to make up a bed in the workshop, if you do not mind the cramped quarters."

"I've slept in worse places." Another truth. Cassius learned from his training that if he were ever captured by the enemy and questioned for information, he would only live to tell the tale if he was able to blend enough of the truth for his story to be believable, with enough false information to protect the empire. Even then, survival was never a guarantee. It seemed to be working well in this situation, however. Only this time, Cassius was the empire.

"It's settled, then. Stay the night with us, and then in the morning we can see what those poultices will have done for Judah's leg."

Cassius accomplished the mission that brought him to this house: a hot meal and temporary accommodation. The knowledge that they were followers of Jesus who was called Messiah and Christ made him want to stay longer. Manipulating their emotions for his own personal gain wouldn't bring his career back. He would still be forced to live a life in the shadows, but it might satisfy a part of his need for justice, which was better than no justice at all.

Cassius smiled courteously and continued eating.

He was already a criminal; he had nothing to lose.

"So those who were scattered went on their way preaching the word." - Acts 8:4 CSB

After the meal, Cassius oversaw the making of the poultice and applied it himself, wrapping Judah's leg carefully. They were all grateful to him for his assistance, but Libi most of all. What he had shared of his story stirred her heart with compassion. It made her think about Rufus, Felix, Phoibe, and now Tirzah who were so blessed to have found a loving home. Cassius, however, sounded as though he never knew the meaning of the word.

"Thank you for showing us what to do, Cassius. I will have Libi help me prepare more tomorrow," promised Chava, taking away the dishes they had used for the poultice now that they were finished. "Libi will get you some blankets so that you do not catch a chill in the night."

"Of course. I will bring them in a moment." Libi smiled and went upstairs to the loft where she slept on the other side of a divider that separated her from her parents, and where they kept the spare linens.

From there she could still hear the hum of their voices as they carried on polite conversation about Cassius' life in Rome, his travels, and the stew. Even though he'd acquiesced to answering all of their questions, Libi could tell that there were things about which he did not wish to speak. Something about the way that he clutched onto his cloak when they were in the marketplace and walked with his head bowed, refusing to make eye contact with anyone they passed on the street told her that he was a man perhaps living in fear. Libi knew exactly what that felt like.

Libi's parents had feared for her life ever since the persecution in Jerusalem, although as she grew older, she realized that their fear for her had certainly developed much earlier than that. As soon as they became aware of her disability, they must have been terrified, and within reason. Some people, from those like the men who had tried to mug her in the agora to Saul of Tarsus himself, kept only darkness in their hearts. She remembered the consequences of such darkness with great pain.

34 A.D., Jerusalem

In the wake of Savta's death, arrangements were made quickly. They bid farewell to their friends in haste and sold nearly everything they had except for a small fraction of what had once been a large flock of sheep, even taking losses when necessary. Dodh Binyamin stayed with Beni in the fields with what was left of their sheep, packed and ready to move. It all came together in a matter of days.

"But where will we go?" Libi's abba asked the question they had all been too busy to contemplate. "Now that we've sold everything, we cannot keep hiding in Jerusalem. Surely there will be more uprisings."

"North toward Phoenicia. Damascus, Tyre, or Sidon maybe," suggested Libi's Dodh Aharon, the eldest of the three brothers.

"We must leave today while the sun is still rising, and no one outside of our family can know of our exact plans until we are settled."

"Saul of Tarsus is a committed man," said Asa with a knowing tone. Before Asa married Shamira, he had been a Levite training under his father to become a priest. After Asa chose to follow Jesus, he'd become a shepherd like Libi's father and uncles, and when he and Shamira were wed, he became a part of their family. Now more than ever, Libi knew her family would certainly be grateful for his insight, even if she didn't understand fully why she had to leave her home. "If he is involved with this in any way, then heading north toward Damascus is our best bet. If we need to keep moving after that, so be it, but where we settle later is not as important as getting away from here now."

"Asa is right," Aharon added. "Pack what you can, necessities only. Who knows that we may have but moments before another attack begins?"

Everyone sprang into action, except for Libi. She wasn't quite understanding what was happening. "Imma?"

As Chava gathered the necessities she spoke quickly, "Libi, remember how you followed us when you could not hear? This is like that once again. God will lead us even if we do not understand what He is asking. He will always be with us, as your Savta said, so there is no need to fear. Only trust. We must hurry, hamuda. Go get your bedroll. Before you roll it up, put some of your clothing in it, but keep it light. You will have to carry it on your back."

"I have it here," said Rut, appearing behind them with her own pack already on. "I put most of Libi's things in my own, so her pack is very light. Come Libi, I can put it on you now."

"Thank you, Rut" said Libi's imma.

"Shamira, are you coming?" said Libi as she and Asa came down the stairs from their rooftop hideaway.

"We will soon," she said, then looked to Asa with wide eyes before she continued. "Asa and I are going a separate way, to say farewell to Eliana and Matthan. We will meet with you again in Damascus." Eliana was Shamira's older sister, who had married Matthan when Libi was still a toddler. She had yet to even think of how she might never see Eliana again. "Try not to grow so much while we are apart, all right, Libi?" She did her best to smile, but Libi was not reassured.

"Aharon," added Asa, "Shamira and I can herd what is left of the livestock we have not sold. That way you all will be able to travel faster."

"I refuse to allow the family to be pulled apart," announced Dodh Aharon.

"Shamira, what if something happens?" said Dodah Elisheva.

"You both know that as long as I live, I will never let anything happen to Shamira. God willing, we will see you again in Damascus; I vow it on my life," said Asa with a sincerity in his eyes that made Libi's lips quiver. She knew he meant what he said, but the idea of them being separated even for a short time made her heart hurt too much.

Shamira nodded and turned to her father. "Abba, it is the best way. You know it is true. The two of us traveling with the sheep will be far less suspicious than our entire family, and this way Dodh Binyamin can travel with Dodah Devorah."

After much more reasoning, he eventually nodded reluctantly and that had been that. They departed immediately.

Only Eliana and Matthan would have known of their plans, and it was better that way. They would not attract attention with their departure.

By the time night fell, Libi couldn't even see the once shining, golden-hued walls that surrounded the great city of Jerusalem. She had fallen asleep in her father's arms, but they did not stop walking. They travelled day and night until they came to Damascus. When they pitched their tents, Libi thought that would be their home once Shamira and Asa arrived, but after overhearing her parents' discussions one too many times, she knew they would not be settling there.

"Tamir," Libi heard her mother beg, "we can make a good life here. Let the children settle. This wandering isn't good for them."

"*Danger* isn't good for them."

"They're not in danger," she whispered.

"You don't know that!" Abba's voice had grown too loud for their cramped quarters. She may have kept her eyes closed and pretended to be asleep, but true rest had evaded her since they had left the only home that she had ever known.

Lowering his voice, he continued, "Chava, beloved, you must trust me."

"Brother," Dodh Aharon had said, interceding between them both, "you can't truly think that people will follow your daughter all the way to Damascus. Only a few people here even know about her or who we are, and they are old friends from Jerusalem."

What was there to know about her? Libi pondered their words.

"Libi's hearing… Her ability to speak is a miracle. Every time any one of us looks at her, we see that. You saw what they did to men like Stephen who dared to speak out about Jesus. What more would they be willing to do to a girl like Libi, an innocent caught up in the middle of this? She is living proof of the very message they are trying so hard to destroy."

"I understand your fears, brother, I do. Are you so sure that you must keep going? Have you prayed about it?"

When she heard nothing, Libi opened one eye and saw her father nod in the dim light of the night. "We will go to Antioch, where no one will know us. It is a large city. It will be easy for us to get a fresh start there."

"Antioch!" said Dodh Binyamin, whisper-shouting from the darkness. "That is a far journey, even farther considering you will have your family with you. You'll be traveling for weeks! Why not settle in Tyre or Sidon? We could build up our flocks in the surrounding wilderness, and make good money trading in the nearby sea ports."

"I would travel a thousand weeks if it ensured the safety of my family and I know both of you would do the same," her father answered. "We prayed to God for years to heal our little girl. There is nothing I won't do to keep her safe. I think we must each make the choices that we think are right for our own lives."

Libi opened her other eye to see both of her uncles nodding their heads solemnly. Although they were agreeing, none of them looked happy about it.

"Stay a few more days then," said Aharon. "Rest, recover, resupply. When Asa and Shamira arrive, they will want to give us news and also say farewell to you. This parting will not be easy on them, Shamira most of all."

They did exactly that, and all the while Libi never let on that she felt confused until the day of their departure.

"Imma, I don't understand. Did I do something wrong?" Libi felt so ashamed that she was somehow the reason for so much sadness among the family. "Why does Abba want to leave?"

"Libi, miracle child, many people loved Jesus. They thought He was a great man who said many profound things and performed wondrous miracles."

"Like my hearing?" said Libi, gesturing to her ears. Although she no longer needed her hands to communicate basic messages, sometimes the old habit stuck with her.

She remembered the day that Shamira had taken her to the Temple to meet Jesus, convinced that He could heal her. She couldn't remember many details of her life before sound as she had been so young at the time, but even though she couldn't understand the words her cousin had spoken to her, she understood things in different ways. The emotions in Shamira's eyes, the expressive way she communicated, and the way her mouth formed words like "Libi," which she knew was her own name, and "healed." The way she smiled when she spoke the words allowed Libi to understand the message even if she couldn't understand it word for word.

Then Jesus had called to her and motioned for her to come to Him. She did so, but nervously and not knowing what to expect. Whatever He was going to do to make her like the others, would it hurt? Libi didn't know who Jesus was, but it felt like He knew her, and that made her feel brave enough to approach Him.

He touched her ears, and when He did, it felt as though all the sounds in the earth suddenly filled her mind at once, unlike anything she'd ever imagined. She knew birdsong and music as though she'd heard them all her life, and they were beautiful. The movements she'd often observed her family members make with their faces and mouths were words that she suddenly had at her disposal to use, without any explanation other than that it was a miracle.

"Yes, Libi, like your hearing. Your hearing is one of those miracles that Jesus performed, but many people believe that Jesus' miracles were not real. Some do not believe in His message and think that it is wrong," her mother explained.

"But it is real, Imma," said Libi, still confused. Why would people think anything different?

"I know, Libi, but some people might not believe us. Some people may think we are lying, and that could make them angry. Your father wants to take us somewhere that we will not be recognized, where no one knows about you or the incredible gift that Jesus gave you. Where there are not so many angry people. Do you understand?"

"Only a little…"

"This will keep us safe, Libi," said Imma.

Shortly thereafter, they departed from the land of Phoenicia. Days before, she travelled with a small caravan made up of only her family and woke up to their loving embraces each morning. Now she travelled with a much larger caravan and awoke to the faces of strangers. Even though the amount of danger she was in had not changed, her fears had. In her heart, she would never fully understand how anyone could not believe in Jesus, but because of people like that, they had been displaced from their home, and now they would be displaced from each other. A few weeks prior, Libi tasted the last of her Savta's dates, sang the last of her songs to her grandmother, and been held in her arms for the last time and she hadn't known it. Then she shared her last embraces with Shamira, Rut, and all of her other family members. How many other lasts would she endure? Despite her confusion, Libi trusted her Imma and Abba. They had always known what was best for her in the past, surely they would continue to take care of her in the future.

43 A.D., Antioch in Syria

Libi was already priceless in her family's eyes, but the miracle had amplified their need to protect. Even her brothers gave her more attention. They had been children at the time, but they too had developed an instinct to watch over her. Libi didn't mind though; she was grateful for what they had found here in Antioch. A new home, a thriving business, and the freedom to worship their God.

"Libi? Are you all right?" called her imma, checking on her.

She must have been lost in her thoughts for some time. "Yes, Imma, one moment."

Libi pulled the blankets from the basket where her family kept them during the warmer months when the extra layers were not necessary. Tucking them into her side, she began to descend the steps back down to the main room where her parents sat at the table while her brothers were unrolling their mats and getting ready to sleep.

"I'll take these outside and check on Leah and Rachel," said Libi, passing from the ladder to the loft to the front door.

"Don't be too long, hamuda—it's dark and the night is growing cold."

Libi smiled backwards over her shoulder as she opened the door. "Yes, Imma. I'll be careful."

As soon as she was outside, Libi gazed up. She could make out some of the stars shining between the buildings that surrounded their home, and the glow of the moon provided more than enough light for her to see her way through the courtyard to where the animals were kept. She rested her spare hand on the *mezuzah*, the first thing her father had put up when they purchased their new house in Antioch, and thanked God again for all He had done for them.

Judah betrayed her from his resting place on the ground, pointing his nose toward his leg and groaning. "Don't you dare keep Cassius up all night, all right? He is a guest in this house, not here to attend to your every need. You must rest if you want to feel better."

"Hee-haw!" the donkey shouted at her.

"Goodnight, Judah," said Libi as though she were admonishing a misbehaving child.

"Baaahhh! Baaahhh!" called Leah and Rachel, Libi's goats.

"Shalom, my girls! Did Abba take good care of you today?" she smiled, approaching her prized possessions. Her father had bought them as an investment. Their utility was never-ending, but to Libi they were more like her children than mere work animals.

"I saved these for you from my dinner," said Libi, smiling and revealing a handful of grapes that had been served alongside the stew and bread.

Eagerly, the goats approached and each stole a cluster from her palm. Leah came first, much to Rachel's dismay. "There's no need to be jealous, Rachel, there's enough for both of you."

"Baaahhh!" Leah groaned.

"Leah, Abba has been thinking about looking for a mate for you. Now, one would think with the prospect of a suitor that you'd be more concerned about watching your figure," Libi joked. "There, there. Both of you quiet down now. No doubt Cassius will be tired, so you shouldn't expect any grapes from him either. Go to sleep."

Libi looked at each of her goats, searching their eyes for confirmation that they understood. They stomped their hooves a few times, but after a bit, they bowed their heads and backed further into their enclosure.

"Do the chickens have names?"

"Oh," exclaimed Libi, seeing Cassius emerge from the workshop. His face was partially obscured by the waning light of the moon, half in the dark, half in the gentle glow of the silvery-white light. Although his appearance was startling, something about the way the stars illuminated his face made him hard to look away from. It was as though he glowed. "I'm sorry. I did not hear you approach."

Cassius waved a dismissive hand in the air. "The donkey is Judah; the goats are Rachel and…"

"Leah," she finished.

"And the chickens?" he asked.

She laughed. "Chickens don't have names."

"But goats do?" he raised an eyebrow.

"The goats are named for the wives of one of our faith's patriarchs," Libi explained.

"Doesn't seem like a very flattering way to honor the patriarchs of your religion," Cassius surmised.

"I suppose, but perhaps if you knew the story of Jacob, then their names might make more sense."

"Enlighten me, then," he said, folding his arms across his chest, entreating her with his eyes.

"Well, it's a bit long, but I suppose to summarize it: Jacob went to work for Rachel's father, Laban. When Laban asked what his payment should be, Jacob made a deal to work for Laban for seven years in exchange for Rachel's hand in marriage, because he was deeply in love with her."

"*Seven*?!" said Cassius, his eyes popping out of his head. "What kind of girl is worth waiting *that* long to have?"

"Just you wait! Jacob worked for seven years, but when the wedding day finally arrived, it was Leah, Rachel's unmarried older sister, who was presented to him instead."

"He didn't notice?"

"Laban tricked him. It is a custom that Jewish women wear heavy veils at their weddings, you see."

"But why would he do such a thing? After making the man work for seven years, why would he cheat him out of his bride?" Cassius was invested, and that made Libi happy. If he was interested in these stories, surely he might be interested in hearing the stories of their God and the Savior who had come to redeem all people, himself included.

"It was *also* a custom that the younger daughter could not marry before the older daughter. Leah was older and their father was probably determined to make a match for her, so he tricked Jacob into marrying Leah instead. When Jacob awoke the next morning, he was furious. He approached the girls' father, demanding to know what had happened. It was Rachel he loved, and Rachel he wanted. Rachel's father told Jacob that he could have Rachel too, if he agreed to work another seven years."

"Another?" Cassius interjected, mouth agape.

"Mmhmm," she nodded. "He agreed, and was also married to Rachel, but his life was not without hardship after that. Being married to both Rachel and Leah was difficult."

"Ha," Cassius scoffed, "I can imagine. Understanding one woman is hard enough, but two?"

Libi's back straightened, and Cassius must have sensed her reaction.

"Sorry," he said, stepping backwards, "it has been a long time since I've been a guest in someone's household and shared polite conversation. It would appear that I am more than out of practice."

"It's all right," said Libi, blinking and looking away, now embarrassed. Was she talking too much? Sometimes she didn't know when to stop.

"Wait," he said, stopping her before she could move past him and return indoors. "What happened in the story?"

Libi blushed. "God blessed Jacob through both Rachel and Leah, taking what could have been a disastrous union and turning it into something fruitful. Jacob had twelve sons who became the twelve tribes of Israel, our people. Because of Jacob's faith in God, he was blessed beyond measure. Many times over, God took what could have been bad, and used it for His glory."

"Hm," Cassius responded. Libi could tell by his tone that he was not satisfied with such an ending. "What about Rachel?"

"What about her?"

"You said they were in love. How could she still love him even after he married her sister? I know that you said he was tricked, but truly, to make *such* a mistake? One would have to wonder if he'd ever really loved her at all…"

Something in Cassius' voice made Libi wonder if his questions referred to more than the story of Jacob and his wives. The intonation with which he had said the words "in love" made her wonder if he had any understanding of love, even outside of a romantic context.

"According to the story, Leah bore Jacob many sons, but Rachel struggled to conceive. I believe that Rachel might have been jealous of Leah, but she still bore Jacob two sons of her own. Those sons became Jacob's favored sons. I think that shows that despite the difficulties and trials they endured, they were close to each other and that Rachel loved him until the end of her life."

"But why did she love him? He doesn't exactly sound like the ideal man if he can't even tell his betrothed from her sister."

"Perhaps she loved him on a deeper level, or she saw something in him. His faith in God, for instance."

"Perhaps," said Cassius cynically.

"You don't believe it?" Libi asked.

"Never mind. I still don't understand the names of the goats."

She laughed lightly. "Well then perhaps I am not as good of a storyteller when my audience isn't made up of children. I hope I haven't bored you too much."

"Are you… Some kind of tutor then?"

"A tutor?" she repeated with disbelief, having never been asked such a question before. "No, but I do help Taliah, a friend of the family, take care of her children from time to time, and they love to hear stories and sing songs."

"I see," said Cassius.

"Libi," Imma called. "Are you finished?"

"Almost, Imma! Just settling the animals," she called back, before turning to Cassius again. "I must go, as I am surely keeping you from your rest."

"If you weren't, I'm sure Judah would be."

She nodded and laughed lightly. Despite his rough appearance, he clearly had a sense of humor and a more lighthearted side. "Here are some clean linens."

"Thank you," he answered, turning suddenly.

Something about his demeanor hardened when he looked away from her, as though he were hiding a part of himself. Then, seemingly realizing Libi was still in his presence, he relaxed. Libi waited patiently for him to continue speaking. She could tell by the way his shoulders rose and fell that there was more he wanted to say.

"Your family is… very kind to me, even though I have nothing to offer in return."

"We would do the same for any traveler or person in need."

Cassius huffed. "It's that kind of attitude that lands someone in trouble like you were in earlier today. You should really be more careful. You never know who you might be letting in your door."

She smiled confidently. "I have faith in God's plan."

"Your 'God' allowed Jacob to be tricked and Rachel to suffer the consequences. I'm not exactly sure I'd put my faith in Him. How do you know that you can trust me?"

His words caught her off guard and gave her pause, but she reminded herself of Savta's last words to her. Jesus had commanded them to share the love and joy of the Lord with all people. Every day she woke up in Antioch, she chose love and joy. She had to so that she could overcome the fear and anxiety that settled in her heart after the attacks in Jerusalem, and find peace in the life she'd been given which was so different from the life she'd once imagined for herself and for her family. This day had been no different. She chose joy.

"I don't need to trust you. I need to trust my God," she answered. "He brought you to our family for a reason right when we needed you."

Cassius smiled.

"But," she continued, her boldness surprising her, "I also trust you, Cassius. Your actions in the agora were those of a good man. I do not think you would do me or my family harm."

Cassius stepped closer to her, closing some of the distance between them. She heard straw beneath them crunching. As the warmth of her breath met the night air it turned to fog. If he had been of a Jewish background like her family, he would never have come so close to her.

He opened his mouth to speak, and Libi's breath hitched wondering what he was going to say. Outside of family, she had never been this close to a man before, or spoken so many words beyond polite conversation.

"Libi," her mother called again. "Is everything all right?"

"Coming!" Libi jumped backwards, realizing that she'd lost herself in his eyes.

"Goodnight, Cassius," she paused. Then, she opened her mouth to add something, without even understanding why she felt so compelled to say it. "I will pray for you tonight before I lay my head down to sleep."

"You should pray for your family. Do not waste your prayers on me."

"I will pray for you all the same." Something about the events of the day and the nature of Cassius' arrival into her life emboldened her. "I told you, I see goodness in you. I am almost never wrong about a person's true character."

His jaw clenched, and he turned away from her, disappearing into the darkness. "Remember what I told you about being wary of strangers."

ANTIOCH'S DAUGHTER

"Now faith is the reality of what is hoped for, the proof of what is not seen." – Hebrews 11:1 CSB

The sun had barely risen before the nameless chickens began pestering Cassius with their incessant squawking. Did the Jewish people have a story about a group of squabbling people? If so, such names would have suited the chickens.

It was just as well that he had been woken from his sleep. It gave him time to roll up his mat and get out of the way before the family began their morning chores. He rolled his blankets tightly as the military had taught him to, placing them on the nearest table in better condition than when he'd taken them. For sleeping on the floor of a carpenter's workshop, Cassius was more well-rested than he'd been in years.

"Hee-hawww!" A groan came from the courtyard. It was the donkey, Judah, as Libi and her family called him.

Cassius followed the noise and responded, "So you decided to live another day, soldier."

"Hee-hawww! Hee-hawww!"

"Patience, patience. I'll get you a fresh poultice," Cassius muttered, walking over toward the beast to remove the wrap around his leg so that it could be washed and changed. Even though he'd only been here one night, he was starting to sound like Libi, talking to animals. Perhaps she was onto something though; his words seemed to comfort Judah and he quieted down.

"Haha!" A deep, resounding laugh came from the doorway, followed by the clapping of hands. It was Tamir. "He is determined, as we thought. Too stubborn to let one man's folly render him lame."

"He's not healed yet," said Cassius, reminding them, "but it looks as though the wound has begun to drain already. I was just going to change the dressing."

"We'll be sure to keep him off of his legs, but he's clearly in much better spirits." said Yuval, coming out of the house to join them. "Thank you for all of your help."

"Yes, thank you," Tamir echoed. "God sent you to us for just such a time as this."

There they went again. Their prayers and praises reminded Cassius of his mother and the way that she prayed and prayed to her little stone idols. Cassius never could keep them straight, and there were times he was sure she hoarded more statues than there were gods to dedicate them too. *We must pray to the gods for good fortune, Cassius,* she would say any time that he questioned her. She threw away what fortunes she had, and in the end, she became like her little idols: stone-cold and lifeless.

"Judah! You're all right!" Libi exclaimed in a sing-song voice as she floated toward them, kneeling beside the donkey.

"He's *better*," said Cassius, still stressing that last bit of information.

"Better because of Cassius," Tamir added.

"This is wonderful news! I can already tell that he is not in as much pain. Thank you, Cassius, for all you've done." She smiled while petting the beast.

"It was nothing," he said, carving a smile onto his face like the sculptors carved the stone statues that lined the streets of Rome, the city he had once called home.

"Ah, well, I have chores to do," said Libi softly, "I'll let you be. I wouldn't want to bother you."

"I was almost finished washing his leg," Cassius replied, unsure of why she was speaking in such hushed tones.

"Oh!" Her face reddened. "I was speaking to Judah, but of course the same applies to you." She bowed her head and rose from her kneeling position in the enclosure.

"Our Libi milks the goats and gathers the eggs from the hens. Come boys, let us go inside and get ready to break our fast. Cassius, you may join us when you are ready," Tamir said, gesturing to his sons who followed him inside. How did this family move and converse so easily, and why did he constantly feel like an outsider and a welcome guest at the same time?

When Judah's leg was cleaned, Cassius helped himself to what he needed for the fresh poultice, warming some milk over the embers of the fire. After the poultice was made, he got into position to wrap the leg, wrapping the new cloths around once, twice, then unravelling it to do it again several more times before getting it right. The dulcet tones of Libi's voice as she sang distracted him from his work.

"I love you, Lord, my strength and my rock, my fortress and my deliverer. You are where I seek refuge, my shield and the horn of my salvation. You are my stronghold, worthy of all praise…"

Her voice seemed to lift and carry far above them, the animals, the workshop, the smell of sawdust, and even the noises of the busy city of Antioch. It was beautiful and enchanting and mesmerizing all at the same time. Cassius' hands fumbled over the cloth. For a brief moment he closed his eyes, letting his mind be occupied only by Libi's song. The words snapped him back to reality—words of praise for a God he still didn't believe existed.

"Pretty words," said Cassius sardonically, ignoring the feeling of his heart softening.

He looked at Libi out of the corner of his eye, still feigning deep concentration on his own task.

She paused, stood up straight, and replied, "Thank you."

Her voice was as sweet as birdsong, and the way she stood with the light hitting her just so made it impossible not to notice her beauty. The smooth, fine locks of her light brown hair became like liquid gold when exposed to the sun. She stood demurely, full of grace. Either she hadn't noticed that Cassius did not mean his words sincerely, or she was simply choosing not to notice.

"Although they're not my words," she continued.

Cassius feared he had accidentally started a conversation.

"I'm sure you're going to enlighten me."

"Only if you want me to," she smiled, and then turned her back to him and faced her nameless chickens instead. Heat rose in his chest, and he couldn't believe that he felt jealous of fowl.

"No, tell me. I'm interested." What was he saying? This woman affected his reasoning skills in more ways than one.

"All right then," she said, coming toward him with her basket. "The words come from a Psalm of David, one of Israel's old kings. It is a song of praise that David wrote after the Lord delivered him from King Saul hundreds of years ago."

"Who was this 'King Saul?'"

"Another one of the old kings, but he grew power hungry and cared more for serving himself than for serving God. David was said to have been a man after God's own heart, and he was anointed by the prophet Samuel to be Saul's replacement and to bring the nation of Israel back to the Lord."

"And yet the nation of Israel still crumbled to Rome hundreds of years later."

Libi sighed. "That may be true, but that was no fault of God. That was the fault of the people who turned away from him. David's words of praise still ring true in dark times as well as light."

"How do you know that?" Cassius asked, then waved a hand in

the air. "Never mind. If it involves another one of your ancient stories, then I don't need to know."

"It's all the same story, Cassius. The story of God's love for His people."

"From my point of view, all gods are the same. Myths made up for mere comfort."

"I'm sorry that you feel that way. I hope I have not upset you." He knew that it hurt her and that she disagreed with his assessment, but it was the truth of how he felt. He couldn't take it back.

"I suppose I don't understand how someone could believe in any god, let alone one they could not see. I grew up surrounded by gods. From the little idols of my mother's own curation to the large, towering stone gods that lined the Forum where the commanders of the Roman Army would make prayers and sacrifices after a victory. It all seemed like too much to me. Too much to be real."

"Our God doesn't accept sacrifices like that," said Libi proudly, a grin spreading from ear to ear.

"How could that be true? Your people have a great temple in Jerusalem. I've seen it."

"My family and I believe that Jesus was and is the Son of God sent to earth, and that His life is the sacrifice that covered all mankind when he died on the cross and rose again."

Cassius had seen him dead, so he knew that much was true. Of course, he hadn't actually *seen* anyone take the body, but there was no other explanation for what Cassius had witnessed and the disgrace that followed. The alternatives sounded too much like a dream to be true. He had been barely more than a boy then, his size and experience making him appear a little less than a full-grown man. Whether he'd been fooled by tricks of light or allowed himself to be overtaken by a handful of untrained men did not matter. Either way, he'd let his pride get in the way of doing his job, and the choices he made still haunted him.

"Whether or not your Messiah rose again seems to be a matter of opinion," said Cassius to Libi, remembering the past with unyielding clarity. Land, titles, a purpose—that was all he'd ever wanted. Now he was essentially right back where he began, except he was dining with and staying under the same roof as the followers who started the rumors that ruined his life. Whatever gods were watching over him, they seemed to have a very twisted sense of irony.

"You wouldn't say that if you'd seen what we've seen," said Libi.

"And you wouldn't say that if you'd seen what I've seen," said Cassius, stopping himself before he revealed too much.

She continued instead. "Maybe I haven't, but perhaps I'll understand someday if you ever choose to share it with me, and someday after that, you might also come to understand what I believe."

"I may come to understand it, but I can't say I'll ever agree with it," said Cassius.

"I wouldn't force you to. That is a personal decision."

"Personal, and not for me." Cassius snapped.

She straightened her lips, and once again Cassius felt a sting inside of him. Why couldn't he speak kindly to this girl just once? All she ever did was be kind to him. Could he not repay that, even slightly?

Then again, why did he care?

"I think I'm finished out here," she said calmly. Too calm. "The food will be ready soon."

"I'll be there in a moment," he said, and when he said it, he noticed an added spring in her step. Perhaps he could make up for whatever harshness he'd displayed toward her... Aside from her beliefs, she herself had nothing to do with what happened. Cassius was more to blame than anyone else; time allowed him to see that clearly. "And... I'm sorry for what I said."

Libi nodded. "I know."

He found his place around the table and sat down, taking a piece of bread, some cheese, and fresh water to satisfy his hunger and thirst. He scarfed down the appropriately sized helpings with ease, yet his stomach still yearned for more. How long had it been since he'd eaten properly cooked, regularly timed meals? He must be sure not to get used to this kind of living—he wouldn't have it when he inevitably went back on the road again.

While he was here, though, he gave himself permission to overindulge a little. Taking another serving of the foods spread before him, he kept eating.

"So," said Tamir. Cassius dropped what food he was holding in his hands down onto his plate to give the man who was now his unlikely benefactor undivided attention.

"Yes?"

"I've been talking it over with my sons and with Chava. We know that you have no other place to stay while you are here in Antioch, and we'd like to offer you a place to stay in our home. That is, the same lodgings we've already given you."

"That's very kind, but I will be moving on soon," Cassius reminded him.

"Well, you see, I wasn't quite finished. There was a bargain I'd hoped to strike up with you. We'd happily give you food and lodging *and* a small wage, in exchange for your help with Judah and around the workshop. You said you had some carpentry skill, and we have what feels like more orders than we can keep up with."

"Aren't you well-staffed enough on your own?" said Cassius, gesturing to the brothers.

"Having you around might speed things up and help us actually get ahead of schedule, and we would certainly appreciate you staying on to help with Judah. As I said before, we were but humble shepherds before we came to Antioch, and while we can care for an animal, having someone around with your knowledge would be handy. The wage wouldn't be much, but considering that you would also have food and lodging, it would be adequate for your situation."

"I don't know." Cassius hesitated.

"I know that you said that Antioch is not your home and that you are merely traveling through. But even if you only stayed for a little while, long enough to teach Yuval what you know and help a little bit here and there, it would be appreciated. I won't ask you for a long-term commitment."

His eyes drifted across the table toward Libi and her wide gray eyes. What was she thinking? Did she want him to accept? If she did, Cassius still wasn't sure if it was because she wanted to indoctrinate him into her religion, or because she perhaps felt some pull toward him, similar to the way he felt about her. Something in him beckoned to know her more, and although he tried to fight it, his interest in her was becoming increasingly relentless.

He tried to focus his mind on his main goal. If he were employed, he would be trusted more. It was the perfect way to find out where this family kept their money. Then, when he was ready to leave, he could disappear when the timing was right with enough money to buy passage on any ship sailing away from Rome. This time, Cassius would make sure that he wasn't the one at a loss.

"All right, I accept," he replied.

"Good! It is an answer to prayer!" said Tamir.

If he believed in their God he would agree, because he had just been provided a perfect escape and a way to get enough money to leave this land once and for all. All he had to do was avoid the effect that this family, and especially Libi, seemed to have on his feelings. He would not make the same mistake twice. He learned his lesson before. Cassius now understood that sometimes the greatest enemy to his survival could be himself. He would not allow his heart, his emotions, or his feelings to get the better of him. Not this time.

"Give thanks to the Lord, for he is good; his faithful love endures forever. Let the redeemed of the Lord proclaim that he has redeemed them from the power of the foe" - Psalm 107:1-2 CSB

"What were the races like?" asked Yuval.

"Hm?" replied Cassius. It had been one week since he began working for Tamir, and it was an adjustment, to be sure. They liked to carry on with conversation or singing while they worked, whereas Cassius often lost himself in a task completely. He was still learning how to navigate the day-to-day routines of this family. At this moment it was only Cassius and Yuval out in the workshop, waiting for Tamir and Gilad to arrive so that they could start their workday.

"The races. You said you were from Rome, and I know they have lots of chariot races there. We have a circus here in Antioch, although I'm sure it's nothing compared to the circus in Rome, even though I've never been to either."

"Oh, well, I suppose in that we have something in common. Aside from watching from the tops of the hills and sneaking around to look at the horses beforehand, I've never actually been to a circus myself."

"Then how do you know so much about horses and donkeys?"

Coming up with answers like this that didn't reveal too much from his past was getting tiring.

"I told you; I've been around."

"I'd like to get a horse someday. They seem like magnificent animals," said Yuval.

"A horse wouldn't really do you much good here in the city. They can be larger than donkeys but they're not nearly as strong. Their greatest asset is their speed, which is what makes them good in battle," Cassius explained without thinking.

"*And,*" he continued, "That is also why they are so popular for chariot races."

"Oh?"

"For your needs, Judah will suffice. A horse may be faster, but in a city as crowded as this, you may as well walk."

"The city has been surprisingly calm as of late," Yuval replied.

"Calm?" Cassius raised an eyebrow in question, his mind briefly drawn back to the protective instinct he'd first felt toward Libi. Had it not been mere days since he'd played a part in rescuing her from thieves? He would hardly describe such a place as calm.

A third voice joined their conversation outside. "I hope you two are getting along," said Libi with a small smile spreading across her face, the heat from the rising sun coloring her cheeks.

"Libi," Yuval chided, "have I ever been anything but civil?"

"Of course not, brother," she answered. "I brought you a fresh jar of water and a basket of dates to snack on." Libi set the items on a nearby table.

"Where is Abba?" asked Yuval. Cassius was wondering the same thing. How much of his job around here would simply involve making conversation?

"He is inside, still talking to Imma."

"And my twin?"

"Gilad is 'helping' put away what's left of breakfast, or rather finishing it off."

"Well, he better hurry up," said Yuval. Turning to Cassius as if to explain, he added, "He's better than I am at detailed jobs."

"I need him to help me first with my cakes," said Libi. "You know I always have him taste them."

Yuval frowned. "Yes, that must be a strenuous task indeed. I will go inside and see how long Abba will be. Cassius, the projects we have to finish by the end of today are already laid out—the broken wheels and the set of four chairs. You can help yourself to the tools if you'd like to get started, although the wheels will probably take two of us."

Cassius nodded and answered, "Understood." He went toward the chairs. Two of them were already finished. The pieces were cut for the third and fourth and just needed to be assembled. It wouldn't take very much time, so long as all of the pieces fit together appropriately. Armed with a fair bit of knowledge from equipment repairs he had assisted with and a good amount of common sense, he took a mallet in hand and set to work attaching remaining legs of the chairs.

Libi had not followed her brother inside. Her eyes staring back at him as he worked made him nervous, so instead of his normal stoicism, he chose to speak.

"You make cakes?" he asked. The words tumbled out of his mouth awkwardly.

"I do," she said, perking up. "Cakes and rolls and loaves… I sell them in the marketplace sometimes."

"Is that why you were there the day we met?"

"Oh, no, that was a simple errand, or it was supposed to be."

"Ah, yes," he said as he paced from one side of the workshop to the other to retrieve another one of the chair legs, reminding himself how much easier it would have been to have walked away from this family and stolen a meal somewhere else. "The herbs for your mother."

"Mmhmm." She nodded. "Have you done this before?"

"What?" asked Cassius, not fully listening to her while he focused on what he was doing with his hands.

"Carpentry," she said, "I was just curious if it had been something you'd done for a long time."

Was there something he was doing that was wrong? Self-consciousness made his jaw clench. No, he was doing it correctly, but for some reason unbeknownst to him he hated the idea of appearing as a fool in front of her. It wasn't only her eyes, alluring as they were. It was everything about her. Her presence, the way she moved, the way she spoke, and the way everything she said sounded like a melody to which Cassius wanted to learn the harmony. He reminded himself to resist these urges.

"To be honest with you," he began, wiping his forehead, "I never did much other than repairs. I don't know anything about very skilled work, but when I look at something I am able to see how it is meant to be and put it that way."

That was true. He had always been a visual learner, learning how to hold a sword by copying Servius' movements and understanding battle strategy by seeing it drawn out. He had even stolen his first loaf of bread from the busy Roman Forum by first watching another waif do the same. But why had he told Libi as much? Did it threaten his ruse?

"That's all right. My father never practiced carpentry before either, but he learned as he went along in order to provide for our family when we came to Antioch. Yuval and Gilad too, while Imma and I brought in what extra coin we could by baking. Now that I'm older, I bake most of the things to sell on my own."

"Of course," said Cassius, not really thinking as he hammered the last leg into place and flipped the backless chair right side up on the floor. He put some weight on it to see if it rocked. It didn't. He turned to Libi again and continued, "So far, I think I'm doing all right."

"Indeed!" She smiled. Knowing that he had brought a smile to her face gave him a strange sense of pride.

As a small reward, Cassius couldn't resist taking a date from the basket she'd brought out. He'd tasted them at dinner the night before and knew how delightful they were. Rome had groves of dates, and his mother used to prepare them in a similar fashion, but they could not compare to the dates that grew farther south. These were even sweeter than those from his homeland, and even though it had not been long since they'd broken their fast that day, he couldn't stop himself from eating more.

Although Cassius was strong and very muscular, Libi could tell that it had been a long time since he had enjoyed the pleasure of food readily available. In every meal he had shared with her family since his arrival, he always seemed hungrier than the rest of them. After hearing bits and pieces of his story, Libi decided that she had been right about Cassius. He was not a man who would hurt her. Like Libi, he was someone who had been hurt by others. There was once a time when her family had struggled to live on the bare minimum in order to survive, so she felt she could relate to him, even if the exact details of his past were a mystery. He seemed to enjoy the dates, taking one after another. At this rate, Yuval might not get any, but that wasn't very important. Libi could always make more, and she was happy to know how much Cassius liked them. It was, so far, one thing she knew for certain that he felt kindly toward.

He glanced back and forth between the chair he was working on and the finished chairs on the other side of the workshop. "These chairs are being carved?" he asked.

Libi had listened to enough of her father's dealings to know the details of most of the projects he worked on. "Yes, my father has always been good at carving since we were children. He used to carve toys for us out of wood he found in the fields when he was shepherding. The buyer of the chairs wanted the first letter of their family name carved into the seat back, but I don't know which one it's meant to be."

"It's alpha," Cassius replied, "*A*."

"You can read?" she said, hoping that her tone did not contain too much shock.

"Mmhmm." He simply nodded, taking another sip of water from the ladle, allowing some of it to drip down his chin where a shadow of a beard grew.

"I always wish I could read, so that I could understand the letters we get from our family members myself. I'd like to read them sometimes before everyone else hears them and be the first. Sometimes I miss my aunts, uncles, and cousins terribly."

"You have many?" said Cassius.

She couldn't stop her grin from spreading across her face. "Oh, yes! There is Dodh Binyamin and Dodah Devorah, and their children Benayahu and Rut—although they aren't children anymore. They're all older than me with families of their own. There is also my Dodh Aharon and Dodah Elisheva, and their daughters Eliana and Shamira. Almost everyone lives in Phoenicia now, except for Eliana who lives in Jerusalem, but she married when I was very small. Shamira and I were especially close. I looked up to her when I was young."

"You do even now," said Cassius. Had she been babbling? "Your eyes give you away. They… *glitter* when you talk about your family, like the sun shining on a river."

Heat colored her cheeks and she wished very much that she had something to hide behind. "Perhaps I should leave you to concentrate on what you are doing."

"No, I don't mind listening to your stories. It helps me focus," he said.

"All right," she said slowly, contemplating her next words,

"Shamira is eight years older than me, but in a way I grew up in her shadow. We used to all live together in Jerusalem—"

Cassius' brow furrowed.

"Should I stop?" she asked.

He shook his head.

"Well, we used to all live together in Jerusalem. Shamira married Asa. They have been in love for as long as I can remember—"

Cassius coughed. Or had he cleared his throat? Libi wasn't sure. She thought it best to skip forward a bit in her telling of her family's history.

"Now Shamira has children of her own. Two! A boy and a girl, Eliel and Yemima. I've never met them, but I hear about them in the letters they send whenever they get the chance."

Even though Libi knew he was distracted and not really listening, it was nice that he tried to remember the names and stay engaged in the conversation. Truthfully, she enjoyed having someone to talk to that wasn't a member of her family.

"How did you end up here?" said Cassius.

"It has to do with some of what I told you before."

"About the Jesus rising from the dead," Cassius interjected. His eyes widened and he looked directly at her, almost as though he had surprised even himself with what he had said.

"Please don't say that," Libi whispered, "I know you don't believe it, but it's not another story to me…"

He cleared his throat. "I should have been more careful with my words—I got caught up in my work and didn't think. You can keep sharing if you want."

Libi was more than aware that they came from two completely different worlds, but his own expression seemed to imply that perhaps their worlds might be able to converge. Even if they never saw things exactly the same way, perhaps it was possible to find common ground here in Antioch, where so many people of so many different backgrounds lived.

"We came here because of something Jesus did for me… *To me*… When I met him in Jerusalem."

Her heart fluttered. She remembered every second of that day. The way Jesus had smiled at her. The way He had brushed her fine hair out of her face, tucking it behind her ears. The way that His words were the first sound she ever heard, and that those words called her from that day forward to be His witness. Sometimes, to reach someone's heart, a story just needed to be told. Words just needed to be spoken. An act of kindness, an act of compassion, even an act of love, just needed to be offered.

"Was it bad?" said Cassius, as if that was the kind of answer he was expecting.

She briefly remembered the words spoken to her by her mother on their journey to Antioch when she was younger, about how dangerous telling her story could be, but even after the time she'd spent with Cassius, she didn't feel any fear in his presence.

"Cassius," she said, forgetting all manner of appropriate conversation, "As a child, I never spoke a word or heard any sound, no matter how loud."

After stopping one moment to make sure he was really listening, she continued, "He made me hear."

What did she mean *"He made me hear?"* How could a person have been born and raised deaf, only to be standing before him now, able to speak and sing and say so much, sometimes *too* much? It didn't make any sense. It couldn't make sense. A person born deaf could not be made to hear—not with any medicines he was aware of, anyway, and Rome was one of the most advanced cultures in nearly every field.

"How is that possible?" he questioned, dropping his tools on the worktable, and forgetting everything that he harbored in his heart. All of his anger, hatred, and prejudice had been temporarily replaced by a combination of wonder and astonishment.

"You've heard of Him. You know that they have said He had the power to perform miracles. It was my cousin, Shamira, who took me to see Him. He was healing others—the blind and the lame. She called out to Him on my behalf, He came to me, touched my ears, and spoke to me. At that moment, it was like a door opened that was always closed before… When things became dangerous for believers in Jerusalem, our family left. Most settled in Phoenicia, but my father brought us here."

She said it like it was a simple story, easy to understand, but it was the complete opposite. It was highly possible she had created a false memory, or that her family around her had made up the story and told it so often that she believed it herself, but that didn't feel right to him. Servius Arrius had taught him once that if he ever had to lie about something, be it military tactics, battle strategies, or army secrets, to make the lie as believable as possible. If it strayed too far from the truth, from reality, it would become unacceptable. It was better to ground a lie in as much truth as possible, filling the story with mundane details. Why include such outrageous details in a story such as this, if they weren't true?

"You don't believe me, do you?" said Libi. Cassius looked up at her once again and noticed how her gray eyes glistened, moistened by tears.

Cassius bit his lip, trying to come up with an adequate response.

"I don't believe in much anymore," he said, and it was the honest truth.

"Everyone believes in *something*."

Thankfully, they were interrupted by her brothers and father rejoining them in the workshop. He spent the rest of the day and the days that followed sanding rough edges out of freshly cut wood, using a mallet to fit pieces together like a puzzle, and carving out patterns where none had existed before. No matter how hard he tried, he couldn't carve Libi's words out of his mind.

They lingered there every night when Cassius laid his head down to sleep, and every morning when his eyes first opened to the break of dawn.

What *did* he believe, and could he *ever* believe in a God who seemed to have abandoned him at every turn? His heart still felt hard on that matter, but it was softening toward Libi, and to her stories. A Messiah was meant to be a savior, according to all that he heard. Was it possible that Cassius could be saved? Compared to this family, he was vile and deserved none of their kindness. Cassius was starting to feel a sense of guilt. That guilt led to despair, and despair led to hopelessness.

The longer he stayed, the harder it would be to leave, but Libi, her silvery-gray eyes, and her talk of impossible miracles and second chances captivated him. Every night he remained under the roof of their workshop, he tossed and turned as he knew he should roll up his bed, shake the dust from his feet, and run without looking back. A shadow of an unfamiliar emotion—hope, perhaps—kept him from ever taking those steps. "One more day," Cassius would say in the dark of the night.

He was losing track of how many times he'd made that promise to himself, and losing track of why he chose to stay with them in the first place.

10

"No one serving as a soldier gets entangled in the concerns of civilian life; he seeks to please the commanding officer." — 2 Timothy 2:4 CSB

43 A.D., Jerusalem

There was one name in the world that Servius Arrius detested more than any other. One name he wished with all of his might to blot out from his memory in the same way conquerors and kings of old would blot out their failures in battle from the records of history to preserve their own legacies. One name he hoped never to hear again, nor ever utter from his own lips. That name was *Cassius.*

How could Cassius have been such a fool? The problem with that question was that Servius knew exactly how, because he had been very much like Cassius when he was younger.

He had been shouting in the Roman Forum for nearly half a day and to no avail when he met Cassius. He had no new recruits to speak of; not many citizens of Rome had any desire to take up arms and fight for the glory of the empire. He didn't blame them. Everyone there already had titles and wealth, or else they wouldn't be shopping where the prices were almost always double the actual value of the goods being sold.

Although he had originally chosen that spot because there were so many people, Servius quickly realized that he needed to rethink his strategy for finding new soldiers. The people there wore fine, swarthy linens and soft, brightly colored tunics—the exact opposite of the roughhewn clothing and heavy armor they would be issued by the Roman army. Their hands were the hands of artisans and politicians, not the hands of laborers and warriors. Servius had nothing to offer those people that they didn't already have.

He saw right through Cassius from the beginning when he asked for his age and Cassius responded with a clear lie. He had been tall for his age, but closer examination of his green eyes revealed to Servius that at the time he didn't have the maturity to match his appearance. Servius never had any sons of his own, though he'd longed for them, but something in Cassius' spirit made him feel like kin, which is why on that day he had made the rare choice to allow his heart to overrule his head. He made the exception and allowed Cassius to enlist, taking him under his wing. Servius knew that he didn't have what it would take to be a true soldier, but he thought that if Cassius did prove himself then he could give him every advantage a father would normally give a son. He could have even passed on the name of Arrius, formally adopting him upon his retirement. The only thing that stood in Cassius' way was himself. Ambitions were a good thing, but too much ambition only made a man's head too big for his helmet. Servius recalled many instances from Cassius' training that should have served as warning signs, but maybe he had his own ambitions for Cassius that clouded his judgment.

32 A.D., The Imperial City of Rome

"Agh!" Cassius cried out, bringing a hand up to clutch his forehead. He'd just been struck by Servius' sword during practice.

"Here," said Servius, moving closer and pulling out a cloth to absorb the blood. "You know you'll never win a battle if you hold yourself like that. You can't crouch down or cower in fear, you must be strong. Stronger than you think you are. You must believe it. That strength will make the other men cower before you. They will take one look at you, how you carry yourself, and even this scar, and they will fear you. Let them think it is a war wound."

Cassius' shoulders slumped and the tip of the dull blade he held in his hand hit the ground with a metallic thud. Although Cassius had not been trained in archery yet, his eyes were already well practiced in the art of shooting arrows. If looks could kill, his green eyes might have been the first weapon to bring Servius Arrius to the ground.

"I am strong!" Cassius grunted.

Servius chuckled. "Even if you are strong physically, it's strength here that counts," Servius held his hand to his chest.

"Here?" repeated Cassius, not understanding.

"Here," Servius added. "Strength of the heart. Courage. Confidence, not to be confused with overconfidence, mind you. That can be as deadly as cowardice."

Cassius looked down at the ground, and twisted the hilt of his blade around in his hand. He bit his lip and continued, "What if I gain all the courage and confidence I need in this training, but then the moment I step foot onto my first battlefield it all leaves me? Then what do I do?"

"Then you pray to Mars that the gods might look down favorably upon you."

"And if they don't? If they choose not to?"

"Then you die on the battlefield or flee as a traitor. Either way, you end up dead, but such risk is the price you pay in service to the empire, in the hope that one day, the empire repays that price back to you."

He saw the way that Cassius started to lean backward, feeling the urge to give up. Servius continued, but softer this time, "A soldier's life is a risky life, Cassius. But every day that you choose to roll up your mat, tie your sandals, and leave your tent, you take risks. The gods could just as easily strike you down with lightning as they could allow you to perish on the battlefield. Learn to fight, Cassius. Learn to be strong. Learn to survive. Learn to see the greater strategies at work. If you do, one day you can retire a wealthy man with property and land of your own. You won't have to serve any empire; you'll be your own emperor. Do you understand?"

Cassius nodded, his posture already improving.

"All right then," said Servius. He lifted his sword and touched it to Cassius' own, letting the clanging of the two blades ring out in the air. "Go and get that cut cleaned and bandaged. We can practice again tomorrow."

"I want to keep practicing now," said Cassius, tightening his grip on his sword. "A real soldier in battle would not have time to have his wounds bandaged."

Servius laughed, but indulged him and took up his own sword once more. "One more duel. Then you *will* get that bandaged before it causes you any trouble."

43 A.D., Jerusalem

Cassius never did learn to see the greater strategy. He never understood that life was a war and not a single battle. Cassius couldn't, wouldn't wait for opportunity to strike. He didn't know how to take advantage of a situation. He was shortsighted, as Servius had predicted, and it was that shortsightedness that had gotten him in trouble. Servius hadn't been there that night, but he'd heard different versions of what happened from the others. The soldiers all admitted to having fallen asleep on duty, an offense punishable by death. It was the possibility of that punishment that probably made Cassius run, but what Cassius was unaware of was the fact that no one wanted to see anyone die over this mistake. It would only kindle the flames of the Messianic rumors, the rumors of a leader who would aid the Jews in their uprising against Rome. Better to let them live to tell the tale that they'd fallen asleep and the man's followers had taken the body, than to silence their voices altogether.

But Cassius hadn't thought of that.

Servius' mind knew that he never should have let Cassius enlist in the Roman Army in the first place, but Servius' heart had been drawn to him. Of all his many achievements, having a child to call an heir was not one of them. Perhaps Cassius could have been that child somehow, and perhaps that was why Servius had always taken a shine to him even though the odds of both of them surviving their respective twenty-five-year commitments were slim. He'd been hard on Cassius more than once, but that was just as any father would do when raising their son. Had he been too hard?

No, he'd been foolish to ever grow so attached to a recruit. There was a reason Rome frowned on its soldiers having relationships or commitments outside of the military. Soldiers were merely soldiers. Pawns to the empire who lived and often died in service, as Servius always expected he would do as well.

Instead, Servius now neared the age of retirement, and he couldn't decide if that particular quirk of fate—his surviving after all these years—was a blessing from Jupiter or a curse from Mars. While the fates had ensured that nearly every one of Servius' battles had been victorious, they had also left Servius alive. Other gods had seen to it that Servius' life was not worth living. He'd outlived all of his blood relatives, and couldn't say that he had a home to go to after his years of service were finished, or even friends he could spend time with that would make the long days more agreeable.

"Pilus Prior," a soldier's voice and the sound of boots running in the mud pulled Servius from his own thoughts. It was just as well too, for they were such a dark place that he dared not dwell among them for too long.

"A message has come for you. A rider brought it moments ago." The man panted for air.

"You sound as though you ran it all the way here from Rome yourself. Stamina like that, or the lack thereof, will do you no good in the battlefield if these orders are what I think they are," said Servius, taking the scroll in his own hands.

"Are we being deployed to Britannia?" asked the soldier, who would be about Cassius' age now if he were still alive somewhere.

"Never you mind it. Leave me alone to read this."

"As you command." The man saluted and turned back toward his own station.

Servius wasted no time in breaking the seal on the scroll and rolling it out before him. *Britannia!* What an honor it would be for Servius to lead a group of men there. Control of the lowlands was imminent, but there was still work to be done. Servius Arrius had an impressive record. As he'd spent the better part of the day reminding himself, most men his age were either retired or dead. At least there he had a better chance of dying an honorable death. Servius had received many honors over the course of his career, but a posting to Britannia? That would be the greatest honor of them all! They had to ask him. Why wouldn't they? He was more than qualified, and perhaps a change of scenery would do him well. Then he could put everything about Judea—Cassius included—behind him. He couldn't imagine a better way to conclude his years of service!

Then he read the words inscribed on the page.

They were the exact opposite of what Servius had thought he

would read. The only thing that prevented him from crumpling the parchment into a ball and throwing it into a nearby fire was his code of honor and duty to the empire. It was an official scroll, and he could not ignore it.

Many of his men would go on to Britannia, but Servius Arrius would not be leading them. Indeed, in regards to Servius, the letter contained only congratulatory remarks on his many years of service, followed by details of how he was to be relieved of duty, and a notice informing him that he was now eligible to collect on the rewards he'd earned during the past twenty-five years. In what was probably supposed to be a gesture of goodwill, the letter also told of how the powers that be would be happy to recommend him for any number of administrative government positions in a city of his choosing. The realization that he was no longer the young soldier with a bright future began to sink in, and he decided that the gods' decision had most definitely been a curse. Servius had grown old now. His only enemy was time, and it had an unfortunately sharp sword.

As Servius contemplated the many routes he might take and the many cities he might choose to retire in, he made the decision to do most of his traveling by land, stopping every so often to check the conditions of the Roman army encampments and the general attitude toward the empire in each major city. Even before he could leave, he still needed enough time to organize the men and their new leader, and prepare whatever he would need for his last journey as a true soldier before he would spend the rest of his days accepting a courtesy position training new recruits or lazing about some government business. How long had he fought, in the hopes that he would never have to return to his homeland again? Everyone he had ever known for any great length of time was long gone now, but what else was he to do? In a few short weeks, he would depart from Jerusalem, where he had last seen Cassius before he had been branded as a traitor.

Cassius still had a price to pay for what he had done. If he was smart, he would have made sure to run far enough away that Servius would never catch him. But then again, if he'd been smart, he never would have run like that in the first place. Servius would be traveling north through Samaria, Phoenicia, Syria, Antioch… Perhaps their paths would cross again.

If they did, Servius would see to it that justice was done.

"Give us today our daily bread." — *Matthew 6:11 CSB*

43 A.D., Antioch in Syria

Libi stepped out from under the covering of her father's workshop and into the street to look up at the sky. The sun was cresting the horizon, casting faint golden hues onto the puffy white clouds that floated overhead. Cassius had been with their family for several weeks, and even now she could hear the sound of him, her father, and her brothers talking and teasing as they worked. Judah made a full recovery in that time thanks to Cassius' efforts, but Libi had not spoken to him alone since she told him about her miracle. *God's miracle.* The miracle of Jesus. Gatherings of believers came and went several days each week, none of which were attended by Cassius. Somehow, he made himself disappear, even when they would meet in their family home. Libi also visited Taliah multiple times since Cassius' arrival; with a new babe and another on the way, it was her pleasure to come alongside her dear friend.

While God was working in their lives and they waited upon His answers, Libi found it best to keep busy. The distractions kept her from worrying too long over Taliah's situation, or thinking too much about Cassius and his presence in her life. Keeping her hands working and her mind concentrated on other tasks was also a method Libi often employed so that she would not easily be overcome by feelings of discontent. She found that if little time was left to be idle, then she rarely had enough time to think about what she didn't have in life—a husband, children, a way to serve that was truly her own. Instead, whatever time she had was devoted to praising God for the blessings He did send her way. That didn't mean she was entirely immune to the pangs of her heart, but rather than overwork a problem, she would leave the leaven to do its work. Like a batch of bread dough being left to rise, she would leave her prayers and worries with God. He knew the desires of her heart better than any.

On this day, Libi set aside many tasks to complete before she could go to the agora, which was why she had risen with the chickens. Today was one of the days she would take her breads and cakes to the agora to sell before the gathering of believers, so that she could tithe her earnings and bring whatever was left of her goods to share with the others. Baking was a multi-day activity. Days earlier, she had begun to mix her ingredients so they would have time to rise. Now, she would use that dough to bake the loaves. Once the rest of her chores were completed, she went inside and sat at the table with everything she needed. Slowly, Libi began kneading and shaping the rounds, singing songs of praise as she did so. Long ago, she worked out precisely how many choruses to sing while working the dough in order to achieve the perfect consistency.

Once they were kneaded thoroughly, she moved them to the clay oven to bake, and then she started working on some of her specialty cakes.

"Imma?" called Libi.

"Yes, hamuda?" said her mother, poking her head through the door.

Libi reached for a basket of dates and figs on the table. "Are you going to use these?"

"That depends… Do you have plans to make some of your sweet treats?"

Libi smiled and nodded her head.

"Go ahead, I have no use for them today."

"Thank you," said Libi, already taking out what she would need for her cakes. She had memorized a variety of recipes for things like barley cakes, wheat cakes, flat cakes, round cakes, but her favorites to make were nut cakes. It was an easy dish that was all preparation and no actual baking over a fire, which meant that the honey loaves could be baked on their own without crowding the oven. Whenever she had the chance to use dates, she always felt as though she were honoring her Savta and putting her own special spin on the recipe that they were still never able to replicate. Libi added a bit of pepper to the mix and kept mixing. Once that was fully combined, she wet her hands and began to form the cakes into shapes like her mother had taught her to, and coated them in sesame seeds. That was a trick she'd learned from another Roman baker she'd met in the marketplace who told her that many of the people north of Antioch preferred their nut cakes that way, and when Libi implemented it into her recipe, her sales nearly doubled.

She took the nut cakes and set them aside to firm up a bit, then went to prepare some baskets and linens so that she could transport her goods to the marketplace in time for the afternoon crowds.

Her Imma turned the corner and came in the back way. "Everything looks delicious, as always."

"Did you happen to take notice of the honey loaves?"

"They're nearly done, and they're perfect, just like you."

"I'm hardly perfect, Imma," said Libi.

"Well, you've always been perfect to me, since the day you were born and I counted ten precious little fingers and ten precious little toes." Chava wrapped her arms around Libi and gave her a tight squeeze from behind. Libi reached up to hold her mother's hands in her own and smiled.

"I always loved being held by you when I was a little girl," said Libi.

"And I loved to hold you, miracle child."

At the mention of the miracle, she turned all of her attention to her ears, marveling at the way she could hear so many sounds. Carts, animals, Judah's boorish grunts, and the chickens squawking. Libi briefly giggled at the memory of Cassius asking her what their names were on his first night in their home. "I am just a girl, blessed by God."

"You may be 'just a girl' to everyone else in the world, but to your father and me, you will always be our miracle, our precious Libi, and we will guard you as such."

"I know, Imma." Libi straightened, realizing that she had worked herself into a sweat all morning and was now incredibly thirsty. She took the back of her sleeve and wiped her forehead, shrugging her shoulders and working out the knots in her back. She went to get some more water from the barrel, leaning over it to gaze at her own reflection and make sure she didn't have anything on her face.

"You must guard your heart too, sweet Libi," Imma whispered quietly. "Remember, he is not a believer."

"Imma, what do you mean?" Libi asked, genuinely surprised by the suggestion.

"Am I mistaken in thinking that you are perhaps fond of Cassius? He has been here for weeks now, and I thought that maybe you might be feeling something... He is new and undeniably handsome, after all."

"No, Imma, not in that way," said Libi.

"Hm, maybe it is the way I have seen him look at you then. Think nothing of it, but remember, sometimes when we say that our actions are motivated by a desire to serve God, we are really using that 'excuse' as a way to impose our own will on His. If you say that you do not have such feelings, I will believe you, of course."

Although she felt an inexplicable pull toward him, she knew she could not entertain any thoughts of marriage to him or love between them, other than the love of friendship, unless he shared her faith. She still prayed that God would help her and her family to reach him and show him what it meant to be a believer in Jesus, but that was all. Or so she thought... Was it possible that her mother had seen something that she hadn't realized was there? Now she was confused, and felt a bit guilty that perhaps she had made an impression that was not a good reflection of her heart.

If Cassius came to know the truth of Jesus and His message, Libi would rejoice and sing God's praises, not because it meant something for her, but because it meant that another lost sheep had found its way home. She would not use the name of the Lord and the power of Jesus' message for her own gains.

She *would* however be spending even more time in prayer if she was to be successful in those commitments. As much as she tried to hide it, her heart did long for marriage—to have someone who knew her better than anyone else on earth, and whom she could rely on. But more than marriage, her heart longed to honor God. She did not want to step outside of His will for her life and make the erroneous mistake of thinking she knew better than He did.

"Oh, Lord," she prayed silently, *"Build a stronghold around my heart, for my feelings are muddled... I pray that if it is your will that Cassius comes to know Jesus, you would allow me to be your vessel in sharing that light with him, but let my intentions be only for your glory, not my own desires. I trust you to provide me with a husband, but only when the time is right and when it is your will. You know better than I do."*

Libi appeared in the doorway. How could she look so perfect after having spent the entire morning working and baking loaf after loaf of bread? It didn't make any sense, but neither did his feelings for her. Her silvery gray eyes captivated him, but he shook his head, trying to force himself to focus only on his work.

"Shalom, Abba," she said to her father, and then nodded cordially to the rest of them. First Yuval, then Gilad, then Cassius. Libi's eyes seemed to linger on him for longer than they had stayed on the others. Cassius reached a hand up instinctively to smooth out his own hair. "How is the work today?"

"It's… It's…" he stuttered, trying to remember what she was talking about. Work. Carpentry. What was he holding in his hands? Or better yet… What was it supposed to be?

"It's going quite well," said Tamir. Had Cassius heard him chuckle? "Cassius is almost finished with one of our larger orders that he started last week. He's an incredible worker!"

He felt Tamir come up behind him and pat him on the back. "Yes, well," Cassius coughed out, "I'm only trying to earn my keep here." *And maybe some other things,* Cassius added silently.

Although he no longer cared about earning their trust for the soul purpose of using it against them. Instead, he was beginning to want their trust because it was something he actually desired. This family always seemed so happy, so full of joy and light. Cassius wanted more than their money; he wanted their happiness too. He didn't want to take it; he wanted to share it.

He wouldn't mind if he could earn Libi's heart along the way either, but some part of him doubted that she would ever love him if she learned the truth about who he was and where he had come from. Cassius' intentions when he had rescued her had been honorable, for the most part, but they had devolved into more nefarious plans once he learned she was a follower of Jesus, a believer in a mythical Messiah.

But what if He wasn't a myth after all? For weeks now, Cassius dined with this family and listened to their prayers before they broke their fasts in the morning and the evening. He heard their religious proverbs and phrases sprinkled in throughout conversation. He even had the pleasure of listening to Libi sing her songs of praise on more than one occasion, with that beautiful but so distracting voice of hers. All of the time, they sounded genuine. Was it possible that they actually were?

Maybe if he accepted their Jesus, he too could live a life so perfect.

Perfect.

That was one thing he could never be. He closed the curtain in his mind where he had briefly allowed light to enter, retreating into the familiar darkness once more. He'd had the chance at a perfect life. After a few years in the military, he would have been given land, honors, and money, among other potential gifts and rewards for faithful service to the empire. All of that had been taken away from him by people like Libi, Yuval, Gilad, Tamir, and Chava. When Jesus' body disappeared, so too did Cassius' only chance at a life more worth living than the one into which he had been born.

"Nevertheless," said Tamir, "we are grateful for your help, but if you keep working at this pace then we'll run out of work for you to do!"

"And I am grateful for the roof over my head," said Cassius. Then he added with a joking tone, "Of course, I can always try to work less, if that would be preferable."

Tamir chuckled. "I'll be right back, boys. I'm going to see how your imma is doing."

"All right, Abba," answered Yuval and Gilad to their father. Cassius laughed under his breath at how they occasionally managed to speak with each other almost as if they were one. Greeks and Romans had many superstitions about twins, but most of them did not cast twins in a flattering light. Cassius thought in particular about the myth of how Rome was founded, by a set of twins called Romulus and Remus who were raised by wolves and birds. In the old story, Romulus killed Remus due to his own anger, and the city of Rome was named after him, for he was the one who had been victorious and built the first city walls. Yuval and Gilad were nothing like the barbarous twins of legend and lore. They got along quite well with each other for the most part, as Cassius imagined any brothers would. By now, he had learned they were not as different as he once expected them to be. While Yuval was taller than Gilad, Gilad's outward appearance was deceptive. He was just as strong as Yuval, although his personality was much softer.

"If it is true that you might be able to finish early today with Cassius' help, then can one of you take me to the agora this afternoon? I have more cakes than I have baskets," asked Libi.

"I can help with that problem," said Gilad, adding a wink at the end.

"I don't need you to eat them all, brother," Libi joked, "I need someone to walk with me."

"Yes," said Yuval, "We certainly don't want another incident. I don't think Imma's heart could take it."

"I don't think Abba's could either," added Gilad.

This entire family seemed to revolve around protecting Libi, but after getting to know her kind nature and innocent spirit, Cassius could understand why. Had he not only known of her existence for mere moments before deciding to come to her aid? There was something special about her that made it easy to want to guard her like precious treasure.

"She should learn to defend herself," thought Cassius.

"What?" she gasped.

Had he spoken that out loud? Now thinking of it, he wasn't sure if he had meant it as a serious suggestion or as another one of his remarks he usually kept to himself.

"No, wait," said Gilad. "That's… actually a good idea."

"It is?" said Libi. "Do you agree too, Yuval?"

"I do, surprisingly. We won't always be by your side at every moment. It's impossible, and in a city such as Antioch, you are bound to run into more than one situation you'd like to escape. I'm not sure why we haven't thought of it sooner."

"Well, I wouldn't go anywhere without one of my brothers. I don't think learning how to defend myself is necessary."

Now that Cassius had seen that Yuval and Gilad agreed with him, the idea made a lot of sense to him. "Libi, you were with your brothers when those two thieves came upon you in the agora. It is like they have said. They cannot defend you every moment."

Libi sighed. "I trust God to defend me in moments where my family cannot. After all, He sent you, didn't he?"

Cassius answered, "I understand your God calls you to have peace with all people, but does your God not also call you to act in some cases?"

"Yes, He does!" said Yuval. "Libi, God sent David into battle with Goliath, and David emerged victorious."

"And," added Gilad, "think of the story of Moses and Aaron. God called them to speak before Pharaoh on behalf of all of the Israelites."

"The same with Esther before the Persian king!" Yuval spoke with a kind of competitive edge. It seemed as though the brothers were now accidentally engaged in some sort of contest to see who could come up with the most examples from their people's history. Cassius now felt called to end it before the conversation veered too far away from Libi, who was supposed to be the focus. Her protection was the most important thing.

"What about your cousin?" asked Cassius. "The one you told me about—Shamira. What if she had not pursued Jesus so relentlessly? What if she had chosen not to act then?"

Libi remained silent for a moment, crossing her arms over her chest. Her eyes widened. They were moist, perhaps from tears unshed, and resembled pools of molten metal. Had Cassius overstepped by bringing her family into the discussion? Was the story she had shared about Shamira too personal?

"We have no way of knowing," she whispered, "but I suppose

the Lord would have provided somehow, if it was His will."

"Well, I would certainly feel a lot better if I knew that the Lord provided you with the ability to defend yourself, if the worst ever happened," said Cassius.

"You would?"

Cassius cleared his throat. "I would. It would mean that there would be one less young woman in distress for me to rescue."

"Do you make a habit out of rescuing young women in distress?" asked Libi with the same humorous tone she used to address her brothers.

"I, uh… Not *usually*…" Cassius looked to Libi's brothers who snickered in the corner, raising their eyebrows and going red in the face. He turned back toward Libi, trying to ignore them. "Not until I met you."

There were a lot of things he hadn't done until he'd met her. He hadn't cared for another person besides himself since his mother had died. He hadn't made such an effort to please someone since Servius had been his commanding officer. He hadn't worked so hard in a single day that by the time night fell he was utterly exhausted, but completely satisfied by what he had accomplished. He hadn't stopped to pray to God before partaking in a meal, any of the gods. He hadn't tried so hard to maintain good manners, ever. He hadn't let himself be a part of a family. Somehow, he felt like these people were his family. They treated him better than a hired hand, and although Cassius had lived in many places before and called other buildings and tents "home," he'd never felt like he belonged anywhere as much as he did under the covering of Tamir's workshop.

"All right," she replied, startling Cassius from his thoughts.

"All right?" he asked, still beguiled by her beauty. "What do you mean?"

"If you wish to teach me to defend myself, I'll do my best to learn."

"You will?" Cassius could not hide his surprise at Libi's

relenting.

"*But*, I have no intention of ever using that knowledge. I don't think I ever could," she said, shaking her head.

"Lord willing, you won't have to," said Gilad.

"What are you going to teach her first, Cassius?" asked Yuval, smirking and leaning back as though he were a spectator and the workshop was a hippodrome.

"Me?" said Cassius. "You're her brother. You teach her."

"It was your idea. Besides, I'm better at offense," said Yuval, throwing up his fists in jest.

Cassius rolled his eyes, "Fine, but if you are so good at offense then you can be the one she fights off."

"Fine by me." Yuval laughed.

"I have to fight my own brother?" said Libi, her pitch rising ever so slightly with each word.

"Would you rather fight me?" Cassius quipped.

Libi coughed. "Show me where to hit my brother."

Cassius moved behind her. "If you want to attack someone, the best way to do so is from higher ground. You're tall for a woman, so that gives you some advantage, but if you are being attacked it's unlikely that you'll see it coming. You need to know how to react quickly. Yuval, grab hold of her shoulders."

Yuval did as instructed.

"Now, Yuval is taller than you, yes?"

She nodded her head.

"All right, the quickest way to fend off someone from this position, that is, if they're holding you from the front, is to kick the man between his legs. Use the force of your knee and jerk your leg upward as though you were about to climb a ladder."

"You don't have to practice that, Libi," said Yuval, leaning backwards before straightening his posture.

From behind, Cassius saw Libi's ears turn red. Yuval shot him a warning look, but Cassius couldn't keep his lips from twitching. After bearing the brunt of so many of their jokes and tricks, he was glad to be on the winning side for once. Was this what it was like to have brothers? It was a friendship, the likes of which he hadn't even come close to experiencing since his brief military days.

"Let's keep going. I'm going to show you how to make a fist, all right? Give me your hand."

She did, but slowly. When he finally clasped her hand between his, he felt a surge of energy rush through him.

"Show me how you'd make a fist naturally," he said, keeping hold of her wrist.

"Like this?" she said, clasping her fingers around her thumb.

He shook his head. "No, keep your thumb outside, and curl your other fingers toward your palm." With his other hand, he moved her fingers as such.

"Why?" she said.

"If you hit a man hard enough, you're likely to cause more damage to yourself than to your opponent if you hold your thumb like that. The force from the punch will reverberate back onto you, possibly breaking bones."

She winced at the suggestion.

"But, if you hit him like *this*, clenching your fist tightly, he'll be the one suffering."

Libi let her hand fall. "I told you; I don't want to make anyone suffer."

"This is only practice, Libi. With any luck, you'll never have to use this information."

"With *God* by my side, Cassius."

Shaking off her brother's grip, she turned back to face him straight on with her mesmerizing metallic eyes. Enamored by her grace, he repeated, "With God by your side." Was he truly mesmerized by her, or was he starting to accept her ideologies as his own?

Satisfied, she turned back around and resumed her position.

"Remember what I said about height advantage? It is better to strike down on your opponent, but if your opponent is coming down toward you, it's better for you to strike upward. Does that make sense?"

"If your opponent is looking down on you, strike up, but if your opponent is looking up at you, strike down," she repeated the summary of the lesson.

"Yes! Now, take your fist and curl your arm toward you, so that the back of your hand is facing your brother. Then, move upward and strike him here, in this direction," said Cassius, reaching around her and pointing to Yuval's abdomen.

She did as she was instructed, but with little force. Yuval didn't even flinch.

"You'll have to learn to strike harder than that," said Gilad with a haughty laugh.

Libi sighed.

"You won't hurt me, I promise." Yuval smiled. At that, she seemed to relax, and Cassius went on showing her the best places on the front of the body to strike. Over time, she grew more confident with her jabs, and Cassius decided she was ready to move on with the lesson. If all soldiers were as quick to train as Libi, the Roman Army would've already captured the whole of Brittania by now.

"Now let's talk about how to attack from behind."

"Why would I need to attack from behind? That doesn't sound like self-defense," protested Libi.

"Maybe not, but what if you were abducted? Held hostage? Say that your kidnapper took you and hid you away. You would have no way of escaping unless he turned his back for a moment, and your chances at getting to safety would be even better if you could render him defenseless, even if it was for only a moment, to give you a head start. Yuval, turn around so I can show her the weakest points."

"Would I strike upward still?" she asked, lifting both of her arms and making petite fists.

"You could, but since his back is to you, it would be better if you had a weapon. You can make almost anything into a weapon; some pottery, a plank of wood, a large rock—hit your captor on the back of the head with any of those and you're sure to render him unconscious. But weapons like that aren't always readily available… You should consider carrying a knife."

"A knife!" she exclaimed. "Oh, I could never use it!"

"And you would never hit anyone either—it would only be another precaution, Libi."

"Here," said Gilad, "this one is too dull for carving."

Gilad tossed the tiny blade in Cassius' direction and it landed between his feet. It was a good thing the younger brother had such good aim. "Hold it like this." Cassius held her arm and demonstrated the proper motion several times until she could do it on her own.

Libi dropped her hand to her side. "I think that's enough lessons for today."

"Very well," said Yuval. "Gilad can take you to the agora now."

"Me? I took her last week."

"Yes, but I want to finish these projects and we both know I'll get them done faster than you."

"But we still have—"

"Brothers, please," said Libi, moving between them. "Every moment that passes is a moment that I'm not selling my cakes. Can't one of you take me? I need to hurry if I am to sell as much as possible before this evening's gathering."

"I could take her," Cassius uttered before he could even think about what he was saying; another thought that he had meant to keep to himself. It was a good thing he was no longer a soldier expected to carry discreet battle plans in his head. Loose lips could lose wars; the only thing he was losing now was his pride.

Yuval and Gilad looked at him and nodded their heads in sync with each other, but Cassius cared little for their reactions. His eyes drifted down between them, where Libi stood with eyes wide.

Had she grown to have some sensible measure of distrust in him, or did she still think so highly of him that she would trust him with her life? After his years on the streets, he didn't think he could ever desire anything more than food and money, but he'd been wrong. Cassius had grown to crave Libi's approval above all else.

"I promise you that I would make sure no harm comes to her," said Cassius, bowing his head slightly.

"I think that's a fine idea," said Tamir, emerging from the house once more. "You've already proven that you are a man of strong morals by protecting our Libi that first day. You may go with Cassius to the marketplace, hamuda. I trust him, and this way, Cassius can join us for tonight's meeting."

Cassius presumed the meeting in question was one where they would gather with other believers. He had managed to avoid going to the previous meetings by pretending he had fallen asleep, exhausted after the day's work, but he sensed this was Tamir's way of telling him that attendance would be required going forward if he wanted to remain here. He supposed it was only fair that if he lived under their roof, he followed their customs as much as possible. After all, how dangerous could a group of believers be?

Libi smiled cordially at her father before picking up her baskets, "All right. Will we see you at Taliah's then?"

"Yes, we shouldn't be too much longer here."

"Very well then. I will see you later, Abba, Yuval, and Gilad." Libi kissed her father on the cheek and turned toward Cassius. Cassius wiped his brow, washed his hands in the basin, and then led the way out into the street.

"So… What do you do at these gatherings? Should I bring something?" Cassius asked once they were a little bit farther away from the workshop.

"Oh, you don't need to bring anything but yourself. We meet at least once a week to listen to each other's testimonies, pray, offer encouragement… Things like that."

Cassius cleared his throat, "Will I… Will I be welcomed? I am not…"

"A Jew?" said Libi. "It is as we've told you before, Cassius. We could not live in a city like Antioch if we only associated ourselves with other Jews. You will be welcomed with open arms, Cassius. Do not be afraid."

Afraid? Cassius had slept countless nights alone on the streets, come face to face with the sharp edges of a sword on more than one occasion, and more recently, lived on the run from the law for years. What was it now that filled him with such fear?

"Let the whole earth shout triumphantly to the Lord! Serve the
Lord with gladness; come before him with joyful songs." —
Psalm 100:1-2 CSB

Cassius stood beside Libi in the center of the agora. Slowly, Libi's sweet cakes began disappearing. During a lull in business, Libi turned to face Cassius, and he straightened his back. "It's a very good day for sales. So many customers at this time of day is incredible!"

"What makes your bread special from other breads sold at the agora?" asked Cassius, knitting his brows together. "I'm not trying to be rude. I just wonder when there are so many others to choose from, why choose your cakes? Especially if this time of day is normally slow for business, as you've said."

Libi ran the back of her hand across her forehead. "Perhaps it is because mine are sweeter than the rest."

"So is your smile. That's probably why people buy from you more than anyone else."

The sound of Libi's laughter echoed throughout the marketplace, and it soothed Cassius' soul like pure honey. "I do not think *that* is why they purchase from me."

The way she couldn't accept the compliment openly endeared her to him. The women in Rome, women like his mother, adorned themselves with jewelry or fine cloth to make themselves appear beautiful, but Libi was beautiful without even trying. It wasn't anything she wore or did to herself, it was something in her spirit that became apparent any time she smiled, laughed, or opened her mouth to speak a kind, gentle word.

"I think that's exactly why they purchase from you. I mean, have you seen the balding man selling herbs and spices? What about that one—the one who keeps strutting about with samples of textiles and a wart the size of a great hippodrome on the end of his nose? You're certainly better looking than they are."

"Cassius," Libi said, scraping her foot on the ground and fumbling with the cakes remaining in her basket.

"What?" he said, tittering. "As far as I'm aware, you still have all your hairs on your head, and I've never seen any warts on your face. Unless you are very skilled at applying pigments and beautifying ointments to hide more unsightly features—*which I doubt*—you are certainly more approachable than the others."

"All right," she giggled. "I will thank you for your compliment, only if you *please* stop flattering me at the expense of others."

"I'll accept those terms," said Cassius puckishly.

"Good," she said, sighing as she looked around the agora. The sun had fallen low behind the buildings, leaving them in almost complete shadow. The transition was quick and jarring. "I suppose we ought to make our way to the meeting soon. Those who have dinners to prepare are likely already gone."

"Now? But we have so many extra cakes." Cassius lifted the baskets he held to show they were still weighted with goods.

"We can't sell them if there are no customers, Cassius."

"Sing." He blurted out the idea inspired by merchants and entertainers he'd seen on the streets of Rome. Her lilting melodies were almost as addicting to listen to as her dates were to eat; they were sure to attract attention, and attention would bring more customers for her.

"What?" she gasped.

"Sing one of your songs. I know you have many in your head." He gestured to a stray lock of hair that had fallen across her forehead. She brushed it back.

"I can't sing in the middle of the agora! What would people think?"

"They would think to themselves, 'What a beautiful woman singing such beautiful songs!' They will come closer to hear you, and when they do, they will smell your cakes and buy them."

She shook her head and began walking in the other direction.

"*One song*. One song, and then we can go to your meeting."

She parted her lips barely wide enough for her breath to escape her lungs. He listened to her faint humming and laughed. "Louder, louder!" he cheered, clapping his hand against his thigh in an effort to give rhythm to her vocalizing. She squeezed her eyes shut, but raised her voice louder and louder with each breath. As Cassius had predicted, a small crowd of onlookers assembled around them, all of them as entranced as Cassius had been the first time he heard her sing. As she continued with her song of praise, people began to approach her with coin. She would take it and hand them their cakes, all the while never breaking up the song.

The more she sang, the more people began to crowd around them, seeming to emerge from the shadows to find out where the source of the music was coming from. Although they'd made a few sales, Cassius decided to encourage them even more.

"Sweet cakes! Sweet cakes for sale," he called, "come and buy your sweet cakes here." He set down the empty baskets he'd been holding at Libi's feet and took the fuller basket from her hands. For a moment she faltered and raised an eyebrow at him, but he waved her on and gave her a look that he hoped would encourage her to keep going. Then Cassius went into the crowd.

"If you think she's a good singer, you should taste her sweet cakes and see how good of a baker she is," said Cassius to one potential customer. They reached toward the basket. "Ah, ah, ah." He stopped them. "The melodies are free. The cakes will cost you." They pulled some coin from their satchel and Cassius gave them cakes in return. He repeated the process with as many others as he could find until the basket had less than five cakes left, at which point Libi's melody came to a close and the crowd had all but dispersed or moved to other stalls.

Cassius trotted back toward her and showed her the basket.

Her hand flew up to her mouth. "Cassius! How did we sell so many?"

"It was your singing that brought them here. I only encouraged them."

"And the coin?" she said, already stacking the baskets to make them easier to travel with. Cassius held out his fist and revealed her profits.

"Oh, Cassius! We must go at once!"

"Of course." He smiled. "We don't have enough cakes left to host another performance."

She laughed, and again his chest swelled with a foreign sensation as they walked. Life in Antioch was not as bad as he once thought it would be. Perhaps he could afford to settle down, find somewhere more permanent to live, and even call it "home." He'd never had a home before, but if he was going to pick any place, this large city was as good as any. It certainly had its flaws; overcrowding was one of them, but that could also be seen as a blessing. It afforded him the anonymity he craved after his past. Antioch also had Libi. Was it possible that she could be a part of his future?

As they walked, he allowed Libi to take the lead in their journey since she alone knew where they were headed, but he did not stray more than two paces behind her. Some of his soldier instincts still remained very much intact, which is why he continually looked from left to right, scanning his surroundings for any warning signs of suspicious behavior or aggressors lurking in the shadows. It was not long before he noticed the scraggly boy who seemed to be trailing Libi from the opposite side of the street. Cassius knew the type, for he had once been such a street urchin, hungry for more than food. The boy's gaze stayed locked on the purse that jingled with coin at Libi's side, and Cassius knew at once what the boy was trying to do. He was a pick-pocket, or he was trying to be. He wasn't a very good one at least, or Cassius would not have noticed him. He was being far too obvious, not blending in with the crowd or even trying to, and blinded by his objective.

Cassius cleared his throat loud enough for Libi to hear. The jerk of her head back toward him caused the boy to also take note of Cassius.

"Is something wrong, Cassius?" said Libi in her usual sing-song voice.

"Nothing's wrong at all." Cassius smiled in Libi's direction but shot the would-be thief a warning glance. The boy seemed to have gotten the message and turned away. Satisfied, Cassius refocused his attention on Libi.

"Perhaps your performance attracted too much attention."

"What do you mean?"

"Anyone could hear the way your coin purse rattles with every step you take. I'm worried about petty thieves trying to take advantage of your good fortune."

"I understand. I will give it to the elders as soon as we get to Taliah and Keinan's house, and then they will decide what to do with it."

"Give *all of it* to the elders?" Cassius balked. All of that hard work and she wanted to give the money away?

"My baking is one of the ways I serve."

"Is it not enough to open your home to weary strangers? You must also give your money away after you've earned it?" Cassius had spent the majority of his life with nothing. He couldn't imagine being in a position of prosperity, and then freely giving his wealth away. What about stability? Security?

"The Lord always provides for our needs, and one of the ways He does that is through giving. When I give my money to The Way, it is given to those who need it. The poor, the orphaned, the widows. If I were ever to be in such a position myself, I would hope that the giving of others would also sustain me. It is also a way that we show we are grateful to God—when He gives so much, even up to His own son, we should be able to give back to Him, that all we have might be used for His glory and to serve His purpose. That can be money, but it can also be talents or services too."

"Hm." Cassius nodded.

"But you're right, Cassius. There is a lot of money, and I would feel safer if you carried it. I wouldn't want to repeat the events of the day that we met, after all."

Leaving Cassius little room to argue, she practically shoved the purse into his hands. His wrist nearly faltered when he felt the full weight of it. At that moment, it hit him. This bag was full of coin, more money than he made in the past several weeks working for Tamir's carpentry business once the cost of his food and board was taken out. He could take the whole thing and be gone in an instant, or at the very least, he could swipe a part of it and it would still be enough to get him started on his next journey, in addition to what little wages he'd saved. Libi would probably be none the wiser. It would still be heavy to her. He could make the swap quietly and while they were walking and she would never know the difference. Was that not the whole reason he had agreed to living under Tamir's roof for as long as he had? To take advantage of them? Did Cassius not despise their people, The Way-followers?

"Thank the Lord for you, Cassius. If not for you and your ideas, we would not have such a sum to protect. I am sure that this is a part of God's plan for helping Taliah and Keinan."

Despite the muggy heat of the evening sun settling over the city at dusk, Cassius felt himself break into a cold sweat. Try as he might, and he tried many times as they continued their journey, he could not make his hands move the way he wanted to. What was wrong with him? This wasn't the first time he'd tried to steal something, and it probably wouldn't be the last.

Then he realized… even if he had all the money in the world, would he ever truly be free?

"I hope you know where you're going," said Cassius. "I don't know of this Taliah you speak of, but if we get lost, I know your family will blame me. I've seen how much they love you, and they *adore* you. I'd hate to see what they would do to someone they despise."

Libi laughed. "I know where I'm going, Cassius."

"It seems like we're heading back to your home," said Cassius. His tone was unusually low, as though he were under a great amount of stress. "Are you sure?"

She was used to his questions, but his unease seemed most peculiar. Libi wondered what could have his mind so occupied, but settled that perhaps he was simply nervous to meet more believers, and wanted to get there in ample time, which she could guarantee that they would.

"The way to Taliah's home involves going toward my home from the agora, but turning off and heading up one of the cross roads. You'll see."

"Very well then," he grumbled.

All of a sudden, Libi's eyes happened upon something *magnificent*. It was stunning. Perfect. An answer to prayer. Only once before had the Lord's hand seemed so evident in her life and the lives of those around her, and that was back when she lived in Jerusalem. "Oh, Cassius! Look at that!"

Libi's steps quickened, and she instinctively gripped her dress and raised the hem enough to ensure that she wouldn't trip in her excitement.

"Look at *what?*" He muttered. "There is nothing to see here."

Looking through his eyes, Libi could see why he would be so unimpressed. To everyone else, what Libi saw was a dilapidated, run-down house that had certainly seen better days. The roof... Well, saying the roof needed to be repaired would be putting it politely. Broken pottery was visible through the windows. A fine layer of dirt and ash coated the brick walls where fire had scorched it, and the main door seemed to hang crooked on its hinges. Still, where others might see disaster, Libi saw possibility.

"Cassius, look at this house! It's perfect!"

"Perfect for what? Firewood?"

Libi saw a man emerge from the doorway, covered in dust himself and coughing tremendously. She did not hesitate to approach him. "Excuse me, is this building for sale?"

"Who's asking?" He snarled.

"I am," said Libi.

"You? What do you want with a house like this?" said the older man.

Libi straightened, holding herself with more confidence. "That isn't what I wanted to discuss, I'm afraid. I merely asked if this building was for sale?"

The man groaned. "What would a young girl like you want with this? Fire took out the roof, and it's a mess inside."

Libi tried to smile graciously in an effort to assuage the older man's temper. "I apologize, you're clearly working very hard to restore this building to its obviously once grand conditions. It was foolish of me to assume you would have time to answer my questions just to satisfy my own curiosity."

She turned to go and heard Cassius whisper, "Now what are you doing?" But Libi had a plan. She could tell from the condition of her perfect answer to prayer that restoring it would take time. A lot of time. Given the fine clothing this man was wearing, or what was visible of it underneath all of the grayish-debris, he most likely wasn't the type to do manual labor. He might not have had the time, but Libi did and she knew where to find help. She could envision it all in her head so clearly that she could practically reach out and touch it; this building, with a little bit of work, would make an ideal home for orphans and those in need. It was a traditional Roman *domus*-style house, and from what Libi could tell, extended far back with a spacious courtyard of its own. It likely had many rooms, or it would once it was fully restored, and with a building like this, the believers could help countless individuals in need. Taliah and Keinan could oversee it, or another volunteer, and Libi could help take care of and teach the children, and even cook if necessary. It could be used as a gathering place for meetings, or a shelter for those in need.

"Wait," said the man, stopping Libi in her tracks.

She turned around and put on a hopeful face. "Yes? What is it?"

"This isn't the only property I own in this city. Some of the previous tenants started a fire and destroyed this place, then took off, leaving me at a loss. The repairs will be costly, but it's the time I'm worried about. In all the time it takes to make this place livable again, I won't be making anything off of it. If you're really interested, I might be able to negotiate a sale." The man nodded at Cassius.

"Don't look at me," said Cassius. "She's the one with all of the money."

The man made a kind of incredulous face, but did turn his attention back to Libi. "Very well, then. I *might* be able to negotiate a sale, but you're so young. Most women your age are more interested in getting married and making a home in their husband's household."

"Oh, it wouldn't be for me alone. There are so many in this city who've come upon hard times… This could be turned into a kind of shelter for them, a place they could stay until they are able to find something for themselves."

"A shelter, eh?" The man ran his fingers along his jaw, resting his hand under his chin for a moment to ponder the idea. "I don't think I've ever heard of such a thing… Not here anyways, but it would clean up the streets considerably, and *that* would increase the value of the other properties I do own…"

"What would you consider to be a fair price?" asked Libi.

The man named an exorbitant number, and Libi knew he was starting the bid much higher than the property was actually worth. Libi would not let him get away with that. She had seen similar bartering tactics within the agora, and knew from observation how to negotiate down to a fair price.

Libi replied with another number far lower than what she was willing to pay, and he countered again. The process repeated over and over again until Libi was satisfied and they'd met somewhere in the middle. "You drive a hard bargain for a woman," said the man.

Libi smiled ruefully. "But do we have an agreement?"

The man looked down at the ground, then back at the building, then up at the sky, and back at Libi, before finally answering, "We do."

"Oh, thank you! Of course, I don't have all of the money with me right now."

"Well, I should think not." The man laughed. "No one would ever carry that amount on hand."

"Well, I don't actually have the money at all, but I know where I might be able to get it."

"Might?" the man asked, raising another incredulous eyebrow.

"If you'll give me one day to talk to some people and make some arrangements, I can be back here tomorrow at this time precisely. If I'm not here, you're free to make dealings with someone else, and neither of us will have lost anything, but if I am here, we'll both have gained something. You'll have earned money which you can take to invest in another property that doesn't need nearly as much care, and I'll have earned *this*."

The sight of it took Libi's breath away. Even if it would take a lot of work, she knew its very existence was proof that the Lord always answered prayers. She couldn't wait to tell Taliah, and only hoped that everyone else at the gathering would be able to see what she saw and take the necessary steps.

"Yes, but why anyone would want *this* that badly is beyond me… Still, you are a good negotiator and I agree to your terms."

"That's wonderful! And you won't change your mind about the price?" Libi asked, wanting to make sure she had all of the details exactly right before she told Taliah and Keinan.

"I'm a witness," said Cassius, who had been rather quiet throughout the whole exchange. "I'll remember exactly what he agreed to."

"There, you see? Fair is fair. I will see you tomorrow," said the man.

After a few more pleasantries, Libi and Cassius continued on their way to Taliah's house. Libi had earned a good portion of what was needed to pay for the building on the sales of her bread alone, and she knew there would be a collection of tithes this evening. The only other expense they would have would be labor and repairs, but Libi had a few ideas on that too…

13

"For where two or three are gathered together in my name, I am there among them." — Matthew 18:20 CSB

"Cassius? Cassius?"

He wasn't sure how many times Libi called his name; he'd been too deep in his own thoughts. He snapped to attention as though she were a military commander and he were still a trainee. It was the fact that he could not seem to escape her command that had him so concerned. Would this growing infatuation be his weakness? His downfall?

"Cassius? Are you well?" she asked again. They stood outside the doorway of what he could only assume was the gathering place.

"I am fine." He snapped his reply a little too gruffly. During their walk from the agora, Cassius realized he would never be free from his crimes, but he would also never be free from the hold Libi had on his heart. He needed to remain cold so that he might be able to calculate his next move with a clear head, or like many other instances in his life, rashness might be his undoing.

It was Libi who knocked quietly on the door when they arrived.

A woman who did not appear much older than Libi's age answered, "Shalom, Libi. This must be Cassius?"

Cassius merely nodded in reply. His mind was too preoccupied to come up with anything else.

"And how are you, Libi? Were your sales today successful in the marketplace?"

Libi's smile beamed. "Thanks to Cassius' help, I earned double what I am used to, but that's not the only blessing. I think I have found a solution to the housing concern, but it will require the help of everyone here."

"Oh, the Lord does provide, doesn't He? I look forward to hearing all of it, but truly, it is good to see you."

"It is good to see you too, Taliah."

"We must thank God for sending you, Cassius. It seems as though you entered our lives at just the right time, if all I've heard is true."

Cassius wanted to cringe… He did not deserve such kindness. If these people knew the truth about his past, then they would know they were practically opening the gates of a lamb's pen to a lion.

"Oh, Cassius, may I please have the coin now so that I can add it to the collection box?" He handed it to her quickly, wanting to be rid of the temptation and done with the whole affair.

Taliah welcomed them to the crowded but spacious room and Libi joined the women while Cassius went toward her brothers and stood next to a window where he could also keep watch. In an unplanned coincidence, he was also next to the collection box which was being generously filled up with coins in varying denominations, including what Libi had donated.

Suddenly the temptation to steal began to grow again. There would most likely come a moment when they all went to their prayers and he could slip away unnoticed. He knew Libi's family would be hurt and saddened if he were to make off with the box, but they'd get over it—in fact, they'd likely pray for him.

However, he also now knew of Libi's hopes to use the money to start a shelter for the needy, and he briefly dared to wonder what his life would've been like if there had been such a home for himself and his mother to go to all those years ago… Would things have been different then? His thoughts were interrupted when a young man he didn't know began to lead them in songs. In order to fit in and not seem suspicious, Cassius did his best to try to join in and look like he was one of them.

In a moment which could not have been more awkward for Cassius, his eyes locked onto Libi's across the room. The movement of his lips and the way he feigned song must have been convincing, because she appeared quite pleased. How he wished he could genuinely make her happy and end the deception. Without the deception, he feared she would never be able to love him, and with the deception there was no way he could stay here under the pretense. Not with the conscience he'd unwittingly developed, and that Libi and all of her goodness and songs inspired. When he was with her and her family, he felt like he could be a better man, but such dreams did not last long before they turned into nightmares. Cassius felt trapped.

A man that Cassius could only assume was also the owner of this house, Keinan, as he recalled, stood up and made an announcement. "It is good to see all of you, and to hear of God's blessings in your life. As you know, we are still awaiting the return of Barnabas to our city. Tonight, we will be blessed to hear from Tamir, who has agreed to testify about how he and his family came to believe in Jesus as the Messiah in Jerusalem years ago and share a message from his heart. Tamir, would you stand?"

At this, Cassius became even more interested. Would Tamir share the same story that Libi had? Of miracles and resurrections and the deaf suddenly being made to hear? He watched Tamir rise with bated breath and waited for him to begin speaking.

Tamir started, "Most of you know me as a friend, neighbor, and carpenter. You know me as husband to Chava, who is one of the most hardworking and steadfast servants of the Lord I know, and who I am honored to be married to. You know me as a father to three young adults, all of whom I could not be prouder. Though for some of you, especially those who are newer to our community, there are things you might not know about the man I was before I came here. Only God could restore a life as broken as mine.

"Most couples who've been married for any length of time will tell you that a happy marriage isn't always an easy marriage. It takes work to build something with strength, but for the longest time, I wasn't interested in building anything. Instead, I hid from my troubles. I ignored the two sons who needed their father's guidance as they grew from boys to men. Every time I looked at my daughter, I mourned that I could not take on her burden myself. I built a wall between myself and my wife because I couldn't see at the time how much we both needed each other to get through the trials ahead of us. I tried to handle everything on my own… but no mortal man can do that and triumph.

"I do not tell you this to burden you with my own shame, but to show you how truly great our God is. My family have extended grace upon grace toward me, and I have tried my best to live a life that is worthy of their love, but the truth is that I was worthy of nothing when Jesus came into our lives. He healed Libi from her affliction, setting into motion multiple other healings that would take place. Healing where I believed it was impossible. Healing between myself and my family. Healing between myself and my wife. Even healing between myself and God, whom I had turned away from for all of those years. In turning back toward Him, all things were made new. He had been there all along, of course, but it took a true miracle—*miracles*—for me to see Him.

"I did not deserve His grace, yet His words and actions pierced my heart. It would have been enough to have hatred melt away and to be washed over with peace, but Jesus did more. *So much more.* How could I not follow Him? My only regret is not leaning on the Lord sooner. I implore those of you listening: whatever you may going through, do not wait for anything, but see His mercies *now*. Feel his presence *now*. Let your life be transformed *now*. There is nothing He cannot heal. Nothing He cannot take and use for good."

Cassius was no longer looking at the collection box. His eyes were intent upon Tamir as the powerful story unfolded. Cassius thought of all the shame that weighed him down; of things he had done that kept him chained to a life of darkness. Tamir's story, probably like many others in this room, proclaimed being freed from burdens and finding peace, but Cassius couldn't help but feel that his story was more complicated. Did the forgiveness of their God extend even to himself? He longed for the kind of lifestyle that Tamir and his family lived in; one filled with reconciliation and restoration. They certainly had their share of troubles and risked persecution for what they believed, but they trusted God would be with them no matter what circumstances should befall. What would it be like for Cassius to put his trust in their God too?

All this day he felt as though he had been wrestling with two choices. Turning back toward his old ways to save his own skin, or turning toward Libi, only for her to eventually hate him if she ever discovered the truth. What if there was a third option? What if... all things *could* be made new, as Tamir said? What if the impossible really was possible? Cassius thought of the task he'd been ordered to participate in the night of their Messiah's execution. It was Cassius who helped pierce His hands and feet with the nails that kept Him affixed to the cross. He had been the one driving the mallet. Could that be forgiven also?

Tamir's next words made Cassius shudder, for it seemed as though he was reading his own mind. "For those of you who think you can never be forgiven or that your sins are greater than the work Jesus did on the cross, you are thinking too highly of yourself. Our sins may be great; His grace is greater. When Jesus was crucified on that cross, it wasn't just *soldiers* who drove the nails through his hands and feet… It was *each and every one of us*. Every course you ever took that pulled you from God, every sinful action or even thought drove those nails deeper into the cross. Yet through the resurrection, we have hope. There is no heart He cannot make new, no sin He cannot forgive, no debt He cannot wipe out. I know most of you here are believers like me, or you came because you are still curious about our faith. I urge you, if your heart is pounding like my heart once did, then He is speaking to you and reaching out, wanting you to accept that grace for yourself."

In that moment Cassius knew; he knew it more than he'd ever known any truth in his lifetime. He wanted this restoration, he wanted to become a different person, and if faith in the man called Jesus Christ was the way to it, then Cassius would take on that faith for himself. His conversion was not quiet; he began to weep and he fell to the ground. "Please…" Cassius choked on his own sobs, "Show me the way."

Without sparing a second, Tamir and other men gathered around. Tamir guided Cassius in his own prayers, showing him how to speak to God. There were no idols involved, no sacrifices. He could simply pray and bear his heart. By the time he opened his eyes, he was already feeling like a different person. Although he'd only been a true believer for a mere matter of moments, he already felt clean and in more than a physical sense. He felt light. He felt his shackles beginning to fall off. He felt the beginnings of *freedom*.

After that, more of the men witnessed to him and explained the fundamentals of their beliefs. Tamir asked Cassius some more questions, and when Cassius answered agreeably, they took him to be baptized. A nagging thought pestered him… This should have been the greatest night of his life as he poured out his hurts, admitted he needed a Savior, and declared his belief in Jesus as the sacrifice that covered his sins. Although he'd confessed to being a sinner in need of redemption, he hadn't told them all of his sins. Was he really forgiven, or was Tamir just saying those things about no sin being too great to forgive because he couldn't begin to imagine the kinds of atrocities Cassius had committed under the guise of preserving the Roman Empire and his own life? He was sure that their God—now *his* God—knew the depths of his betrayal, but if these friends and other believers found out, would they reject him? Would he once again be a cast-off? A disgrace not only to his country, but to the community of Way-followers he'd just begun to call friends? No, Cassius thought it better to push those thoughts deep, deep down inside of him. After all, if it was true that he had become a new person by believing in Jesus, then what he did in the past shouldn't matter to anyone. Should it?

"It's a wonderful idea, Libi, and I'm sure we can find someone who will be interested in helping to run it," said Taliah.

"The first thing we have to do is actually *purchase* the building. Then we can figure out how exactly it's going to run. What do you think, Imma?" Libi looked to her mother for encouragement, and saw that tears filled her eyes.

"I think it's a beautiful idea, and I am so thankful to God for blessing me with a daughter who wishes to bless others in such immense ways. I am sure your father will agree, and even be amenable to helping with the repairs."

"Thank you, Imma," said Libi.

Taliah smiled. "I'm going to go call the children back in; I let them play after your father finished speaking and they became restless, but the night is growing dark and they need to start settling down for the evening. After that, I'll find Keinan and tell him of what you have shared. I think the men are almost done and ready to finish for the night, so it will be a perfect time to gather everyone for one last announcement."

"Thank you so much," said Libi.

She followed Taliah with her eyes as she moved to the other side of the room where the men were mostly gathered around Cassius, who had only moments ago taken a leap of faith and become a believer in Jesus Christ. Her heart soared with the revelation that he had been so moved by the Holy Spirit, and Libi wanted to tell him how happy she was for him, but it seemed as though more than Cassius' beliefs had changed in the last few hours. Libi suddenly felt nervous to speak to him. For the first time since Jesus had given her the gifts of hearing and speech, she felt at a loss for words. She wondered what it was that suddenly made her heart flutter in a way it never had before, and why she felt like she was seeing Cassius for the first time.

Keinan's voice disrupted Libi's thoughts and drew her attention back to the front of the room. "If I could have everyone quiet down for a few moments, there are a few more announcements to be made and then you can all go home. Of course," Keinan laughed, "there is no hurry. My wife and I are happy to host you all for prayer and fellowship as long as you like, although as I look around, I do see a few tired eyes."

"Abba…" At that, little Omri came running to the front of the room, stretching his arms toward his father. "I'm sleepy…"

The little boy yawned as Keinan picked him up and everyone laughed when he closed his eyes and rested his head on his father's shoulder. "Some of us are more tired than others, I see," Keinan joked. "The first matter we wanted to discuss is the matter of the tithes and offerings, which you know go to support the widows and orphans among us, as well as those in need within our community. There is one among us who has a proposition for how to use this month's offerings that I think is most noble."

Then, in a moment Libi could not have been less prepared for, Keinan gestured to Libi herself. "Libi *bat* Tamir, would you please tell everyone of what you told my wife?"

Nerves overtook Libi at once. She never expected that she would be the one who would present the idea to the Way, but then again, it was her idea. How was it that she had no problems speaking to Cassius of things like Jesus' teachings, His resurrection, and even the most personal details of her miracle, specific things she'd never even told Taliah, but couldn't share an idea that she had pursued with such confidence earlier that day with people she'd known and trusted for years?

"Go on," she heard her mother whisper from behind her, but as she looked at the crowd, she found that it was Cassius' encouraging smile that gave her the confidence to speak.

"On your way here, some of you may have seen a building damaged severely by a fire. If you've seen it, then you probably know it's hardly in a condition that's suited for living. Quite the opposite, in fact… The man who owns the building would like to sell it, and… And I think that we should use the money that we've collected to purchase it."

Libi paused for a moment, briefly overwhelmed by the many sets of eyes staring back at her.

"Tell us why you think we should purchase it," Taliah called out from the back of the room, where she stood with Felix, Rufus, and Phoibe, cradling little Tirzah in her arms.

Libi nodded her thanks for Taliah's reassurance and pressed on in her speech, "As Keinan said, the money we collect is used to care for those in need. So often women and children in difficult situations have nowhere to go. Why, it was only a few weeks ago that Taliah and I found Tirzah, left because her mother couldn't care for her. I propose we buy that house, fix it up, and turn it into a shelter. A place the needy could come to for help."

"Who would run such a place?" A voice called out.

"Volunteers," Libi answered confidently, "myself included. I would be willing to help in whatever way that I could, cooking, cleaning, and such."

"If the place has been damaged by fire, how will we restore it?

Surely, we'll need even more money for that," said another voice.

In yet another sign from God that He worked all things together, Libi's father spoke up and added his voice to the discussion, "I would donate the labor of myself and my two sons to such a cause. I would also donate my tools and any supplies that I can. Thanks to Cassius' help, our business is far ahead of where we need to be, and what work we do have won't need to be finished for some time."

"But what about the money… Can we even afford such a place as this?" Each person who spoke up raised valid points, and Libi prayed to God for the right words to win them over. In truth, she did not know the exact answers to every question, but she still had faith.

"I think so," said Libi.

"How much did the man ask for it?" said Keinan.

When Libi told him the amount, Keinan laughed. "My friends, whatever doubts you may have about this endeavor, I strongly suggest you ignore them. At such a good price, this would *have* to be God's will. Shall we put it to a vote then? All in favor, raise your hands."

Libi could barely bring herself to look out at the crowd, but when she did, tears flooded her vision. Every hand in the building was raised upward to heaven.

"That's settled then. Anyone who wishes to help or donate to the reconstruction can speak to Tamir, and those who are interested in volunteering to assist with the upkeep of the house should speak to Libi or Chava. Shalom and goodnight," said Keinan, and with a clap of his hands, the crowd began to disperse.

What felt like another hour passed before Libi and her family were finally able to leave, as so many had come up to them with ideas for how to help and questions about what would be needed. Of course, not much could be answered until they had a better idea of what they were going to be doing, but many friends and individuals committed to helping however they could. After that, it was a quiet walk home; Libi and her mother walked, carrying the now empty baskets in front of their waists. They were followed closely by her father, brothers, and Cassius, but she didn't dare turn around to sneak a peek at them. She kept her eyes focused on the stars, lost in prayers of thanksgiving. What an extraordinary day this had been! The Lord had provided in more ways than Libi had thought possible, from touching Cassius' heart with her father's testimony, to her abundant sales in the marketplace, to the man willing to sell his building for such a bargain price. Yet even in the midst of such abundant blessings, Libi had a sense that this was only the beginning of God's latest miracle.

"Therefore, everyone who hears these words of mine and acts on them will be like a wise man who built his house on the rock. The rain fell, the rivers rose, and the winds blew and pounded that house. Yet it didn't collapse, because its foundation was on the rock. But everyone who hears these words of mine and doesn't act on them will be like a foolish man who built his house on the sand. The rain fell, the rivers rose, the winds blew and pounded that house, and it collapsed. It collapsed with a great crash." -
Matthew 7:24-27 CSB

The day after the gathering of believers, Libi returned with enough money to purchase the ash-covered domus that would become a haven of hope where people could come in search of a meal, a safe place to sleep, and a message of hope. The landlord couldn't accept the money fast enough before he ran off, leaving them to deal with whatever remained of what was once a grand house in the city's center. After that, Libi, her father, mother, brothers, and Cassius walked through the building, inspecting it and making notes about what would be needed.

"Can't you see it, Abba? Won't this be the perfect place?" said

Libi, filled with anticipation for the dream to become a reality.

He chuckled to himself. "Were it not for your enthusiasm, I wouldn't believe it, but I can see it through your eyes."

Chava nodded enthusiastically. "Through this, Libi, who knows how many more will come to have miracles of their own, both big and small? God is good."

"Amen to that," Yuval began, "*but* no amount of enthusiasm is going to get this place fixed up without some serious physical labor. What do you think, Abba?"

"The structure seems sound. The parts of this building which have been touched by flames can be repaired, although it may take a significant amount of time. Not to worry, Libi, replacing materials and reinforcing the structure here and there is far easier work than rebuilding entirely from the ground up. The roof will be our first priority, and then we can start the repairs on the interior."

"Seems to me like we should get started now, doesn't it?" asked Cassius. "No time like the present to start getting some of the larger, unsalvageable pieces out of here. Then we can get a more accurate idea of exactly what materials we'll need to gather and return tomorrow."

"Cassius is right. We'll begin by picking up the bigger pieces of rubble and sorting them into piles of what can be salvaged and what cannot."

"I think we should make it into a competition to see who can move the most pieces—you men, or us. My daughter and I together are stronger than we seem, you know," said Libi's imma, giving her shoulder a squeeze.

"Don't I know it?" Libi's abba grinned. "This will not be an easy task, mind you. It certainly won't be finished in a matter of days, but the more we do now, the easier it will be to recruit volunteers in the future. Nothing built in a great hurry is everlasting. The best things come in time, so we'll all need to learn to be patient and trust in God. Things won't always go exactly according to plan, no matter how much we try to avoid it, but God is the master overseer. Every challenge for us will be another opportunity to strengthen ourselves, our faith, and our work. Understood?" They nodded in agreement. "Good. Now let's get started!"

"Abba?" whispered Libi, moving toward where her father now stood in the center of the *atrium*. "Before we begin, can we stop to pray? I want God to be involved in this, as you said, from the very beginning."

"Thank you, Libi, for reminding me. See what I mean about nothing being built for endurance when it is built in a hurry? When we rush, we forget to rely on God, and He's the very one we should be keeping at the center, *always*. Let us gather and pray that He will bless our work here."

Her father extended a hand to her, and she extended one to her mother. Together, her whole family and Cassius bowed their heads in prayer as her father petitioned God to see that their labor would be fruitful and that He would guide them throughout the process.

After uniting in prayer, they used what was left of the daylight to start cleaning up around the house and sorting things into piles of what could be repaired or repurposed, and what simply needed to be discarded. Libi's father, thankfully, came up with many ideas for how to use even the smallest of materials to ensure that there would be very little waste.

They rose early the following morning and took as much as they possibly could, now having assessed the kinds of tools and materials that would be required to complete the job.

"It is a blessing that the walls are made of brick," her abba said. "Some have cracks in them, but most are just covered in soot and dirt. When we are finished, no one will be able to tell the difference between the old and the new. More than anything right now, the whole place needs to be cleaned."

"That is why we brought these," said Chava, lifting buckets and rags. Libi and her imma set to work scrubbing, washing, and bringing in load after load of clean water. The men divided into teams, with two taking steps to reinforce the walls, and the other two beginning the process to mend the roof.

When the work began, they were all very lively and excited, but their collective pace gradually slowed as the course of the day went on and as their energy and enthusiasm were spent. As Libi passed through each of the rooms, singing songs while she worked to pass the time even quicker, she couldn't help but imagine what they might be used for some day. The domus was built around a spacious atrium, which one entered through the *vestibulum* facing the street. Each of the other rooms were built off of the atrium, forming a long rectangle. Libi imagined the vestibulum of the home being full of light so that when people stepped inside, they themselves also instantly felt lighter. Passing through the entrance, they would notice the rooms and alcoves of varying sizes on the left and the right sides of the atrium, with a spacious *culina* in the back of the house. She delighted when thinking about how much one could bake in the spacious culina, as opposed to the small clay oven and cramped quarters to which Libi was accustomed.

The smallest of the bedrooms which could not house many people would make perfect living quarters for the caretakers of the home. Libi spun around in the center of one such room and envisioned where someone might put a table to sit at and make notes about the household expenses and what would be needed for each month. It could go up against the wall next to the door. Opposite it could be a bed, and under the high-up window there might be a small trunk to store personal belongings. Of course, this was all hypothetical. Libi herself would not be the caretaker of the house, she had only come up with the idea. It was up to others to decide who would be the best fit to run this ministry.

Just then, a breeze traveled through the window, making what was once a curtain blow into the room. Libi looked at it and shook her head; it had so many holes in it and was so blackened from smoke that it might as well be torn down and used as another rag. Letting her hands fall from her hips, she moved toward the window with one arm outstretched. She reached up as high as she could and began to tug, and then tug again when it still did not budge.

"Now, now, don't be difficult," Libi talked aloud. With a grunt, she gave another tug, but to no avail.

"Can I help?" asked Cassius, who now stood in the doorway where Libi had been moments ago.

"Oh," she said, startled by his sudden appearance. "This curtain is ruined… I was trying to get it down, but…"

"Here, let me," replied Cassius.

Cassius wasn't much taller than Libi was, but as he lifted his own arms to tear the curtain down, she couldn't help but notice his broad shoulders and toned appearance. She realized she was staring and quickly looked away, but she heard Cassius chuckle ever so quietly and knew her extra attention had not gone unnoticed. She felt her cheeks redden and, although she couldn't see for herself, she worried that her face was even redder than dates.

In one swift motion, Cassius pulled the curtain off of the wall and it fell to the ground in a pathetic, shapeless heap. They both bent down to pick it up, and for a moment, their hands touched. Libi's breath hitched and she withdrew her hand, looking at Cassius to gauge his reaction. He didn't look away from her at all, and she feared she would get lost in the forest within his brilliant green eyes.

"Here you go," he said, handing her the rolled-up ball of tattered cloth. This time, his voice was low and husky.

"Thank you, Cassius," she whispered. Although she had noticed his appearance before and had taken note of the unusual hue of his eyes, something felt different now, as though a door opened where she thought there was only a wall. The road bent in a new direction she'd never noticed before. From a lake of still waters, a rushing river of possibilities now flowed.

As easily as she had envisioned what the walls of the house they stood in might look like once they were restored, she now envisioned a future with him. Violent flashes like memories flooded her mind, only none of the memories had happened yet. She imagined Cassius dressed in fine robes, and herself crowned with a wreath of flowers as though they were celebrating their wedding day. She saw herself again sitting beside Cassius around a dinner table, their faces lit only by the dim glow of lamplight and herself round with child. He carved toys for their little one as her father had done for his children so long ago. Then she saw the two of them older, each with stripes of silver and white hair to show their age, surrounded by children and grandchildren who all had her fine brown hair and Cassius' colorful eyes. She saw them serving together in this very house, only any remnant of the fire damage was gone, and it was full of smiling people. She saw it all so clearly, not like the kinds of dreams she had when she slept. When she awoke, she always remembered those dreams being slightly blurry and almost shiny. This felt as real as the cloth she held in her hands.

The cloth!

"I'm sorry, I don't know what I was thinking. I must be tired." She wondered what he must have thought, standing there next to her for who knows how long while she played make-believe as though she were still a child. She was not a little girl anymore, and Cassius was not a little boy.

What was it that now drew her heart to him so strongly? What had changed in these past few days? It was as though God had pulled back another curtain, only this one changed not how she saw the world, but how she saw Cassius. She had rejoiced that Cassius had taken such a bold step in his faith, and she prayed for him and praised the Lord alongside the other believers, but that had been the joy of seeing someone come to know the Savior she so deeply loved. Now her heart stirred in a different way, and a strange and anxious spirit she had not been familiar with before caused her to wonder if Cassius might have similar feelings.

"It's all right. Do you need help with anything else?" he asked.

"No, but… I did want to tell you how happy I am for you. We have all prayed for you since you came into our lives, and I'm glad that you have found a relationship with our Lord."

Cassius smiled and nodded. "Someday I hope I will be able to tell you the story of my life and of that night at the gathering in full. I never expected any of this to happen when I came to Antioch, or that my entire life would be changed. A large part of that is because of you."

"Me?" asked Libi.

Before Cassius could open his mouth to continue, another voice distracted both of them.

"Libi… Where are you? Come and see what I've found. I think some of this furniture they left behind is still good!"

"Coming, Imma! I was gathering some of the old linens up." Libi moved to the doorway, tossing what was left of the old curtain into the pile with the rest of the blankets and things she had found that were beyond a simple wash or mend.

"Do you need my help?" asked Cassius.

For some reason Libi found herself incapable of meeting his eyes, nervous for the first time in his presence and conscious of every move she made. "If you'd like, you can help me put these things with the rest."

"All right," he replied, taking on the small task without hesitation. Libi felt silly standing there and watching him, when she knew there were other things to which he probably had to attend.

"Thank you, Cassius."

"You don't need to keep thanking me; I'm happy to help."

"Well, thank— " she caught herself before she could finish the instinctive response. She cleared her throat and began again, "I'll thank God for bringing you into our lives, then."

"And I shall thank him for bringing you, Libi, into mine."

Cassius stretched his arms and groaned. After a long day's work of more manual labor than he had been used to since beginning his work for Tamir, his muscles were sore in places they hadn't been sore since the earliest days of his military training. They'd spent a little more than half of the day working on the domus, and what was left before the evening meal tending to other jobs back at the workshop. He leaned back onto his mat and peered up through the cracks in the ceiling at the few stars he could see from where he had made up his bed. The stars shined silver; *like Libi's eyes*.

Had he imagined the way Libi looked at him earlier? Was he wrong in thinking there was something different in her eyes, something more than simply kindness or courtesy? For weeks now, Cassius had fought against the growing affection he'd felt for her. He tried to distract himself from the pleasant melodies of her songs, and avoid caring for her or her family at all, because such feelings of attraction would have only hindered his once-dubious plans. Ever since they'd raised the money for this building together, and ever since he had now come to share in her faith—which seemed like a lifetime ago, even if it was only a matter of days—he stopped trying to fight his feelings. He had fallen in love with this woman, and he accepted defeat, but it did not sting as he thought it would. It did not hurt or weaken him. Instead, it made him feel stronger.

He couldn't help but notice how she seemed to be rendered speechless in his presence, which was unusual for a woman like Libi. She always surprised him before with her candor in conversation and outgoing personality. Then there was the moment when their hands had briefly touched. Her breathing had quickened and she had looked at him in a way she'd never looked at him before. The memory of it made Cassius smile like an emperor on his throne, only Cassius' throne was the hay beneath his body that softened the otherwise hard-packed dirt.

For the first time in his life that he could remember since his mother had passed, Cassius felt hope for the future. He felt like he had a chance, and it hadn't come by any of his own doings. When he was younger, he had put all of his ambition and cunning energy into advancing in his military career to earn land, money, and titles. In his own folly, he had lost all of that, and now when he least expected it, he was faced with possibilities again. But exactly how far could his dreams go? He knew that her people had specific marriage customs, but he wasn't quite sure what those were or what rules and actions they entailed. Oh, how he wished he'd had a real father of his own to teach him these things. A father who could have helped him avoid the mistakes and missteps of his past. In the areas of fighting and war, Cassius had been well-trained, but in matters of the heart, Cassius had little experience and next to no sources on which to rely.

He knew one thing for certain: If he intended to present himself as a proper suitor for Libi, he would need to prove himself. He had earned Tamir's trust that first night when he had rescued Libi and helped to heal Judah, their donkey, but that was the kind of trust that men shared when they worked together. It comprised of respect born out of friendship. Cassius needed to earn his trust in such a way that Tamir *and* Chava would trust him with the one thing most precious to them in the world: their daughter.

There would be many more days of strenuous labor, but he would do it again and again. He would work from sun up until sun down for seven years or more if he had to, like the man in the story Libi had told him all those nights ago. Back then he had questioned what kind of woman would ever be worth so much sacrifice. Now he didn't have to ask, for he knew exactly what kind of woman was worth so much. It was Libi. It would always be Libi. It was her goodness, her songs of praise, and her continuous choice to see the good in him that first began the process of softening his heart and demonstrating to him the kind of life he could have if he gave himself over to God.

Although his mind swirled with visions of her and her silvery eyes, he had to do his best to fall asleep, or else he would be of no help to anyone the next day. He would need his rest now and in the nights to come if he was to work hard enough and make himself into the kind of man Libi deserved. Cassius never wanted her to know of the stone-hearted man he'd been and the kind of dastardly deeds to which he'd been so calloused. He squeezed his eyes shut as tightly as he could and then he whispered into the darkness, "Goodnight Judah, Goodnight Rachel, Goodnight Leah." He pulled the blankets around his body and smiled to himself. "Goodnight to all of you nameless chickens too."

15

"Many plans are in a person's heart, but the Lord's decree will prevail." - Proverbs 19:21

43 A.D., On the Road to Tyre

Servius Arrius could postpone the inevitable no longer. After everything that needed to be carried out in order for the transition of power to occur had been done, Servius bid farewell to the bed he'd called his for the past several years. He said farewell to the familiar tents, training areas, and halls that he had come to know as well as the back of his hand. He even felt a twinge of remorse once he had ridden far enough away from the city to no longer be able to see its walls. As wretched as his time there had been, he would miss it.

Why couldn't he have been sent anywhere else but Judea? Why did the gods insist that he spend the last good years of his career in a dusty, dry wasteland where he would deal only with the petty squabbles of dissatisfied occupants of the city, rather than in active service? If Servius had known then that all of his glory years were behind him, soon to become distant memories, he might not have tried so hard to ensure that *Pax Romana* lived on in a place as far from Rome as Jerusalem was.

When Servius began his administrative post in Jerusalem, he had initially achieved remarkable success. As Pilus Prior, he was the most experienced man among them all and kept order within the cohort. He was not the most popular, but he made sure that he was at least the most respected. Where other officers in a cohort would accept bribes from their men to look the other way when they wanted to take an unofficial leave of absence or explore a form of entertainment otherwise prohibited by the laws of the Roman army, Servius would execute the law without faltering. He never needed to accept bribes from his men for insubordinate behavior because those in his command feared him too much to even attempt such actions. What good had it all been for now? He'd received no promotion, no special commendations. Just the pension in the exact amount that was promised to him.

Of all Servius' regrets in his career, the biggest he carried was allowing the young Cassius to enlist in the first place. It was one of the only times he'd ever faltered in his exact execution of the law, and it set into motion a chain of events that would lead to the even darker black mark on his career as a soldier: the incident with the Jewish man they crucified. In the fallout of the whole ordeal, the Roman Army, Pontius Pilate, and the chief Jewish priests ended up in cahoots to cover up a scandal that could rival those of the Roman imperial dynasty. It was the only time Servius had ever compromised, and his career suffered ever since. Perhaps if things had gone differently, Servius might have one day adopted Cassius after a long and glorious career for both of them. Although he was not his own by blood, he would have liked to have a son. Someone to carry on his name. Perhaps he could have given Cassius the name of Arrius, but "perhaps" was not what was.

He left his group when they arrived in Tyre. They were to continue their travels by sea, whereas Servius would travel by land. When questioned about his decision to spend so much time wandering, he informed the others that he had intentions to campaign for possible positions in government, or look for a province where he might be useful or at least find good land. Although it was uncommon for an officer to live long enough to retire, it was not uncommon for such an officer to seek out other roles within public service.

Pursuing such a career would, of course, be the most natural action. His father had been a politician, and his father's father had been one before that. The name of Arrius was associated with justice and leadership, and his given name, Servius, meant to serve or preserve. Quite literally, he had been bred and trained since birth to carry out the empire's best interests. In reality, Servius had no such political ambitions. He simply didn't want to return to his homeland, which was now haunted by too many ghosts from his past.

When the last of his company boarded the ship that would take them to fierce battlegrounds and lands yet unconquered by the greater empire, Servius made his way to a nearby military camp. It was familiar, having been constructed to match the strict specifications that all Roman camps had to follow. It was a large rectangle, roughly two-hundred paces long, clear of trees but near enough to a water source to be sustainable, and with only four heavily fortified entrances, one on each side of the camp. He approached the nearest gate and made it known who he was, where he was coming from, and what his intentions were. The guard on duty went to report to his commanding officer, then came back to welcome Servius to the camp.

"Greetings! My commander wishes to speak with you in the *principia*."

"Greetings to you too. I can find my way there, if you will find someone to take my horse."

"Of course," said the guard. Servius dismounted and handed the young man the reigns.

Servius needed no help finding the principia, or headquarters of the camp. Like as any other camp was designed, this one had only two main streets, the *via principalis* and the *via praetoria*. The principia and the commander's tent were marked with flags. He ducked his head under the entrance and greeted the officer inside.

"You are the visiting officer," said the other soldier. He matched Servius in rank, but not in years. Servius felt like an old fool in his presence. A lame horse that couldn't do the only thing he'd been trained to do anymore.

"I am," he answered, "Servius Arrius; myself and my men were encamped outside of Jerusalem. We've been recently reassigned and now I am heading north."

"You have men with you? My guard told me you were unaccompanied."

Servius cleared his throat. "They departed today by sea, but I will be traveling by land to collect what is owed to me on my retirement."

"Taking the long way around, then?"

"I've been told I might receive a recommendation to a number of local government offices upon my official retirement. I supposed I would see what was out there and where I might like to settle now that I am… unattached."

"Aha, I see. Well, I for one would return to Rome in a heartbeat if I were in your position. I am convinced there is no city so great as that of our emperor's, even in all of my travels."

All of *his* travels… Not only did this young man match him in rank at an age many years his junior, he probably also had more real experience than Servius, seeing all sorts of cities and lands he could still only dream about. At his age, it was unlikely he'd ever see more than what he already had.

"Yes, I will agree that I have yet to see any city east of it that comes *quite* close…"

An awkward silence fell between the two strangers, until the other officer began again, "Hm, well, I'm not certain we have any available tents for higher ranking officers…"

"I am capable of sharing a tent with *auxiliaries* and *legionnaires* if necessary."

"Well, I could hardly see fit to put an officer of your standing in with the— "

"It is no trouble, I assure you. I simply wish to have one night's sleep, food and rest for my horse, and I will be on my way."

"All right, then. If that's the way you see it, you can claim any available bed that you like on either side of the via praetoria, and dine with my men for the evening and morning meal. Can I arrange anything else to make your stay with us more comfortable, Servius Arrius?"

"I would appreciate knowing your name," said Servius. Although he had an onslaught of questions about where Servius had come from, who he was, and what his intentions were, the young officer conveniently forgot to extend to Servius the same courtesy of familiarity.

"Yes, of course. I am Marcus Valerius."

"Valerius?" said Servius, taken aback. Many things made sense now, for nearly every citizen of Rome knew of the Valerii. Among their lineage were some of the most decorated generals, esteemed statesmen, and influential magistrates. It was said they even had their own special place in the Circus Maximus in Rome. That kind of reputation came with certain privileges—the kind of privileges which would make one's time in the Roman Army much more agreeable. It was not on sheer strength in battle that this young Marcus Valerius had come into such a position; this was likely a courtesy posting as a part of his political career. Men like Marcus would use the military as a stepping stone, not as a lifestyle as Servius had. He had given everything to the army, believed in it, and what they could do. Those like Marcus believed in only what it could give themselves. Rather than serve the empire, they expected the empire to serve them. If Servius had come with a name like Valerius, he might have seen the shores of Britannia.

A sudden commotion came from outside. Servius moved away from the tent's leather opening to make space for a lower ranking soldier who was panting for breath. "There is a disturbance among the men."

"I'll take care of it," said Marcus, straightening his armor. "Care to join me, Arrius?"

"Of course," Servius obliged. Together they exited the tent to see two soldiers holding another between them.

"What seems to be the problem?" asked Marcus in a tone much less jovial than the one he had used to converse with Servius. It seemed as though he was trying to sound in command, but to Servius, his tone was still not very harsh.

"This man was absent from drills yesterday. He was found today stumbling drunk in the streets of the city while these officers were on patrol," explained the tribune.

"He was found today, stumbling drunk and with *a woman*," added the soldier who gripped the accused man's right arm.

"Ha!" Marcus laughed. "Is that all? Douse the man in water. He reeks of drink and sweat. Then have him tied up and see to it that he gets nothing but water and barley for three days, rationed. After that, send him back to be drilled."

Marcus gave all the men who had gathered a nod and signaled for them to disband and follow his orders.

"Pardon me, but only three days on rations?" said Servius.

"Do you object to my methods of discipline?"

"The man deserted without warning, gave no indication that he planned to return, and was negligent in fulfilling his other duties. You intend only to ration his food?"

"What would you have me do?" Marcus shook his head, his brows getting closer and closer together with each word he spoke.

Servius could think of many options, but chose not to list them out loud. "Something he will remember longer than it takes for him to come to his senses?"

"I'd rather have my men like me than fear me. They're more likely to respect my word then, wouldn't you say?"

Servius blinked in disbelief. "Reduction of rank, at least? Or reassignment of duties?"

Marcus chuckled. "He's an auxiliary infantryman, I can't reduce his rank anymore when he isn't even a proper citizen."

"Discharge?"

"Discharge would probably be exactly what he thinks he wants. A man of your age must know that a soldier is likely to seek certain kinds of solace every now and then, eh? I let my men have their fun, they respect me in their own way, and I know that they're happy with their living conditions. Disgruntled men have less to fight for."

"But men who are allowed to run wild with no disciplinary recourse are far more likely to run in the face of battle. Their loyalties certainly won't be to you."

"How many battles are we really likely to see here? These are peaceful times, and we are far removed from any active combat."

In thinking of it, Marcus Valerius was likely to never see battle no matter where he was stationed. His family influence would take care of that.

"He won't enjoy the taste of barley and the humiliation of being tied up any more than corporal punishment, I assure you." Something about the way that Marcus spoke made Servius feel on edge, as though Marcus was deliberately being condescending and talking down to him. "In a few days, he'll be back to normal and probably won't risk such a thing again for several months. Although the wine in these parts of the world is said to be very tempting…"

Servius didn't respond.

"I am speaking in jest, but I can see that you've taken some offense to my words. I would remind you that you are only a guest here, and I am the one in command. Why don't you find somewhere to rest and recuperate from your travels? I will not hold any of this against you."

Against Servius? The Roman Army did have standards, and in many cases, death was the punishment for crimes of even less severity. It was Marcus who should be ashamed. Was the reality of the Roman Army just compromises and rescissions of honor as opposed to strength and integrity? Had everything that Servius worked for and fought for been a fraud, with the real advantages being given only to those who were wealthy or had influential families? His past efforts seemed aimless, as he now felt.

He politely thanked Marcus for his hospitality and made his way to an empty bed where he laid down his head and kept his eyes shut for the rest of the afternoon until it was approaching dark, although he did not sleep. His mind was too restless for such things, as he now called into question every decision that he had ever made.

As the smell of food wafted toward him, he begrudgingly rose to grab what he could from the evening meal, and forced himself to eat despite his melancholy mood. He took some bread and stood near a fire, where he heard Marcus again talking to another soldier.

"That man came by again, today," said a voice Servius did not recognize.

"Which one?" asked Marcus.

"The one who was wondering what we were going to do about the thief who stole a month of his earnings. The farmer who sells his crop in the city's marketplace."

"That delusional old man? He reported that theft months ago. What does he think we would still be doing about it?"

"We did tell him when it happened that we would try to find the perpetrator, but we never could."

"What description did he give of the thief?"

"Average to tall height, strong build, a distinctive scar across the left side of his face cutting through his eyebrow, green eyes, and dark hair which he specifically reminded me was cut short, like the military style."

Servius dropped the loaf he'd been holding and it fell into the fire, quickly engulfed by the flames. Instinctively, he drew his arms close to his chest so as not to draw any undue attention to himself.

"He thinks it's one of us, doesn't he? Because the man resembles a soldier?"

"That would explain why he's so persistent."

"What good is a month's wages to that man, anyway? He will make more."

"Apparently this man considers it a fortune."

"Ha! No one here matches that description, and I don't have the time or patience to deal with it. Besides that, who knows how far the thief could have gone by now? Next time that man is here, tell him I'll arrest him for disturbing the peace. *My* peace, that is."

The other man laughed and cheered, "Pax Romana!"

Servius paid no more attention to their conversation. Marcus Valerius may not have known any soldiers that matched that description, but Servius did. He remembered the exact day that Cassius had gotten that scar too, because it happened during his training. Servius had given it to him. Indeed, there could be many men with hair cropped short in this area, many with green-tinted eyes too, but such a distinctive scar? And had Cassius not been a thief and a street rat when Servius had first met him? Cassius was alive, and with that knowledge, so was Servius' own spark of ambition. Maybe he could right at least one of his wrongs from the past twenty years of service.

Servius' name was one that implied absolute service to sustaining the Roman Empire, and he had been named as such by his family to set him up for success. Those were the ideals he had tried to live his life by: service, no matter where he was called, and justice, no matter what the cause. Although civilian law had much clearer distinctions on punishments for various crimes, as Marcus Valerius demonstrated, military law had more opportunities for different interpretations. This would be his last mission; to find Cassius and see to it that "justice" was done. He remembered once again what he had said to Cassius regarding the soldier's life.

"What if I gain all the courage and confidence I need in this training, but then the moment I step foot onto my first battlefield it all leaves me? Then what do I do?" Cassius had asked.

"Then you pray to Mars that the gods might look down favorably upon you."

"And if they don't? If they choose not to?"

"Then you die on the battlefield or flee as a traitor. Either way, you end up dead, but such is the price you pay in service to the empire in the hope that one day, the empire will repay that price back to you."

When Cassius fled, he probably hoped that he would never have to see Servius again. When Servius had joined the military so long ago, he hoped his career would be full of much more glory than it had turned out to be. It seemed that the gods and their twisted sense of destiny had other plans on both accounts.

16

"Now these three remain: faith, hope, and love—but the greatest of these is love." — 1 Corinthians 13:13 CSB

"Shalom!" called out a feminine voice. "We've brought food and water to sustain you."

As the weeks passed, the days grew cooler, but Cassius barely rested long enough to notice. He straightened and wiped the sweat from his brow, seeing that it was Taliah, her children, Libi, and Chava all approaching with baskets of food and jars of fresh water. He knew what he was working toward and enjoyed being a part of a team again, rather than on his own. Keinan was a good man, and he'd quickly become friends with him as he had with Gilad and Yuval. Together with Tamir, the group worked on the house, but it was still a lengthy process that occupied most of their days. Just as they had taken their time ensuring that each board placed in this house was put up with care and consideration so that it would last, Cassius too was making his moves very carefully. He prayed as often as he could, training his mind to think of it as his first line of defense rather than his last resort.

"It is very welcome, my wife," said Keinan, passing Cassius on the right and going to take the basket his wife carried.

"How are things going?" asked Chava.

"Extremely well," said Tamir. "The roof is almost finished, and soon it will be time for you all to come in and start helping with some of the smaller details, furnishings, and such."

"The time has gone by so fast!" said Taliah, eyes wide. "I will have to start speaking to other members of the community and seeing if anyone has anything to donate."

Cassius took a ladle and helped himself to water, quenching the ferocious thirst he hadn't had time to notice accumulating in his throat. One cup full, then another.

"I had not expected that it would be done so quickly," said Libi, "but perhaps I should have! The Lord always provides when it is His will, doesn't He?"

"Indeed," agreed Taliah.

"Truthfully," Tamir began, "it is all thanks to Cassius. He's worked more hours than the rest of us combined. If I didn't know better, I would say he was trying to impress me or win my favor for some reason."

"I wonder what that reason could be," said Gilad, putting a little too much emphasis on his words.

"Is that the sun, or are you going red in the face, Cassius?" teased Yuval.

"Just thirsty," he replied, interjecting very little into the conversation. Was it too soon to approach Tamir about Libi, or were his feelings so obvious that everyone around him already knew? Briefly, he risked a glance at Libi to see how she reacted, but she was sitting with the children.

Cassius had come to learn all of their names, though not without great difficulty. All of them were so blessed to have found a loving home. Cassius himself had been an unwanted child left to the streets, but now even he was beginning to feel like he had a home. One of the things he loved the most about the newfound faith was that it didn't matter who you were—broken on the outside or the inside—because of Jesus, you could be redeemed. Cassius certainly had a lot of reasons to need redemption, and there were still some nights where he woke from nightmares about things he had done in his past, but he would remind himself that those things didn't matter anymore. What mattered was how he lived now, or at least that was what he had been told. He still had so much to learn to be as wise as Keinan or Tamir.

Omri played between the two older boys, who swung discarded scraps of wood as though they were swords. Libi held the infant Tirzah on her hip, with Phoibe clinging to her other arm. Briefly, Cassius let his mind imagine that Libi carried their children in her arms, and the thought made him excited and terrified at the same time. If they ever were to be together—if it was God's will as they always said, and as Cassius was learning to say—would Cassius know how to be a good father? He knew one thing for certain: He would try his very best to become a good husband.

"Cassius," said Felix, waving to him. "Could you come here? Rufus and I have a question."

"And me! I have a question too!" Omri said, jumping up and down.

"Don't bother him too much," said Taliah with a tone that reminded Cassius of how his mother used to speak to him when she sensed Cassius might do something he shouldn't, which was most of the time since he had been such a mischievous child. "We came here so that they could have a rest from their work, not so that Cassius, Gilad, and Yuval could entertain you."

"It's all right," said Cassius. "I don't mind."

"Well, you might after all of your energy is spent because of my boys." Taliah laughed.

"It's no trouble at all, really," Cassius smiled and walked over to join Libi and the children.

"What's your question?" Cassius asked.

"Is it true that this *whole* place was destroyed in a fire?" asked Felix.

"Well—"

"Did you have to build *all* of these walls from the ground up?" Rufus added before Cassius could finish.

"Mostly—"

"I want to see *everything!*" Omri sighed. "Will you show me?"

"I thought you only had one question?" Cassius laughed.

"One question, each," Felix corrected.

"*Well,*" he said. Cassius scooped Omri up into his arms and tossed him into the air, catching him again and making him laugh as he sat him down. "Perhaps if you ask them one at a time, and give me time to answer, then we can satisfy all of your curiosity."

"That's fair," agreed Felix, whom Cassius had a feeling would grow up to be a great negotiator. "Was this whole place destroyed in a fire? Did you have to build it all up again?"

"Yes, and no. It was very damaged, but Libi could see it for what it was: a solid structure. All we had to do was fix it a bit. Sometimes when things get broken, people might have a desire to toss them out or give up on them completely, but with time and patience, they can be made to look new, like this place. Some new bricks and beams here and there, some sweeping and washing over there… and it looks as good as new."

"I hope that when I am older, I will be as strong as you. I would build dozens of houses even bigger than this one!"

"Ah, but you're forgetting, Felix. I didn't do all of this alone. I had your father's help, and Tamir's help, and Gilad and Yuval's help as well. We all have weaknesses, that's why people work better together. Like a great cohort or *century* in the Roman army—each man has his place on the battlefield. Some are skilled archers, while others are best on horseback or carrying swords. Some are great leaders who have the skills and foresight to predict where to send their troops, while others play supporting roles. It is the same with us here. Tamir is good at very detailed work, while your father and I can do more heavy lifting. Yuval and Gilad work well as a team because they are brothers—they know what the other is thinking and are skilled communicators. We each do what we can, and ask for help with what we can't. You have your own strengths, Felix, and you have your brothers, Rufus and Omri. Perhaps the three of you will someday make a great, formidable team."

"That sounds like something Libi would say when she is telling one of her stories," said Rufus.

"Oh, yes!" yelled Phoibe excitedly. "It's like King David and his best friend, Jonathan!"

"Yes," Libi smiled, "or Moses and Aaron. Remember, God called Moses to deliver the Hebrew people from Egypt, but when Moses feared he would not be able to speak well to Pharaoh, God sent his brother Aaron with him. You might also think of Ruth and Naomi, who bravely stuck together even after hard times fell upon them. Ruth's selflessness toward her friend Naomi was what stuck out to Boaz in the story and turned his heart toward her. You know they married at the end, but did you also know that Ruth was King David's great-grandmother?"

"She was? Oh, I didn't know that," said Phoibe, her face turning toward the sound of Libi's voice. "I think I would like to serve others like Ruth, and like you, Libi." Phoibe smiled dreamily.

"Your parents are great servants to others as well, you know."

"Oh, I do! I love them and you very much."

"And I love you, Phoibe. All of you are like family to me. I remember the day each of you entered Taliah and Keinan's lives. You were all such blessings, and I know you will each go on to bless others in your own way. Look at Cassius—he could not have known that his coming to Antioch would enable us to help so many others thanks to his gifts in carpentry, but because of God, so much has been made possible. Cassius was able to use his skills and his gifts of diligence and strength—not only physical strength, but strength of character—to help us bring this old house back to life. Who knows how many will now have a place to sleep and eat and call home now because of his efforts and God's faithfulness?"

Was Libi saying these things to teach the children a lesson, or because she returned Cassius' feelings? In the time he had grown to know more about Libi and who she was, Cassius had come to realize she was nothing if not completely genuine. Although he first balked at the way she always chose to see only the good in a situation, it had become one of the things he loved most about her, because it encouraged him to do the same. Libi wouldn't have said those things if she did not truly believe them, and the idea that she did hold Cassius in such high regard stirred his spirit, giving him hope and making him want to act even more boldly in his efforts to win her heart and Tamir's approval. In Rome, all that two people had to do to be married, technically speaking, was to announce their intent to live together as husband and wife. Certainly, there were other ceremonies and customs that were often involved—but they were just that. Customs. Formalities. He didn't know everything about how people like Libi's family went about getting married, but he gathered that it was a great deal more complicated.

"I wish I could see it all. I mean, really see it," said Phoibe, who turned her face downward.

"I can describe it to you," said Libi, "the same way I describe places in the stories I tell you."

"Oh, I know, but I really wish I could see it sometimes. Like today, I truly wish I could see everything that has been done. I know this will help so many people, and maybe even other children like Felix and Rufus and me, but I still wish... Sometimes..."

"I know," said Libi, pulling the girl closer to her.

"I have an idea," said Cassius, once again interjecting into a conversation more than he ever would have in the months and years before he had been changed by his experiences with Libi and her family. "Why don't we all go around to each of the rooms, and you can all give your advice on how you think they should be used. Think of one thing that stands out about each room to share with Phoibe."

"That sounds wonderful!" said Phoibe, whose face instantly brightened. Cassius looked for approval in Libi's own silvery-gray eyes next, and when he saw her eyes sparkling like rippling river water lit by the sun at high noon, he knew he had done well.

"What do you think, Libi? Can we?" said Phoibe.

"Ask your parents first," she reminded them, smiling gently.

The children turned toward Taliah and Keinan, who both voiced their approval. Libi gave Tirzah back to Taliah, and then the rest of them headed off through the house. The house that would've been just what Cassius had needed all those years ago, and that would be there for all of the children to come who were just like Felix, Rufus, Phoibe, and even little Tirzah, so that none would ever have to grow up feeling as though they were unwanted.

"All right, we are now in one of the rooms that line the east-facing side of the building. Rufus, would you like to go first?" said Cassius. Libi followed, guiding Phoibe with a gentle hand on her shoulder and observing how Cassius kept the boys engaged.

"Um… It has windows that are very high up on the walls. The sun would come right through this one in the morning, so it would have lots of light during that part of the day."

"Imagine it, Phoibe. You wake up with the heat of the morning sun kissing your face, gently waking you from slumber for another day," Libi filled in Rufus' own points with her own explanation, emphasizing feelings that Phoibe could relate to the physical characteristics of the room.

"Perhaps it would make a nice bedroom then? It sounds like it would feel very safe and full of light for someone who has been very sad or alone," Phoibe suggested.

"I love that idea, Phoibe!" Libi encouraged. "What do you

think, Felix?"

"Maybe… To me, I see a room that's big enough for many beds, but I wouldn't want to sleep here. I would want to rest in the mornings, and it'd be hard to do that with the sun in your eyes."

At this, all of them laughed.

"And what about you, Omri?" said Libi, patting the child's head.

"Horses!"

Cassius chuckled. "A room for horses, eh? I suppose they might appreciate the sunlight, but maybe not the lack of space to run free." Cassius moved to muss the boy's hair, and Omri shook his head in reaction. Libi smiled at the way he was so natural with the children; so different from the stoic man she'd met in the marketplace, yet so familiar.

"How big is this room?" asked Phoibe. "I can't feel the light from the window where I am, but I can hear a little bit of an echo on the walls and I feel a slight breeze…"

Libi knew measurements wouldn't be of much use to Phoibe, so she tried to think of something else to say. She thought of the days before she had the gift of hearing, and how her family had found alternate ways to communicate with her. She remembered the different signs they used to use, the way they spoke with their hands and gestures, with facial expressions filling in the context. They used her sense of sight where she would have otherwise relied on hearing.

"Here, Phoibe," said Cassius, breaking Libi's train of thought. "Give me your hand."

"All right. Where are you taking me?" asked Phoibe.

"Place your other hand here, on this wall," Cassius said, helping the girl to find it. "Good," said Cassius, directing her steps. "Now walk forward and count how many steps you take… One… Two… Three… Good, keep going."

"Four… Five…" she carried on counting.

"Now we're coming to the corner, so prepare to turn."

"This is how we do it at home," Phoibe explained. "My abba put wooden beams on the walls that I could hold onto… I can follow them anywhere I need to go in the house."

"Your father is very smart to come up with such an idea," said Cassius.

"Oh, yes. I still use my hands to find some things though."

"Hm…" said Cassius, matching each of her steps. "Rufus or Felix, do you still have those wooden beams you were playing with?"

Rufus shrugged. "We left them in the atrium."

"Go and get one of them and bring it here, please," Cassius instructed.

"What for?" asked Phoibe, leaning her head to one side. In no time at all Rufus returned and passed the narrow piece of wood to Cassius.

"Thank you," Cassius said, taking Phoibe's hands and wrapping her fingers around the end of it. "Hold onto this. You may need to use both hands because of its size, and the length isn't quite right for your height, but drag it out in front of you. Side to side—yes, that's it!"

"What is it supposed to be doing?" asked Phoibe.

"It does what the wooden beams that your father put on the walls for you do. It will guide your steps, whether there is a wall there for you or not. Go on, use it to find obstacles in your path."

"Ouch!" said Felix, bending down to rub his ankle.

"Felix! There you are!" Phoibe laughed.

"Now you've got it!" Cassius smiled. "With a stick the right size, you can go anywhere."

"Here you go, Rufus. Perhaps Abba can make me a stick of my own," Phoibe extended her arm out toward the sound of Rufus' voice, and reached again for Cassius' hand. He took it and guided her back to the wall of the room so that she could continue to get an idea of the size and shape of the space.

"Do you feel the light touching you now? We're coming more

and more out of the shadows. The sun is hitting your hand, the one that I hold, and now your arm, and now…"

"I can feel it on my face!" Phoibe exclaimed. "It feels warm, but there is a nice breeze, and I can hear all kinds of sounds from here if I listen carefully."

"Good!" Cassius nodded.

"Oh, Libi, I know what this room would be perfect for!"

"You do?" asked Libi, emphasizing her interest. "What?"

"This could be a room for you to tell stories in, and teach children like me all the songs that you sing. You could put tables and chairs in it, and make it a place for learning. The window will carry the sound of your singing out into the streets for all to hear it. Oh, Libi, you have such a beautiful voice! Imagine how many people might hear it, and then come inside."

"I agree with Phoibe," said Cassius, now looking straight back at Libi. Perhaps the breeze was stronger than Libi realized, because she felt a chill go down her spine that made her shiver.

Felix and Rufus began snickering, breaking the intense moment.

"What's so funny, boys?" said Libi, raising her eyebrows at them.

"Nothing," said Rufus, still laughing.

"Well, it must be something," said Libi. Were they playing some sort of prank? Had Felix made a kind of joke? Or was it something about Libi's appearance that drove them to such foolishness? Instinctively, Libi reached a hand up to smooth her hair.

"I think I know what they're laughing at," said Phoibe, an impish smile spreading across her own sweet and innocent face.

"What is it?"

"Cassius thinks Libi is pretty!" Omri blurted out. His voice lowered to a whisper and he continued, "I think she's pretty too. When I grow up, I'm going to marry her."

"Haha! You are too young to marry Libi," replied Felix, all of the children collapsing in a fit of giggles.

Libi had initially been embarrassed by Omri's outburst, but she found his second admission to be endearing. She didn't want to hurt his feelings by laughing with the others, so she did her best to straighten her face. "That's enough, children. I think we should go back and sit with your parents now. Perhaps it is time for you to enjoy a snack. Felix, take Phoibe's hand."

The children did as they were told, knowing Libi well enough to associate that particular tone of voice with order.

"After you," said Cassius, stepping away from the door, "future wife of Omri."

"Well, he's such a charmer. How could I refuse?" she said as she stepped into the light of the atrium, following the children at a modest pace, although they moved much quicker than she did in their excitement.

Cassius raised an eyebrow. "He certainly has an eye for beauty, and he is likely willing to wait many, many years, like Jacob in that first story you ever told me. I can understand why."

Libi's expression no doubt revealed her shock, but hopefully it did not also expose her delight. For the first time she could remember, she questioned her miracle. Had she truly heard him correctly? He may have been teasing, but even in his lightheartedness, his words had been personal. He recalled to her their earliest conversations, and in the same sentence, he said that she was beautiful. The most handsome man she'd ever met thought *she* was beautiful! She took her next steps more swiftly, anxious to join the larger group, but a part of her heart now stayed behind with Cassius, knowing his feelings toward her.

When she was sure she was far enough ahead of Cassius that he could not see her, she mouthed her thanks to God for putting him in her life, and then added a prayer that he would stay in her life for a long, long time.

"Pleasant words are a honeycomb: sweet to the taste and health to the body" — Proverbs 16:24 CSB

"Cassius? You're still working?" said Tamir, coming into the workshop. "Why don't you put whatever it is away for the day and rest before the gathering?"

Cassius smiled, genuinely smiled, which was becoming a regular occurrence. In relinquishing so much of the control he held onto for so long, Cassius realized that he never experienced victory so sweet as when he surrendered to God.

"It is not any work task that keeps me here this evening. It is… a gift."

"A gift?" Tamir raised an eyebrow. "Is this gift, by chance, for my daughter?"

"Well, it might bring her some happiness," said Cassius, biting his lip. Cassius had never a good strategist or a good communicator. He had always been a man of action and impulse, much to the chagrin of Servius, who had tried to instill in him an appreciation for seeking the counsel of others. "I apologize if I should have asked you first. The materials I've used are scrap pieces. Anything else I've needed, I've purchased using savings from my wages. It has cost you nothing, except the use of these tools I've borrowed."

Tamir offered a smile, but a queasy feeling settled in Cassius' stomach and prevented him from returning the gesture. He'd been held at the point of a sword, but he'd never been as scared as he was now. What if it was too soon? What if Tamir had already made up his mind about Cassius, and never intended to see him as a suitor for his daughter?

"Of course, you can use the tools, Cassius, and I never would have suspected you of stealing supplies. May I ask what this gift is?"

"I'd rather keep it a surprise, if that is all right."

"Certainly," said Tamir. "But, Cassius, I do not wish for there to be any kind of mistake or misunderstanding about this. Are your intentions with this gift to perhaps win the affection of my daughter?"

"Well, I… I mean, I'm not sure that… That is to say…"

"Because if they *are*," Tamir raised an eyebrow, "then you should know that you do have my blessing to pursue such things."

Cassius breathed a sigh of relief.

"*But,*" said Tamir. Cassius knew there must have been a catch. In a war, no emperor or king would ever be so quick to give up his treasure to another, no matter how powerful, and Cassius knew that there would never be another treasure as valuable as Libi's heart. He had underestimated her, certainly. Like her family, he saw her as innocent and unable to understand the ways of the world. However, that innocence was her strength. She always saw the best in others, and her capacity to serve and show love to those who needed it the most was unmatched.

Cassius knew he loved Libi. No other possible explanations for the passionate feelings he carried within him existed. His soul had been set aflame by God, but in his heart, embers burned for Libi. They were constant, always there, ever present, and always keeping him warm. Still, how could he express such things? Even if Tamir were to approve of him as a suitor for her, how would he ever be able to be an adequate husband to Libi? Her words were a salve that mended all wounds. Cassius didn't know how to harness such words with his lips, so he set his hands to work instead. Hopefully, it would be adequate.

"There are probably some things to discuss," Tamir continued, "expectations and such."

"Yes, of course." That was exactly what Cassius had been wondering about. He shifted back and forth on his feet and waited for Tamir to elaborate.

"In these months I have known you, I have come to think of you as another son. I was grateful when God brought you into our lives when we needed you. You have been an invaluable help to me and to our entire community. I rejoiced with you when you chose to accept our faith as your own, and the memory I have of praying over you with the other men is one I will treasure, as we all watched you take your first steps as a believer. I feel as though I understand your character, and would be happy to see you and my daughter have a long and happy future together, *if* that is what she wants. As such, you may court her favor, and should she return your affections, a formal betrothal can be arranged."

"I'm sorry, Tamir, but I don't know what to… In Rome, things were very different. I'm not sure what traditions are expected." If only he had a father of his own to ask these questions to; then he would not have to feel like such a fool in front of his potential father-in-law.

Tamir must have sensed his shame, because he gave Cassius a pat on the shoulder and an encouraging smile. "Typically, a man might give a gift to his intended or pay a *mohar*—bride price—to the father or family of the bride. The intention to marry would be announced publicly, and then a formal agreement or *ketubah* would be written up dictating the length of the betrothal and any requirements before marriage."

"Requirements?" asked Cassius.

"Nothing out of the ordinary. It is important that you have a place of your own in which to live. Monetary stability. A means of providing for your family. When such requirements are met and the length of time agreed to in the ketubah has passed, the man may come to collect his bride. There would be a small ceremony, followed by a feast, and then they may go off together as man and wife to the home of the groom."

"Hm," said Cassius. He'd had a roof over his head for the past few months, though it was not a home. Saving up enough coin to buy a proper house would take a long time, but seven years or seventy times seven, he would do it for Libi.

"Do not worry, Cassius. These are hard times for many of us; if it reaches this point with both you and Libi and if she expresses to me that she would like to marry you, I am sure an agreement can be made. She is our miracle child, and I would only give her to someone who I knew valued her as much as we do. I sense that you share in those feelings, therefore, if you both feel amicable toward such an arrangement, we can work out the finer details later. I value her heart first and foremost. Until she has made her choice, I suggest you pray about it."

"Yes, pray," affirmed Cassius.

"It is like I said when we began our restoration work on the shelter: If you want anything in your life to last for any great length of time, you must seek God's will for it, and make Him the foundation for every decision. Your faith is new, but God is your foundation. It may take time for you to build up wisdom, but it will come when you seek it out. Seek out such wisdom regarding my daughter, and I assure you, all will be well."

"I will." Cassius nodded.

"I know. You remind me of myself years ago. My relationship with my wife had been built on the right foundations, but somewhere along the way, we lost track of such things. It revealed the cracks in what we'd tried to build by taking shortcuts, but even when you fail, Cassius, you can always start again. It takes perseverance, and I know you have that. Now, I've taken up enough of your time. You must hasten so that we can meet the other believers on the mountainside."

"Mountainside?" asked Cassius in confusion.

"Yes, Barnabas, a man who visited and taught us for a while, returned this week with another teacher. Barnabas was greatly loved by our community and there are many who will be thrilled to see him again. Since we are expecting such a large crowd for his return, we are meeting on the mountainside outside of the city. It is often safer there. There are caves nearby, should we need to hide from persecutors, although Antioch has been mostly accepting of our faith. Do not forget, Cassius, many of us come from Jerusalem where we saw loved ones lose their lives in the name of Jesus."

"I see. I'll be ready in a few moments."

Nothing in Cassius' life had been built on a strong foundation before, but Cassius knew that would change immediately. He wanted his newfound joy to last, he wanted his relationship with Libi to last, and more than anything, he wanted the hope he found in the message of Jesus to last. He would take great care building these foundations.

"Lord of lords," Cassius prayed in his mind and heart. *"Help me, with everything."*

Before Libi could see him, he wrapped his gift in cloth and held it close to his side. He wanted to see the look of surprise on her face when he unveiled it, and did not intend for anything to spoil it.

"Oh, I'm so excited for this evening! Barnabas will have returned *and* we'll be able to share the good news that the restoration work

is almost complete. Soon Taliah and Keinan will be able to move in," said Libi while trying to pack up the baskets of bread and refreshments she and her mother had prepared for the gathering.

"I am not so sure Taliah and Keinan will be the ones moving into that house," said Chava.

"Why not, Imma? They're perfect for such a task." As far as Libi knew, it had always been the plan for Taliah and Keinan to take over the running of the house, with the help of volunteers, of course. They were natural leaders within the church.

"I think Taliah's time might be coming sooner than any of us suspected. In any case, it would be a difficult thing to ask her to balance a newborn of her own and the care of young Tirzah and the other children, along with the running of a house so large as that one."

"*Jehovah Jireh*; the Lord always provides. He will provide in this too, Imma. I know He will! We must pray." Libi couldn't imagine the Lord not providing as He always did before. She had no reason to doubt that He would leave her prayers unanswered in this.

"Your faith inspires me every day," said Libi's mother. "I will join you in these prayers."

"Is everyone ready to go?" Libi heard her father ask from behind her.

"I am!" said Gilad, swiping one last piece of bread from the basket their mother was wrapping up.

"It's a wonder Libi and Imma still have food to bring to the gathering," joked Yuval.

All of them laughed, and Libi took her basket in her arms and turned to face her father as he stood in the doorway. When she looked to meet his eyes, she noticed that he seemed taken aback. No laughter, no words. He looked at her in a way Libi had never seen before, and his eyes glistened with tears.

"What is it, Abba?" questioned Libi, approaching him. Although she was taller than most young women her age thanks to the height of both of her parents, she still had to look up to meet his gaze. "Aren't you excited to see Barnabas?"

"Yes, *ahava sheli*," he said, using a nickname he'd rarely used since she'd been a young child. "I suppose sometimes I forget that time has passed, but then I come inside expecting to see all of you children as… Well, small children, and I'm continuously surprised at how much God has blessed me."

"Oh, Abba, God has blessed us all to have you and Imma as our parents. Should we hasten to the gathering so that we aren't late?"

"In a moment. Chava, boys, would you please go outside? I have something that I need to ask Libi first."

Imma immediately followed his instructions, nodding politely. Yuval and Gilad followed her out but not before giving Libi some teasing looks. She returned their knowing looks with her own confused expression.

"What did you need to ask me, Abba?"

He took in a deep breath, held it for a moment, and then puffed it out. "Libi… What do you think of Cassius?"

Libi's own breathing hitched. She had spent much of the past few weeks thinking about Cassius, but she now failed at stringing words together to summarize all of those thoughts. "I… I think very highly of him, of course. He has been a guest of our home and has done great work for you, so I am told."

That was hardly an adequate summary of her feelings, but she had never expressed love for anyone outside of her family before, and had certainly never thought of how she might explain those feelings to her own father. She kept the emotions she felt for Cassius close to her heart, unsure of what to do with them.

"You hold no interest in him for any other reason then?"

"No!" Libi exclaimed, and instinctively reached up to cover her mouth. Her eyes went wide, realizing all she'd said with a single word. Her father seemed to half-chuckle in response. "That is," she tried to speak more calmly, "I am quite fond of him, Abba. I think we all are grateful to God for placing him in our lives at such a time as this."

"Am I wrong in thinking you might be a little more grateful than the rest of us?"

"No, Abba, I don't think you'd be wrong," Libi admitted, realizing that she had begun to sway back and forth on her feet. She continued quickly, allowing her words to blend together, "I never thought of him like that when he first came to stay with us, but after he accepted Jesus and became like us in his beliefs, I started to feel differently. I noticed qualities in him that I hadn't seen before... or at least, I hadn't seen in *that* way. He is strong, not just physically, but I think he is strong of heart as well. When he sets himself to do something, he does it with everything in him. He perseveres where others might give up. He is not one for many words, but he finds so many other ways to express himself through what he does for others... He's... He's..."

Libi realized how much she'd said in such a short period of time, and felt her cheeks blush.

"I understand," said her father, now equally as red.

"If it is what you wish, I will put such feelings away immediately, and never speak of them again. I trust you to find a man for me to marry someday, when that time comes." Her father would always do what he thought was best for her, and would never deliberately put her in a situation that might cause her harm.

"Libi, *ahava sheli*, my miracle daughter in more ways than one... I am only asking you these questions because Cassius has already made his interests known to me, but I told him that I would not approve such a match without knowing how you felt about the matter first. Libi, if he is the man that you wish to have as your husband, I would agree to a betrothal between the two of you. There would, of course, be many requirements he would have to meet. However, I do feel peace about this even though we have only known Cassius for a short time. As you said, I think God brought him into our lives for a reason. If this is a part of His plan, His will, then who am I to stand in the way? You have said that you hold affection for him."

"I do, Abba."

"Cassius may speak to you this evening. If, after that, you are still interested in pursuing a relationship with him, we can discuss the details and requirements for a betrothal to take place. It will take time, Libi. Like I have said before and as I told Cassius moments ago, nothing built in a hurry— "

"Is everlasting," Libi finished the phrase. "I know, Abba. I want to have a relationship like you and Imma have. One that lasts and overcomes all things. I will come to you and consult you on everything and not hurry into anything."

"Good," said Tamir. "I am glad we have had this talk, but now that we know your feelings are mutual, take care to make sure the two of you are never alone or far from a group of others so that you might be held accountable. I know I can count on you to honor my wishes in this."

"Yes, Abba, I will do as you ask."

After a few more quiet moments, Libi and her abba exchanged looks that said what words never could, and then they went to join the others and began the journey to the mountainside gathering of believers. *"Thank you, Lord,"* she prayed, *"Please help me to follow your will for my relationship with Cassius. I know you have sent him into our lives for a reason. For a time, I believed that it was just so that we could minister to him and share your message of love, but if there is indeed another, deeper reason, please bless our union. I know all good things come from you."*

Her heart had wings, and she felt like she could fly away into the big, billowy clouds that floated overhead. It all felt so *right*. How could it not be from God when everything seemed to have fallen into place so perfectly? Although she looked forward to her next conversation with Cassius now more than ever, she also felt that she might never be able to take a deep breath again. Every thought she had was held captive by the possibility of what he might say and what might become for both of them.

18

"The Lord's hand was with them, and a large number who believed turned to the Lord. News about them reached the church in Jerusalem, and they sent out Barnabas to travel as far as Antioch. When he arrived and saw the grace of God, he was glad and encouraged all of them to remain true to the Lord with devoted hearts, for he was a good man, full of the Holy Spirit and of faith. And large numbers of people were added to the Lord. Then he went to Tarsus to search for Saul," — Acts 11:21-25 CSB

"Libi! I can hear your voice. Will you come closer?" called out Phoibe. Libi turned to see her, carried in Keinan's arms and followed by Felix and Rufus. Taliah walked behind the rest of the group with Tirzah in her arms and Omri clinging to her side.

"Coming, Phoibe!" Libi answered. "Imma, do you have everything you need, or do you still require my help?"

"I think I can manage fine," said Chava.

"All right then," said Libi, turning to go toward where Keinan set Phoibe down on a large rock right against the face of the mountain. The older children gathered there while the rest of their family carried on toward the larger group. Libi waved to Taliah in passing—she had so much to tell her, but it would be best to discuss it away from younger ears. She would wait until she had a good opportunity to share all that had changed between herself and Cassius.

"I will come too," said Cassius. "I have something to give Phoibe."

Libi's eyebrows furrowed. "What is it?" If Libi's mind were a chariot, she could have raced circles around any circus or hippodrome in that moment. Her imagination reeled with curiosity.

"Ah-ah-ah," said Cassius, waving a finger in the air. "I'll only reveal it to Phoibe."

"Hm…" Libi sighed as they walked toward the children, passing Taliah and Keinan who carried on with their youngest two children toward the other believers. "Phoibe, was it difficult getting here?"

She shook her head. "My abba guided my steps until it became too rocky for me to walk on my own, and then he carried me."

"I believe I can help with that," replied Cassius.

"You can?" said Phoibe, her voice pitching up.

"Here, I made this for you," said Cassius. From underneath the cloth he'd been carrying at his side, Libi marveled as Cassius revealed a smooth wooden walking stick, made perfectly for Phoibe's size. "Take it in your hands and see if you can tell me what it is."

"Is it a… Oh! Oh, Cassius, is it a stick for walking!"

"Yes, it's for you to use the way you did when we walked around the rooms in the domus. Remember?" Libi's heart fluttered. Surely, Cassius was the man for her. The cane itself was solid and sturdy, and would no doubt hold up for a long time. It was the perfect size for Phoibe to hold, and every consideration had been taken into account for what would make it the most beneficial for her. When had Cassius worked on this, on top of everything else he'd been doing? His actions showed true selflessness and care. Libi would be proud to serve by his side.

"Yes! I held it out in front of me and it felt like I could see the space around me… Like how I see with my fingers and hands, only I could feel things an even farther distance away." Phoibe turned back and forth excitedly.

"Phoibe," Libi began, kneeling down beside her, "it's a beautiful walking stick, and perfect for your size! Do you feel how Cassius has rubbed it smooth so it will not splinter? And here at the top… There is a leather strap for you to put around your wrist!"

"That way, you won't be able to lose it," Cassius explained.

"Oh, thank you, Cassius! Do you think I could use it now?"

"Certainly," said Libi. "The ground here is even enough that you shouldn't have any trouble practicing. Take the cane in your hand and…"

"I'm walking!" shouted Phoibe. "Oh, I must find my abba and imma to show them."

Libi laughed and turned her head over her shoulder, calling out, "Rufus! Felix! Come out of the caves and walk with your sister."

"Coming!" She heard them call out, echoing each other.

"Is it safe for them to play in the caves?" Cassius asked.

"They don't go very far," explained Libi.

"Besides," added Phoibe, "my brothers know them very well. Whenever we're here early before the gathering starts, they often play in them."

In a huff, she heard Rufus come first. "What is it? Oh, a walking stick!"

"There is a strap that goes on my wrist, and I can hold mine out in front of me to tell where the ground goes up and down, and where things are in front of me. Now I will be able to go anywhere!"

"It looks really good, Phoibe," said Felix.

"Felix," Libi began, "take your sister's arm and walk with her while she practices. From what I can see, the gathering is about to begin. The three of you best hurry to sit with your family."

"All right," the two boys said in unison.

Libi and Cassius settled into step with each other, a few paces behind the children, but still in full view of the rest of the gathering of believers. When she was certain she could speak to Cassius without Phoibe's sharp hearing interfering, Libi whispered in a low voice, "That was a very kind thing you did for Phoibe, Cassius. I don't even know how you had time!"

"I made the time." He shrugged. "Libi, please understand. I didn't just do it for Phoibe. I did it because I wanted to show you that... That is, I hoped it would make you happy. I wasn't sure what I could make for you, so I—"

"Cassius," she interjected. Libi knew words were not his strength, and she wanted to make sure he knew how much she valued his actions. "A gift for Phoibe is the best gift you could have given me. I want for nothing, but Phoibe has wanted for the whole world. You've just given it to her."

"Libi, in these past months…" his voice trailed off again, but this time Libi was patient. She looked at him and encouraged him to go on with her eyes. "You and your family have meant so much to me. When I first met you all, I was a bitter man without much hope or goodwill, but you all played a part in giving me a new life. That is, the life I received through your God."

"Our God," she corrected. "He is *our* God, Cassius."

"Ours." He nodded. "I have spoken with your father because I have realized that my affections for you have grown beyond gratitude. Libi, I *care* for you. Is it possible that you could care for me too? Or… grow to care for me?"

Now it was Libi who was speechless. What was she meant to say? She couldn't very well run back to her parents and ask them for their advice.

"If that is not what you wish, then forget this conversation ever happened. I do not want to trouble you, but I cannot go on without knowing what I am working for, or if I should put such feelings aside."

She realized she hesitated too long and now he was beginning to doubt himself, which was the exact opposite of what she wanted.

"Cassius, please don't mistake my silence for a lack of affection. I do care for you, very much."

"You do?"

"Yes. I think God brought you into my life for a reason, and not only to save me that first day in the marketplace."

"Libi, I cannot promise that I will be a faultless husband if we were to marry. I will probably make many mistakes, indeed, as I already have in every part of my life, but I promise I will always try to learn from my mistakes so that I never repeat them. Will that be enough for you?"

"Yes, I think it will." She smiled. "I would be honored if you spoke to my father about a betrothal."

Of course, it *would* be there in the mountains, where Cassius would finally declare his love for her. The green grass that covered them brought out the stunning forest tones in Cassius' eyes. She looked at the scar that crossed his eyebrow again, knowing that Cassius, like all men and women, carried more than one scar— some seen and some unseen. While she still wondered where they came from, she also knew that in time she would come to know each scar's story and Cassius himself in an even deeper way.

"We should join the others, as you said. The gathering is almost beginning, and I am eager to hear this Barnabas speak. So much has been said about him since I've been among your family," said Cassius, quickening his steps. Libi matched his pace.

"I think you'll like him. He's a very wise man, and it's said he's brought someone else to us who is supposed to be another great teacher and communicator of our Lord's message," said Libi, clasping her hands together.

Cassius did his best to follow along with the songs of the believers, which were becoming more and more familiar to him. Although he had no real talent for singing, he sensed that it did not matter. The believers did not sing because their voices were beautiful; they sang because joy compelled them to lift up the name of their Lord. Cassius certainly understood that. At this moment, he could dance through the streets if he had any concept of rhythm—maybe even if he didn't. Libi affirmed that she felt likewise toward him, and to know that he was working toward their union gave him the strength and confidence of a hundred men.

Finally, after so many years of feeling like a directionless, wayward failure, he had a future, and not like the lofty plans of his youth. He may have saved Libi that first day in the marketplace, back when he'd thought of her as nothing more than a foolish girl with a foolish nature, but if the truth were to be told with all of the facts laid out plainly, then anyone could see that it was Libi who had saved him. She did not come into his life with armor and sword to defend him, but she broke down the walls surrounding his heart and infiltrated the deepest part of his soul with her generosity and tender words. Certainly, he made it difficult for her, yet she persevered. She never lashed out. She never treated him with contempt. She never looked at him with pity, she just kept giving him kindness after kindness, and it was exactly what Cassius needed to help him see the truth. Swearing his allegiance to a caesar he would likely never meet was one thing, but to a God who knew him by name and would not only call him into battle, but fight alongside of him? That was a different matter entirely.

"That's Barnabas," Libi whispered, gesturing with her hand when the singing died down.

"Greetings to all of you believers in Antioch," welcomed

Barnabas. Cassius straightened to get a better view. Cassius could see he had wide eyes with lines around them as though he smiled often. His voice was low and deep, but jovial sounding. It seemed to echo off of the mountains and back toward the whole crowd. Cassius could both see and hear why this was such a good spot for meetings of this size. There were more people here than he had ever seen gathered all at once in Taliah and Keinan's home.

"It has been some time since I have been with you all here, but before I talk about myself and where I have been, I want to say that I am increasingly awed at how fruitful you are as a group. I have heard talks of a home being built, to be sustained by your generosity so that those in need will have a place to go. This is a wonderful way for you to reach out to those in need and minister to others, and I myself am eager to see this place and hear more details of the progress you've made and how it will be run."

Cassius looked at Libi, whose head was bowed, keeping her wide silvery eyes out of view. He noticed the color of her cheeks darken and the corners of her lips turn up. She may have been humble, but Cassius was proud. He had doubted whether or not such an undertaking was justifiable, but that was before he had come to accept Jesus as His Lord and Savior, and put his past fully behind him. Once again, Cassius was grateful he never needed to dwell too long on those times again. As Tamir and others had said to Cassius when he joined their faith, the God they shared made all things new. Late at night when Cassius was haunted by nightmarish memories from when he'd been at his lowest, it was all he could do to repeat those words over and over again. *All things new. All things new. All things new.* " Only after some time had elapsed was he able to fully believe it and rest in that promise. There were times when doubt crept in and made Cassius wonder if it really was all that simple, but whenever he struggled, he simply clung again to his battle cry.

All things new.

"I have also been blessed to see other ways in which you have been blessings to others. In my limited time with some of you, I have heard tales of your acts of kindness and selflessness and the ways in which you have joined together as one to proclaim the good news that Jesus is risen!"

"Jesus is risen!" Cassius heard other voices repeat from all different directions. Cassius let those words wash over him, cleansing him yet again. It was more than a phrase. It was a promise of redemption for what he had done in his worst hours.

"I am glad to be with you all once more," Barnabas continued when things had quieted down yet again. "I have missed you since I left, but you all must know that I did not leave because the work was finished. In fact, I left because I felt the Lord telling me that there was more work to be done, so I went out in search of someone that I call a friend. I have heard him proclaim the message of our Lord in ways I never could, and when I last saw all that God was doing here, I knew I had to go and get this friend so that he could come and witness it also."

"Who is this other teacher?" called someone in the crowd.

"This man who I am about to introduce will certainly have time to share his own testimony with you in his words, but to give him a proper introduction, let me say… This man is proof that God can use anyone in any circumstances for His will. He is proof that God can take what was broken and make it new. His life shows that there is no such thing as too far away for God to reach. As in the songs we just sang, even the darkness is not dark to our Lord. There is nowhere we can go to flee from his presence. That is why I believe this man will be such a great blessing to the community you have built here, where the word of our God and the message of our Savior is being preached among both Jews and Gentiles. We are all God's creation, and this man's testimony will show that no matter where we are, where we come from, or where we intend to go, God can always lead us in another direction for His purposes."

From this description, Cassius had a feeling that he would like this man, whoever he was. Perhaps if Cassius heard from more believers who had been in as dark of places as he had in his life as a non-believer, it would strengthen his faith even more.

"Do you know of whom he speaks?" Cassius whispered in Libi's direction.

"No," she murmured. "In any case, Barnabas is well loved and respected by our community. He is a good man, full of the Holy Spirit and strong in his faith. If Barnabas vouches for this teacher, he must be genuine."

"Hm," Cassius mumbled, half-listening to what she was saying and half-focusing his eyes to see who among the crowd would come forth matching such a description.

Barnabas gestured for a man to join him. The man had his head covered, and in the shadows, Cassius could not quite see his face.

"Please, allow me to introduce you to *Saul*," said Barnabas.

The man called Saul removed his covering. He was humble in stature, but with striking features that one was not likely to forget. Cassius watched for the crowd's reaction, expecting smiles or verbal greetings. While some watched in quiet anticipation, a few seemed to lean backward as though in disbelief, eyebrows knitting together and heads turning.

"That man is the same one who persecuted us in Jerusalem!" said one in the crowd, after what felt like an indeterminable period of silence.

"It's a trap! That's Saul of Tarsus!" said another, and soon even more voices followed until their words were no longer intelligible.

"It *is* him! Abba, it is! " Libi shrieked.

She jumped to her feet in distress, as did some of the others. Cassius rose along with Tamir. "Who is he?" asked Cassius.

"You… Don't you know?" said Libi, tears now streaming down her face.

Cassius turned back to see if the man in question would offer a response. Barnabas lifted his hands and called out, "Please, do not react in such haste but hear what he has to say. He is not the man you knew; I am willing to stake my own life on it."

That was a kind of loyalty Cassius had rarely encountered, even among soldiers. "What are they talking about?" he spoke.

"That man… Saul…" Libi gasped for air, clinging to Tamir. "He… He…"

He watched Libi collapse into her father's arms as she fainted either from fear or shock. Instinctively, Cassius lunged toward her, but he knew it was not his place to touch her or hold her like that. Whoever this man was, he had struck terror into Libi's heart, for Cassius had seen such looks before, but only on the faces of those who had come within an inch of their deaths, barely surviving to tell the tale.

19

"Ananias went and entered the house. He placed his hands on him and said, "Brother Saul, the Lord Jesus, who appeared to you on the road you were traveling, has sent me so that you may regain your sight and be filled with the Holy Spirit." At once something like scales fell from his eyes, and he regained his sight. Then he got up and was baptized. And after taking some food, he regained his strength. Saul was with the disciples in Damascus for some time. Immediately he began proclaiming Jesus in the synagogues: 'He is the Son of God.'" — Acts 9:17-20

The mountains were melting. All around Libi, they no longer looked like mountains. They appeared instead as ominous waves of darkness. She feared she might drown in their black shadows until her eyes began to focus again, taking in the darker hues of greens and grays that made up the landscape around her. She rubbed her eyes with the backs of her hands until all things looked as they were meant to look. She was still frightened, but not by tricks of her own mind.

In broken pieces, memories began to flood her brain. Not just memories from the moments before she had fainted, but memories from long ago. Memories of screams, hurried footsteps, scraped toes, and salty tears. Memories of Savta's dates scattered on the streets, forgotten and left to be trampled on, and then… memories of Savta.

Libi thought back on that horror-filled day and the nights of dread that followed when all her Abba could think about were imaginary scenarios where only the worst happened. For weeks they travelled seeking safety and peace and healing; all of it had culminated when their family separated and they continued on to Antioch. It was in Antioch where they were supposed to be safe, and they had been, until now.

"Why, God? Why have you done this? Are we to lose our lives now, just when we had become whole again?" Libi prayed, for the first time in her adult life truly questioning the will of the Lord. Of one thing she was certain: this could all be blamed on one man, and his name was Saul.

It was Saul who spurred on the tension in Jerusalem. It was Saul who oversaw the stoning of Stephen, which then turned into a great persecution of all believers throughout the city of Jerusalem, and throughout Judea. It was Saul whose name haunted Libi's nightmares. Whatever Barnabas might have said, Libi knew in her heart that wherever Saul went, pain and devastation followed him. Even now he could be here as a spy, plotting his next moves to destroy The Way.

There must have been some kind of mistake.

"Libi? Are you all right?" She heard her father ask. As she came back to her senses, her movements became frantic again. Libi gripped her father's hands in her own tightly and began to plead with him.

"Abba! Abba, we have to leave!" She knew it would not be safe to stay in Saul's presence any longer than necessary.

"Please, everyone," Barnabas beseeched the crowd, but Libi blocked out his voice.

"Tamir, we must take Libi home. The color has all but drained from her face! I am worried for our daughter's health," said Chava in tones that reminded Libi of when she had been ill as a child and her mother had taken care of her. Home was exactly where Libi wanted to go.

"I… I am not sure…" Tamir hesitated.

"What?" Chava interjected. While the two of them exchanged glances that carried more than a thousand words, Libi began to shiver.

"I think we should hear what Barnabas has to say."

"But your daughter!"

"Abba, you must remember what happened in Jerusalem even better than I do. How can you stay here and listen to this now?" Libi cried.

She straightened her back to look her father in the eyes as he answered softly but firmly, "But is that not our calling as followers of Jesus? To proclaim His message to everyone? What makes this man different? Why should his testimony not be heard?"

"His… *testimony?* Abba, how could a man like that change?" For the first time since the miracle that opened her ears, she raised her voice in protest to her own father. She wracked her brain for possible answers as to why he could even begin to consider lingering in Saul's presence, but she found none.

"I do not understand," Cassius interjected. "What has this man done? How do you know him?"

"That man is no teacher, but a persecutor of our faith! Cassius, it is because of him that we were driven out of Jerusalem! He took part in the persecution that led to the death of my *savta!*"

Libi dug her fingers into the cool dirt beneath her, tearing up clumps of grass and sediment. She pushed off of the ground and stumbled to a standing position. "We cannot trust this man, Cassius. This is not the kind of man who can change." Whatever vision and focus she had regained since her fainting spell disappeared again when her eyes welled over with tears. She prayed that if her father could not see reason, that Cassius would be sensible. Cassius had defended her before in the marketplace. He knew what kind of darkness inhabited the world. He had to see how irrational it was to remain in Saul's vicinity. Surely, Cassius would help her convince her family to flee while they still could!

"I… I remember you telling me about this, but I still do not understand. When I became a believer, your father told me that God makes all things new."

"Yes, He does," sighed Libi. "But this man's faith cannot be genuine. He must be trying to trick us!"

"But—"

"But what?" said Libi. What was left for him to question? Did nobody see the dangers as she did? It was as though she was back in the streets of Jerusalem, but she was the only one wanting to run, while the rest stood still.

"What makes him any less deserving of redemption than a man like me?"

"Cassius, you are a *good* man. Whatever is in your past cannot be anything compared to what this man has done."

"That's not true," Cassius answered quickly.

His tone was cutting and surprising to her. For a moment, all of her tears came to halt. "What do you mean?"

"If that man cannot be saved, then there is no hope for me either." Cassius' jaw hardened and a very different expression slid across his face compared to the one he had born moments earlier. It was a familiar expression to Libi, because it was one he bore constantly during his first weeks working for her father. He had been a stranger to her then, and he looked again like a stranger to her now.

"No, Cassius, this is different."

"Libi, you must stop… There is so much about me you don't know."

Libi felt bile rise up in her mouth. "What are you trying to say?" She coughed, choking on her own spit and tears.

"I thought I could be forgiven, but perhaps I should have known that I didn't belong with people like you from the start. I don't even know what I was thinking."

Libi watched as Cassius' eyes darted back and forth and he slowly moved farther away from her. Saul's presence alone was enough to stir up conflict—Cassius would not be saying such things and speaking in riddles Libi could not decipher if he were not here.

"Cassius, you're not making any sense. This is confusing all of us—I am sure we can figure this out." Libi felt as though she were shrinking inside.

"I didn't learn about carpentry or the care and keeping of livestock from a father I never had or a mentor that never existed. I was a soldier in the Roman Army. I learned such things to survive. I was in Jerusalem all those years ago. I was there when Jesus was crucified. *It was me.*"

Libi shook her head. "You're lying. This can't be true! You never said anything about—" Before she could even finish the thought, Cassius continued with more confessions.

"I put Him on the cross."

"Please, Cassius, stop saying these things!" She squeezed her eyes shut and willed the sun to go backwards in the sky and make it so this day never happened. Not only this day, but all of the days going back to her Savta's death. If only she could open her eyes again and be back in her Savta's arms, making up songs of praise without a care in the world and no painful memories whatsoever of a man called Saul.

"Libi," she heard her father try to speak.

"It was my hands who drove the nails through His. It was me who was assigned to guard His tomb before He resurrected, and on that morning when I awoke and tried to make sense for what my eyes saw but my heart could not believe, I fled out of fear for the consequences of that day. I have stolen, I have cheated, and I hung Jesus of Nazareth on the cross. *It was me.*"

"No!" She screamed with everything she had left within her, which wasn't very much at all. Libi raised her hands over her ears, struggling to believe what she'd heard. She had no words left for Cassius. How could this be happening? Where was God's will in all of this? This was the mountainside where so many believers gathered together time and time again to worship Him. Where was His presence now? She couldn't feel it at all anymore.

"Cassius, Libi," her abba said as he moved between them. "That is enough. This is not the time or place for this discussion."

Libi turned her face away from Cassius and clung to her abba like she had when she was still a little girl. She couldn't bring herself to look at Cassius even a moment longer. If she did, it would only add to the list of painful memories that had been forever burned into her heart. Moments ago, she had been certain she would marry this man and share a life with Him. She had been so certain that it was what God wanted, but this couldn't be God's will.

Libi was the miracle child whose mother and father did everything they could to protect her and keep her safe. She was the one who had been born deaf, but whose ears had been opened by Jesus who was the Christ. Although she had seen the persecution of believers firsthand, she had made it to Antioch. She had survived, and she had kept singing songs of praise to God as Savta had told her, because even though it had been the hardest thing she had ever endured, she knew God was good. She knew He had a plan. Why would He now allow this? None of it made any sense. Her faith felt so far away and out of reach.

"Please, Abba, please let me go home now… Everything hurts," she whispered, barely able to speak at all.

She felt her father shift awkwardly on his feet, "I'm sorry, Cassius. I—"

"You need not say anymore, Tamir. I will be on my way. I am sorry for everything." Libi heard the sound of Cassius' footsteps walking, no, running away, and hoped it would be her last memory of him.

"Yuval, Gilad—one of you should take your mother and sister home. I will hear what Saul has to say and join you this evening." It was Yuval who offered to walk with them, and Libi was grateful, for he was far less chatty than Gilad, though why her father insisted on staying to listen to Saul, Libi could not fathom.

On the walk home, Libi couldn't stop herself from shedding even more tears. She wept for the life they once lived and the home they shared in Jerusalem. She wept for all the atrocities she heard that Saul had committed. A small part of her even wept for Cassius, as the full weight of his admissions began to settle. She realized with increasingly painful clarity the depths of his betrayal; he never lied to her directly, but he neglected to tell her the truth she deserved to know as the woman who would have been his wife. Tears fell until her eyes burned, and she could keep them open no longer. She had never felt more broken, and even with her family surrounding her, she felt completely alone.

Cassius didn't know where to go at first. He stumbled as he ran from the mountainside, then lost himself in the city of Antioch. Although he'd come to know the city almost as well as he'd known Rome in his time there, it all seemed unfamiliar now. He didn't belong here. He needed to get his things from Libi's house. Cassius hurried in that direction, hoping he could get there before she returned with her family.

He opened the door to the workshop, and was relieved to see no one inside. Hurriedly, he made his way to the corner where he kept his things. He pushed aside the roll of linens to retrieve his satchel of coin and other personal items. Thankfully, he did not have very much to pack. As he was tying his things to his belt, the door at the other end of the workshop creaked open. Cassius halted his movements and looked up like a thief who had been caught in the act, even though he was not guilty of taking anything that wasn't his.

"Cassius," said Yuval. Both men stiffened awkwardly as they looked at each other. "I don't think now is a good time for…" His voice trailed off. It appeared he was as unsure of what came next as Cassius himself.

"I came for my things. It will take me but a few moments, and then I will be gone."

Yuval cleared his throat. "Let me get what remains to be paid of your wages." He moved to go back into the main house.

"No, keep it. I don't want it."

Yuval stilled. "If you insist."

"I do." Cassius took one last look at the place where he had dared to hope for the first time in over a decade, and mentally said farewell to each beam and board. He doubted very much he would be back.

"Yuval… Is Libi… I mean, is she…"

"She's hurt, Cassius. I think we all are. Perhaps it is best that you leave."

Cassius nodded his head in woeful understanding. "Tell the others that I said farewell… or don't. Whatever you think is best."

"Where will you go?" asked Yuval.

"Does it matter?" asked Cassius, anxiously eyeing the door.

Yuval's eyebrows moved closer together. The lines that appeared on his forehead made him resemble his father even more closely. "I cannot speak for everyone, but I do not want to see you harmed any more than I want to see my sister hurt."

Cassius heaved a long, shaky sigh. "I don't know where I'll go."

"Well… Take care of yourself, at least."

Cassius would have laughed if the words had not stung so much, but isn't that what he had always done? Taken care of himself? He bid Yuval farewell and went out the door, not stopping to look back. There was nothing else he could say or do now.

He started walking again, not paying attention to where he was going. Yuval had said Libi was hurting, but what of Cassius' own anguish? Gradually his pace quickened, but he couldn't outrun the memories. No matter how hard he tried to ignore them, they lingered still in his mind and forced him to relive the pain over and over again.

"This is not the kind of man who can change."

"This man's faith cannot be genuine."

"You're lying. This can't be true!"

Libi's words echoed in his mind, awakening other ghosts from his past and inciting them to join in the torture.

"I told you never to come here, again."

"He is a mistake."

"I don't care what happens to the boy now."

Along with the voice of his father, the only thing Cassius could remember of the man, he heard his mother's screams and cries just moments before she was brutally murdered in cold blood, all because she had dared to *love*. Cassius had done the same thing, and although Libi hadn't driven any daggers through his heart, it hurt as much as any other mortal wound.

"You could be just as large of a threat to yourself."

"You're too arrogant."

"That was not a request from your friend, that was an order from your Pilus Prior!"

Servius Arrius' voice came next, still bearing his constant tone of disappointment, reminding Cassius that he was and had always been a failure. If he hadn't run from his post, would things have turned out any better for him? Would there have been some way he could have avoided punishment or found another way to survive? Better yet, what if he hadn't been born, as his father had suggested? For a flash, like lightning, Cassius felt that his father was right. His life had not been built on a good foundation. His life had been built on sinking sand. He never really stood a chance.

Unable to stand it any longer, Cassius fell to the ground, striking the rock-solid earth beneath him with his fists and crying out a wordless plea to God. *"Why did you allow me to be born into this world when there is no hope for me in it?"* he prayed. Was he allowed to be angry at God, or was that another sin to add to his list of reasons why he would never be good enough for anything or anyone? He was angry, regardless of the answer. *"If you are a real, living God and if it is true that you care for people unlike the stone idols my mother kept, then why did you allow this to happen? Why was I born from my parents' lust instead of love? Why did my mother have to die before she could raise me? Why is it that every time I try to walk through an open door, the world shuts it in my face?"*

Cassius waited, but he wasn't sure what he expected to happen. Despite Cassius' passionate pleas for an answer, the world around him remained calm as the sun set on yet another day Cassius knew he would live to regret. He realized that he must have looked like a fool, on his hands and knees in the middle of the city of Antioch. Broken, he rose to his feet, shaking the dirt and rocks from his clothing. When he finally looked up, he was astonished at how the One True God answered his prayers so directly.

It was Libi's house.

Not the house she lived in, but the house for which she had fought. The grand domus that would be a home to children like Cassius, motherless or fatherless or both. The house that would be a refuge for women like Cassius' mother who had nowhere else to turn to except places of darkness. The house that now, with the gleam of the setting sun behind it, seemed to glow like a bright light for the whole world, or at least the whole city of Antioch.

Libi… Her words began to echo again in his mind again, but this time they were joined by memories of his own hasty replies. Her rejection had been more painful than any wound inflicted by sword or spear, but he was not wholly innocent of being hurtful. It was Cassius who put those tears in her eyes, and not only with the words he had spoken in that conversation. No, he laid the groundwork for that from the first day he saw her when he had plotted against her family; the foundation of their relationship was built on secrets he'd never admitted and lies he'd never confessed. The truth of his past was ugly, and the more he thought about it, the more he realized Libi was right. A man like him did not deserve forgiveness.

He needed to do something, *anything*, so instead of wallowing in darkness, Cassius went into the house. His belief was all he had left, so he chose to lean into it instead of run away from it. Taking a mallet in hand, Cassius set to work. He would finish her house, and beyond that, he didn't know. It wasn't the first time that Cassius had been a wanderer without any plans for the future except survival, but this was the first time that he would do so with God at his side. He would trust in Him, even if he didn't understand everything about Him yet, and he would hope that it would be enough.

With each beam and brick that Cassius drove into its proper place, he tried to atone for his sins. He pushed himself harder and harder, releasing every bit of anger he'd ever harbored and letting go of every sorrow he'd endured. He kept going until his hands were blistered and until those blisters bled, lighting lamps when the sunlight faded completely and moving from room to room as he accomplished every leftover task with zeal.

In the still of the evening when Cassius had nearly finished, a slow creak startled his pensive concentration. At once, he set down his tools quietly. Was it Tamir, perhaps? Cassius wondered if he should run, but then he reminded himself, his days of running away were over. But what if it was someone else? Someone who had heard his confession and feared him as much as Libi feared Saul?

"It doesn't matter," Cassius reminded himself. He had given up control to God.

"Is someone in here?" called out a voice. It was Keinan's.

"It's me, Cassius," he said, coming downstairs and toward the entryway where he saw Keinan standing with Barnabas and Saul. Cassius was taken aback by their presence and wondered if it would be better for him to keep speaking or be silent. Surely, they must have heard the truth about him

"Cassius, did you do all of this?" Keinan's jaw dropped as he looked around. "What happened to your hands?"

"I… There was work to be done, and— "

"Are we to understand that you are one of those responsible for bringing this idea to life?" said Barnabas. His eyes were wide and full of warmth somehow, not hatred. This was not the greeting Cassius had imagined.

"Your work here is admirable," added Saul. "What you're doing here will be an incredible testimony of God's faithfulness to both Jews and Gentiles."

Cassius struggled to come up with a response. Should he tell these men the truth if they did not already know, so that there would be no false pretenses? "I only did some of the building work, which is now nearly finished. What are you all doing here?"

"Cassius is being modest," said Keinan. "He works harder than anyone I've ever met. Barnabas, you met Tamir and his family the last time you visited. You know how quickly his sons get work done, but Cassius here can do the work of five men, and I think he just proved that."

"No, please," said Cassius. "I don't want your praise."

"Are you to be involved in the running of this place also?" asked Barnabas.

Cassius' stomach hit the floor. He was certainly not the right person to fulfill that kind of a role. There were too many sins in his past that disqualified him from being able to do something so important. "I don't think so… In fact, I was getting ready to leave. Leave Antioch, that is."

Keinan's brows furrowed. "Leave Antioch? Why?"

Cassius' shoulders drooped. "I have nowhere to go, and I do not think I am welcome among the others anymore. The truth is… The truth is…"

How was he to say it? The way he had spoken to Libi had not been so kind, but there was no kind way of putting it. He was a monster.

"Cassius," Keinan interrupted him before he could find the words to finish, "we know what the truth is. Tamir told us after the gathering."

"He couldn't have told you everything, or you wouldn't still be standing here. Don't you know what I've done?"

"Maybe not everything, but Cassius… I think that you should come with us," said Keinan.

"With you?" said Cassius. "But what of Taliah? Your children? I shouldn't."

Yet again Cassius was dumbfounded at the overwhelming grace these people possessed; grace he once treasured from Libi, before she became aware of his past.

"Barnabas and Saul are staying with us on our rooftop. You will be but one more guest. In any case, it would be better for you to have a good night of rest before making any rash decisions. You may have seen some of our community at their worst today, but that does not mean you need to leave. At least not right away," Keinan said, clearly trying his best to assuage Cassius' conflicted feelings.

Exhausted, Cassius breathed out and said, "Why do you want me to stay with you? Why do you care?"

"I would guess," answered Saul, "it's because Keinan feels that it would be valuable for you to hear my story. As you may have gathered, I once had a very *different* reputation, but it was only after an encounter with Jesus, who is the Christ, left me blinded, that I was finally able to see."

20

"For all have sinned and fall short of the glory of God; they are justified freely by his grace through the redemption that is in Christ Jesus." — Romans 3:23-24 CSB

"Is she all right?" Libi heard her father ask from below, finally coming home after what seemed like an eternity.

"She didn't eat anything, and she hasn't spoken since we returned," said Chava. "My heart breaks for her, and all of us. What now, my husband?"

"I am not sure… I didn't have time to tell you before we left, but before this all happened, Cassius expressed to me his interest in marrying Libi."

"Well," said Libi's mother, "I had my suspicions that such a thing might happen one day. But what about what he said? And what about… *Saul?*"

Libi squeezed her eyes shut and then opened them again. Her eyes still stung, but when she closed them, all she could see were memories of the horrible things that had happened that day, and memories she'd long since buried from years before.

She heard her father's footsteps moving closer to where her

mother was sitting. "I know how this may sound, but I believe in what Saul is saying, Chava. How could I not? Is it not the very message we have been sharing and clinging to all this time? That with God, all things are made new? It is my story too."

"But it was because of Saul that we were displaced from Jerusalem and forced to come here and separate from our family. Do you regret that decision?" questioned Chava.

"No, I don't. I know in my heart it was the right decision for us at the time, and I also know that if we hadn't, so many blessings might never have come our way. This home, the workshop, the community of believers … The road getting here was not easy for any of us, but you must know how much I love you for standing by my side through it all."

Libi blushed overhearing their conversation and the affectionate words exchanged between the two of them. How she wished she could have had such a relationship with Cassius, but she couldn't find it in her heart to forgive him. Why had she not been more wary of him? He had warned her from the start, but she had not listened. She foolishly believed he possessed a good heart, but how could someone truly good have done all of the things Cassius confessed to doing?

"What do you think about Cassius?" asked Chava. "Yuval told me that he came and got his things, but did not say where he was going." She was glad that he had left quickly without making things worse. She couldn't imagine having to face him again so soon, or maybe ever.

Libi heard her father sigh deeply. "Do you remember what I said all that time ago when I shared my testimony at the gathering of believers, the same night that Cassius joined our faith?"

"I do," her mother replied softly. Libi hoped her father would elaborate, because in all of the commotion of the building of the house, she had nearly forgotten it all.

"I didn't plan it, you know. I had no way of knowing that what I would say would apply to Cassius so literally. It must have been

God working in my heart to reach his. I told Cassius when he confessed to me regarding his feelings for Libi that it had to be her choice, and that whatever choice she made, he had to respect it, and he most certainly did that."

"Do you have any idea where he might have gone?"

"Keinan was looking for him after the gathering. Perhaps he found him," said Tamir.

"Does Keinan know?"

"Yes… My beloved, I have to believe in what I said when I gave my testimony. I cannot be standing one foot in and one foot out of my faith. Even if it is hard, I have to give others the same forgiveness I have been given. It is the same way with Saul. If I pick and choose when to show grace and when not to, then I am a hypocrite. No better than the Pharisees all those years ago. Can you understand, my love?"

"I understand and I agree," said Chava. "Although I worry for Libi. She has never had to face something like this before, and I know Saul's appearance was unexpected. She is haunted even now by memories of that day…"

"The day my mother died," Tamir finished. "Neither that day nor this day are a surprise to God. I have to believe this, Chava."

The door opened again from beneath the loft. Libi recognized the voices as those of her two older twin brothers. "How is Libi?" asked Gilad in an unusually low voice.

"She didn't speak a word the whole way home, and after I saw her and Imma safely home and watched Cassius leave, I returned to hear the rest of what Saul had to say. Is she talking yet?" said Yuval.

"There is no change." said Chava. "Give her time."

"I always knew Cassius was hiding something, but I supposed he had his secrets as any of us do. I had no idea it was so…" Yuval's voice trailed off.

"Nothing Cassius has done is worse than anything you or your brother or anyone else has done. Remember that, Yuval, before you let your temper get ahead of you."

How could her abba say that? How could he brush what Cassius had done aside as though it didn't matter?

"I know, Abba. I am sorry," said Yuval.

"Imma," Gilad whispered, "may I try talking to Libi?"

"You can, but I'm not sure if she will be ready to talk back yet," said Chava.

"I just want to try," he replied.

Gilad had always been the softer of her two brothers. Although she had never been as close with Yuval, she knew he would jump to her defense in an instant if she called on him. While Gilad was strong of heart, and Yuval had physical strength, they both shared their strength of character.

"I will go and settle the animals for the night," said Yuval.

"I have some things to prepare for tomorrow," said Chava.

"I will help you," said Tamir. "Then perhaps we can *all* get some rest."

One by one Libi heard them all exit. All except for Gilad. She recognized his gait pacing the floor. After a few silent moments, she heard him climb the creaky ladder to the lofted room.

"Libi?" He said quietly. She did not turn to look at him. "Libi, I know you're awake. I can see your shoulders shivering."

He came around to her side and sat next to the window, pulling the curtain back. "You know, every time I see stars I think of Sabba."

"And Savta," she muttered.

At that, the corners of Gilad's mouth turned up. "And Savta's *dates*. We never have been able to make them quite the same, have we?"

"No."

"Libi, are you all right?"

She searched his eyes to see if he was being serious. Of course, she wasn't all right. "Gilad… I don't understand. I don't understand how Abba can be saying all of those things. I don't understand how he can be so open to hearing Saul speak… I don't understand how he can forgive Cassius so easily."

"I don't think forgiveness ever comes easily to anyone, Libi, but I know Abba forgiving Cassius does not mean that his heart doesn't hurt for what you are going through. Perhaps if you'd heard what Saul had to say about his testimony then maybe you'd understand."

"I could never understand, *especially* not coming from a man like Saul," she said.

Gilad breathed in a deep breath and held it for a moment, before letting it out slowly. "You know, I had come to see Cassius like another brother in these past few months. I saw the way he looked at you and the way you looked at him… It was the way Abba and Imma look at each other. I thought you had come to love and care for him?"

That was the most painful part of it all. She had cared for him, but she now realized she did not even know him. "Gilad… He was not who he made himself out to be. How can I care for someone I don't even know?" Libi briefly wondered how many other women he might have convinced of his affections in an effort to gain something. Every notion she'd ever had about the good in the world had been shattered. "You heard what he said… He was one of those who put Jesus on the cross."

"You know that it had to be, Libi," said Gilad.

"He could have refused," she replied.

"Libi, he was a soldier in the Roman Army who had been given orders to follow. Besides that, Jesus had to die so that He might be raised to life. Through His sacrifice, He paid the price for all of our sins, Cassius included. I know you know this."

"He could have been lying about his faith too, Gilad!"

"I don't think so," he whispered. "I was there when he prayed for his salvation, and with the men when we blessed him with our own prayers and encouragement. I believe he was genuine in that, Libi, as I still do, but even if I didn't, that's between Cassius and

God."

Libi was so confused. She needed the counsel of a friend who could understand the complicated feelings in her heart and knew her deeply. She needed the counsel of her cousin. "Oh, Gilad! I miss Shamira so much."

"I know," he said. "Your relationship with Shamira was special."

"It was more than special, Gilad. She was always there for me. *Always.*"

"Do you think it would help to talk about this with Imma?"

Libi shook her head. "No, I'm too embarrassed."

"What about Taliah?"

Libi shook her head again. "Taliah is my friend, but I am not as close to her as I was to Shamira. I wish we all still lived together in Jerusalem, Gilad… I wish things had never changed."

"I understand," he said, nodding in the shadows. "Libi… What if I helped you write a letter to Shamira?"

For the first time since the gathering of believers, Libi's heart began to lift. "Oh, Gilad… Do you think it would reach her?"

"We can try, if it might bring you some peace? I'll fetch something to write with, and then you can tell me what you want to say to her. I won't repeat a word of it to the others, I promise."

"Thank you, Gilad!" Hope began to spring up in Libi's soul. They received letters every so often from their uncles in Phoenicia, which was much farther south than Antioch, but Libi had never been able to write one back, at least not one so personal.

When Gilad returned with writing implements and parchment, Libi laid her soul and heart bare. Forgetting that she was really talking to her brother, she told Shamira every detail of how Cassius had come to Antioch, how she had desired to build a shelter for those in need, how Cassius had become a Christian and helped with that work, how her feelings for him had developed, and everything between. She ended the lengthy letter with the account of Saul's arrival and his conversion story, and with a plea for advice and prayer.

"How will it get to them?" Libi pondered aloud.

"I will find a rider first thing tomorrow morning who is heading to Tyre or Sidon. Beni and Asa are often there trading at this time of year. I have faith it will reach them."

"Thank you, Gilad… You are the best brother I ever could have asked for," she leaned forward to embrace him in her arms.

He chuckled lightly. "I won't tell Yuval you said that, for both our sakes. It's been a long time since we played as we did when we were children, but I know he would still win in a wrestling match. Best we keep that between the two of us too." Gilad winked and Libi smiled. Finally, she could rest her head on her pillow and sleep. A message from her dearest cousin would be just what she needed to help her sort her feelings out. She prayed that whatever rider Gilad found would be swift, and that either Asa or Beni would be in the right place at the right time.

Cassius sat on the rooftop and stared out at the stars. Weeks ago, they had brought him such comfort. He dreamed underneath them of a new life with Libi. Now he looked out at the vast expanse and felt so small. Even as a young recruit to the Roman Army, Cassius' over-inflated sense of self made him prouder than he ought to have been, but now he was humbled as low as the dust.

Cassius heard some footsteps and a few grunts and grumbles coming up from behind him. It was Saul.

"Looking out at the stars?" he said, moving to his own bed roll.

"Mmhmm." Cassius nodded.

"You did not seem to eat much." Saul's observation was true. By the time they returned to Keinan's home, Taliah had put the children to bed, but left out some food for the rest of them. Cassius tried to be polite, but he had lost his appetite, among other things.

"I wasn't very hungry," said Cassius.

"I expected more of a reaction from you earlier," said Saul. Cassius noted that he was being very direct, and he wasn't sure how to respond to that. What made this man so bold and confident? In a very strange way, Saul reminded him of Libi. She too had been bold in her faith, although she expressed it very differently. He twinged again at the thought of her and how she must have been feeling.

"The daughter of the family I was staying with, Libi, was born deaf. She was healed by Jesus. I was surprised when I first heard that, but after learning more, I could not deny it. Perhaps that is why I did not react more strongly, but there was one thing that confused me. You said your encounter with Jesus did not heal you of blindness, but *left you blind*, and now you see. How can that be?"

Saul rubbed at his temples and sighed. "To tell my story is to tell of great pain, but it is also to tell you of Him, and that is why I share it freely. I will not try to hide from my past, for there is no other way to explain it. I was an avid scholar of anything to do with the Law—Jewish Law, that is. When Jesus walked the earth, I did not know Him, or perhaps I refused to know Him. I was so focused on keeping things as they were, I could not open my eyes to see things as God wanted them to be. As much as I talked about Him, learned about Him, and memorized His words and commandments, I did not fully know Him. If I had, perhaps I would not have committed the sins that I did, but it had to be that way."

"What do you mean?" He wondered where Saul's clarity came from. Cassius himself spent much time pondering why certain things happened in his life, things that made his life significantly harder in more ways than one. How did Saul know?

"I think perhaps when I finish the story, things will be clearer. You see, after Jesus' resurrection, which I did not believe at the time, I used my power and influence to persecute those who followed His teachings, thinking that I was doing what God would want me to do: preserve the old ways, and extinguish any fires started by the deviant. In my misguided zeal, I watched on while believers of Jesus were stoned to death or imprisoned. I entered homes and ordered the arrests of men and women for their crimes of faith. Soon, however, this belief in Jesus spread beyond the walls of Jerusalem. I was still unable to see the truth, so I went after them. It was on the road to Damascus where Jesus spoke to me."

Cassius narrowed his eyes at Saul, squinting in the dark of the night to see his facial expressions. "He spoke to you directly?"

"There was a blinding light all around me, of such intensity that I fell to the ground. I heard His voice say to me, 'Saul, Saul, why are you persecuting me?' I called out to ask who the voice belonged to when He responded, 'I am Jesus, the one you are persecuting, but get up and go into the city, and you will be told what you must do.' The light faded, but it wasn't only the light that I could no longer see. I was blinded. I spent three days in total darkness, refusing food and water. In that time, I felt a range of emotions from confusion to anger to sadness to fear, and then… to humility. After three days, the Lord sent a man called Ananias to me, and he healed me. At once, something like scales fell from my eyes and I was overcome by the Holy Spirit. I had never seen more clearly than when I could not see at all. It took taking away my sight for God to show me the light. I was baptized immediately and began to regain my strength, but since then, I have been proclaiming Jesus whenever and wherever possible."

"I still don't understand what you meant when you said, 'it had to be that way,'" Cassius admitted after a moment of silence. He thought of Libi and her pain, her separation from her family. Even though it had been a long time since Cassius' mother died, he could still feel the pain of losing loved ones like it was yesterday. Did that really have to be? Did Libi have to endure that? If Saul had recognized Jesus sooner, none of that devastation would have happened.

"It is true: I intensely persecuted The Way and sought to destroy it. I advanced in my Torah studies beyond many of my contemporaries, out of devotion to the traditions of my ancestors."

Cassius nodded his head as he listened.

"But God used all of my fervor that I once had for the law, and turned it for His grace. All of the knowledge I'd gained enables me to preach His word and carry on the good news that is the salvation offered through the resurrection of Christ. My story, painful as it is, tells of His power. Were it not for His amazing power, I would not be standing here today. He is the only one who could redeem me after all of my actions. My hope is that others who hear of my transformation might be struck by the same realization that Jesus is the way, the truth, and the life."

"It didn't seem that many people felt that way today," said Cassius.

"Yes, at first some were taken aback, but most stayed and listened, later rejoicing with me and I with them at the overwhelming goodness of the One True God we all serve. There are still those who have not yet heard of how I have taken up the faith I once sought to destroy, but I know that His grace is sufficient for me."

"How?" Cassius' voice cracked as he asked the question. "How do you have such confidence? How are you able to tell of such things without feeling utter shame?" The more Cassius heard Saul's story, the worse he felt about himself. Saul had been able to use his past to do great things, but what could Cassius do? Lead an army? He probably couldn't have even done that.

"There are times when the enemy may use our past to destroy us, but it is as I have already said: I know that God's grace is sufficient for me. Therefore, I will most gladly boast all the more about my weaknesses, so that Christ's power may reside in me. So I take pleasure in weaknesses, insults, hardships, persecutions, and in difficulties, for the sake of Christ. For when I am weak, then I am strong."

"That is what I want; to know that God's grace is sufficient for me. How can I be like you? What do I have to do to earn it and be deserving?" said Cassius. He felt his body begin to sweat. Although they were outside and under the stars, he felt uncomfortably hot despite the chill of the night air.

"Do you not believe that by God's grace that you have been offered salvation through Christ's sacrifice?"

"I do… But I have done such horrible things," said Cassius, his voice breaking off. He had always wanted a proper name and titles, but the only titles he'd accumulated were thief, cheat, and murderer… How could he ever add Christ-follower to that list? "You don't know all of it."

"Then tell me," said Saul. Cassius was afraid to look him in the eye, for his gaze had grown so intense.

"I… I was born from an unmarried woman, and my father was already a married man," said Cassius.

"And?" said Saul.

"And my father killed my mother when I was a child."

"And?"

"To survive, I became a thief, stealing from others when I needed to and sometimes even when I didn't."

"And?"

"And… I lied to join the Roman Army. I took every opportunity to prove myself no matter who it hurt or what it cost. I was sent to Jerusalem where I executed whoever I was told to execute. Making jokes, taunting, tormenting others, and I… I…"

"Say it, Cassius."

"I killed the man called Jesus of Nazareth, the man I now call Savior. I nailed his hands into the cross myself," he coughed out the words, barely intelligible between his jagged breaths. "I was to guard His tomb. When I awoke and saw that it was empty on the third day, I ran and abandoned the other soldiers who were with me because I was afraid of being punished, and I've been running ever since!"

In quick succession, Cassius began confessing every detail to Saul of who he was, filling in every gap of his story, sharing how he'd come to Antioch, and all that had transpired between him and Libi and her family in the past few months. Words began to tumble out of Cassius, confessions that he'd long kept hidden. There was relief in sharing all of these things. Cassius had kept them pent up inside for so long, believing that speaking about them would only bring about greater pain, but he found no judgment in Saul. Only a listening ear. Cassius never before realized how badly he needed to be heard.

Tears poured down his face, wetting his beard and then puddling on the rooftop. Finally, when he had come to the end of his story, Cassius whispered, "I killed him. I killed him and others and I've never stopped regretting my part in it." For the first time, Cassius admitted out loud how his past haunted him in ways he'd never understood before.

"And I persecuted his followers," said Saul, matching Cassius' own tone. "We have *all* played a part in nailing his hands and feet to the cross. We play that role daily, whenever we sin, in ways both great and small. We are the ones who drive those nails deeper and deeper into those wooden beams. So, I'm asking you, what makes me any greater than you?"

Cassius looked down in shame. "I thought it was that simple. That I could become a Christ-follower and my past wouldn't matter. That I could forget about it and never have to think of it again."

Saul nodded his head in understanding. "I have lain awake at night tormented by the memories of their screams. Even in sleep, I have not been given rest, for I have woken from nightmares where all I could see were their faces. Sometimes I too have wished I could forget, but I can't, Cassius. Our pasts are a part of us. They remind us why we need God's grace in our lives. If we forgot that, how could we ever be able to minister to others? You must come to understand that God has a plan in everything. Libi was born deaf, so that others might hear of that miracle and in turn, hear of the glory of God and the hope of Jesus as the risen Savior. Now, as you have told me, she speaks and sings His praises, never failing to encourage others of His love. I myself was figuratively blind to the love of God, and it took a miraculous encounter with Jesus that left me physically blind before I could see the truth; that I had been blind all along. I endured that trial not just so that my own eyes could be opened, but so that I could help others open their eyes as well."

Saul stopped and took a deep, shaky breath before continuing, "Perhaps, Cassius, you have lived your whole life empty, wanting, always hungry for more, so that you could experience the fullness of God's love and demonstrate to others what that love looks like in action."

"But how can I ever be forgiven for what I've done?"

"Twice now you have tried to start your life anew. The first time you tried to bury your past, forgetting about it, but in that you were fighting the full healing that God offers you. The second time, on this very evening, you have tried to make up for your past by your own efforts, but no works of human hands could ever surpass the grace that comes from an infallible savior, Jesus Christ. You are still fighting that grace. There is nothing we can do to earn it, nothing that we can do that will ever make up for it, but God gives it to us and it is enough. To be a follower of Christ does not mean you are like Him exactly, but that you are living every day in the never-ending pursuit of *becoming* more like Him than you were the day before. You have that desire and it burns in your heart, does it not?"

Cassius clutched his chest. It felt as though there were a great fire burning within him. The way Saul described it was exactly how he had felt since the moment Libi's family had made him aware of the truth. "It has taken over me. All my ambitions before it have ceased to exist. Every part of my mind, heart, body, and soul pushes me farther and farther into directions unknown."

"That's the Holy Spirit, Cassius!" exclaimed Saul, a broad smile stretching across his face. "It's the presence of the Lord Himself that surrounds us, covers us, and guides us, endowing us with love, joy, peace, patience, and so much more. We do not have to keep our God in a temple, or worship Him as we would an idol. He is here and with us now. That desire to know Him, to be like Him, and to do His will on earth—*that* is what it means to be a Christ-follower."

"Even if God has forgiven me, how shall I... How *can* I continue on with my life, carrying the weight of my wrongs? How do you do it, Saul?"

"Can I remind you of something? *It is finished.* Not just Jesus' sacrifice on the cross. Creation is finished. The fall of humanity— the first act of sin—is over, done with, and finished. The miraculous birth of Jesus is finished. The crucifixion is finished. His resurrection to life after three days in the tomb is finished. The only thing that isn't finished is your acceptance of that fact, of your new life, and of the glorious plans that God has yet to reveal to you when you stop living in the past and start living in Him. Why do you continue to punish yourself for something that is already long past in the eyes of the Lord?"

Cassius let those words wash over him, and as they did, he felt the stain of his actions wash away too. He closed his eyes and mouthed them over and over again. *It is finished. It is finished. It is finished.*

"There is no secret," said Saul, "He has made a way for both you and I to live a life freed by grace. Accept that grace. Accept it day by day if you have to, hour by hour, breath by breath. Wear that grace as you would wear armor. You were a soldier once so you know what it means to protect yourself. You know that strong armor is a necessary factor in winning a battle. You cannot win if you are the easiest foe to defeat, so you cover yourself in all of your most vulnerable places, protecting yourself. You've been wearing a kind of armor your whole life that has made you untouchable by nearly everyone, except for God Himself. When you met the family of Tamir, you slowly started to remove your armor, allowing you to understand the depth of Jesus' sacrifice on the cross. Now that you have acknowledged and accepted Him as your Savior, the Christ, and the risen Messiah, you must put on a new kind of armor. The armor of God."

"Armor of God?" replied Cassius. Something made the hairs on his arms and legs stand up.

"Yes. You see, the things of this world will try to pull you away from God. They will try to distract you from pursuing Him and chasing after Him with all of your heart. If you want to live in grace and live by grace, then as you already know from your military training, you must arm yourself. Rather than metal and leather, you must take up a spiritual armor. A belt of truth, for discerning the influences of the world from the influences of the Holy Spirit. A breastplate of righteousness, to guide your actions. Sandals of readiness for the gospel of peace. Use your faith as a shield from darkness, wear your salvation like a helmet, the most important piece of armor, and always keep the word of God in your heart as you would keep a sword at your side. Study it, learn it, and know it, so that when trouble comes your way, you will be well-equipped to withstand it. Let the Holy Spirit guide you in everything."

"You ought to write all of that down." Cassius tittered awkwardly, unsure of what else to say.

Saul chuckled lightly to himself and responded, "Maybe I will, someday, but as for right now, do you understand, Cassius?"

"I understand," he affirmed, not more to himself than to Saul. He had always thought his life had been a battle against the gods and their trickery, but in truth, his life had been a battle fought by God out of love to win his soul.

"Saul... Would you teach me more?"

21

"Trust in the Lord with all your heart, and do not rely on your own understanding; in all your ways know him, and he will make your paths straight." — Proverbs 3:5-6 CSB

In the weeks that had passed since the "incident," Libi had not left her home. She was not ready to face the world. Over time, things returned to a kind of normal. Her father and brothers went back to their work, and activities around their house resumed. Libi went back to her baking, which she usually sent with her family when they went to gather with the other believers for meetings. Her family encouraged her to join them, but they didn't force her. She was not ready to face Saul, nor was she ready to face Cassius again. Anytime she thought of either of them, her stomach filled with a queasy feeling that made it difficult for her to breathe or think clearly. Instead, she spent all of her days at home baking and helping her imma around the house and waiting anxiously for a letter from Shamira. She needed sound advice and wisdom from someone she knew with whom she could be completely vulnerable.

As Libi kneaded bread inside her home, there was a sudden

knock at the door that broke her concentration. Wiping her hands on her skirt, she stood to go and see who it was. Her father and brothers were in the workshop, so it must have been someone they knew. "Taliah!" Libi exclaimed as she welcomed her friend inside. "How are you?"

"I am doing well," Taliah said, cradling her belly. "I came to see how *you* were."

"Me?" asked Libi incredulously, although she knew she was probably the talk of their community.

"Yes, *you*. You know Cassius has been staying with us, don't you? Along with Saul and Barnabas?"

Libi bit her lip and turned her back to Taliah, taking up her kneading again. "I heard." As guests to their community, it was only natural that Saul and Barnabas would stay with Taliah and Keinan, who had become such leaders among them.

"Is that why you have not come to visit? The children miss spending time with you."

Libi shook her head. "Oh, no, I have just been so busy lately."

Taliah took a deep breath and stepped closer to Libi. "I know how hurt you've been, Libi, and I—"

"Please, don't say any more." Libi raised a hand. "I need time, Taliah. I'm sorry."

"All right… We've been busy too you know, gathering the last of the furnishings and provisions needed to open up your house."

"It isn't *my* house," Libi reminded her. "It was only my idea, but I am pleased to know that the men were able to finish it."

"The men? Don't you know?"

"Know what?" Libi shook her head.

"The men didn't finish it. Cassius did it by himself. We've been collecting donations and filling it these past weeks, preparing to open the doors."

The news shocked Libi. "He… He did? But why?"

"I think he felt it was as important as you did. He's a very interesting man, Libi," said Taliah.

Libi didn't need to know how interesting Cassius was. However, knowing that he had been the one to finish work on the house warmed her heart, which in turn made her feel even more confused.

"Taliah… Why are you telling me this? Why are you here?" Libi asked, setting aside the kneading again.

"If it upsets you, then forget I mentioned it. I only came to see if you were planning to come to the gathering at the end of this week? It will be on the mountainside again. The weather is just right for it, and since Saul and Barnabas arrived, our numbers have only continued to grow."

"I don't know, Taliah. I am not sure I am ready," Libi answered. A part of her wanted very much to be ready. She wanted to put aside her hurt and welcome Saul, if he really was as good of a teacher as everyone made him out to be. She also wanted to forgive Cassius, if he really was genuine in his faith as reports of his actions seemed to suggest. Still, painful memories of not just their time together but of her childhood and her early years in Antioch kept her from being able to forgive either of them. Her soul was weary and she longed for worship, but her heart was fearful of facing the world.

"Would you consider it, Libi? For me?"

"I feel like there is something more you are not telling me, Taliah," said Libi. "Why is it so important to you that I am there *this* week?"

"As much as Keinan and I would like to take on the running of the shelter, we've prayed about it and it doesn't feel right for us. My time comes closer and closer with each day, and I know when the child is born that he or she will require all of my attention in those early months. I've talked to several others, but none have stepped forward. I think *you* could be the perfect person for the job, Libi."

"Me?" Libi's jaw dropped. "I only came up with the idea, Taliah. I couldn't be in charge of it."

"Libi, don't you see how this could be the answer to all of our prayers? I have seen you with my children and with others; you have such a great capacity for showing love to those who need it. You are a gifted communicator. You are a diligent worker at everything you make your mind up to do. It was your vision to put this whole idea together. You are the one who saw it first. What if it was God's calling to you all along?"

"How could I run such a large house?"

"The same way you help with the running of this one. Baking, cleaning, taking care of people. You would be given a portion of the tithes to help pay for expenses. It wouldn't be much, but I know you could get by, and surely there would be other volunteers to help you."

"I am an unmarried woman, Taliah. Who would accept such a thing? I couldn't live there alone."

"Your brothers could stay with you, or it could be worked out so that you don't have to be there all the time, or your family could help. I don't know all of the answers, Libi, just as you did not know all of the answers when you first presented the idea of buying this house to me, but God does. You are the one who thought of this; at the very least, you should be one of the ones responsible for its upkeep. Keinan is in full agreement with the idea, and if you are at the meeting this week then we will nominate you formally and put it to a vote. As it stands though, you are the only candidate."

"Taliah, I…"

"Pray about it, Libi. That's all I am asking. If you are not at the next meeting, then we will continue our search elsewhere, but please pray in the meantime."

Libi looked into Taliah's eyes and could see that she was searching for some kind of agreement. "All right," she conceded, "I will pray about it."

"Very well! I will pray for you also, but I must go now—I promised Keinan I would not take too long. It felt good to see you again though, after all this time."

"It was good to see you too, Taliah," said Libi, knowing that it was not a lie. She'd spent so much time hiding, she had forgotten how much she desperately needed fellowship. Taliah was right; Libi did love to serve others. She had missed playing with Phoibe and telling stories to Omri and chasing after Felix and Rufus and cradling sweet baby Tirzah…

Libi and Taliah embraced before Taliah went on her way again, leaving Libi to ponder all that she shared. She kept on working until the sun set, bringing the evening calm with it. All was quiet and Libi was deep in thought when she heard another set of footsteps behind her.

"Libi?" said Yuval, entering the room where Libi sat at the table.

"Yes?" she replied. "Are you looking for something?"

"No, actually, I was looking for you."

"Me?" asked Libi, wondering what it was Yuval had on his mind.

"I just wanted to say, we may not have always been as close as you and Gilad, but I hope you know that I am always on your side. I would fight a thousand foes for my sister," Yuval confessed.

"He could do it too, with my help," Gilad joked, coming in the open doorway behind him.

Seeing the two of them together made Libi grateful she had brothers who would always care about her. "Thank you, both of you," she said, smiling.

"All we want is to see you happy," said Gilad.

"And you haven't been as happy as you used to be," said Yuval. "You used to sing while you baked. Our house is too quiet without your voice."

"Of course, I have done my *best* to try and fulfill that role," said Gilad. He placed his hand on his chest and began to belt out melodies of his own far too loudly and confidently.

Libi couldn't help but burst into laughter, laughing so hard that her eyes began to water and her belly began to ache. "That doesn't sound like any song I've ever heard," she said, wiping the tears from the corners of her eyes.

"But *that*," said Yuval, pointing at her. "That laughter sounds like the Libi we know and love."

"Are you doing better, sister?" asked Gilad.

"I am… Taliah had some… *interesting* things to say. Did you know that Cassius finished the work on the house by himself?" A silly question, she realized, because otherwise they would have been working on it themselves. "Why didn't either of you tell me?"

"We weren't sure if you wanted us to speak about him to you, or if it would be too difficult," said Gilad.

Had she really been *that* distant, that they feared even the mention of Cassius' name would hurt her feelings? Maybe it would have in the beginning, but she had hoped she was recovering from the heartbreak.

"Taliah said… She thinks that I should be involved in the running of the house. Can you imagine that? Me?" Libi explained to them.

"Have you spoken to Abba or Imma about it yet?" asked Yuval.

"Not yet, but as I am unmarried, she suggested that we could all be involved with it as a family. I worry that it is too much to ask…"

"I would do it," they answered in unison, although each with their own inflection. Libi laughed again.

"You would?" asked Libi.

"Taliah is right. You are your best when you are showing love to others, and there are so many in this community who need to hear your heart." The tender words from Yuval brought tears to her eyes.

"I wasn't sure I'd ever be able to use my heart like that again," Libi admitted.

"Whatever you need, we'll help you with it," said Gilad.

"So will we," added Libi's abba, coming inside with her imma. They must have overheard the conversation from the courtyard.

"You will?" said Libi, overwhelmed. The few drops of tears she'd already had in her eyes began to multiply and overflow.

"We know how much joy an opportunity like this would bring you, and in truth, your passion for this mission has spread among all of us," said Tamir.

"You have always been our miracle child, *ahava sheli*, but now you can share that miracle with so many others who need to know of how good our God is. It's a very short walk between our house and the domus. The work may be hard and the days may be long, but it would be easy enough to go back and forth between there and here, and well worth it too."

"Oh, Abba! Imma!" Libi rushed to their arms to embrace them. "Thank you!"

"Don't cry, my daughter," said Tamir.

"It is all right, I am shedding tears now because I am so very happy, and so very grateful for all of you. I can see it now, Abba. I wouldn't have been able to do any of this if God had not led you to Antioch. Maybe I don't understand everything, but I'm beginning to," she explained.

"Jehovah Jireh, Libi. The Lord provides for our needs, He always has, and He always will," said Tamir, holding her tightly in his arms.

A sound from outside the workshop interrupted the warm embrace Libi reluctantly pulled away from. She, her parents, and her brothers straightened and she wiped away her tears.

"Who could it be?" she asked. "Do you think Taliah has returned?"

"Likely not. It is probably a customer. I will see to them," said Tamir. He crossed the room and exited.

"Shall we get this room cleaned up so that we might enjoy the evening meal, then?" suggested Chava.

As they all moved to ready the room, Libi heard another noise from the workshop. She recognized it as her father's voice, but could not place the tone. It was somewhere between a laugh and a shout.

"Everyone, come at once!" he called. "Someone is here that you must see!"

Libi blinked several times, forcing her vision to focus, and when it finally did, she almost could not believe her eyes. Better than any letter, standing in the workshop beside her abba was Asa, Shamira's husband.

"Asa! Asa!" Libi squealed with excitement and ran to greet their visitor, who leaned against the entryway to the workshop. She clasped his hands in hers. It had been so many years since she had seen her extended family, and although the letters were plentiful, nothing could compare to seeing a familiar face.

"Asa! You're here?" Gilad and Yuval asked in astonishment, although Yuval's voice was much deeper than Gilad's, which seemed to lilt upward with more surprise than confusion.

"It is so good to see all of you," said Asa, whose beard had grown much longer than Libi remembered it. Amidst his dark hair there were now a few locks of gray. "You two are men now!"

"I dare say I'm taller than you," said Yuval, standing up on his toes for added height and raising his eyebrows.

"I won't challenge you on that." Asa chuckled. "And Libi…" He stared at her, stroking his beard which was equally tinged with gray hair throughout as the curly mop on top of his head. "You are not the small child we remember. When did you get so tall?" He asked quizzically.

"I suppose with these two for brothers, I had to catch up eventually," she quipped.

He let out a deep breath. "Shamira would be so filled with joy if she were here to see how you've grown."

"Thank you, Asa." Libi smiled.

Chava pushed between them all. "Asa! You must come in at once! I will set an extra place for you at our dinner table. You've arrived just in time!"

"Dodah Chava, Dodh Tamir. It is so good to see all of you."

"Well, it is not often we receive family visitors here, as I'm sure you can imagine. Come inside immediately and enjoy some food and drink; then we can catch up on all that has happened in Phoenicia since we last saw our family," Tamir persuaded, ushering Asa inside with Chava following close behind.

"At least we got to greet him." Gilad nudged Libi in the side.

"Imma will keep him talking for hours before any of us will be able to have any words with him, but I am glad he is here."

"Me too," Gilad replied. "I knew the letter would arrive, but I didn't think Asa would be the one delivering a response."

"Neither did I," Libi whispered, "Thank you for convincing me to write it."

Asa arrived in time to break the evening fast with all of them. They dined over bread and stew. Imma had even pulled together a spread of cheeses, dates, and figs, sparing nothing from their stores for Asa's visit. As they ate, Asa told them about his journey from Phoenicia to Antioch, how he'd ridden with a fast-traveling caravan of merchants from the seafaring port of Tyre with news to bring to the family and some business to take care of in the city.

"These are delicious," said Asa, popping another date into his mouth. "Exactly like Savta used to make."

"Not quite like Savta used to make. We know she stirred them in honey and pepper, but we still can't figure out what else she added to make them so special. She always kept her recipe hidden from us," said Libi.

"Cinnamon?" guessed Asa.

"Tried it," Libi replied quickly. "Too sweet."

"Coriander, then?"

"Not sweet enough," said Chava.

Asa laughed. "It will remain a mystery to us all then. I'm sure if Savta were here, she would be laughing at all of our guesses and still never revealing whether we were right or wrong. She would keep handing them to us even after our bellies were full."

"But you would never be able to refuse my imma, regardless of the excuse," said Tamir.

"Never," Asa echoed.

"Tell us, Asa, how is Shamira?"

Asa leaned backwards on his cushion. A grin spread across his face and created new lines around his eyes that hadn't been there when he and Shamira first married. They were not the kind of lines that resulted from a frown, however. Libi could tell these lines came from smiles and laughter and a life well lived.

"Shamira is as well as she ever was. Strong of health and strong of will. I am continually in awe of the gift God has given me through her. Our children, Yemima and Eliel, grow taller every day. Eliel has his mother's spirit and quick wit, and Yemima has her fair looks and gentle heart. By the time I arrive home it is very possible that they will have a new younger brother or sister to watch over and play with some day."

An impish grin took hold of Asa's face, and Libi clapped her hands together. "Another sibling? Shamira is with child again?"

"And you left her at a time like this?" Chava said, mouth agape.

He chuckled. "It was she who sent me here, and you all know that when Shamira wants something, well, she can be very persuasive."

"Shamira sent you? Whatever for?" said Tamir.

"She received a letter from Libi telling of recent events, and her heart ached. She wanted me to come and see how things were. That reminds me, a traveler never arrives at the home of his gracious hosts without gifts." Asa reached for his satchel, while Libi's imma sent her a questioning glance, no doubt curious about the contents of the aforementioned letter. Libi nodded and smiled with her eyes, trying to communicate that all was well. Then she turned her attention back toward Asa's rummaging.

"Dodh Tamir, these are from Aharon and Binyamin. They are letters about business in Phoenicia and other family news."

"No doubt they are still wishing I would bring my family back, either to get in on their business or bring mine to theirs. I will enjoy reading these later. Thank you, Asa," said Tamir.

Asa nodded. "Dodah Chava, this is from Devorah and Rut." He revealed a beautiful length of cloth, woven together with many striking colors. "Rut made it herself. We often say that she is the sole reason our wool turns such a good profit at the markets in Tyre. Her talents at spinning set ours apart from others. The garments she makes are so fine that when she wears them in the marketplace, it makes everyone want some of our wool, but whether our wool is actually any softer than others or if it is just Rut's skill remains to be seen."

"She was always very talented, even when we lived in Jerusalem," said Chava.

"I hope these gifts will suffice as thanks for hosting me without notice. If it is too great of an inconvenience, I am sure I can find somewhere else to stay."

"Somewhere else? No, of course not," said Chava. "There is always room in our house for any guest the Lord chooses to send us, especially family."

They continued to eat until every last bite was gone from their plates. Libi helped her mother to clear the dishes and then went to get fresh linens for Asa to make up his bed. She shuddered briefly, remembering how she had done the same for Cassius when he had first arrived, not realizing who he was or what kind of impact he might have on her mind and heart.

"Asa," she said, approaching him. "I brought these for you."

"Thank you, Libi." He smiled graciously and placed the blankets with his other things. "May I speak with you privately?"

"Certainly," she said. She had hardly been able to say much of anything during the dinner conversation. She looked forward to catching up with him; he had already spoken briefly about Shamira and their children, but Libi wanted to know the details. What were their interests? Who did they resemble most? She followed him outside and waited patiently for him to speak, reluctant to barrage him with questions immediately.

"You know, I didn't just come bearing gifts for your abba and imma. I brought something for you too," he said.

"Me? I hope Yuval and Gilad don't find out or they will certainly be jealous," Libi joked, but she was very eager to know what he had brought. He pulled some parchment out of his cloak and Libi knew instantly what it was. "Another letter! Is it— "

"From Shamira? Indeed."

"Did she… Did she tell you what I wrote to her?" She wondered if all this time Asa had been pitying her in his mind. Libi had written her first letter to Shamira in the thick of heartbreak and confusion. She would be horrified to know that Asa had been privy to her most intimate thoughts and feelings all this time.

"Don't worry, Libi. Shamira would never break your confidence in that way. She did tell me that you'd grown to have feelings for a man called Cassius, but that something had happened that caused you great distress. She was so concerned for you; you know how big her heart is."

"Yes," Libi sighed, "Shamira loves with everything in her."

Asa's eyes seemed to gloss over thinking about the wife he left at home. They were a perfect match. Libi's heart turned at the thought of how she hoped she would find such a match in Cassius. Now the thought brought her nothing but despair; they had been complete opposites from the start. Was she being selfish? Was he right when he had called her a hypocrite? Thinking about it now since time had passed, she felt her heart softening. She was beginning to see that the blame wasn't only one-sided.

"Her love for you made her sick with worry. I promised her that I would deliver this to you personally, to make sure it arrived as quickly as possible and without incident, if it would ease her stress."

"I feel horrible that you might miss the birth of your next child because of me!" said Libi, the pang of remorse hitting her like a waft of hot air from the clay oven. Libi knew it would be impossible, but more than anything, she wished she could return with Asa and be with all her dear family.

"Shamira has her mother and Dodah Devorah with her to take care of her. She is in good hands, and if this helps reduce any of her anxiety on top of the unavoidable strains of childbirth, I am more than happy to do it for her. Would you like me to read it to you?"

Libi blushed. Would it say anything incredibly personal or private? She supposed however, there was no better option.

"Yes, please."

"All right, it begins, 'My dearest cousin, Libi, first I must begin by saying that it is me writing to you. Can you believe it? My first real letter. I have asked Asa to teach me to read and write so that I will be able to communicate with you and my sister more personally, and he has been a faithful and patient teacher. My hand is not quite steady yet, but I know that you don't mind.'"

"You're teaching Shamira to write?" Libi interrupted. What an incredible gift!

"Mmhmm. She's better at it than she gives herself credit for too. It continues, 'By now you know, there is no feeling like the feeling of loving another person in a way that is deeper than the love we show our friends, our family, even our own parents. But you are also aware that there can be no greater sacrifice than to love a person so wholly. Perhaps this Cassius is the one for you, as my Asa is to me,'" Asa paused to clear his throat, "'or perhaps he is not the one that God has in mind for you. Either way, I shall keep you in my prayers as I always have.

"'I confess that I was amazed to hear about Saul. You know as well as I do the depth of pain our family endured due to the persecution in Jerusalem, but if what he says is true, the man we remember no longer exists, and I rejoice at his transformation. What I am about to say to you may come across as harsh or unloving, but you must understand that I am saying what I have to say because I love you. You do believe in a miraculous God, don't you? If you don't, then you may hold to the feelings you shared in your original letter. If you do, then you must accept all people as He accepts all of us.

"'Dear Libi, Savta's songbird, the heart of our family, you have lived an extraordinary life. You have been surrounded by those who have loved you every day since the day you first drew breath—a day I remember well. You have been loved and cared for by all of us, especially your parents, who sought to protect you from every possible form of danger or harm. Perhaps I myself played a part in this sheltering, but I fear that until now, you have never truly had to face the outside world. Your circle of loved ones has been made up of so many people who share your beliefs, your background, your understanding of the world. Your faith in God is strong and your love for Him is incredible. That has been clear to me from even before you could speak the words yourself. Without that one miracle, your ears would still be closed and your songs unsung. Therefore, it stands to reason that you cannot deny the existence of a miraculous God. So, my next question to you is this: What makes a sinful man any less deserving of redemption than a deaf-mute child of a miracle? The same God who opened your ears opens hearts as well. You either believe in that, or you don't. There cannot be anything in between.

"'I believe that God could change a man like Saul just as He changes all of us. I wish I could be with you right now, to hold you, to comfort you, to whisper into your ears that everything is going to be all right. Unfortunately, I am limited to this parchment, but hopefully the words on my heart have been inscribed in a way that will give hope. I know that you have very strong feelings for Cassius, and that those feelings which were once quite bright with potential are now very dark with uncertainty. I would never advise you to pursue a relationship if that relationship was not what you felt was right, but I must tell you: love is the only way. Even if it is never to be a great romantic love story, you must learn to love him in some capacity, because God loves all of us. Yes, all of us, no matter what we've done, and His love never fails. I love you too, Libi. Take care, be continually devoted to prayer, and write me again whenever you wish. Now that I can write back, I can assure you that you will always receive a response from me, even if it does take me a little bit of extra time. Your cousin, Shamira.'"

By the end of it, Libi was moved to tears of gratefulness to God. It was easy to feel loved when surrounded by family, but it was much harder when those people were far away. Asa's presence was a reminder that even if she didn't see it, she always had an army of relatives lifting her up in prayer.

"Are you all right?" asked Asa, folding the parchment and taking a bit of cloth from his waist belt and handing it to her. Libi nodded, both to affirm that she was all right and to thank him for the cloth which she used to dry her tears.

"I am sorry, Asa. You've travelled days and nights all for this. I'm sure this isn't a very pleasant visit."

"Don't worry about it, Libi. You are my family as much as you are Shamira's, and as you know there is nothing she could ever ask of me that I would not do for her or our family." He smiled and chuckled lightly, and Libi could tell he was trying to lift her spirits.

Still, there were thoughts that taunted her after he had finished reading Shamira's letter to her. "Asa... Could I ask you a question? Or would you prefer I didn't?"

"You can ask me anything, Libi, and I will do my best to answer. But are you sure you want to ask me? Not someone else, like your mother perhaps?"

"No, no... You read Shamira's letter, so you know what has happened. I'd like to speak to you, as a friend. A cousin."

"Of course," he said. She handed the cloth back to him and he took it, exchanging it for the letter for Libi to keep. "I understand what you mean."

"Do you think… Do you think Shamira is right? I mean, I know she is right, but… I can't understand it. Cassius hid the truth from me—from all of us. He said he wanted redemption from his sins and to become a believer in Jesus like us, but he…"

"He what?"

"He has spent years on the run, stealing, cheating, and doing terrible things. Before that, he was a Roman soldier—one of the very same soldiers who nailed Jesus to the cross. You were there, Asa. How could someone do something as horrible as that?"

"From what I understand, all of those things happened before he became a believer."

"Well, yes, but…"

"But? It is as Shamira says, Libi. You either believe in a miraculous God, or you do not. There once was a persecutor named Saul, but that man no longer exists according to what you have told us. He is now a teacher who follows the same beliefs we do, because he is made new by Jesus' sacrifice. It is the same way for all of us, Libi."

"How can I show love to Cassius, even as a friend? Every time I think of him, I think of what he's done. Visions, *horrible* visions of him flood my mind. I see him with a mallet in hand, nailing our Messiah to the cross. How can someone like *that* change?"

Asa sighed deeply, and Libi wondered if she had said too much, or if he perhaps did not want to answer her. Perhaps he didn't even have an answer. He stroked his beard for several moments, and then he straightened, opening his mouth to speak again.

"I know how you are feeling right now. Maybe not exactly, but close. I remember the night of the crucifixion. I remember being so lost and not knowing what to do. I had overheard some of my father's conversations that day, and I knew at once what he aimed to do. I had always known my father could be cruel, but some part of me held out hope that he would see the error in his ways, and that our relationship would be reconciled and restored. I ran to your family's home and told Aharon and Shamira all that was happening, and for whatever reason, Shamira's father acted more like a father to me than my own that night. He saw my pain, he saw my concern, and he saw Shamira's fears too, and he agreed to come with me and see it through to the end. We followed the trail of onlookers to the house of the high priest, and it was there that I heard my own father, as a member of the Sanhedrin, cry out for Jesus' death."

Libi had been a child at that time, and had been a hearing child for less than a week. She had been too young to consider all of the possible ramifications and far-reaching consequences of Jesus' very existence. In many ways, she had never known a world without a Messiah. Libi had never had to consider what He meant to those who had not always lived in the light of God's love, for it had become as second nature to her as her own hearing. She imagined what that moment must have been like for Asa, and how much pain he'd had to endure.

"I was furious. I was enraged. I was many things, but most of all, I was hurt. I'd felt so betrayed by the man I had called abba for all of my life, even if his love was only a thing of my imagination. I ran from that house, burning in anger. I felt like I couldn't breathe. My palms began to sweat. I tasted bile in my mouth. My mind was neither here, nor there. I felt like I needed to get away. It was Aharon who stopped me—I remember he grabbed hold of me, and I remember thrashing, trying to break free. I was convinced that all I needed was to be alone, but he wouldn't let me have that. He wouldn't let go; he just told me to stop. He called me 'son.' That word and the way he refused to let go... I realized in that moment that I had never really had an earthly father. Not in the affectionate sense, anyway. I'd never been held. I'd never been chased after, not like that. I began to cry and weep for the life I'd lost."

"Asa, I am *so* sorry," said Libi.

"Don't be. I've gained much more in my new life, my relationship with God, and the incredible gift He has given to me through Shamira and our family, but I remember at the time hating my father. I hated him and everything for which he stood. I wanted to curse his name. But Shamira, so strong and full of wisdom even then, reminded me that hate for others has no place in our hearts if we truly believe in God's love. It wasn't easy, but nothing ever is. All of the pain didn't vanish instantaneously. I was able to forgive him eventually, not only for his actions as a part of the Sanhedrin, but also for the many ways in which he had hurt me before that. He had not been the kind of father I wanted, the loving one that I wished I had, but the Lord helped me to see that his sins were no greater than my own. I also learned that I had a loving heavenly father who would never abandon me. When Jesus was crucified on that cross, it wasn't just soldiers who drove the nails through his hands and feet. It was each and every one of us."

All of a sudden, realization filled Libi's mind like light filled the dawn. "That's it!" Libi exclaimed.

"What is?" asked Asa, taken aback.

Ever since she had overheard her mother and father talking the night that Saul came, she had been trying to remember what it was her father had said in his testimony that had reached Cassius' heart. She had been too devastated in that moment to ask of what he spoke, but she remembered it now as clear as day. "My father said the exact same thing when he shared his testimony on the night Cassius was saved. He talked about how there is no life or heart that He cannot make new, no sin He cannot forgive, no debt He cannot wipe out. Oh, Asa! I understand now! I understand how wrong I was…"

"It is easy to let hurt and anger cloud our thinking, but what is most important is what we do when we realize we've made a mistake."

"I know…" Libi sighed, exhaling the elation she'd felt

momentarily and inhaling once again the pain and fear she'd been living with since the last gathering she'd attended. "Asa, I am worried I will not be able to do it. I know now how wrong I've been in my thinking regarding both Saul and Cassius, but I am still so…" She couldn't find the words to describe the myriad of emotions, so instead she let the thought hang between her and Asa, hoping he would understand what she didn't know how to say.

"Your mind knows the way but your heart is not ready, is it?" asked Asa.

She nodded her head. "What if I am never ready?"

"In those months before Shamira and I were married and when I was working as a shepherd, sleeping each night under the stars with your family's flock, I had a lot of time to think. Although I was a shepherd by then, a part of me never stopped being a student. I spent much time pondering David, the shepherd-turned-king, and trying to remember as many of his psalms as I could, imagining the contexts of how they were written. There was a line from one psalm in particular, written during one of the lower points of his life, that stood out to me and that I spent a great deal of time thinking on. The line is a prayer of surrender which reads, "God, create a clean heart for me and renew a steadfast spirit within me." My heart was not clean then. I still wrestled with resentment toward my father, and as I considered that psalm, it became more and more clear to me that there was nothing I could do to free myself from that resentment. Forgiving my father was too difficult for me to do on my own. I needed God to give me a new heart, a clean heart, free from bitterness and restored by His spirit. It was His strength, not my own, that helped me to forgive. You can pray for a clean heart, too, Libi. He is faithful, and He will help you if you ask."

Libi did just that. She prayed that God would make her heart new, wash away every last bit of the pain she still carried, and help her to forgive those she struggled to forgive. Whether or not Cassius was still in love with her was of little concern to her now, but finding the opportunity and strength to forgive him and ask for his forgiveness in return meant everything to her. Libi knew what she had to do. She had to love Cassius regardless of anything he had ever done or could do, for that was how Jesus first loved them.

22

"For we know that our old self was crucified with him so that the body ruled by sin might be rendered powerless so that we may no longer be enslaved to sin, since a person who has died is freed from sin. Now if we died with Christ, we believe that we will also live with him, because we know that Christ, having been raised from the dead, will not die again. Death no longer rules over him. For the death he died, he died to sin once for all time; but the life he lives, he lives to God. So, you too consider yourselves dead to sin and alive to God in Christ Jesus." —
Romans 6:6-11 CSB

"Would you like to come with me to the agora today, Libi?" Asa asked her early that morning. "I want to purchase a special gift for Shamira while I am here. I know that she will not be expecting it, which will make the reward from the surprise that much sweeter. I could use a woman's opinion, if you wouldn't mind?"

Libi glanced at her imma for approval. "Will you need my help today?"

Chava smiled back at her. "Not today, *ahava sheli*. You should enjoy yourself."

Libi's mother patted her on the cheek and she blushed. Libi may not have felt completely restored, but she was getting there. She still needed to make amends with Cassius, and hoped she would see him at the gathering at week's end, which Libi now knew she would be attending. Turning to Asa, she replied, "I would be happy to come with you and help you pick out a gift for Shamira."

"Very well then," Asa cheered. "We shall leave after we break our fast! Perhaps we can also visit this shelter I've heard so much about."

"Oh, yes," said Libi. "I haven't seen it since the work was completed, but it's a very large domus not far from here. If Taliah or Keinan are there, I'm sure they'd love to show it to you as well."

The sun was high in the sky by the time they were ready to head to the center of Antioch's trade district. Libi tugged at the shawl around her shoulders. It was the same one she had been wearing that day in the agora when she first met Cassius. Perhaps wearing it once more would help her find him again.

She walked side by side with Asa through each street, careful not to get lost or separated or let her mind wander. First, they approached a jeweler's stall. There were many fine items hanging near the back, kept away from wandering hands of street vagrants, that were made of beautiful metals and contained precious gems. The seller stood protectively in front of his displays, and Asa and Libi stopped two paces away from him so that they could gaze at the contents.

"Ah! Can I interest you in something pretty for your lady?" the seller grinned.

"This man is family to me; I am simply here to offer an opinion. It is his wife who will be receiving the gift as a surprise," Libi explained, nodding toward Asa.

"I see, I see." The seller began to rattle off a list of what he had available, beginning with his most expensive offerings. Libi noticed how Asa listened to the man, politely letting him finish his speech before gesturing to a small display of more plain and simple adornments. He leaned toward Libi and pointed with his finger to one of the humbler items, a simple pendant.

"Do you think Shamira would like something like that?" he whispered.

Libi looked at the piece, modest and striking. "It is very beautiful, Asa."

"I sense that you do not think it is the best idea."

Libi bit her lip, careful to consider her words. "I am not certain if it suits Shamira's personality. It can't be denied that it is an extraordinary gift, but I'm sure she would enjoy any gift so long as it came from the heart. Maybe you could try to find something that she could have with her every day, or that she could use on a regular basis? Something that might be more practical with three children underfoot?"

"This is why I brought you with me," whispered Asa discreetly. Then, turning back to the seller, he continued, "Thank you for showing us your wares. I will keep them in mind and consider them."

"All right," the seller replied, "but know that jewelry of such quality is difficult to find. If you want the best in fine metals, you should come to me."

"I certainly will. Thank you again!"

The two of them turned to leave that stall and continued to walk through the marketplace. All around them different sellers and craftsman shouted about their offerings, each of them trying to overpower the others. They passed by basket weavers, metal workers, wood workers, sculptors, and so much more. They were nearing the end of the agora and Libi was beginning to wonder if she had given Asa bad advice. By the time they returned to the first jeweler's stall, it was highly possible he could have already sold the necklace Asa had admired.

"I am sorry, Asa, I am not seeing anything else."

"It's all right. It's not wise to buy the first thing you see anyways. You should always consider a purchase before making it. Let's head back and see about the pendant. Perhaps it can be made more suitable for everyday wear."

"That's a good idea," said Libi.

As they began to head back toward the middle of the agora, the busiest area, Libi's ears adjusted to the high volume of noise. It was then that she heard a faint voice coming from behind her that she had almost missed.

"Bracelets… Bracelets… Pretty bracelets for sale…" The voice sounded as though it belonged to an elderly woman.

"Asa, wait," Libi called.

"What is it?"

"I heard something…" Her voice trailed off into a whisper as she focused on all of the sounds around her. Mentally, she blocked out the sounds of hagglers, wooden carts, and families having conversations. She listened for the elderly woman's voice, but found it hard to identify its origin. She craned her neck, hoping it would help.

"Bracelets… Bracelets…"

This time, Libi could distinguish a direction. "Come this way!"

She led Asa back to the end of the agora to a shadowy space between two larger stalls. There was an elderly woman there with a wrist full of humble bracelets. From the appearance of things, she was having trouble selling them. She seemed frail and lonely, by the empty look in her eyes. Libi approached her slowly.

"Excuse me, those bracelets on your arm are quite beautiful," said Libi, offering a congenial smile.

"You think so?" Instantly the elderly woman's face brightened. She spoke with a thick accent that was hard to place, telling Libi that she had probably lived in this cultural epicenter all of her life. "I make them myself in all different colors."

The woman shakily lifted her arm to proudly display her creations.

"I've never seen anything else like them!"

"Others make them with silver or gold, but I do not have any of those things. I paint the wooden beads with dyes I make from plants and berries I find, and tie them together with string. They're as good as any of the other bracelets you see here," said the woman, now suddenly withdrawn.

Libi took the woman's other hand between hers. "They're *better,*" she insisted.

"Asa," she said, releasing the woman and turning toward him, "I think you should buy one of these bracelets for Shamira. She can wear it every day as a reminder of you. It is not as dear as silver, but it will be dearer to her because you gave it to her."

Asa nodded. "You are so right, Libi. How much are they?"

The woman named a meager price. Together, Asa and Libi chose a bracelet with a natural hue for Shamira. Libi noticed how Asa paid the woman triple what she asked. Her eyes lit with wonder. "I know of only one group of people who would be so generous. You are Christ-followers, aren't you?"

The old woman proceeded to ask them questions about who they were, where they had come from, and the spirit that surrounded them. Although Libi never imagined she would be sharing the message of Jesus as their Lord and Savior in the midst of the agora when she set out that morning with Asa to search for a gift for Shamira, she was amazed at how God gave all things a purpose.

"Where can I find your people that I might learn more?" she asked.

Libi proceeded to give her specific directions about the mountainside, where to find them, and when they met. "With so many of us, it is usually easier to meet outside. A cool breeze often blows through and makes it very enjoyable. Do you think you could find the way there? If not, I can give you the names of some who lead smaller gatherings in the city and might be able to help you."

"Child, I know the place you have described well. I am there every week gathering berries and plants to stain my beads. I will certainly be able to find you."

"That's wonderful news!" Libi exclaimed.

"Is there anything else we can do for you?" said Asa. Libi had not realized how far the sun had slid to the side of the agora, cloaking them all in the shadows of the afternoon.

The woman laughed lightly. "No, you have given me more than enough."

"Do you have a place to stay?" asked Libi.

The frail woman gestured to the pouch now full of coin thanks to Asa's generosity. "I will sleep better than I have in years thanks to you, and I will see you again on the mountainside."

Libi smiled. "I will be praying for you until then—Oh! I did not even get your name. I apologize for my rudeness, but would you tell me, that I might keep you in my prayers?"

"My name is Iulia. And you are Libi? And Asa?"

"Yes," Libi confirmed. They exchanged a few more pleasantries before they parted ways, but Libi was already counting the days until the next gathering of the believers, an excitement she hadn't felt since Saul first arrived, but that she could now hardly contain.

"That was a very good choice, Libi. Shamira will love this bracelet, even more after I tell her the story of Iulia. How did you spot her? I would never have noticed," said Asa, still turning the bracelet over and over in his fingers.

"I heard her voice and turned around," Libi explained.

"In these crowds? I think Jesus did more than open your ears that day in the Temple," Asa teased. Now that he had said it, Libi also found it curious how she'd been able to pick out the feeble voice of Iulia in the midst of the mid-day commotion at the agora.

"Libi," Asa continued, "even with the extra coin I gave to Iulia, I have still saved much more than I would have if I'd purchased that pendant. I saw someone earlier selling parchment and inkhorns, among other things. With the money I've saved, I'd like to purchase some new writing implements for Shamira to go with the gift of the bracelet. It will be something she can use to write you, which I'm sure she is going to want to do a lot of when I tell her all that has transpired during my visit."

"Oh, that's a wonderful idea, Asa!"

"Good! I'm glad you agree. It won't take me long to purchase, and then we can be on our way to visit this grand domus I've heard so much about."

Libi nodded in agreement, and Asa led her back through the agora the way they came, stopping only once he found the seller he had been seeking. Libi didn't feel the need to focus so intently on what was being said, so while Asa asked questions and bartered for a good price, Libi let her mind wander. Her eyes meandered over the pens, penknives, and ink sets. She looked at the parchments and writing samples and admired their beautiful designs even if she couldn't decipher the symbols.

Another customer cleared their throat behind her.

"Oh, pardon me," she said, stepping behind Asa to give the others more room to browse. She turned to offer a polite smile before coming face to face with Barnabas, and behind him, Saul. Libi recoiled in shock. The world began to spin again, as it had that day on the mountainside.

"Libi? Are you all right?" said Asa. He shuffled the items he'd purchased under one arm, and steadied her with the other. Then, seeing the other two men now face to face with them, he straightened his posture and spoke in a more formal tone. "Shalom to both of you."

Barnabas nodded and turned toward Libi. "Am I right in thinking you are one of Tamir's children?"

Libi nodded slowly, before stuttering a response. "I am Libi bat Tamir, his d-d-daughter. This is Asa, a v-v-visiting family member."

"I thought I recognized you. Saul, her father is the carpenter who donated the building supplies to the shelter."

"An admirable work it is, too. Your community is doing great things, and I hear the idea for it came from you?" Saul looked at her for confirmation, but Libi found herself unable to answer him.

Libi changed her mind. She wasn't ready for this at all. She should have stayed home this day; it was still too soon, the emotions of the previous weeks still too raw. How could she have a conversation with this man as though nothing had happened? She couldn't. "We were about to leave."

She turned to go, but was stopped by a gentle hand from Asa who whispered so only she could hear, "Remember Shamira's words, Libi."

She swallowed hard in an effort to hold off the tears that would inevitably come, and turned back to face Saul. When she looked into his eyes, she saw how his expression had changed. He was noticeably discomfited by her reaction to him.

"I beg your pardon, Libi bat Tamir, but I cannot help but feel I have wronged you in some way," said Saul, breaking the silence that had fallen upon the group. "Would you tell me?"

Libi's lips quivered and her hands began to shake. All of the grievances she'd ever bottled up inside, all of the negative thoughts she'd held in her heart but never dared to speak aloud rushed to the forefront of her mind. It was not something he had done, but many things that had happened because of him. Things she'd never truly confronted until recently.

"I was there in Jerusalem," she said, the strength of her voice faltering. "I was there the day Stephen died."

Libi watched as his face turned white. She closed her eyes to stop tears from flowing and continued, stronger with each word, "I remember walking with my family as laughter turned to screams. I remember cutting my feet and scraping my knees as we ran for safety. I remember watching my beloved savta die from injuries she sustained at the hands of persecutors, and I blame you. I blame you for leading the persecutions that led to my savta's death. I blame you for my family being forced out of Jerusalem. I blame you for so much of the pain and loss I have felt over the last ten years, and…"

Libi stopped to look at Saul once more, seeing how his shoulders heaved up and down with rapid, unsteady breaths. In that moment, she was comfortable with the idea of turning away from him and never speaking to him again, but echoes of Shamira's letter and Asa's counsel convicted her. God did not desire a comfortable relationship with Libi. He desired a close one, and that required letting go of the resentment she held onto, and falling in to faith.

She believed in her heart the message of salvation through Jesus, but the anger at the past still remained. She knew she could not relinquish it without His help, so she closed her eyes, took a deep breath, and focused all of her mind, heart, and soul on her prayers.

"God, help me in my weakness. I know you have always provided for me throughout my whole life, even when I have not seen it. Provide for me now the strength to forgive what I cannot forgive. Show me how to love this man and see him as you do. Make my heart like yours. I am consumed by a fire of anger and hurt I cannot control, but I want to be on fire for you. I cannot do this alone. Help me."

She opened her eyes once more, now seeing that Saul had lifted his hands to his face to catch his tears. With all the faith she could muster, she breathed out the words, "I *did* blame you, but now I *forgive* you."

With one swift motion, she pulled the lightweight shawl she wore from her shoulders and held it out to him that he might dry his tears. "Thank you," he whispered, not broken, but humble. When he took the cloth from her hands, Libi felt all of her loathing go with it, and she found herself crying with him.

Though she had not seen it before, she saw clearly now how that pain which she had tried to bury in the depths of her memory for so long and avoid confronting had affected her spirit the way a little bit of leaven made the whole loaf rise. By God's grace, He removed the pain that leavened her heart, and filled her instead with a new understanding of His spirit.

Love—God's love—was the only way.

More words were exchanged between Libi, Asa, Saul, and Barnabas before they finally parted ways. Saul and Barnabas had their own purchases to attend to, and it was getting later in the day. While there was still sunlight left, Libi led Asa up the streets to show him the domus as she had promised to do earlier. It was well-removed from the agora, but still within Antioch's trade district. Only a few businesses lined the streets, and they were not nearly as crowded or loud. "It's here," she said, gesturing to the grand door between two shops.

She entered first before Asa, and called out, "Taliah? Keinan? Is anyone here?"

There was no response, but the door was ajar so they moved through it. When they were both fully inside, Asa pushed the door closed. "Your descriptions were very accurate! From the street, it does not look like much, but it's quite spacious inside. I can see how this would be useful for helping so many people."

Libi beamed. "Yes! Come into the atrium and I will show you around. Perhaps we will find the others in one of the rooms."

Libi explained the layout as they walked further into the center of the house. "So much has changed since I was last here…" she said, marveling at how the domus was unrecognizable compared to the state in which she and Cassius found it. "There had been a fire, and the previous owner was convinced the cost and time to repair it would be too great, which is why he was so eager to sell. Looking at it now, perhaps he would think he made a mistake. Abba and the others were able to do so much with so little."

"The Lord provides," said Asa as he looked around at all sides.

Libi strained her neck toward the culina. "Taliah?" She called out, hoping for a response, but still none came. "That's so strange… I thought for sure we might see the others here, but they must have all gone already."

Suddenly, there was loud screaming and shouting outside of the domus. The commotion was strong and sudden, making Libi jump.

"Stay here," said Asa, hurriedly, "I will see what is happening."

"Where are you going?"

"Wait for me—I am going to see what the trouble is." His movements were quick as he dashed across the atrium, swinging the door at the end of the vestibule open. Libi turned and retreated deep into the house, hiding herself in the darkest corner of the culina, where she began to pray fervently over whatever was happening outside. Maybe it was because of Asa's presence, but she couldn't help but think back to the persecution in Jerusalem.

She began to pace back and forth in the room, her hands brushing over the repaired tables and donated cookware that lined the walls. Finally, after what felt like an eternity had elapsed, she heard footsteps behind her. "Asa, what happened?" she asked as she turned around, only it was not Asa who greeted her. It was someone unfamiliar.

Before she could even think of what to do, the stranger lunged forward, blocking her from escaping. "Don't scream," he ordered.

Libi could barely breathe, let alone scream. At the sound of his voice, she recognized him instantly—he was one of the two thieves who had tried to rob her that day in the agora when Cassius had saved her. Where was Cassius now?

"What… do you… want?" she said, her voice trembling.

He moved even closer, and Libi felt bile rising up in her throat. "Keep quiet. I'm warning you—call out for help and you'll be dead."

"Oh, Lord, please protect me. Show me your hand as you showed it so clearly with Saul. Please!" Libi prayed silently,

hoping that God would answer quickly.

Cassius had been at the domus earlier that day with Keinan. They'd spent the better half of the morning bringing in the supplies and linens that Taliah had gathered. He had learned so much in his weeks spent with their family, and he would be forever grateful to them for the kindness they had shown. Cassius felt more secure than he ever had in all of his life. He had no more fears, no more desires to run. Even if he still had things chasing him, he only cared about chasing after two things: God first, and Libi second, if she still wanted him.

Now, in the afternoon, Cassius was the only one who remained to finish sorting the donations. Keinan had left not too long before, and Cassius promised to follow him as soon as he was finished. He puttered back and forth in one of the upstairs rooms that they had designated as storage, moving usable items to one side and the things that needed to be repaired to the other. Cassius picked up a crate and set it down with the other usable things. He thought he heard a door open, but rationalized that his mind must have been playing tricks on him. He carried on with his tasks, the sounds of gentle conversation drifting in through the window and drowning out any other figments of his imagination. As soon as he'd settled into a rhythm again, he heard a scream coming from outside, followed by shouting, and he knew he hadn't imagined it.

Without thinking, he dropped everything and flew down the steps, practically falling into the atrium. It was then that he realized the door to the main entrance was ajar. Cassius must have forgotten to set the latch in place after Keinan and the others had left earlier that day. Now aware that he may not be alone in the domus, he became very alert of his surroundings. He heard an unfamiliar voice coming from the culina at the back of the house, followed by a much softer voice that was very familiar, and very dear to his heart.

Libi was here, and how or why she came did not matter. She was in danger.

All of his military training came back to him in a heartbeat. He stepped away from the center of the atrium into the shadows, moving swiftly along the walls until he was right outside the culina. He turned the corner very slowly, unsure of what to expect. There she was, beautiful, kind, gentle Libi, being held at knifepoint by a rough looking man. He was one of the very same men Cassius remembered fighting off that first day in the agora. Cassius' arm instinctively reached to where his sword had once been strapped at his side; even after all these years, there were some movements his mind could not forget. Realizing he was unarmed and that he had no weapon, his pulse started to race. He clenched his fist, seeing how the attacker had Libi pinned against the wall so he could not see Cassius. That meant he had surprise on his side.

"Don't... want to... do this... please," said Libi between jagged breaths.

"Quiet, girl," said the foe.

"Don't... want to do this..." she repeated. What did she mean?

"Don't you move now, *silver-eyes*," he ordered. "I remember you from the agora. You were lucky then, but you won't be so lucky this time. Stay quiet or I *will* kill you. I need to find a way out of here." The man turned his attention away from Libi for a moment.

Time seemed to slow down. Cassius watched as her hand slipped ever so swiftly to the folds of her dress at her side, from which she pulled out the hidden blade he had trained her to use what felt like a lifetime ago. It dawned on him then that when she said, *"Don't want to do this,"* she wasn't talking to the attacker. She was talking to herself! She didn't want to use the knife! She never had—she only accepted it after Cassius insisted. She kept a firm grip on it, precisely like Cassius had taught her to, fully prepared to defend herself, but Cassius would see to it that she did not have to bear that burden.

For barely a breath, his eyes locked on to hers. He lifted a finger to his lips to encourage her to remain quiet. Then, he lunged at the attacker from behind, pulling him from Libi and pushing him into a corner. "Get away from her!" he growled in a low tone he didn't know he could reach.

"Cassius!" he heard her cry out.

"You're not going to hurt her," he said.

Thanks be to God for helping him find Libi's home, where Chava had seen to it that he had been well fed and where Tamir had given him a job that once again kept him active, restoring his strength to near where it was when he had been a soldier. After a few well-timed jabs, the attacker fell to the ground and struggled to get up. Without thinking about it, Cassius grabbed the nearest thing to him—a jar—and threw it on the man's head, knocking him unconscious.

"Is… he…" Libi asked. Cassius turned and could see how her lips quivered and hands shook.

"No," said Cassius, trying to assuage her fears. "Go upstairs, quickly. There should be rope or something else in one of those rooms that we can use to tie him up before he comes to his senses."

Without a word, she left and returned with the rope. Cassius wasted no time securing the man's bonds.

"Did you come alone?" he asked. "Are your brothers with you?"

"No, I came with— "

Another man entered the room. He was someone that Cassius did not recognize. Older, taller, and with wild-looking hair. "Libi, are you all right? A man in the street is saying he was robbed by two men. They found the first, but the second is—" He stopped talking suddenly when his eyes landed on Cassius and the intruder.

"Asa," said Libi, rushing to his side. "The second thief is here.

He came in here to hide, but Cassius fought him."

Cassius cleared his throat. "Perhaps one of us should go and get the authorities before this man awakens."

"I will go," said Asa, leaving and returning with local officials who took the thief into their custody. Cassius and Libi stood nearby in the atrium and listened while Asa explained what transpired. Cassius wanted to say something more personal to Libi, but he wasn't sure of how to break the silence. Thankfully, she broke the silence for him.

"The Lord provided you to save me. I called out to Him in prayer and He answered by sending me you, *again.*"

"I'd say you were fairly close to saving yourself. You didn't need me." He smiled back, feeling the tension all around him ease. "Besides that, you had… Asa." Cassius couldn't help it if he said the man's name with a hint of disdain. Cassius had never seen him before in all of his time spent with Libi and her family, but weeks had passed since then. Perhaps she had found another suitor, one more well-suited to be her partner in life. The man was older than she was, but he did not seem like a bad man. Were it not for the situation, Cassius may have been able to find reasons to like him.

Libi half-suppressed a laugh and Cassius gave her a questioning glance. "Cassius, Asa is the husband of my cousin, Shamira. He is visiting our family, and I only brought him here to show him what we had done."

"Oh," said Cassius, trying not to sound too relieved. Now that she said it, he remembered the many stories she had shared of him and Shamira from her time in Jerusalem. Perhaps Cassius could call this man a friend after all; it would certainly be easier to like him now that he knew he was not after Libi's heart.

"I *did* need you, Cassius. There is something I must say…"

"You don't have to say anything."

"I do! I am… I am full of regret for the way I acted. It seems that today is my day for making amends."

"What do you mean?" asked Cassius.

"Earlier today, in the agora, I met Saul. He was with Barnabas, who recognized me. I tried to leave, but Saul could see how I reacted to him and he asked me what he had done. I couldn't help it after that. There were so many things I wanted to say to him that I hadn't even dared to think about in years… I told him everything I felt, and then… I told him I forgave him."

"You *forgave* him?"

She nodded her head. "Yes, I did, but not by my own strength. It isn't mere coincidence that Asa is visiting at this time, you see. After everything that happened, I asked Gilad to help me write a letter beseeching Shamira for advice. I had no idea Asa would personally deliver a response, but he did, and in Shamira's reply she reminded me of the truth that I had forgotten: that the same God who performed a miracle by opening my ears also opens hearts. I prayed and asked Him to open mine, that I might be able to see others as He does, and find the strength to forgive what I have not been able to forget. He is faithful, and I know now that I was wrong that day on the hillside. The truth is that I was not strong enough to forgive, but God has—*is* helping me. I forgive you too, Cassius"

"Libi, I should not have lied to you. I should have told you the truth from the beginning."

"I would have judged you, just as you feared. Although I wish you had not felt like you needed to keep it from me and that things had not happened the way they did, I am grateful that I got to know you for who you are now first. Can you ever forgive me for how I acted?"

He looked into her eyes, her silvery gray eyes that were unlike any that he'd ever seen, so wide and full of unanswered questions, and smiled at her. Was this not the reconciliation he too had prayed for over these past weeks? "Yes, I can."

"I wish we could begin again. Start over between us."

An idea sparked inside of him. "Then why don't we?"

"What do you mean?" Suddenly her misty eyes flooded with

confusion instead of remorse. "How can we do that?"

Cassius straightened, taking two small steps back as any appropriate stranger would do before making a new acquaintance. "My name is Cassius. I am a soldier, or I was a soldier in the Roman Army. I deserted after Jesus arose from the grave, although at the time I did not believe what my own eyes had seen and fled for fear. I have spent the years since then living on the run and doing all kinds of things I'm not proud of, but I'm not running anymore. I've come to realize that all those years I spent running from God, I should have been running toward Him. I have been learning from a man called Saul who has been helping me as I look for the best way to address my past, but I have given that also completely over to the Lord. I don't know what my future holds, but I know that I am not the same man I was before. I have heard of a woodworker in this area who at one time had room for another man in his employ. If he is still in need of help, I would very much like to speak with him. What is your name?"

She stared at him pensively, and after a few too many moments passed, Cassius started to wonder if he had made a mistake. Did she think he had gone mad? She began to smile and the usual sparkle returned to her bright eyes, and he knew he'd finally done something good.

"My name is Libi. Follow us home and I will introduce you to my family. I'm sure they would love to get to know you and learn about who you are. *All* of who you are."

"I would be delighted to, Libi." The sound of her name rolling off of his lips felt like ointment on a wound. It cleansed him and healed him. "And I look forward to getting to know you."

23

"Above all, maintain constant love for one another, since love covers a multitude of sins." — 1 Peter 4:8 CSB

The officials finally left with both thieves in tow. While they had been talking, they learned that those two criminals had been wanted for some time as suspects of thefts happening all over the city, but no one had ever been able to catch them until that day. Libi was grateful they would no longer be on the streets, but as they left, her heart filled with compassion and she was compelled to pray for them. They had done wrong things, but in the eyes of God, they were the same as her: in need of a Savior.

"Well, that's over now. I apologize that I was not able to formally introduce myself before. My name is Asa, and I presume you are Cassius?"

"Yes, I am." Cassius nodded.

"I have heard much about you." Asa smiled. "It is good to finally meet you."

The exchange warmed Libi's heart. Although she did not know if she and Shamira would ever see each other again, or if she would ever have the pleasure of introducing her dearest cousin to

Cassius, she was happy that he could meet Asa.

"I've invited Cassius to join us for dinner," said Libi. She knew the invitation would come as a shock to her family, but she also knew that they would welcome him back again if she did. After all, Gilad had told her that Cassius had been something close to another brother to him.

"If you'll give me a few moments to collect my things, then I will be happy to join you both," said Cassius.

"All right, we'll wait outside for you and then we'll all walk together," said Asa.

When Cassius was out of earshot, Libi spoke to Asa in hushed tones, "I have forgiven him, Asa, and he has forgiven me. I didn't think it would ever be possible, but God is so good!"

"I'm glad for both of you, Libi. Thanks be to God!"

When Cassius exited, making sure to secure the door this time, they all turned to go. They walked at a moderate pace, Libi walking faster than usual, anxious to tell her family of what had transpired. When they finally arrived, Libi saw her family gathered together in the workshop. She nodded to them all, communicating that this was what she wanted, and they greeted Cassius as they would have weeks ago.

"It is good to see you, Cassius, we've missed having your help here at the workshop," said Tamir.

"I have been staying with Saul and Barnabas, as you know, and they have been teaching me more and more about the Lord and His love for us. Still, I have missed you all too, and grieved the choices I made and the way things were left between us. There are things that trouble me still."

"Cassius," began Tamir, "you do not need to say anything to us."

"No, please," said Cassius, "I need to ask for forgiveness from *all* of you. I can barely forgive myself when I look back on my life and what I've done... but as for you all, I must confess that when I originally accepted your offer of employment, Tamir, my intentions were not honorable, but rather I had hoped to steal from you. It wasn't until I spent more time with you, learned more about your story and about God that my heart began to change. By God's grace, I am freed from the man I used to be, but I am continually striving to be a better man that I am. I know it is a great deal to ask, but I would like to come back as your hired help, if you can find it in your heart to trust me."

Libi looked to see how her abba would react. His brows furrowed as he turned his back to Cassius, now facing the workbench. Would he not say something? Then she saw her abba pick up the biggest nail he could find, along with a mallet. Libi held her breath, unsure of what he was doing.

He walked past them all to the door that faced the street, placed the nail in the frame, and turned to face his family. "*It was me,*" he said. Three hard swings drove the nail firmly into the beam.

Yuval was next to step forward. He picked up another nail and took the mallet from his father's hand, repeating the words as he drove a second nail into the wood with a single, heavy blow. When he was finished, Gilad already stood at his side with another nail and did the same.

Asa followed, and then, to Libi's own surprise, her imma whispered from the back, "My son, may I have a nail, please?"

"Do you want me to drive it in for you?" said Yuval, low and under his breath as he placed the nail in her grasp.

"No, Yuval," she said, shaking her head as tears ran down her cheeks. "It was me, too." Chava did not hammer as hard or with the strength of the men, but with each swing, Libi was reminded of the price Jesus paid for their salvation. She had been a child then, and had not been at the crucifixion herself, but she saw the weight of it now in a way she never had in the past. Before her imma could turn around, Libi had already moved to her side, ready to take the mallet in her own hand.

She turned toward Cassius and added her admission to the others. "It was me."

Libi's own vision blurred as tears filled her eyes. Although at first her father's movements stunned her, she understood now what he meant. This action spoke louder than words ever could. Cassius may have held the mallet that day, but all of their sins put the nails in Jesus' body. Finding her own nail, she positioned it next to the others and swung the mallet with all her strength. The sound sent chills down her spine and made all of the hairs on her arm stand up. She struck a second time and a third. With each hit, her arms grew weaker, but the nail barely moved into the wood. She shook her head, still holding the nail in place, but unable to continue. "I was *so* wrong…"

Suddenly, Cassius was at her side. She lifted her eyes toward him in trepidation. He looked at her and then to Tamir, raising his eyebrows. Libi saw her father nod. Cassius placed his hand over Libi's and took the weight of the mallet, helping her drive it through with the others.

Cassius withdrew from her side, and after a few more moments of silence, Tamir once again raised his voice, "Cassius, none of us are without sin. For any of us to hold the past against you would not be fair. I know I speak for my entire household when I say that we already forgave you, and I would be honored to have a man of your skill and passion working in my shop. Now it is us who must ask your forgiveness, for ever giving you cause to doubt the reaches of God's grace."

Cassius nodded his head, the start of a smile cracking across his face. "God makes all things new," he said, pausing to wipe the tears from his eyes. "Let us go inside for the evening meal and rejoice in that."

Libi's heart fluttered, for she knew it was true. If she had thought she had known joy before, she had not even come close. This was joy: to fully depend on the love of God and be confident in His power, knowing that His love and grace was so much stronger than any earthly thing.

Libi breathed in the crisp morning air as she stood with her family outside of the domus. *Her* domus. Asa stayed with them until the next gathering of believers where Libi was appointed as caretaker of the shelter after a vote by the community, before leaving to return to Phoenicia. Although Libi ached to think about the distance between them, she understood now better than ever the extraordinary way in which God kept them together through the Holy Spirit. The faith they shared united their hearts, and she gave thanks for that. When the vote had been taken, Libi kept her eyes squeezed shut, praying that the Lord's will would be done. She thought again back to the psalm Asa shared with her in which David asked God to create within him a clean heart, and restore to him the joy of salvation. God had been faithful to Libi in the same way, because although she had strayed, when she returned to Him, the broken pieces of her life—even the ones she'd long forgotten about—all began to come together again. When she opened her eyes, she saw God's faithfulness yet again, as the care of the domus was officially given over to her.

Iulia, the woman who made the bracelet Asa purchased for Shamira, had been there also, sitting near to Libi and her family. She did not say much before the speaking began, but when she left, she let Libi know that she would return. Libi could see after that why Saul drew so many crowds and kept people coming back to hear more. His messages were full of passion, and made so many things clear that once seemed difficult to understand. If anyone had told her months ago that she would be sitting down to hear a man who had once persecuted her family and so many others preach to her on love and forgiveness, she would not have been able to believe them. Things had changed so much for her and her family in that time. Her love for God remained, but her understanding of His love multiplied tenfold.

Love had been exactly what Saul spoke about at the last gathering, and while Libi might have once been surprised by the timeliness of such a sermon, she knew that nothing was a surprise to God. Saul talked about the attributes of love: patience, kindness, not self-seeking nor irritable, keeping no record of wrongs, finding no joy in unrighteousness, but rejoicing in the truth. In the days since, Libi repeated the list over and over again in her mind, trying to keep them in her heart so that she would remember them and put them into practice in her everyday life and in her role as caretaker of the domus. They described exactly how she wanted to love others going forward: bearing all things, believing all things, hoping all things, and enduring all things.

Now she waited with her family for Taliah and Keinan to arrive so they could begin making the final arrangements. Libi needed to move some of her personal things over, as well as determine what the most efficient uses of the space would be for her. Lists needed to be made so that the culina could be stocked with grains and herbs, and anything they needed that hadn't been donated would have to be purchased.

She counted on her fingers all of the things she would be asking Taliah about when she arrived with Keinan. "Baskets and bowls… I'd like to keep up with my baking if I can… I'll have to talk to Taliah about what is already collected… I'm sure it will take time to get the word out… How long do you think until we can open the doors, Abba? Imma?"

Chava smiled. "One step at a time, Libi."

"Oh." Libi laughed lightly. "I am getting ahead of myself, aren't I?" Her imma was right. So long as they leaned on God in everything and took care not to stray from Him, He would lead them as He always did. One step at a time.

"I have never been prouder to call you my daughter, *ahava sheli*," said Tamir, putting an arm around her affectionately.

"I always knew that God had called you for a special purpose, ever since you were healed by Jesus that day outside the temple so long ago," said Chava. "I believe this is that purpose. We are *both* proud of you!"

"All of the glory belongs to God. None of this would be possible without him." Libi pulled away and turned her head toward the street. "Look, Taliah and Keinan are coming."

Cassius was with them too, and even though she had seen him at the gatherings and when he started working with her father once more, Libi was still eager to see him again.

Cassius had wrestled with his feelings for Libi ceaselessly over the past few days as he transitioned back to working with Tamir as a carpenter while still living with Taliah and Keinan, asking God for guidance on what to do next. He prayed constantly, *"Lord, if these feelings are not from you then take them away from me. Do not allow me to burn for what you do not will for me to have."* Still, the feelings he harbored for Libi that now felt stronger than ever before did not subside. Things had changed—of that much, he was certain—but he did not want to presume Libi's feelings. He needed answers for his heart and likely for hers. As he walked with Taliah and Keinan to meet Libi's family at the domus, he knew that he could wait no more. He needed to speak to her personally. He let the others greet and make small talk before he cut in.

"Libi, you look well," he said, greeting her with a smile. "This role suits you."

"Thank you," she said, returning his gaze, before turning back to address the group. "Shall we go inside and begin? I have so many questions for you, Taliah, about the inventory of—"

"Libi," he said quietly, not meaning to cut her off. "I was wondering if I might have a word with you privately."

She blinked at him, before replying softly, "Very well, if it is all right with the others."

Cassius looked beyond her to Tamir, searching his eyes for approval. "The rest of us will step inside the vestibule and begin discussions," he said.

Cassius nodded in understanding, then he turned to Libi. The two of them remained in the street just beyond the threshold of the domus, but still in full view of the others.

"I must first say congratulations. I don't think they could have picked a better person for the job of caretaker," he said.

The corners of her lips turned up and she replied, "I was so nervous that all I could do was close my eyes and pray that God's will would be done… I was shocked, but I am so thrilled by the opportunity! I can see it now, Cassius. I can see so much clarity in my past and the things I used to question; I know now why I was born deaf and healed by Jesus. It was so that I could do more than proclaim His name—it was so that I could help children like Phoibe, Rufus, Felix, and others know that they are and have always been enough, as my family did for me. As painful and difficult as it was, I also see why God took us out of Jerusalem. It was so that we could serve Him here in Antioch. Who knows, but perhaps if we'd never had to leave, we'd never have opportunities to serve like *this*."

"You know," said Cassius, moving his sandals back and forth on the ground, "I don't think I ever told you of my mother. Her name was Laelia. I loved her as any child loves their mother, but she did not always make the wisest decisions. I think now it is because she felt she had nowhere else to go. No one to turn to. She was killed when I was a boy at my father's order, and I witnessed her murder. You see, they were not married when I was born, and I suppose he didn't want her to cause trouble for him, because by that time he was already married to someone else. I grew up an orphan after that, but I think that if my mother had a place to go like the shelter you've envisioned… If there had been someone like *you* there for her, perhaps things would have been different."

"But look where you are now," she said, stepping closer to him. "Every step you took led you to this moment. You have come so far."

"Only because God has carried me this far." He took a deep breath and began again, asking a question for the second time that he'd hoped he would only ever have to ask once. "Libi, it was here at this house that my feelings for you truly began to grow. It was here where I fell in love with you and where I think you began to feel similarly, but so much has happened since then. My heart is not the same as it was when we first met. Like the domus, we've both experienced drastic change. It happened exactly as it should, for I see now that I had much to learn about God and myself before I could commit to such a relationship. However, I must know, do you still have feelings for me? Are your thoughts captivated by me as much as mine are by you?"

He noticed her cheeks flush with color. His heart raced trying to guess what emotion she was feeling. Embarrassment? Anger? Dare he presume affection?

"I have spent these last days praying for you, Cassius. I have been asking God for guidance as well, asking that He would help us to fix our relationship, even if it never went further than friendship. Above all, I have prayed for your happiness, but the truth is, yes. I do still have feelings for you."

He breathed out a sigh of relief. "Libi, I want you to know that I have put a lot of work into learning more about myself and how Jesus' sacrifice covers me. When I spoke to you the first time about our future, we didn't have the right foundation in place for our relationship to grow—that was completely my fault. I don't know all the traditions, so perhaps even now I am going about this the wrong way, but what I do have is a heart full of love. I love *you*, Libi, and I want you to be my wife."

"Cassius, I—"

He held up a hand, stopping her from responding. "There is one thing more you must consider. A life with me would not be easy—

and there may be more to endure."

Libi's brows furrowed. "There is more?"

"Much, but this is what you must know now: given the nature of my desertion from the Roman Army, I am unsure of my future. I will always have my past hanging over me, and while I would pray that we can enjoy a long and happy life together and that God provides a way to free me of my past completely, there is always the possibility that one day I might have to pay for my actions."

"How might you have to pay?" she asked, wrapping her arms around her body.

Telling the truth to her was painful, but he learned the hard way that the pain which came from telling the truth rarely exceeded the pain that would follow if he tried to hide it again. "The punishment for desertion… is death."

She gasped, and Cassius wished there had been a more delicate way to say it.

"I don't know if there is even anyone left who would even still be able to identify me, or if they are even looking, but if we were married, your life could be affected by the choices of my youth"

"I see," she whispered, her eyes no longer focused completely on him.

"I know this is a lot to consider so please take your time in answering. It isn't fair to you, and you deserve so much more than what I can offer, so I promise this will be the last time I ask. If you say no, I will follow Saul or Barnabas wherever they go and never return to you again. Libi, will you marry me?"

He waited what seemed like an eternity for an answer. His breath became shaky. His palms became sweaty.

"Libi?" He asked again, searching her gray eyes for an answer.

"Yes," she said. Her voice did not falter. "Yes, I will marry you. We are both imperfect, but God in his perfect goodness has brought us together. I believe in miracles, Cassius. How could I not? I will pray that the Lord provides yet another miracle to free you from this burden, and I will do so by your side as your wife."

He wanted to encircle her in his arms and draw her near to him. He wanted to sing, he wanted to dance, he wanted to shout! This was neither the time nor the place, so he simply leaned toward her ear and whispered words that only she could hear, "You have made me the happiest man alive." Then, offering Libi his arm, he led her into the domus to share the news with her family, and continue on with the work.

Later that evening, once again at Keinan's home where he still stayed, Cassius had great difficulty falling asleep. He could probably count on one hand the times in his life when he'd been given to tears before he came to accept his need for a Savior; now it seemed like he could not stop. He felt so unworthy of the vast love, grace, and mercy that was being showered upon him. Tears streamed down his face as he looked toward the heavens and gave praise to the Lord. Wedding details had not been discussed, but as far as Cassius was concerned the ceremony could not come soon enough.

PART THREE

"My soul, bless the Lord, and all that is within me, bless his holy name. My soul, bless the Lord, and do not forget all his benefits. He forgives all your iniquity; he heals all your diseases. He redeems your life from the Pit; he crowns you with faithful love and compassion. He satisfies you with good things; your youth is renewed like the eagle. The Lord executes acts of righteousness and justice for all the oppressed. He revealed his ways to Moses, his deeds to the people of Israel. The Lord is compassionate and gracious, slow to anger and abounding in faithful love. He will not always accuse us or be angry forever. He has not dealt with us as our sins deserve or repaid us according to our iniquities. For as high as the heavens are above the earth, so great is his faithful love toward those who fear him. As far as the east is from the west, so far has he removed our transgressions from us. As a father has compassion on his children, so the Lord has compassion on those who fear him." —
Psalm 103:1-13 CSB

ANTIOCH'S DAUGHTER

24

"A time to love and a time to hate; a time for war and a time for peace." — Ecclesiastes 3:8 CSB

Servius Arrius' journey was coming to an end. He would not be able to stave off the inevitable for much longer. There was only so much time that he could spend "campaigning" for jobs within local governments. Sooner or later, he would have to find a place to settle and collect on his pension, whatever good it would do him then.

From Tyre, where he had first heard whispers of Cassius' presence, he traveled to Sidon and then inland to Damascus. Finding nothing there, he returned to the coastal cities of Tripolis, Laodiciea, and Rhossus in Syria. Some that he questioned had faint memories, others had *feigned* memories they were only willing to part with for a certain amount of coin. Servius quickly learned to tell the difference between such people, knowing that the latter likely did not possess any real leads that would aid him in his search. Others gave vague descriptions that sort of matched Servius' recollections of Cassius, causing him to dwell among them for longer periods of time.

In each town and city he passed through on his journey, he tried to conceal his identity by stationing himself in marketplaces and lower-class areas hoping to catch Cassius in the act of theft. Even with all of his plotting and planning, his search had come to no avail. Now he arrived in Antioch, and the idea of finding Cassius and bringing justice to him was becoming less and less appealing. As loathsome as Servius found the idea of returning to his home, he was growing older, and with that age, he found that he grew weary faster than he used to when traveling. There was a time in his youth where he could march on foot for hours on end in any weather or terrain, but now Servius could hardly stand to sit atop of a horse for too long.

It was possible he'd overreacted when he heard mention of a man that matched Cassius' description. He had no real way of knowing whether or not Cassius was still alive, or even still in this part of the world. All he was acting on were things he'd heard while at the encampment of Marcus Valerius and his men. Since then, he'd based every travel decision off of indistinct testimonies from unreliable witnesses. This was not the way a soldier of his level and renown conducted a search; at least, it shouldn't have been.

As he rode his horse down the center of the busy Antioch streets and felt the gazes of a hundred or more onlookers watching his every move, he made his decision. If he did not find Cassius in this wretched city, he would move on once and for all, board a ship sailing east, and face whatever ghosts waited for him.

He approached a building with what looked like a carpenter's workshop at the front of it. Once there, he dismounted his horse. He desired to walk on foot for a while and get to know the streets of the city he would be resting in for the foreseeable future, and surmised that a carpenter would likely have a place to stable animals. He also desired some food to eat, and preferably not the kind the army rationed. "Is anyone in there? I have silver to pay you if you will stable my horse and bring me food and water," he called out to the inhabitants.

Servius heard shuffling footsteps from inside, but no immediate response. "Is anyone there?" He called out again, letting the reigns of his horse fall from his hands.

The door opened and a figure emerged. He was older and had a beard, but he had the same scar, blunt hair, and green eyes of Cassius.

"No…" he whispered at the realization. "After all this time?"

25

"Therefore put on the full armor of God, so that when the day of evil comes, you may be able to stand your ground, and after you have done everything, to stand." — Ephesians 6:13 CSB

"Hurry," said Libi. "We're going to be late!"

She and Cassius had a short betrothal before marrying in simple and humble ceremony, very different to the weddings she had grown up witnessing when she and her family lived in Jerusalem. There was no grand feast with loud music, but there had been food and songs. She and Cassius made vows to each other before a group of witnesses and in the sight of God. Many from their community of believers were present, as were Saul and Barnabas.

The typical requirements of a betrothal period had already been met, although in an unusual way. As opposed to Cassius setting aside time to build a home for Libi, in a way he already had, since it was agreed that they would postpone the opening of the shelter until after they were married. They spent their wedding night and the days that followed in the home that Libi and Cassius had built together. Over time, Cassius revealed more and more of his past to her, but none of it ever made Libi question the man he was now.

Rather, it strengthened and solidified her love for him—a man who could overcome so much. There was no other she could ever desire to have by her side in ministry.

When the house was opened formally to those in need, Iulia was the first to come, eventually finding the joy of salvation for herself. Libi had always suspected that the elderly woman had no home of her own, relying on the money from her bracelets to survive. Others came after that, many of which were friends of Iulia. She proved to be instrumental to Libi, often aiding her in the kitchen and helping to spread the word to those she had known on the streets. The many rooms of the house were soon filled with mothers, women, and children all longing for a home and a place of belonging. Some of the rooms had, as Libi anticipated, been converted to places for sleeping. Others were set aside for the purposes of teaching skills, singing songs, praying, and fellowshipping.

It was not as difficult as Libi had thought it would be to run the house, for many who came to stay were often delighted to help in whatever way they could. Some of them came and went. Women married or remarried. Children were adopted. Others remained for longer periods of time. Many were exposed to the message of Jesus Christ and had accepted His grace for themselves, and it was that mission that kept Libi going each day, and allowed her to face each challenge with unwavering faith and joy. The foundations in the house were strong, and Libi knew it. She knew the relationships formed there—with one another and with God—would last, like her father had said when they first began the work of restoring this place and turning it into a shelter and refuge for all.

"I was helping Iulia by bringing some fresh wood into the culina so that she could heat up the food for the others tonight," said Cassius, coming into the room they shared and taking Libi in his arms. In one swift motion, he drew her nearer to him and pressed his lips to hers. The scratchiness of his beard tickled her and she smiled as she pulled away. "Do you *really* want to visit your family this evening?" he said, running his fingers through her hair. "We could just… stay here."

She giggled and replied, "They are expecting us, my husband."

"What can I say in my defense? You beguile me, Libi. I am helpless in your presence, as usual." He leaned in to embrace her again.

Even though they'd been married for some time, he retained the ability to sweep her off of her feet and surprise her with his affection as much as when they first kissed on their wedding day. She doubted those feelings would ever fade. "You know," she sighed, "I never cared for the sound of my name until I heard you say it."

"What do you mean?" said Cassius, tilting his head to the side and raising his eyebrows flirtatiously. "I have always found your name beautiful, like you."

She laughed lightly before continuing, "When I first received the gift of hearing, I would listen to everything. The birds singing. The wind in the trees. The sounds of the animals in the pastures. Even the sounds of people shouting in the streets of Jerusalem. It was all exciting to me, and I treasured each new noise I became aware of, but I never liked the sound of my own name. I don't really have a reason."

Cassius laughed and she playfully swatted at his arm.

"Don't laugh at my expense," she said, although she too found herself unable to suppress her own laughter. "I suppose it does sound rather odd, but the way you say my name, it always sounds so… special. Tender and full of love."

"I do love you, Libi," he said, lowering his voice to a whisper. "I love you more than I ever thought I was capable of loving anything or anyone on this earth."

She closed her eyes and leaned toward him. "I love you as well," she whispered. Even she began to forget about joining her family for dinner.

"I was thinking," he said, taking her hands in his. "Do you suppose I should change my name?"

"Whatever for?" she asked, blinking her eyes several times in an attempt to gather her wits.

"Sometimes I wonder if the name 'Cassius' still feels right. I think of the name and of who I was years ago—"

"The person you never have to be again," Libi reminded him.

"Even so, sometimes I think it would be better if I did not go by that name anymore. If I changed it to something new; something associated with less painful memories."

"You would always be 'Cassius' to me, and even so, I do not think your name is one associated with painful memories. God makes all things new, even you. A new Cassius, but still Cassius. Your name is a testimony to God's amazing power of redemption, and of how He transformed you and made you into who you are today."

"Hm." He smiled. "All things new. You know I used to repeat that to myself over and over again just to sleep at night. Sometimes I still do."

"Do you doubt it?" asked Libi.

"No, not now, but it comes from something Saul once said to me. When I was staying with him and he was teaching me, I told him of how I still wrestled with my guilt over my past and wondered if it would ever go away. He told me that I needed to stop fighting God's grace. I remember him saying, 'Wear that grace as you would wear armor.' So, I armored myself with those words and others."

"Cassius," Libi sighed. "That's beautiful."

"Perhaps that's what we should call this place: The House of All Things New… It fits, don't you think?"

Libi thought about it for a moment and smiled. It fit surprisingly well. Not only had the house itself been literally made new, for when they found it all that remained of it were pieces of charred wood and ash, but all those who entered it encountered that same grace that covers all things. Everyone who came inside had a second chance at life. "I think it's perfect, although I'm not sure if it will ever catch on. It is quite a long name."

"Doesn't matter. That's how I'll always think of it. We should go now, or we really will be late to your family's home for dinner."

"Would you taste these for me first?" asked Libi, moving to pick up the basket of freshly prepared dates she intended to bring.

Cassius obliged. "They're as good as they always are. You know, I don't think I've ever mentioned this to you before, but they remind me of the dates my mother and I used to enjoy as a treat back in Rome."

"Really?" Libi replied.

Cassius nodded as he took a second date from the basket. "Well, they are not quite the same. They are close, but missing a spice my mother used to add."

Libi sighed. "Savta never did give us the recipe she used. We've tried everything from cinnamon to coriander to cloves… They've never tasted the same."

"Did you ever try cardamom?" asked Cassius.

"Cardamom?" Libi's brows furrowed. "Where would Savta have gotten cardamom?"

Cassius shrugged his shoulders. "It is what my mother used. She used to send me out to get it for her. Perhaps your grandmother purchased some from a traveling merchant?"

"Ha! I shall have to see about getting some and trying it myself, but I suspect you are right. Savta always had a few tricks up her sleeve!"

"Perhaps we can purchase some at the agora on our way and test it with your family," Cassius smiled, putting an arm around her and guiding her out the doorway and through the vestibulum to the street.

Hand in hand they walked through the streets of Antioch back to the home where Libi had grown from girl to woman, as was their weekly custom. They always broke bread for the mid-week evening meal with Libi's parents and brothers. Thanks to Iulia's help and faithful service, they were able to leave the house in her care as she would serve the meal to their guests and often clean up afterward, leaving Libi and Cassius time to visit with their family members.

"Libi! You're here," said Libi's mother, opening her arms to greet her and give her the same affectionate embrace as she had when Libi was a small child. "How have you been this week?"

"Very well, Imma," she answered. "A woman who goes by the name Aleta came to us the other day. She's very quiet and stays close to Iulia. I think in time she will open up."

"That's wonderful news," Chava said, smiling. "You and Cassius must both come inside now."

"All right," said Libi, turning to offer her hand to Cassius once more. "Are you coming?"

"I'll be inside in a moment. I want to check on a few woodworking projects before I forget." Although they were given a portion of offerings and tithes to help with the costs of running the refuge, there was still often a disparity of money in terms of what was needed and what was available. To make ends meet, Cassius still worked with Libi's abba and brothers for a wage, becoming an even more skilled craftsman.

"Very well." She nodded to him, before leaning in closer to add in a hushed tone, "But don't be too long."

He brushed her lips lightly with his own. "Consider that a promise."

Cassius could hear the familiar hee-haw of a donkey in the courtyard. "I have nothing for you today, Judah," he quipped. "I have my own work to do." Cassius strode to the work table to run his hands over the wood he would be using to make a bespoke chest, ensuring that it was smooth and without any sharp edges that might splinter. He noticed one particular corner that jutted out misshapenly, and quickly set to smoothing it while he still had it in his sight and on his mind. While he was working, he let his thoughts wander, listening to the sounds coming from the streets outside. Carts passed by, people talked… some laughed, some yelled. He heard the hoof-beats of mules and horses.

"Is anyone in there? I have silver to pay you if you will stable my horse and bring me food and water," called a voice from outside. Cassius wasn't sure if they were addressing him or not. "Is anyone there?" the voice said again.

At once, Cassius' memory ignited with recognition. He hadn't heard that voice for ten years. It was older, gravellier, but it carried the same command that it had in the Roman Forum.

It was Servius Arrius.

Slowly, Cassius set down his tools and moved to open the door and face his old commander completely.

"No… After all this time?" said Servius.

"How can I help you?" Cassius replied, avoiding eye contact and bowing his head the way any civilian would do in the presence of a high-ranking official, although it was clear Servius already recognized him.

"Cassius, who are you talking to? The meal is getting cold and—" Libi said as she entered the workshop, before she halted her voice and her steps several paces behind Cassius.

"Cassius?" She said again, although this time her voice faltered. "What is happening?" She must have sensed the tension in the air. Tamir, Chava, Yuval, and Gilad followed her, perhaps out of their own curiosity.

Tamir took a well-mannered approach and stepped in front of Cassius. "How can we assist you?"

Servius ignored Tamir. He kept looking straight at Cassius. He could feel the way his eyes burned with fire and rage as they had when Cassius had been barely a man and trying to prove himself in all the wrong ways. "Who are these people, Cassius?" He hissed his name. "Don't tell me you've gone and put together a family for yourself."

"They mean no harm," said Cassius.

"So, they are your family! That is a surprise… Last I heard of you, your actions were not those belonging to an honorable man. Should I tell them the truth about who you are, or do they already know?"

"They already know, Servius. Even if they didn't, it's been a long time. Years. Do the soldiers in Jerusalem still remember my name?"

Servius spit on the ground and invited himself into the workshop. "No, no one remembers you, and they shouldn't. You abandoned your post without even a second thought to how it could affect the rest of us."

Petrified in the presence of Servius Arrius and when Cassius thought his earthly strength might fail him, words came to him. Words from the Holy Spirit. *All things new. All things new. All things new.* If ever there was a time to put on the armor of God, as Saul had taught him to do, it was now. Mentally, Cassius envisioned each piece of armor and imagined himself putting it on. First the belt of truth, followed by the breastplate of righteousness, sandals of readiness for the gospel of peace, the shield of faith, the helmet of salvation, and finally, the sword of the Spirit strapped to his side. He prayed to God not for his safety, but for Libi's.

"I was young, Servius. I didn't know what else to do, I saw things I couldn't explain, and I was frightened for what might happen to me," confessed Cassius, knowing there was no excuse for his actions, but wanting to explain anyway.

"You should have come to me. I told you from the beginning what to expect from a soldier's life."

"Would it have changed anything?" countered Cassius.

"Maybe." Servius the tools in the workshop as he would inspect a military encampment. "After it all happened and things quieted down, no one wanted to execute the soldiers who were on guard that day. If they were dead, it would only add to the growing rumors of the resurrected teacher. Everyone agreed that it was better to keep the peace and to look like fools, I suppose, than see that actual justice be done."

"Then what does it matter if I am here?" Cassius asked.

"It matters because you betrayed me!" Servius shouted. When he looked into Servius' eyes, Cassius saw that flicker of fatherly affection he had long since forgotten about, but as quickly as it came, it was replaced again by coldness.

"I will take whatever punishment God wills for me, but do not harm these people. They are my family," said Cassius. He closed his eyes, reliving every happy memory he had shared with Libi from the day they'd first shared their feelings for each other, to the day she'd agreed to marry him, to their wedding, and all of the mundane but perfect moments in between. He thought of her hair, wanting to memorize its fine, smooth texture and the sun-kissed golden locks that hid amidst the darker brown colors. He thought of her silvery eyes which never stopped looking at him with affection, always seeing the best in him and encouraging him to live a life that was worthy of her love. He thought of her lips, soft and sometimes timid, but his, as every part of him fully belonged to her. He prayed to God, *"Never let her joy be lost again... Take care of her as only You could. I gave my soul to you that day at the gathering of believers, but my life has always been in your hands. Whatever is fair to me, I accept, but show Libi your mercy and kindness."*

"'God?' Don't tell me you're one of them now too," responded Servius, balking at him.

Cassius felt uncomfortable, not for himself, but for what he imagined Libi's family must be going through witnessing this encounter. *"Lord, make your justice swift for their sakes, that they would not have to endure this much longer. Your kingdom come. Your will be done."*

"I am. I believe in the One True God, and I believe in the resurrected Messiah," Cassius spoke with firmer resolve than he'd ever had before, strengthened by the Holy Spirit that now felt so near to him.

"Do you take me for a fool?" Servius' eyes narrowed. "What sort of lie are you trying to peddle? That you actually love these people, and their deranged beliefs?"

"It's the truth, and as I have already said, I will take whatever punishment God wills for me," Cassius said, bowing his head and stretching out his arms with the palms of his hands facing upward. "Do what you must."

His brows furrowed. "The Cassius I knew was a soldier who possessed the strength of ten men. Will you not even fight for yourself?"

"If you are looking for that Cassius, then I am afraid he is no longer here. The man you see before you now is the new Cassius, a different man entirely, for I have been completely and wholly transformed by my beliefs. If you wish to take me prisoner, then do so now without causing these innocent people any more distress."

"Cassius, no!" Libi rushed to his side. He felt her shiver against his chest and it hurt him deeply to know that it was his actions—even the actions of a version of himself that no longer existed—that brought them to this moment. That pain was greater than any wound Cassius had ever endured.

Cassius wanted nothing more than to comfort her and make her feel protected, but he kept his eyes affixed on Servius, not looking back lest he lose his courage. "Well?"

He watched Servius run his fingers through his now-entirely gray hair. He looked down and then back up again at Cassius. He could have been mistaken, but he thought it looked as though Servius had tears in his eyes. "You are right. Cassius is dead, and

I will no longer spend my time searching for his ghost." Cassius followed him out onto the street and watched him mount his horse, still too in shock to fully take in the impact of what Servius was doing.

"I shall find somewhere else to stable my horse. I can see that there is no room here," said Servius.

"Servius, wait," Cassius blurted out, unsure of what he intended to say next. What would be appropriate in that situation? There was so much he wanted to tell him, but he couldn't find adequate words. God could have found another way to reach Cassius' soul, but it was because of Servius' actions, from allowing Cassius to enlist all the way to ordering him to guard the tomb of Jesus, that brought him to Antioch, to Libi, and to her family.

"You know that I can't," said Servius, and he was right. Even though they were closer physically than they had been in years, they were still on opposite sides of the world. He cleared his throat. "As I said, the man I'm looking for is gone. I need to be on my way."

Cassius nodded in understanding, and then Servius surprised him by continuing to speak. "Did he… Did Cassius know that I cared for him like a son?"

"He did, and he would want you to know that he looked up to you like a father," said Cassius.

"I would have helped him, you know. It may be hard to believe, but I would have broken any number of laws for him. He was my weakness."

"I made mistakes, Servius," Cassius said, giving up the act of pretending he wasn't there and speaking to his former commanding officer directly. "You taught me so many lessons, but I was still too foolish then to understand them all. I had to follow a different path."

"I hope it was worth it."

"It *is*," said Cassius, his vision beginning to blur, "and I thank you for everything you did and tried to do for me. It is my prayer that someday you find the same peace I found."

"I do not think peace is where my path leads," Servius said, shaking his head. "I have too many ghosts in my past. Too many failures to count."

"You didn't fail me."

Servius nodded. He gripped the reins of his horse tighter and addressed him one last time, "Farewell then… Cassius."

"May God be with you." With that, Servius Arrius urged his horse to go onward, never looking back. Cassius doubted he would ever see him again, at least in this life, but he held out hope that he might see him again in the next. He would keep Servius Arrius in his prayers, because he was the closest thing he'd ever had to a father. As he watched Servius' horse disappear into the crowded streets and on toward the fiery-colored horizon, he felt Libi's presence as she came up behind him.

"How is your family?" He prayed they were not too shaken by the unexpected encounter.

"They all went back inside. They wanted to give you some time," she whispered.

"I am sure they will have questions, but Libi, are you all right? I am so sorry…"

"I am fine, Cassius, just grateful to God that you are still with me. That was him, wasn't it? The man you told me about?" She asked, still speaking softly and clinging to his side as though she might never let go again.

"It was," Cassius confirmed. "He had every chance to take my life or at least take me from you, but he didn't."

"God was at work," she sighed. "He answered our prayers."

"The Lord does provide, even when it seems impossible. He is making miracles happen all around us every day. Let's go back inside so that we can enjoy the meal with your family and talk about all that has transpired." They both turned to go inside. Cassius entered the workshop first, but Libi paused inside the threshold. "What is it, my beloved?"

"How do *you* feel?" she asked. "That must have been difficult for you."

He smiled as his eyes wandered from where she stood to where the nails they'd driven into the frame of the door still remained as a constant reminder of Jesus' sacrifice on the cross and the grace they'd all been given. It had been difficult, but as he had come to learn, life—in any circumstance—was rarely easy. It was only when he finally stopped running from the truth, that he embraced it and found peace. "I feel free, Libi. Finally free."

EPILOGUE

"In those days some prophets came down from Jerusalem to Antioch. One of them, named Agabus, stood up and predicted by the Spirit that there would be a severe famine throughout the Roman world. This took place during the reign of Claudius. Each of the disciples, according to his ability, determined to send relief to the brothers and sisters who lived in Judea. They did this, sending it to the elders by means of Barnabas and Saul." — Acts 11:27-30 CSB

44 A.D., Antioch in Syria

It had been over a year since Cassius first arrived in Libi's life as any great hero would in the love stories Phoibe still loved to hear, and nearly a year since Saul and Barnabas came to teach them. When they first arrived, Libi hadn't realized how many lessons she'd needed to learn, but now she realized that one never stopped learning or growing closer to God. It would take a thousand lifetimes to understand all there was to know about His love, but Libi gave Him each day of the life she had.

"It's been a good day for profits," said Cassius, holding the empty baskets of bread Iulia helped to bake. Although many had come and gone from their house, Iulia remained.

"It has, indeed," said Libi. "I hope it will be enough for the believers in Judea."

"I am sure it will be a great help to them. Besides, Barnabas and Saul stressed that we only needed to contribute according to what we were able. I know it's not as much as you wanted to give, but you give every day, Libi."

She blushed at her husband's praise. Ever since they'd heard about the famine that was going to spread throughout the Roman world, Libi had hoped to get back to baking her loaves and cakes the way she used to so that she could sell them in the marketplace and donate whatever money they brought in. However, she'd been so ill lately that the smells from the ovens made her sick. She could sometimes barely even stand to help with the regular meals, let alone take on any extra duties. "Yes, we must thank Iulia. It is only because of her hard work and selflessness that *this* was even possible."

"And *this*," Cassius added, gesturing to the empty baskets he carried, "is amazing, as you are to me. I'll never fully understand how someone as loving and generous as you could ever look at me in any way that is favorable, but I thank God for you every moment of every day. Every time the sun catches your hair, every time your eyes light up with joy, every time your voice lifts in song."

He leaned in closer and whispered, "Every time our lips touch."

Libi smiled, overcome by his affection. "You always think you are blessed because God gave me to you, but never forget for a moment that I am equally blessed by you. I will always love you, Cassius."

"And I you. Let us make our way to the gathering, so that we can give this to Saul and Barnabas."

She handed him the baskets of bread that remained, and he stacked them on top of the empty baskets he already held, continuing to carry them for her. As they walked on, Libi thought back on all the ways God had worked in each of their lives to bring them to a point where they could serve side-by-side, each a help to the other in every task.

"Cassius, I was wondering…"

"What is it, my beloved?" he asked.

"Do you ever think about that man… Servius Arrius?" She wasn't sure if it was right for her to bring it up, with months having passed without them speaking of him. "I am grateful that you are with me now, but when you described him to me before, you described him as a hardened soldier… A man who knew only duty and loyalty to the empire and to his career. We called it a miracle then, and I believe it was, but why do you think he let you go free?"

Cassius took a deep breath and moved the baskets he carried to his side, wrapping his other arm around Libi and pulling her close. "Servius was the closest thing to an earthly father that I ever had. My real father wanted nothing to do with me. Servius… I don't think he ever wanted to kill me, not really. As we both know, time can change so many things. Maybe his sense of honor and duty might have compelled him to do so once, or his anger at my leaving may have clouded his judgment, but I don't think that is what he truly wanted in his heart."

Libi shook her head. "I still don't think I understand it, but I'm glad that whatever his reasons were, he *did* show mercy that day. The Lord provides even in ways we cannot expect or ever comprehend."

Cassius cleared his throat and continued, "People, soldiers, even myself—I think we have a tendency to believe that hate makes us stronger, and therefore we hold onto it. That isn't the case, Libi. You have shown me more than anyone that love will always be stronger than hate. Love will win in battle every time. Love, even the tiniest bit of it, can outlast hatred. Love," he gestured to his wife, "when nurtured, taken care of, and given time to grow, can drive out hate completely. I pray that one day Servius

Arrius finds the greatest kind of love there is, which knows no limit—not even death."

They walked together in silence for some time before Libi finally spoke again when they were just outside the city. "Cassius, I haven't just been ill lately. There is a reason why I could hardly stand to cook these past few weeks, and why I felt such difficulty rising each morning."

Instantly, Cassius stopped her and turned her to face him. His face was pale and his countenance low. "Is something wrong? Are you unwell? Libi, you must tell me at once."

"No, nothing is wrong." She laughed lightly. "I am with child, Cassius. You are going to be a father."

"Me—a father? And you—a mother?" He asked the questions with widened eyes, and Libi nodded her head.

"Yes! I wasn't sure until recently, but—" She stopped, noticing how he ran his fingers through his hair. "Cassius, are you happy?"

"Libi… Do you doubt?" he whispered. "I have never been happier in my life. When? How soon?"

She smiled. "Not for some months yet. It is still very early, but I couldn't keep it from you anymore."

"Does your mother know?"

"Only you and Iulia… I had to tell her as soon as I suspected it, because she became worried about my health. I thought we could tell my family together at the gathering. Oh, Cassius, can we hurry?"

"I'll get you there as fast as I can," promised Cassius, pulling her in for a long kiss. She lifted her hand up to run her fingers through his black and brown hair, lost in the sensation of his touch and forgetting about everything else around them. "We have so much to thank God for on this night," he marveled when he finally pulled away.

"So much," she echoed. In her prayers she thanked God for the new life growing inside of her womb, and for all of the changes she witnessed in the past year where He had taken something that was old or broken and made it new even when she hadn't thought it possible. There were many changes yet to come. The changes a child would bring, changes when Saul and Barnabas departed from them again, and even the day-to-day changes that were natural to life, but she praised the Lord because she knew that no matter what changes came her way, the love that united Libi and Cassius would sustain them. Not only the love they held for each other, but the love they held for God. That was the true foundation her father had spoken of all that time ago, and she knew it now better than ever. When a life was built on such a solid foundation and when each choice a person made was guided by a desire to grow closer to God, then His love would be their source of strength throughout every season.

God's love was everlasting.

THE END.

Servius Arrius' quest will continue, and Shamira, Asa, and Rut will return in Daughter of the Most High.

Coming soon.

Discussion Questions

1. A major theme in Antioch's Daughter is grace. This includes extending grace to others, accepting it ourselves, and the meaning and depth of God's grace. How did you feel this theme was revealed in the story? What moments stuck out to you? How would you define grace?

2. This story celebrates our Heavenly Father and the way He cares for each of us individually as His children. What are some Biblical passages that talk about how God loves His children? Can you think of a time when you may not have felt deserving of His love, but He lavished it upon you?

3. The first few chapters of Cassius' story portray a small boy walking through a painful childhood. Could you relate to this, and if so, how did it impact you? If not, did it give you insight or grip your heart in some way?

4. As a young man, Cassius enlisted under the watchful, sometimes protective eye of Servius Arrius. Who do you think was most disappointed in the way the relationship ended? Why?

5. In the first part of the book, Libi is living through a "season of waiting" as she waits upon God to fulfill the desires of her heart. Rather than spend time dwelling upon what she doesn't have, such as a husband or family of her own, she chooses to fill her time with acts of service to others and songs of praise to God. Are you in a season of waiting? How can you learn from Libi's example? What habits can you start in your life that will sow a spirit of grace and contentment in any circumstance?

6. One of Libi's gifts is her ability to serve in whatever capacity she is needed, whether that's baking bread and selling it to donate the proceeds, or helping take care of Taliah's children. Is there a ministry or area of service you feel called to? If so, what action might you take to follow through?

7. As a new believer, Cassius struggles with anxiety and wrestles with doubt due to the hurt of his past and the mistakes he made that still weigh on his heart. To combat that doubt, he repeats certain phrases over and over to himself, like "All things new" or "It is finished." This brings to mind the idea of hiding God's word in our heart and knowing what the Bible says, so that we can recall it in times of need. How do you practice spending time in scripture reading and prayer? Have you ever memorized Bible verses? Consider making a list of verses you'd like to memorize, or a list of ways to practice consistency in your personal Bible study.

8. Libi reacts with shock and fear upon recognizing Saul at the gathering on the mountainside and later in the marketplace with Asa. After praying to God for strength, she is able to move from a place of hurt to a place of forgiveness and healing. How do you think you would have reacted in her situation? Have you ever experienced something similar, or struggled to forgive someone? What was that process like? How did you work through it, or how are you still working through it?

9. At the end of the story, Cassius and Libi are expecting a child. What kind of father do you think Cassius will be someday? What are ways God could use his past to influence his approach to fatherhood? How has God used something from your past to prepare you for something that came later?

AUTHOR'S NOTE

Dear Reader,

Another book, another author's note! Writing *Antioch's Daughter* was, by far, the most difficult experience I've ever had as an author, not because of the story, but because of what was going on in my own life during the months I spent drafting and editing it. Those were times of great change and great difficulty, but God's faithfulness was made so clear. Just when I was about to give up my writing because I felt like I couldn't do it anymore because of the stress of the "real world," as well as my chronic health journey making it feel like my creative energy was spent and my imagination was effectively broken, I felt God open doors in my mind that I thought were closed forever. He gave me inspiration and strength to keep pursuing the publication of Libi and Cassius' story, which, believe it or not, is a story I've had planned and been passionate about telling since before Jerusalem's Daughter even had a completed first draft.

I have heard so many stories told to me from friends and loved ones about how they felt "too far gone" to be saved by God. It truthfully breaks my heart to know that there are those out there who struggle with such feelings. It was out of this that Cassius' story was born, because so many of us have at some point or another struggled with the crushing weight of sin. But God is good, and He truly does make *all things new!*

This book was so different to write compared to *Jerusalem's Daughter* in so many ways. Because this story takes place beyond Jerusalem, from Judea to Antioch to Rome and beyond, I got to do so much more research and explore so many more ideas. Some made it into the story, others did not, but I learned a lot and was continually in awe at every turn of how God orchestrates history to declare His name and His glory. In this author's note, I'm going to try and share some of that research with you, answer some questions you've asked, and maybe even some questions you didn't ask but that have such intriguing answers to me that I couldn't help but pass them on! Remember, <u>my work is fiction</u>, but the message of God's redemption is truth.

1. **Were those who guarded the tomb Roman?**

There is much debate as to whether or not it was Roman soldiers or Temple guards who guarded Jesus' tomb. The tomb was sealed and the order was given by Pilate at the priest's requests, suggesting that these guards and authority came from Rome, not the Temple. However, the guards were bribed by the Temple. Why would Roman soldiers have any attachment to Temple authorities? Their allegiance would have been to Rome first, before the priests. Furthermore, the Bible tells us that they had fallen asleep while on duty. If they had been Roman soldiers, the punishment would have likely been death.

This presented me with a research problem as I began telling Cassius' story. I knew that Cassius was a Roman guard from the moment I met him in my mind's eye. I had to now figure out how his story fit within the facts we know from the Bible. I determined that Cassius' core struggle would have been fear. He would have been a young, ambitious soldier, eager to prove himself and his name. I imagined that when he had woken up first and, to his horror, realized to the best of his understanding what happened, he fled, afraid of who would believe him or what the punishment might be. The other guards, therefore, would have woken up later and seen that Cassius had abandoned them and that the tomb was empty. It became entirely plausible in my imagination that they had gone to the Temple first, distraught over what to do. As Servius Arrius surmises in the narrative of this story, killing the soldiers on duty would have just added to the rumors that Jesus was indeed resurrected. By keeping them alive, giving them a story to tell, they would have been able to quash rumors of a resurrected Messiah, and it would've been the soldier's words against the Christian's. Cassius' betrayal would've been frustrating, but it would not have been the greatest concern.

Remember my characters and their stories are Bible-based, but completely fictional. This book is, by nature, ancient historical fiction, and makes no claim to be fact. As much as I would love for Cassius to really be a broody soldier that I could take with me as my bodyguard to all my bookish events, he is still just a character. My mission has always been to write stories that inspire others to return to scripture, not to replace it, but to honor it. Any transgression on my part is not intentional. I always recommend reading the Biblical account first; there is no substitute for God's Holy Word in its original form. Therefore, I recommend the reading of Matthew 27:62-28:15 in your own Bible so that you can learn more about the guards who were put in charge of watching over Jesus' tomb, and come to your own conclusions about who they might have been.

2. Why was glory so important to Cassius? Why did he care so much about having titles and wealth?

When we first begin to learn more of Cassius' backstory, we learn of how his mother begged his father to make him a legitimate son and give him the family name, but Cassius' father (whose name we never find out) refuses. Why was a name so important in Roman culture, that having a name or a title became something Cassius chased after? Ancient Roman culture was built around the family structure. Who your father was mattered. Your last name, or the name of your family, determined to which class you belonged. Extramarital affairs were often expected in Rome among men, but they were considered private. If such affairs were to become known, they would be frowned upon, and there might even be legal consequences depending on the circumstances. It is clear then why Cassius' father would have been so woeful to recognize Cassius as a legitimate son, because to do so would be to admit publicly that they had been unfaithful. Without a family name, Cassius would have been from the lowest class, and he would have had to fight very hard for everything he wanted in life. The army gave him the opportunity to improve his social standing in the hopes that one day he might not have to fight quite so hard.

With so much emphasis placed on identity, it does make one grateful to know that our identity comes from Christ and Christ alone, doesn't it?

Bonus fact: Servius Arrius mentions the idea of claiming Cassius as his heir in the story. Although Roman soldiers were forbidden from marrying, it was not uncommon for them to be with women as though they were married, often fathering children through such unions. If they lived to retire, they might be able to legitimize those children and marry the women formally. In light of that, no one would question Servius giving Cassius the name of Arrius, but does the name "Arrius" sound familiar to you? Well, I named him in homage to the military character of Quintus Arrius in Ben-Hur, one of my favorite Biblical novels. Maybe they were cousins? I believe it.

3. Why aren't they called "Christians" throughout the story?

You may have noticed several different ways of referring to Libi's family and those who shared their beliefs in Jesus as the risen Messiah. They are described with terms like "Followers of The Way" and "Way-Followers." No, this wasn't an attempt to make the word count of this book larger or add pages to the manuscript! It's actually in an attempt to be historically accurate. In Acts 11:26 tells us that believers were first called "Christians" at Antioch. Many believe that this name did not originate from Christians as a way of describing themselves, but rather as a way for other people to identify them. Back in those days, you were often identified based on who you followed. For instance, those who followed Caesar would have been known as Caesariani. Of course, the use of "Christians" to identify people with these beliefs may not have become common universally until much later, but that is one theory as to how the term originated.

4. How did early believers meet and gather? Did they have churches like we do now? What about weddings and other religious ceremonies? How would those have played out?

This was one of those questions that plagued me the most when I was writing, because I struggled so hard to find plausible scenarios for my characters without the typical church-setting and order of things as we know them today. House-churches would have been very common, although what exactly went on in them, we do not know. They probably would have joined together in song and read from Scriptures as they did in Jewish services and celebrations, since that is what they would have known. Offerings might have also been taken to support those within the community. They also may have even still attended synagogues, with their own gatherings happening afterward. The best pictures of the church in action come from the book of Acts, of course.

As far as weddings, no such ceremony like we have existed back then. Formal ceremonies may not have even been required by some cultures, but couples may have had their own traditions, like the reading of poetry, a large feast, special clothes and colors, and even special times of the year for getting married. In many cases, being married was as simple as paying a bride-price and then cohabitating. This was very different from a Jewish wedding, where a betrothal would have lasted for months and there were many religious traditions regarding the actual event itself. So, what did early Christian weddings look like? Well, that is something to be left up to the imagination. Over time, traditions probably would have mixed and mingled just like culture did and just like how Christianity came to be something shared not just by Jews but by Gentiles as well. For the purposes of my story, I did make things for Libi and Cassius much more relaxed than an average historical Jewish betrothal, but to me, it felt right for these characters.

5. Did early believers really meet on the sides of mountains?

Interestingly enough, I discovered that modern day Antakya (Hatay), Turkey, otherwise known as historical Syrian Antioch, is home to the Church of Saint Peter, a church built into a cave on a mountainside. There are many different stories pertaining to where this church came from, how it was built, and what it was used for, but the church we can see at that location today with mosaic tile and an intricately carved facade, although beautiful, was probably not the original architecture. The oldest surviving parts come from the fourth or fifth century, but some people believe that early believers would have hidden from persecution in the original caves. I decided to include a little homage to it in my story by having the believers occasionally meet on a mountainside. It made sense to me that they might have gone there occasionally, especially if they were expecting large groups of people and wanted to get away from the city's center.

6. Where does your research come from?

During some of the earlier periods of drafting this story, I was blessed to be able to use California Baptist University's online library to find scholarly articles on specific subjects, which is where I was attending school at the time for my degree in English. Truthfully though, I have quite the growing collection of books at my disposal on various times and places in history, and several sets of Biblical encyclopedias, commentaries, concordances, and dictionaries. A lot of these belonged to my grandmother when she was alive, who was somewhat of a scholar in her own right, and many of them still have her handwriting in them. Every time I pull one out and see a note from her in it, even if I can't read it, I smile!

7. A lot of Paul's dialogue comes from letters Paul wrote in the Bible, but it seems anachronistic. How do you explain this?

I don't like to use my imagination too much when writing historical figures into my fictional stories. One of my pastors has a habit of repeating himself in his sermons. Not that every sermon is the same, mind you, but he often returns to some of his favorite passages or messages from scripture when he speaks. I think we are all like that to a certain extent; there are things we are passionate about that we may return to over and over again. I based some of my fictional Paul on that idea; he does recall his past multiple times over the course of his writings, repeatedly reflecting on the grace of God which makes us new creations in Him. I do have Cassius mention once or twice that Paul should really consider "writing down" everything that he says. This was a little bit of a quip on my part, because we know through the lens of history that in actuality, Paul's writings account for much of the New Testament.

If you would like some specific references that I leaned heavily on, I encourage you to read Galatians 1, Ephesians 5, Philippians 1 and 3, 1 Corinthians 13, and 2 Corinthians 5 and 12. These all include passages that I pored over and read extensively to prepare my heart during the writing process for Antioch's Daughter, and I believe they reflect the themes of this story well. You can also find the scripture for which the entirety of this story is based on in Acts 2:42-47, Acts 7, and Acts 11:19-30.

8. Why do you refer to Paul as Saul throughout the story, even after his conversion?

As previously noted, the majority of Libi and Cassius' story takes place in Acts 11. You may be surprised to learn that Paul did not immediately begin going by that name after his conversion. In fact, the first record of Paul using his second name is not until Acts 13:9, when he visited Cyprus! In my research, I found that this was most likely due to his location. The names Paul and Saul appear to be interchangeable, with Saul being a Hebrew name, and Paul being the Roman variation. It is likely that he began using the Roman form of his name as he travelled further and further from Jerusalem. Given that the Bible refers to

Paul as Saul during the era in which my story is set, I chose to stick to that name.

9. Who is Servius Arrius, what is he hiding, and does he return?

Servius Arrius has some secrets in his past, but I can't give too much away! He may seem like an unusual choice for a POV character (a character whose "point of view" you get to read from) since he has so little time in this story, except for stories from Cassius' memory. For me, it was important to introduce him to you as the audience now, because he will become an important character in my next book, *Daughter of the Most High*, which will follow another member of my Biblical Fiction Family, Rut, when she meets a particular seller of purple and travels to parts of the Roman world she never expected to see, learning about herself, her faith, and what it means to truly trust in God when things seem so uncertain. This book will cover events in Acts 15 and 16, and themes and messages from Paul's letter to the Philippians, so if you're really anxious, I suggest you scour those passages for clues as to when and where Servius will appear again! Otherwise, you'll just have to wait for the epic conclusion in Book 3.

Wow! That's a lot of questions for one book! There was a lot more I learned in my research that didn't even make it into this story, but if you love learning as much as I do, then I hope you will have enjoyed this.

Now it's time to thank some people… and there's a lot of people I have to thank! First and foremost, though, is God. Like I said at the beginning of this author's note, none of this would have been possible without him. Second, thank you to YOU, the readers! I hope that reading this book will have strengthened your faith as much as writing it completely changed and transformed mine. Miracles do happen.

Thank you to Audrey and Alysha! My greatest friends and sisters in Christ. Alysha, you cared about this story before Shamira's story was even finished. You were always excited for this book, maybe even more than my first! I'm grateful though, because your encouragement reminded me that this was a story worth telling. Audrey, critique partner isn't even a strong enough term for what you've been to me. You put up with so many of my tear-filled rants and frustrated messages about this story. You helped brainstorm even when these characters didn't have names. You gave me kind words when I was ripping myself apart because of doubt. However, you also rejoiced with me wholeheartedly at every victory, big and small. You deserve a Medal of Honor for the friend you've been. I'm sure it was a lot to put up with, but you never made me feel like my late-night texts were unwelcome. I hope I am the same kind of friend to both of you!

Thank you to my pastor and friends at Sunrise Community Church in Fair Oaks, CA.

This is the *Generations of Faith* series, and it was named very intentionally so. My characters' faith has been passed down through their parents and grandparents, as has mine. Without my grandparents' examples, I would not be here today. I am so appreciative of the generations of faith that are behind me, and the legacy of love and service my family holds. Therefore, I must thank my family. I feel you with me every day, whether we are physically together or separated by many miles. You all give me strength. You give me encouragement. You are always there for me, and I am *always* grateful. In particular, thank you to my Grandpa Graves, who celebrated turning 90 this year. You have been such an inspiration and role model to me of what it looks like to truly live a life in service and surrender to the Lord. Thank you for passing down your wisdom, your legacy of prayer, and your steadfast love. May there be many more birthdays to come!

Thank you to my husband. You listened to me describe this plot at least a dozen times, and still can't remember the names of the characters (for instance, that time you called Shamira "Basheera") but you are always eager to help me and listen to me and tell me that my stories are serving a purpose. You have also shared in my research woes from time to time when I have been unable to find the right source I need to back up a claim, and your assistance there has been very much appreciated as well! I thank God for your patience.

Finally, thank you to my Momma, Mommy, *"Mother,"* and Mom, specifically. You were the first Libi I ever knew. You showed me what grace looks like, not just in terms of giving grace, but in being graceful. You showed me what having such a great capacity for love can look like. You demonstrated to me as a child that loving others doesn't make you weak, but that love gives us strength. More than anything, you taught me that love always believes the best. Some may have underestimated you, and sometimes I might have even underestimated you myself, but you are the strongest woman I know.

ABOUT THE AUTHOR

Jenna Van Mourik graduated *magna cum laude* from California Baptist University with a B.A. in English, and received a Certificate in Christian Apologetics from Biola University's Talbot School of Theology. Her debut novel, *Jerusalem's Daughter,* was published in 2021 and is the first book in the Generations of Faith series.

When she's not reading, writing, podcasting, or sharing her favorite books on social media, she's spending time with her husband, Brandon, and toy Australian shepherd, Piper. She strives to live every day according to God's purpose, with what she calls a "Now go!" mindset, in reference to her favorite passage of scripture, Exodus 4:11-12.

Connect with her at www.authorjennavanmourik.com or on social media at @jennavanmourik.